A STEVE CANNON NOVEL

LOST AND FOUND

B. R. LAUE

ISBN: 978-0-9973419-5-9

Brandy Hill Publishing
P.O. Box 1202
Morgan Hill, CA 95038

brandyhillpublish@gmail.com

Join the mailing list (no spam) for advance notice of new books in this
series, and to periodically receive free Steve Cannon short stories.

Cover by Sandy Laue

For Sandy, my beautiful muse

Author's Foreword

World War II was a horrific conflict that dramatically changed every region of the globe. The war in the Pacific was especially difficult for the American forces and a proportionately larger number of cases of what was then called 'shell shock' came out of the watery conflict. More than that, however was the antipodal nature of the enemy the allied forces faced as they pushed their way toward the home islands of the Japanese. Far more than the European theatre, the enmity of the fighting ran deeper and lasted longer.

OTHER STEVE CANNON TITLES

Vegas Wash
A Song For Desmond
The Knights of Nauvoo
The Mayor of Burro Springs

APRIL 5, 1965

THE FRONT OF the Macayo mexican restaurant on Decatur Boulevard looked drab in the midday sun without its night time mantle of neon. Steve Cannon lit a Pall Mall and reached for the envelope on top of the dashboard. He unfolded the newspaper clipping first and laid it aside. It was a two month old article written by the Las Vegas Sun reporter, Rita Malone, recounting the murder of Desmond Rooney and Steve's subsequent investigation of the crime. He opened the one page letter which was written in a strange block script and requested a meeting with the private detective. It was unsigned. He took a last, quick drag on the cigarette before he snuffed it out and headed toward the entrance of the eatery.

There were only a few customers scattered among the red vinyl booths. Steve headed toward a long row of empty ones and settled down in the last seat, his back to the door. He did not bother to scan the faces of the other patrons. If the person he was to meet was here or would arrive shortly, he or she probably knew what Steve looked like from the likeness in the newspaper photo. He ordered coffee and was just setting the cup back onto the saucer after his first sip when he felt a presence beside him. Steve did not look up, but took another sip of the black liquid.

"Have a seat. You'll make us both more comfortable."

After a momentary hesitation, the man moved to the other side of the table and lowered himself onto the bench seat. Steve's cup stopped in midair, halfway back to the table. Steve looked into the first Japanese face he had seen close up since the end of the war twenty years before. Like many veterans of the Pacific, he generally avoided anything even remotely connected to the Land of the Rising Sun. There were very few Japanese in Las Vegas and that had made it easy to sidestep the issue altogether. Steve took a deep breath through his nose and forced himself to engage the private detective side of his personality. He looked into the dark brown eyes set in the weathered face. He guessed the man to be in his late forties and employed in some sort of outside job, judging by the stiff canvas jacket over a faded pair of green coveralls. His mental inventory was interrupted by the sweet fragrance that entered his nostrils and took him instantly back to the jungles of Guadalcanal, when the evening breeze brought the cloying smell of chrysanthemum soap from the freshly killed bodies of Japanese soldiers up the hill to his foxhole. For several seconds he fought to bring his senses back to the present. When he had composed himself, he took another long gulp of the coffee and busied himself pulling his notebook from his inside jacket pocket and laying it out on the table before him. He reached into his back pocket and extracted a pen. When he was done, he looked back into the unblinking eyes.

"What can I do for you, Mr...?" The man reacted with a slight bow toward Steve.

"My name is Kinnosuke Ogawa, Mr. Cannon. Most people call me 'Keno'." Steve wrote the name in the small notebook and waited while the waitress put a cup of coffee in front of the heavily calloused hands that were folded on the tabletop. Keno took the cup in both hands and took a slow sip, looking back at Steve as he lowered the thick white porcelain to the saucer.

"I need your help, Mr. Cannon. I have money, I can pay you."
"Let's not get ahead of ourselves, I need to know what kind of trouble

you are in, Mr. Ogawa, and why me?" Keno looked down at his cup before he spoke.

"You are the one to help me. We may have met before. You see, Mr. Cannon, I too was on Guadalcanal." Steve sat back into the red vinyl and let a long breath out through his mouth. He measured his words and tried to keep his tone as even as possible as he spoke.

"All the Japanese on Guadalcanal were either killed or captured, and most of those we captured chose suicide over imprisonment." The man across from him nodded.

"I was on the last hospital transport ship that left the island for Rabaul. I was delirious with malaria and do not remember the trip or my last few days on the island." Steve fidgeted uncomfortably with his pen and notebook.

"You speak English without an accent, Mr. Ogawa, how is that?" The older man half smiled as he took his second sip from the cup.

"I was born in Yokohama, Mr. Cannon. My parents brought me here as a sixteen year old in 1932. I went to UCLA and graduated in 1936. I went with my father to Japan to attend to family business in 1939. We never made it back. Because I spoke English, I was conscripted into the Imperial army and fought in China before I was shipped to the Pacific."

"And after the war?"

"I came back to find my mother and sister who had been interred in a camp in Wyoming. I married a girl in Japan before I was sent to the Pacific. She died along with my father in Nagasaki. Our only son was with his grandmother in Tokyo and survived." Keno shrugged as he looked away from Steve.

"You still haven't told me your trouble." Keno nodded.

"Maseo, my son, is missing Mr. Cannon. No one has seen him for seventeen days." Steve wrote several lines before asking his next question.

"What do the police say, Mr. Ogawa?" Keno shook his head.

"They say he ran away, Mr. Cannon, but that is not possible. He would not dishonor his family in that way." Steve shrugged.

"I wouldn't know about that, Mr. Ogawa, but if he didn't run away, what do you think explains his disappearance?" Keno Ogawa looked down at his coffee cup.

"I don't know, Mr. Cannon, and no one I have talked to seems to know either." Steve shifted his weight in the booth and stretched his stiff right leg out slightly under the table.

"Give me the name of the detective you talked to, and I will take a look at the police report."

"Thank you for helping me, Mr. Cannon." Keno pulled a thick wad of bills secured with a red rubber band from the pocket of his jacket.

"No, Mr. Ogawa, I have not decided if I am taking your case. Like I said, the best I can do right now is talk to the police. After that, if I decide to go forward, I will let you know." He looked quickly down at his notes so he didn't have to see the disappointment on the lined face.

"Is there a number where I can reach you, Mr. Ogawa?"

"I work at the municipal golf course. You can leave a message for me there. Please call me Keno, Mr. Cannon." Steve looked up impassively and closed his notebook.

*

A few minutes later as he drove toward Fremont Street and the downtown offices, Steve's mind was flooded with images of the buddies he had left in body bags on the hot humid island. He thought too of Skipper, his best friend, who survived the Pacific with him, but was fighting for his sobriety and his life in an LA halfway house. He blinked the tears from his eyes as he parked the red Jeep Wagoneer in the lot connected to the Hall of Justice. A warm spring breeze ruffled through his dark brown hair as he walked the fifty yards into the building.

As he crossed the wide floor of the rotunda, he ignored the main desk and the booking rooms to his right, but continued down a long hallway until he came to a series of closed office doors. He knocked on the second one on the right, and hearing a muffled reply from inside, opened the unlocked door and walked in.

Detective Tam Polhaus was in the middle of compiling the monthly crime statistics for March when the private detective appeared in his office. He grunted a greeting and indicated one of the two gray metal chairs in front of his desk. He continued adding several columns of figures, only pausing to push an ashtray toward his visitor when he heard the click of the zippo lighter. After several minutes he sighed, sat back in his chair with his hands behind his back and regarded Steve with a weary half smile.

"So. What brings you to this part of the woods? I am sure it is something you want from me, or why else would I hear from you?" Steve laughed as he exhaled a large cloud of smoke across the room.

"Well, Tam, if you want on my social calendar so badly, just let me know, I will squeeze you in." He grinned across the desk as he brought the cigarette back to his mouth. Tam shook his head.

"Spill."

"No big deal, Tam, I just want to take a look at a missing person report that was filed last week, that's all."

"What's the name?" Steve pulled his notebook out and flipped through several pages.

"Keno Ogawa. The missing person is Maseo Ogawa, but he also goes by 'Martin'." Tam stood and shook his head.

"I'll go see what I can find out. Stay here and don't touch anything until I get back." Steve waited until the large German-Irish cop closed the door behind him, before picking up the March crime report.

When he returned ten minutes later, Steve was studying the large map of the valley on the far wall. Tam handed several sheets of paper to Steve before he crossed the room and sat down behind the desk. Just as he settled in, he saw the crime report sitting on Steve's chair. He rose wearily and retrieved it, shaking his head at Steve's back as he sat down.

Steve stood and read the three pages before handing the report back to Tam. He sat down in the chair and began to scribble notes in the pages of his notebook. After a few minutes he looked up at Tam, who had resumed his paperwork.

"Not much here, Tam. Who is Greg Alfson?" Tam looked over before resuming his work as he replied.

"New Detective. Just promoted from uniform last month."

"He know what he is doing?" Tam shrugged and leaned back in his chair.

"They break them in on these kind of cases, doesn't look like there is much to miss in this case, how are you involved?"

"His father wants me to look into it, that's all. He's convinced he didn't run off." Tam snorted.

"Aren't they all? Detective Alfson covered all the bases as far as I can see. What more do you want from us?" Steve stood to go.

"It doesn't matter much one way or the other. I promised him I would look over the report. Now I have, and that's where it ends." Tam leaned forward and frowned.

"You're not going to take the case?" Steve shook his head. Tam sat back and grinned.

"You never miss a chance to make us look bad. You could probably come up with this kid half a day, tops." When Steve didn't say anything, but turned toward the door, Tam spoke again.

"You don't fool me. The minute I heard the last name, I knew what your take would be. Christ, Steve, all that happened over twenty years ago, time to let it go." Steve turned back from the door and stared at the detective.

"You don't know how it was on that island, Tam, and only the ones that lived through it ever will." Tam shrugged but did not look away from the hard stare.

"I was D-Day plus three and I saw a lot of bad stuff and so did all the guys in my unit. I don't hold a grudge against the Germans, hell, I'm half German myself."

"Not the same, Tam. It just isn't." Steve turned away, shutting the door behind him as he left the office.

*

Steve drove the eight miles to his modest house on Ringe Lane, just a mile west of the Nellis Air Force Base. Though it was only 2:30 in the afternoon, he poured himself three fingers of scotch and stared out the back door of his kitchen at Sunrise Mountain three miles in the distance. A half hour later, he found himself in his small office dialing the number to the municipal golf course.

"Hello, this is Steve Cannon. Is Lew Mannion around?" He waited and drank the last of the scotch until the familiar voice came on the line.

"Hi Lew, how you been?"

"Yeah, it has been a little while. Listen. This is real short notice, but do you have time to let me buy you a couple of beers, later?"

"Great. Let's meet at Foxy's, it's almost on your way home. Five sounds good, see you then." Steve hung up the phone and picked up his car keys.

The parking lot was nearly full when Steve pulled off the Strip in the shadow of the Sahara Hotel and parked in front of the famed delicatessen. He stood just inside the door and took in the friendly clatter from the busy restaurant. He watched for several minutes before his old friend and the owner of Foxy's, Bernie Gold, spied him and came over, a big grin on his happy round face.

"We must be on the same wave length my friend, I was just about to call you. I need some advice and I need to fill you in on several things, you got some time?" Steve draped his arm around the stout shoulder as they walked toward the door to the back room.

"Sure, Bern, I'm meeting Lew Mannion here at five, and until then, I'm all yours." Bernie closed the large oak door behind them and joined Steve at one of the green felt covered tables that filled the room.

"It's been awhile since you had a card night, Bern, people ask me about them all the time." Bernie laughed and shrugged.

"I know, I know, but the hotel has been keeping me hopping, I must get twenty calls a day and I spend most evenings checking on the day's construction." He shook his head as he headed to the phone. He picked up the black receiver and dialed a one digit number.

When someone out front picked up, he ordered coffee before he turned back to Steve.

"How's Lew been? I haven't seen him or played golf with him for ages. How about you make sure he comes to the next casino night? He always says yes, but never shows."

"I will, Bernie, I will. In fact, I will make a point of it tonight in front of you, then he can't say no."

"That should work. You free Thursday night? I'm trying to schedule a board meeting for the Carmino Lighting company and that seems to be the only night this week that most of the board can make it." Steve shrugged.

"Sure, Bernie, that is fine by me. You need any help setting it up?" Bernie shook his head as he got up to meet the waiter with the carafe of coffee halfway.

"No, just show up, we got a lot of business to get through." Bernie picked up a roll of blueprints that were lying on the table. He unrolled them and setting his coffee cup on one corner, he shifted them around so that both he and Steve could view them.

"Steve, I need your advice on the casino layout here. I know you helped Nick over at the Golden Nugget when they remodeled their casino and I thought maybe you could take a look and tell me if this seems right to you." Steve looked over the plans for several minutes as he finished his coffee. When he was done, he pulled out his notebook and tore a clean page out and began to draw a diagram on the small sheet.

"You have your blackjack pits and your craps and roulette tables placed well, with your poker tables separate and away from the slots which will keep those customers happy, but I think you have a security issue with the catwalks." He quickly drew a line across the middle of the sketch which depicted the whole area of the casino.

"If you have a catwalk that cuts across the center of the casino, you can get more coverage with less people, plus you have eyes in the sky right over the roulette and crap games where your biggest security problems are likely to be. You will also have two more angles on the twenty-one games. Check your blueprints and with your builder, Milton, but I am pretty sure there is a support beam right about there where you could hang a catwalk encased in two way mirrors." Bernie took the piece of paper in his hand and looked back at the drawings.

"I see your point, Steve, I think that will work. I will run it by Milton, but I think it will work. Thanks." Bernie leaned over the table and poured Steve and himself another cup of coffee before sitting down. He looked over the rim of his cup at his friend.

"How you given any more thought to the Head of Security job?" Steve smiled and took a long sip from his cup.

"Yes, Bernie, I have, and I have some ideas if you would like to hear them."

"Of course, my friend, I am all ears." Steve sat forward in his chair and took a deep breath.

"I think that most of the casinos in this town are looking backwards when it comes to security. The cheaters and con artists are getting more sophisticated every year and a lot of money is lost before most of the bosses even realize there is a scam. So, my idea is to build a security team, rather than just have a typical layered organization. Hire expertise in all the areas of concern and then make sure everyone knows everyone else's job as well as making sure that the training is kept up to date and the communication between the casinos all over the city is set up so that if problems develop downtown, for instance, they can be solved before they spread to everyone. I know Nick Montero down at the Golden Nugget would like the idea and he would get the other casinos to sign up." Steve stopped and waited to get Bernie's reaction. Bernie's head bobbed up and down.

"Yeah, I see your point. Hire the talent for the specific threat. But aren't we still going to need someone to coordinate all this?" Steve nodded.

"You are. I want to be part of the team and if you trust me, I will recommend someone soon for the head job, I just want to check with them on a few things first."

"Sure, I will consider anyone you suggest, Steve. Do you want to see your choices for office space?" Steve laughed.

"I did promise you I would finally get modern, didn't I?" Steve smiled as Bernie unrolled yet another set of plans.

*

Steve saw Lew Mannion through the tinted glass windows of the deli as his lanky frame crossed the parking lot and entered the restaurant. He had known Lew since seventh grade and had probably seen him every day of his life until the war. He had played forward on the basketball team and was a scratch golfer even in high school. With the exception of Skipper and Bernie, Lew probably knew as much about Steve Cannon as anybody.

Lew smiled when he saw Steve already sitting behind a large pitcher of beer.

"I see mine, where's yours?" Steve laughed and tipped the pitcher and filled one of the glass steins to the top and handed it to Lew. Steve pushed a chair out with his foot and Lew sat down while Steve poured a glass for himself.

"It's been awhile Lew. How are Brenda and Sam?" Lew smiled and wiped beer foam from his mouth.

"They're great. Sam's going to Boulder High this year and he might even play basketball under old man Jenkins if he doesn't retire in the next three years." Steve laughed.

"I can't believe he is still there. Must be almost forty years he has been coaching. How about yourself? Still enjoying working for the city?" Lew took another long drink of the beer and nodded his head.

"It's not too bad. The politics and the unions get on your nerves from time to time, but overall it's pretty good. I have been running that course for ten years now and I pretty much got it to where it almost runs itself. You are doing well. I saw that big article in the Sun a couple of months back. I don't know who you paid to run that, but you came out looking pretty good." Steve laughed again and poured Lew's glass full of beer.

"Yeah, and I need to talk to you about something along those lines. I know you need to get home to Brenda and Sam, so I will be brief. Tell me about Keno Ogawa." Lew pursed his lips and lowered his glass to the table.

"Why do you want to know about him?" Steve shrugged.

"I'll tell you in a minute. He work for you long?" Lew snorted and sipped his freshly poured beer.

"He was there when I arrived. Not for him, I would've never made it. What he doesn't know about keeping a golf course in shape and playable, especially in the winter, isn't worth knowing." Steve was about to ask another question, when he saw a wistful faraway look in his friends' eyes. Steve waited. Lew looked up and spoke evenly.

"The thing about Keno..." He paused for a few seconds and then went on. "He isn't what he seems at first glance."

"Yeah, I know he graduated from UCLA." Lew shook his head.

"No, it's more than that. You know what Kendo is?" Steve sat back in his chair and nodded.

"It's that stick fighting they do. Saw a lot of their equipment on Tulagi and even saw a demonstration in New Caledonia." Lew shook his head and chuckled.

"Describing it as stick fighting is kind of like saying golf is all beer and colorful clothes. It is a very ancient martial art based on the sword that is really at the root of their culture. Keno is a seventh dan and there are not many of them outside Japan and he is also shihan." Steve frowned.

"What is shihan?"

"It means he is the head of the dojo. They practice every Tuesday and Thursday down at Dula Center, when the basketball leagues aren't playing." Steve nodded. Lew grew quiet again and looked past Steve.

"To watch him go about his work every day, you wouldn't even guess that his son has disappeared. He is a pretty strong guy, in a lot of ways." Steve took a sip of his beer before he spoke.

"That's where I come in, or more accurately, where he has requested that I come in. You know the boy?" Lew nodded and then shook his head.

"Great kid. Worked beside his father summers and weekends all through high school. Smart, a real hard worker. Hard to figure. I am glad you are going to help him out." Steve looked out the window over Lew's shoulder as the sun began to dip behind the Spring Mountains.

"I haven't decided yet, Lew." Steve waited while Lew finished the last of his beer.

"What is your holdup? If it is money, I'll gladly pay for it." Steve scowled. "No. It has nothing to do with money."

"Then what?" Steve gazed into the gray eyes of his friend.

"Ever since Guadalcanal, I can't stomach Japs. I still have regular nightmares and they are always there, in the jungle shadows, just waiting to slit another G.I.'s throat." Steve looked down into the pale yellow beer. Lew's voice was quiet.

"If you don't think you can do it, then don't." He peered into the attached casino where several older women were playing the nickel slots. When Steve didn't reply he looked back at his boyhood friend.

"I was in the Pacific too, Steve, and while I was just a marine quartermaster on Guam, and didn't see any action like you and Skipper, I hated them every bit as much." He paused and leaned in slightly toward Steve. "But I will tell you one thing you can take to the bank. Keno Ogawa is one of the most honorable men I have ever known, including our fathers." Steve sat back and looked into his friends' eyes, but said nothing. Lew shrugged and started to slide his chair back to leave. Steve reached out and placed his hand on the taller man's wrist.

"Give me just a couple minutes more, Lew, I am curious about something." Lew turned back toward the table and waited.

"Tell me a little more about Martin."

*

The round wooden stage in the half finished building was filled with showgirls as Steve sat down at a table near the back of the room and the open double doors he had just come through. Below the stage a thin Cuban man in a pork pie hat played loudly on an upright piano. Steve watched as a long legged dancer in leotard, black tights and pink ballet slippers lead each girl in turn across the stage, slowly repeating the same steps each time and watching the other dancers' feet closely, stopping and repeating a few steps when she saw a problem. The woman's dark blond hair was pulled up into a bun on top of her head and her long graceful arms seem to pull her lithe body smoothly through the complicated routine.

It was nearly seven o'clock when Remy DeMarche signaled the piano player to stop and dismissed the dancers. She was rubbing the back of her neck with a small towel when she spied Steve sitting near the door where several of the girls were already filing out of the showroom. She walked slowly towards him, a small smile playing across her full pink lips.

"Hi ya, Gem, you're looking great up there. Done for the night?" Remy sat down at the small table and began rubbing a sore calf muscle.

"I didn't expect to see you until later, Steve. I hope you don't want to go somewhere now, I am wringing wet, and I need a hot shower and some ice on my toes." Steve laughed and reached for her hand.

"I figured as much. I thought I could give you a ride home, make us some dinner why you shower. Leave your car here, I'll give you a lift back in the morning, how does that sound?" He squeezed her hand gently. She squeezed back as she spoke.

"That sounds great. I had to break up the dancers into three groups and I have been at it since eight this morning. I don't know what I have in the fridge, but I do have some beer and I bought a bottle of scotch." They smiled at each other as they stood to go.

Fifteen minutes later, Steve pulled the Jeep through the white brick gate and curving around on the semi-circular driveway, parked in front of the large two story house that sat on the second fairway of the Desert Inn golf course. The pale blue sky was lit by the last of the sun rays and the small breeze blew with a soft coolness as Steve opened the front door and waited while Remy walked into the round foyer. Steve walked down a short hallway to the kitchen as Remy ascended the large circular stairway to the second floor.

An hour later, Steve gazed across the black dining table that held the remains of the pasta dinner he had prepared. Remy was swirling red wine around in a large glass, her hair, still damp from the shower hung long across her shoulders. The light from the fireplace danced across the rim of the crystal. Steve poured some more from the bottle into Remy's glass and then refilled his as well.

"The girls all looked much improved since the last time I saw them, you must be happy with the progress." Remy smiled.

"I am, I guess. Still a long way to go and the hotel opening is only three months away. Donn Arden warned me that the some of the routines I worked up are complicated, especially for a Las Vegas revue, but this is my chance to do something different and I want Bernie to have the best show on the strip. But it is a lot of work and

I have had to audition more dancers. Luckily, Bernie wants more of a traditional revue in the small showroom as well, so I have don't have to let any of the girls go." Remy looked across at Steve and took a small sip of wine before she spoke again.

"You've gotten quiet since we finished dinner. Is there something on your mind? If so, I would like to hear about it." She smiled at Steve as he shifted in his chair and looked directly into her dark brown eyes. Steve shrugged.

"Just trying to decide whether I take a case or not, that's all." Remy's brow furrowed as she leaned forward slightly toward Steve.

"What is the case about?"

"Missing kid. Early twenties. Works at the Stardust. Been missing for over two weeks. By all accounts he has dropped off the face of the earth." Steve took a sip of the French wine and looked into his glass. When it looked as if he wasn't going to add any more, Remy sighed.

"I don't see the problem. I am sure his parents are frantic over this and you don't need me or anybody else to tell you that you are their best hope." She stopped as she saw Steve looking intently at her.

"They're Japs, that's all." Steve pulled out a pack of Pall Malls and lit one with a gold lighter that sat beside a cut crystal ash tray. Remy waited until he had exhaled the first puff.

"Yes, Steve, I know, but they are just people too. I don't like Germans or what they did to my country when they marched in, but when I meet one, I try to wait and see if I can find something in them as a person that I can admire. And you know, the funny thing is, I usually can." Steve looked over at the earnest face.

"You are beautiful." Remy laughed softly and shook her head.

The logs in the fireplace burned for two more hours after The couple had ascended the curving staircase that led to the master bedroom.

April 6

STEVE DROVE DOWN East Sahara Boulevard toward the rising sun and turned left onto Nellis Boulevard. Two long blocks after crossing Lake Mead Boulevard, he turned onto Ringe Lane. His gravel driveway swept down off the small street and curved in front of his house before meeting up again with the asphalt. From half a block away, he saw the car parked just past his front door. He had never seen the car before but as the nose of the Jeep tilted down the slight incline, he recognized the profile of the man sitting behind the wheel, his arm dangling out the driver side window, a burning cigarette in his hand. Steve parked the Jeep behind the yellow Ford and when he closed the red door behind him, he saw the man standing beside his car squinting into the bright sunlight.

Jack Cathay was eight years older than Steve and while almost as tall, outweighed him by sixty pounds. His close cropped hair was gray and his tan cheeks held the beginnings of middle age jowls. When he spoke he put his most notable attribute on display.

"Hi ya, Cannon." The rough gravelly voice belied the kind expression in the pale blue eyes.

"Jack. I didn't expect to see you for a while." Steve waited to see if there were any indications of the three bullet wounds, visible or otherwise. Jack shrugged and smiled. Steve shook his head slightly.

In the five years he had known Jack, this was the first smile he could remember seeing. Though their history together wound through the twisted tale of the killer Angelo Sorelli, and their so far unsuccessful efforts to bring him to justice, Steve sensed that today was a different day.

"I needed to see you." Jack's voice grew even more hoarse. "I need to say some things." Steve nodded and led the way toward the weathered front door. Once inside, Jack motioned toward the back of the green couch that divided the end of the foyer and the beginning of the living room. Steve nodded back and laid his windbreaker on the green fabric.

"Probably too early for whiskey, Jack. You want some coffee?" The older man shook his head. Steve sat down in a matching chair.

"Yeah, I've had mine already too." Steve placed his hands on his knees and looked at the mobster. Jack cleared his throat.

"I was laid up in that hospital bed for six weeks. Had a lot of time to think about things." Jack looked down at the gray carpet and then back up at Steve. His eyes were a little more watery than when he was squinting at the sun outside.

"You didn't have to do what you did, Cannon, I wouldn't have done it for you." Steve started to say something, but Jack held up a beefy right hand.

"But it don't matter much why you did it, I just want to thank you." Steve sat back into the chair and nodded.

"Thanks for that, Jack. I am sorry about Little Moe." The two sat for several seconds without speaking. Jack broke the silence.

"I guess you probably heard, I left Tommy."

"I heard that, Jack, I guess you have your reasons." Jack shrugged. "Nothing that big, just time that's all."

"How's Tommy taking it?"

"Not good at first, but now he is OK. Gives a chance for some of the east coast talent to move up and show off their stuff. He's covered, so everything is OK on that front."

"What are you going to do now, Jack?" The older man looked out the small window toward Sunrise Mountain. Steve sighed.

"You can't make a career out of chasing Sorelli, Jack, that is no way to live. Tam's on the lookout, some law enforcement agency will get a line on him soon, and if we're lucky, haul him in and that will be that." He stopped when his voice began to betray the lack of confidence they both felt. Jack snorted.

"This may surprise you, Cannon, but you are right about that. Sorelli is most likely in Mexico and out of reach for now. But he won't stay that way forever, he will come back as sure as I am sitting here, we just gotta wait that's all." Steve sat forward and waited until Jack was looking at him.

"Jack, listen to me a minute without saying anything until I am finished, OK?" Steve waited until the gray head nodded agreement.

"Bernie's casino is opening in July. We have been going back and forth on how to set up security. I told him I had someone in mind to coordinate all the security protocols in the hotel. That someone is you, Jack." Steve stopped and waited. Jack shook his head and snorted.

"Why me, Cannon?" Steve smiled.

"I know what you did for Tommy. There isn't a card shark, card counter or cheater that's played here in the last ten years that you don't know on sight, no matter how many goofy disguises they got on. What you don't know about the cashier cage and the counting room hasn't been thought of yet. So how about it?" There were several more moments when neither man spoke or looked at the other. Jack rubbed his large jaw.

"I'll consider it, Cannon, but I'll want to talk with Bernie about it. I need to know that he knows what he is doing." Steve chuckled.

"Sure thing, Jack, but let me ask you. What are you going to do until then?" Jack shrugged.

"Don't know, haven't put much thought into what to do, mostly what I don't want to do anymore."

"I have another suggestion for you, Jack. The first phase of the Casablanca, the part that was the Three Coins Motel and the front part of the building will be ready in two weeks. I am taking office space in there. I need someone to help me set it up, help hire a receptionist, and do some legwork on several cases I am working. Want the job?" Jack shook his head wearily.

"You're a pushy one, aren't you Cannon. How much does it pay?" Steve sat back and smiled.

"I don't know, Jack, you tell me. How much a week for a guy like you?" Jack frowned and rose from the couch.

"Five hundred, plus a gas and meal allowance." Steve stood up and looked the older man in the eye. He extended his hand.

"Done." Jack slowly reached out and clasped the firm shake. "Where you staying, Jack?"

"At the D.I., Tommy's letting me keep my room for a month. When do we start?"

"I'll call you later this week, and we can meet at Foxy's for the time being." Jack looked at the floor and nodded thoughtfully, before turning and heading toward the door.

"See ya later this week." Steve moved his hand through the air in a small mock salute as Jack disappeared through the door.

*

It was just after seven-thirty and nearly dark when Steve walked up the concrete steps and pulled open the door of the Dula Recreational center. The old building sat in the middle of a large park just off the downtown district and held a basketball court, a weight room and two handball courts. The sweaty smell of the gym hung in the stale air of the lobby as Steve walked across the linoleum floor and through a small door that hid a stairway. Two flights up, Steve walked out onto a narrow parapet area that overlooked the spacious court. He leaned on the red pipe railings and looked out over the activity below.

Twenty-five men, almost all Japanese, knelt in a long line across the parquet floor. All were dressed in traditional kendo fashion; thick blue cotton tops and the split blowsy pants that appeared as a blue, floor length skirt when they stood. Arranged neatly in front of each of them were the protective head pieces, the thick gauntlet gloves, the chest protector, and the shinai; a three foot long mock sword made of long strips of bamboo secured with leather strips. As Steve watched, the line bowed deeply in unison, their arms stretched forward and their foreheads nearly touching the floor, before they shifted slightly to their left, bowing once in that direction before resuming their former position. They bowed once more, murmuring several phrases in Japanese. Steve leaned further out over the rail and saw the object of the last bow. Keno Ogawa was seated facing the group from twenty yards away. He bowed in response to the groups' last supplication. For several minutes the men ritually donned their head pieces, chest protectors, thigh protectors and gloves, forming into two long lines when they were finished.

One member from each of the lines advanced cautiously toward each other by sliding his bare right foot along the floor and quickly bringing the left foot to the back of the front foot, before extending the right foot again and repeating the process. When they were within striking distance of each other, one of the combatants held his shinai perpendicular to the floor while the other lunged forward and struck it vigorously several times in a row as the shinai was moved from one side of the receivers' body to the other. With each strike the attacker let out a short, sharp shout. When each man had gone through both lines several times, Keno Ogawa issued several short commands and the men broke up into small groups. While Keno walked slowly among them, the men set about practicing drills that were designed to build endurance and skill. After forty-five minutes had passed, Keno issued another loud command and moved to the middle of the floor. Three men stood opposite him as the others knelt in the same fashion that Steve had observed when he had first come in. The first man in line held his shinai at his side, and took three of the long sliding steps toward Keno, before stopping and executing a small bow which was returned by Keno. The man then drew his shinai in an exaggerated motion, extending it in front of him as he slowly squatted. Keno mirrored his actions simultaneously. They hesitated for three seconds, their shinais pointed at each other from three feet away. They both slowly rose from the crouched position. Keno's opponent let out a fierce shout and advanced toward Keno, the tip of his shinai moving in small menacing circles. They moved around each other for several seconds before Keno's opponent let out a cry and rushing forward swung the bamboo sword deftly toward Keno's head. Keno waited for a split second as the blow descended. Just before it impacted upon his head piece, he stepped quickly to his left, slashing his sword across the man's chest protector as he stepped past him, gliding several steps before turning around, his shinai held at the ready. The man instantly charged again. This time Keno moved forward and met him halfway, stepping to the side at the last second, his shinai cracking sharply on top of the surprised man's wrist. The man turned and bowed slowly. Keno bowed back and coming to the man's side, walked him slowly through the maneuver several times until he was sure that the lesson had been received. For the next hour, Keno patiently worked through all the members of the dojo in the same way, offering advice and encouragement to each in turn. As the men formed the same long blue line as they had in the beginning, they repeated the bows and then began removing their armor. Steve retraced his steps back down the narrow stairway and into the lobby. He sat on a bench near the door and smoked a cigarette. Fifteen minutes later, after all the other dojo members had filed by, Keno Ogawa came through the locker room door, a large blue canvas bag slung over his shoulder, a thin black leather shinai case in his right hand. He stopped in the middle of the lobby when he saw Steve. He bowed his head slightly and gazed impassively at the private detective for a few moments before he spoke.

"Mr. Cannon. I am surprised to see you this evening." Steve stood up, pushed the glass door open and looked back at Keno.

"Do you drink beer, Mr. Ogawa?"

A half hour later, Steve sat across from Keno Ogawa and shifting around in the small wooden chair, surveyed the narrow dining room. Seven blocks north of Fremont Street, Steve had never seen the sushi restaurant. The only other patrons were two elderly Japanese men pushing small black and white objects around on a playing board. A thin Japanese girl with short black hair brought two large brown beer bottles and glasses toward the table. Steve leaned back to give her room to set the lacquered tray between the two men. As she bowed quickly and turned to leave, Keno reached out and stopped her saying something in rapid Japanese. She smiled and giggled slightly at Steve, putting her hand quickly in front of her mouth. She bowed deeply and still smiling, moved away and disappeared behind a curtain. Keno chuckled as he poured some of the beer into Steve's glass.

"That is my niece, Suko. My uncle and my sister own this place. How do you find Japanese beer, Mr. Cannon?" Steve picked up one of the bottles and attempted to read the label as Keno poured the contents of the second bottle into his own glass.

"I have always found it watery and rather bitter, Mr. Ogawa." Keno stopped his pouring for a few seconds. He smiled and hoisted the large glass of beer toward Steve. Steve lifted his as Keno invoked the traditional Japanese toast.

"Kampei." Steve took a large drink of the frothy beer and set his glass down.

"That is pretty good, a little deeper flavor than most American beers." He took another sip and put down the glass when he saw Keno observing him closely. Keno leaned toward Steve, his voice low.

"Why are you here, Mr. Cannon?" Steve took a bigger sip of the beer and put the almost empty glass back on the tray. Keno raised his hand and uttered something toward the curtain. Steve heard the short feminine reply.

Steve waited until Suko had replaced the empty bottles with two full ones and left the table before he cleared his throat. He looked across the table at the bemused expression on the worn face.

"I want to help you find Martin." Steve gazed evenly back at the unblinking eyes. Keno reached out and picked up his glass, the creases in his calloused hands streaked blue from the dye that had leached from the sweaty Kendo uniform.

"You have had a change of heart. Why?" Steve looked out the window at the bright yellow lights of a small shabby casino across the street before he met the Japanese man's gaze once more.

"I can't tell you why. I don't know myself. As I was watching you in the gym tonight, I just decided, that's all." Keno smiled briefly.

"That's not all, Mr. Cannon, but that is all we get to know." He touched his glass gently to Steve's before taking a large drink. Steve pulled out his notebook and pen.

"I need some information. Are you comfortable talking to me here, or would you rather somewhere else?" Keno shook his head.

"Here is best." Steve nodded.

"I know Martin worked at the Stardust. What exactly did he do there?" Keno's countenance changed as he sat back in his chair. He frowned as he turned one of the empty beer bottles slowly over in his hand. Steve tapped the pad impatiently with his pen. Keno held up his hand.

"I am sorry, Mr. Cannon, this is a hard question for me." Steve put down his pen, lifted his glass and took two small sips as he waited. Keno sighed, sat up in his chair and looked sadly across the table.

"He was dealing baccarat. Everyone knew the truth except me. He told me he was in food service. I found out from one of his friends a week after he disappeared." Steve wrote two lines in his notebook before he spoke again.

"I don't want to push too hard on this, but those jobs are not just handed out. Somebody has to have a lot of juice to even get into the dealer school. It took him several months to get through that school. He lives with you right?" Keno nodded.

"He was taking classes at Nevada Southern University. I didn't question him closely." Steve wrote for a few seconds before he pushed the notebook across the table.

"I need names, addresses and phone numbers of all his close friends." Keno looked at Steve before picking up the notebook and directing a stream of Japanese toward the curtain. A few seconds later, Suko appeared at the table, her hands folded in front of her. Keno held the notebook and pen up in his left hand and uttered several sentences in Japanese while he looked at Steve. Suko took the pad and pen from her uncle, bowed and returned to the space behind the curtain. Keno looked down at his beer glass.

"I have met some of his friends, but not all." Steve nodded. "When was the last time you saw him?"

"Friday, the nineteenth of March, Mr. Cannon."

"Where was he heading next, the last time that you saw him?" Keno shook his head.

"I do not know. It was six o'clock in the evening. He was going out. He could have been going to the hotel, I don't know." A few minutes later, the curtain was swept aside as Suko returned to the table, placed the notebook and pen on the tray, bowed to her uncle and left. Keno picked up the pad and pen with both hands and handed it to Steve. Steve glanced at the three names and addresses that were printed neatly on the page.

"In my experience, Mr. Ogawa, in dealing with young people, friends have the most helpful information." Keno nodded and continued to stare at his glass. Steve pulled out his wallet and began to retrieve a five dollar bill. Keno shook his head and quickly placed his hand on Steve's.

"No, Mr. Cannon, you do not pay here." Keno pulled a small

zippered bag from his back pocket. Steve saw the same folded bills that he had seen at the Mexican restaurant.

"How much do I pay?" He looked quizzically at Steve. "For Martin?" Steve sighed.

"One hundred and fifty dollars a day, plus expenses. I don't want any money now. I will give you a bill the next time we meet." Keno slowly placed the roll of bills back into the pouch. From behind the money he slipped out a small black and white photo. He slid it across the narrow table to Steve. Keno stood up and looked down at Steve.

"I am going to use the restroom now. I am weak and sentimental when it comes to my son, Mr. Cannon, but I look back on much loss. Do not hold anything from me, I must know where Martin is. Goodbye." Steve stood up as Keno bowed before disappearing behind the curtain. Steve pulled out the five dollar bill and slipped it under the lacquer tray before he walked out into the warm night.

APRIL 7

STEVE EASED INTO a parking space on Stewart Avenue, two blocks north of Fremont Street, just before nine o'clock. He looked across the street at the yellow stucco, one story building. The 'closed' sign in the window did not stop Steve from crossing the narrow street and rapping on the glass. Just above his hand, 'Las Vegas Dealer School' was written across the door in large green letters. After a few minutes, Steve heard a window sliding in its' frame and looked down the side of the building, just as a head of red curls appeared. Steve smiled and waved.

"Hello, Betts." The head disappeared and Steve waited while Betty Graco appeared in front of him, twisted the key in the lock and opened the door.

"Steve Cannon. Well, I'll be. How have you been, dear? I haven't heard from you in ages. Come on in and have some coffee." Steve followed the short round woman across a small entry way and into a large room filled with gaming tables. Betty led the way into a cluttered office that sat behind a huge glass window that looked out on the floor. She sat down heavily behind a metal desk and motioned to one of the chairs just inside the door. As Steve sat down, she poured two cups of coffee from a percolator resting on a shelf behind her desk.

"Black, right?" Steve nodded as she handed the cup across to Steve. Steve took a sip and looked around.

"Nothing much's changed around here, Betts." Betty took a sip and chuckled.

"And you should see how much work it is to keep it that way. I've had two competitors open and close in the last three years. The big hotels keep telling me I should get bigger. Ha! Quality is quality, and anyone I take on, gets a job and a good one, or they get their money back." Betty laughed and sat back in her chair. Steve smiled and placed his cup on the edge of the desk, one of the few uncovered spaces in the office.

"I won't take up your time, Betts, I know you open in an hour. I just need to pick your brain on something I'm working on." Betty Graco shrugged.

"Shoot. You know if I can help, I will." Steve smiled and took another sip of the coffee.

"I need to know what you remember about a young Japanese boy named 'Martin Ogawa'. He probably went through here in the last eighteen months or so." Betty frowned over the top of her cup.

"Had several boys that fit that description go through here, but the name isn't registering. Why are you asking, Steve?"

"I am looking into a case that involves him. He might be in trouble, might just be a runaway." Steve reached again for his coffee.

She swiveled her chair around and pulled open a file drawer just under the percolator. Steve watched while she thumbed through several inches of paper. When she turned back around, she had a single sheet in her hand. A small photo was clipped to one corner.

"Here he is. I remember him now. Quick study and a very good attitude with customers. He went through the main course and then came back two months later for Baccarat training." Betty handed the sheet to Steve as she spoke. Steve noticed the picture was the same one that Keno had given him the night before.

"Is that still how it works, Betts?" The older woman nodded.

"Pretty much. The casinos still use those dealing jobs as incentives and send the cream of the crop back here for the school. Sometimes, guys with a lot of juice go directly through it. Had the senator's son-in-law go through here last month, without going through the regular course first, but that is the exception not the rule." Steve made a small sucking sound with his teeth.

"Two months is pretty quick to make the grade, especially in a place like the Stardust." Betty nodded knowingly.

"Yeah, but you have to remember that a lot of rich Asians like to play that game and the Arabs think Asian dealers are good luck, so my guess is, that has a lot to do with it." Steve handed the sheet and the photo back across the desk to Betty.

"Thanks for the info, Betts. That confirms some of the facts I have been told." Steve rose and took another sip of his coffee.

"Thanks for the coffee as well. Don't get up, I will show myself out." Steve smiled and put down the cup before he turned toward the door.

"Glad to help, Steve." Betty waved and Steve returned the wave through the glass window as he made his way to the front door. There were several students already waiting on the sidewalk as Steve crossed over to his car.

A block away, Steve pulled into a Seven-Eleven and parked in front of a phone booth. He waited until the coins had finished clanging through the box before he dialed the number. After four rings Steve could hear the click of the receiver.

"Hello?" The voice was young and male. "Is this Ronald Hillman?"

"Yes, who is this?"

"My name is Steve Cannon. I have been hired to find Martin Ogawa. Suko, his cousin says you are a good friend of his, do I have the right guy?" There was a slight pause on the other end.

"He is my friend, yes. But I don't know where he is." Steve shook his head.

"Nobody does, son. But information you have may help me find him. Do you understand that?"

"Yes, I do." Steve sighed.

"Where can we meet? I can get usually get better information face to face, than over the phone. You live on Eastern, right?" Steve relayed the address from his notebook.

"Yeah, it's the big pink house on the desert side of Eastern. Sits off by itself.

"I can be there in twenty minutes. Can you wait for me?"

"Sure, I'll be here."

"Good, Ronald, I will see you then."

Steve tossed his notebook on the seat of the Jeep and drove six blocks, turning right onto Eastern Avenue. A mile later Steve drove by the new high school, Valley High, that was in the last stages of construction. The house sat between Flamingo and Tropicana and it was ten minutes before Steve pulled off on the short dirt road that lead up to the house. Steve climbed out of his car and looked across the desert. In the distance about four hundred yards away he could see the large trees surrounding Paradise Park. He waited for several minutes after knocking on the bright pink door. When it was opened by a tall blonde woman in her mid-forties, it was immediately closed down to four inches as she stared at the man standing on her porch.

"Who are you? My husband is here." Steve smiled and took two steps backward, but the door remained only slightly ajar.

"My name is Steve Cannon, Mrs. Hillman. I just spoke with your son Ronald on the phone twenty minutes ago and I am here to ask him some questions about the disappearance of Martin Ogawa." The woman cut him off.

"My husband and I have already asked our son if he knew where Martin was after the police called."

"I am sure you have, Mrs. Hillman. I need information about other people Martin may have known or was associated with. I also need to corroborate some of the facts I already have. May I come in please?" Steve held out his card. The door opened a little wider and the woman took the card in her hand, turning it over and then reading the front. She frowned and looked up at Steve.

"Ronald is downstairs, Mr. Cannon, but we are leaving in twenty minutes for the horse stables and I don 't want to be late for my lesson." Steve nodded and grimaced as he moved through the now fully opened door and waited on a tile landing that lead to a spacious living room and also to a wide carpeted stairway that led down to the next level. Mrs. Hillman indicated the stairs and Steve nodded toward her as he started down. They turned right and emptied out into a huge rec room.

Steve stopped at the bottom of the stairs. Ronald Hillman was standing in the middle of the room. All three walls that Steve could see were covered with stacks of small wire cages. Ronald was holding a large yellow desert iguana, and as Steve stepped into the room, the loud buzzing of rattlesnakes in two cages near his feet stopped him in his tracks. Ronald Hillman smiled.

"Don't you like snakes, Mr. Cannon?" Steve bent down and looked at the sidewinder and the small Mojave in the two cages nearest the floor. He straightened up before he answered.

"Can take them or leave them, as a rule. But I like to know when they are around before they surprise me." He looked down at the short young man in front of him. The blue eyes were sharp and earnest under a brown Beatle haircut. Ronald lifted the iguana up and disentangled its' claws from his t-shirt. He moved to the opposite wall to place him back in his cage, as several rattlesnakes in front of him began to shake their rattles vigorously. Steve looked around the room and realized that over half the cages held snakes of one variety or another, the rest held different species of lizards.

"Quite a large collection. Where did you get them?" Ronald Hillman closed the door of the cage and turned back to the private detective.

"The lizards I caught mostly around here, or in that big patch of desert between NSU and Tropicana. The snakes all come from the highway that goes out to Red Rocks. They crawl out on the road just as the sun goes down to keep their bodies warm on the asphalt as long as possible." Steve nodded and pulled out his pen and notebook, an act that was met immediately by more buzzing, this time off his left shoulder.

"Somewhere more quiet we could talk, Ronald?" The young man nodded and pointed out a sliding glass door that led to a concrete patio. Steve followed and they sat down under a faded red umbrella in two wicker patio chairs. Ronald pushed the brown bangs out of his eyes. Behind him, Steve could see Mrs. Hillman watching them from a picture window one story up.

"You live here with your parents, right?" Steve looked up from writing the date in his notebook. Ronald scoffed.

"Hardly. I'm twenty-three. I am just here this quarter. I am going back to Princeton in two weeks to start graduate school."

"What is your field?"

"Zoology." Steve smiled to himself.

"Who takes care of the snakes and lizards when you are not here?"

"My little brother, Harry."

"Does he know Martin?" Ronald laughed and shook his head. "He is only sixteen." Steve nodded.

"How do you know Martin?" Ronald looked at Steve directly.

"I have known him since we were in junior high. We went to Western High School together." Steve furrowed his brow.

"Western? This area is zoned so that all the kids go to Las Vegas High." Ronald nodded.

"My folks moved to this house the middle of my senior year. They gave me a waiver for the last semester."

"When was the last time you saw or spoke to Martin Ogawa?" Ronald looked out at the desert over Steve's shoulder.

"The middle of February. We played golf together at the course where his father works."

"Was he the same to you? Did he act differently or talk about things that he hadn't mentioned before?" Ronald shook his head.

"He was the same old Martin, pretty much, except he was a little more outgoing than before. Maybe being a dealer brought him out of his shell, I don't know."

"He get good grades at Western?"

"Pretty much straight A's, like most of our group."

"So why become a dealer, why not college, like you?" Ronald shrugged and fidgeted in his chair. Steve noted that Ronald's mother had left her perch by the window. When Ronald didn't answer, Steve asked the question again.

"Martin always felt bad because his father was a gardener and they didn't have much money, especially for clothes and cars and things like that. Martin became more and more interested in making money. He lied to his father about going to NSU. It didn't surprise me that he became a dealer, especially a baccarat dealer. My dad says those guys can make sixty or seventy grand a year." Steve tapped his pen on the notebook and looked directly at Ronald.

"If Martin needed to go somewhere, somewhere safe, where would he go?"

"You mean if he was sad or in trouble?"

Steve nodded.

"Yes, that's what I mean, Ronald." The young man looked down and picked at his t-shirt where the iguana's claws had made several small holes. When he spoke, his voice was barely audible.

"Suko, he would go to Suko." Ronald looked up at Steve. "His father came here a week ago."

"Did you tell him what you just told me about Suko?" Ronald sighed.

"No, but I told him where Martin worked and what he did." Ronald finished just as Mrs. Hillman walked down three short concrete steps and came over to the chairs.

"We have to go now, Ronald. I will show you out, Mr. Cannon." Steve stood up and put his notebook back in his jacket pocket.

"I may need to ask you some more questions, Ronald, before you go back to school." Ronald nodded and headed back toward the sliding glass door. His mother followed him for a few steps.

"You make sure all those cage doors are closed, Ronald, I don't want to find another lizard hanging on my upstairs curtains." When Ronald didn't reply, she turned and looked at Steve quizzically.

"You know, you don't look like a Cannon. I know Helen Cannon pretty well, how are you related to her?" Steve had seen a walkway that circled around the large pink house and led to the driveway. He hesitated for a second as he started walking toward it.

"No relation, Mrs. Hillman, another family entirely." He didn't wait for a reply but strode around the corner of the house, then slowed his pace as he walked to the Jeep, twenty yards away.

*

Steve walked through the door of Foxy's just ahead of the lunch crowd. He took a seat in a row of empty tables by the window and was reading his notes when a waiter approached him. Steve looked up and smiled.

"Hi, Walter, how have you been?" The tall thin waiter smiled back. "Great, Steve, what can I get you?"

"Pastrami on rye and a beer." Walter nodded and pulled a set of cutlery wrapped in a cloth napkin from his apron, unfolded it and arranged the three implements in front of Steve.

"Bernie know you're here?" Steve shook his head.

"Nope. He's probably busy with lunch spooling up, don't bother him." Walter nodded as he backed away from the table and disappeared into the kitchen.

Steve was halfway through his sandwich and was reading the previous day's edition of the Review-Journal, when Bernie pulled out a chair and sat down.

"I didn't see ya sitting here, until just a minute ago." Steve laughed.

"Yeah, and I told Walter not to tell you, either. I just needed some lunch and some time to think. I didn't want to pull you away from your work." Bernie waved dismissively in Steve's direction, picked up a section of the paper and shook his head.

"Walter has orders to tell me whenever you show. I wonder who he thinks he works for?" They both laughed and then laughed even harder when Walter suddenly appeared back at the table.

"You want some coffee boss?" Bernie beamed up the waiter.

"Sure, Walter, I'll be here for a few minutes, that would be great." Bernie turned back to Steve. Steve folded the paper and placed it near the window. He sat up straight in his chair and took a small sip of the beer.

"Bernie, let me tell you who I think should be the head of security for the Casablanca." Bernie leaned in toward Steve.

"Sure, Steve, shoot."

"Jack Cathay." Steve sat back and drained the last two inches of beer from the glass and looked across the table at his friend, trying to judge his reaction. Bernie sat back and looked out the window.

"Hmmmm." Bernie rubbed his chin and looked back at Steve.

"I see where you are going with this. I hadn't thought in that direction, but that kind of expertise is hard to find. Do you think he would do it?" Steve shrugged.

"I think so. I sounded him out on it pretty strongly. He wants to talk with you, so at this point I will leave it between the two of you. You may get some guff from Tommy Carmino, but I don't see how he can object too strongly, Jack quit several weeks ago. Jack is still staying at the D.I. for the rest of this month. So you can call him there." Bernie smiled.

"Just like Tommy, Jack and I go way back to Chicago, in fact, Jack was higher in the organization than Tommy was at one time. So, I wasn't surprised when I heard that Jack had quit, I guess I always wondered why it took him so long." Walter appeared at the table with a cup of coffee and another beer for Steve. After a small sip, Steve gestured with the stein toward Bernie.

"It was that near-death thing and the fact that Little Moe was killed, and it was Jack's idea to go after Sorelli. Pretty hard to see how it wouldn't change him." Bernie shook his head and took a slow sip of the hot liquid. Steve waited until he put the cup back down on the saucer.

"Bernie. You know anybody in the casino end over at the Stardust?" Bernie made a face.

"Used to know Sonny Turlow, but he has been gone for two years. I heard a whole new crew took over the first of the year."

"I heard that too, I am just checking with everyone to get a line on who has the muscle there." Bernie nodded slowly as his attention was drawn to the obituary section. He held it up and turned the sheet toward Steve.

"Look. Nathan Nessbaum died." Bernie ran his finger down the page and stopped near the bottom. Steve peered at the notice and read the first several lines.

"Didn't know him, did you?" Bernie folded up the paper and set it next to his coffee cup.

"Yeah, I met him once or twice when he was here from Tahoe on business. I know his brother, Sheldon and his wife pretty well. They live out where I do. I heard about it two days ago when it happened. Just keeled over in his casino from a heart attack. They are having the funeral Saturday, he's gonna be buried out at the Sunset Cemetery."

"Are you going?" Bernie nodded his head as he stood to go.

"Yeah, I seem to be going to quite a few lately. Hopefully, they will give it a rest soon." Bernie laughed quietly at his own joke and smiled down at Steve.

"Finish your beer, I have to go do some things in back." Steve waved as Bernie turned and weaved his way through the crowded tables back through the swinging doors that led to the kitchen.

"See you, Bern." Steve took one more gulp of his beer and

slipped a five dollar bill underneath his plate. He walked out onto the sidewalk where the first warmth of spring created heat mirages when he looked across the asphalt toward the desert.

Twenty minutes later, Steve took the blue carpeted steps two at a time as he ascended to the second floor of the Desert Inn Hotel. He paused for a full three seconds at the glossy double paneled wooden door. Large shiny brass letters announced that this was the office of 'Thomas Carmino, Head of Resort Operations'. Steve carefully pulled down on the brass lever and cracked the door an inch. There was no one at the receptionist desk. Steve stepped slowly into the large room and closed the door silently behind him. He heard the receptionist, Miss Horvath, talking to someone behind the wall that separated the waiting area from the back filing space. Steve walked quietly across the carpet, opened the door to Tommy's office, taking care to again close the door noiselessly behind him.

Tommy Carmino was talking on the phone when Steve Cannon materialized in front of his desk. Tommy came out of his chair with a small startled jump, before his face clouded over and he raised his arms incredulously, pointing back toward the reception area.

"What the hell?" Steve smiled at the mob boss as Tommy spoke into the phone.

"No, not you, Marvin, I was talking to another pain in the ass who just walked in here unannounced." Tommy shook his head at the reply from the other end of the line.

"I don't care. Done by Friday or else." He dropped the gold-plated receiver back onto the cradle and glared across the desk at the private detective who was busy lighting up one of his cigars.

"How the hell did you get in here?" Steve shrugged, turned his head toward the door and blew a small blue cloud of Cuban cigar smoke toward the entrance.

"Miss Horvath must have gone to powder her nose, Tommy, how do I know?" Tommy scoffed.

"You must think we are partners or something, the way you

waltz in here and kipe one of my Cubans without asking." Steve smiled as wide as he could.

"Well, I am on the board of Carmino Lighting, Tommy, that should count for something." Tommy shook his head back and forth several times.

"You amaze me, Slick, you really do. That was Bernie's idea, I should have known that was going to haunt me forever, but: Hey!" Tommy sat up at mock attention in his large leather chair. "I guess I got nothing better to do than listen to whatever hare-brained request you are going to hit me with now, right?" Steve laughed and shook an inch of ash off the cigar into a crystal ashtray.

"Well prepare yourself, Tommy, you are going to get a kick out of this one." Steve waited a full five seconds as he took a deep drag on the thick cigar and blew the smoke out of the side of his mouth.

"I need you to give me a two hundred-fifty thousand dollar marker I can take across the street to the Stardust baccarat room." Tommy Carmino's eyes glazed over for a split second before he exploded.

"You want what, Cannon?" Tommy stood up and leaned out as far over his desk as he could. Steve looked up at the two purple veins in Tommy's forehead. Steve smiled with a closed mouth and then put the cigar to his lips and talked past it.

"Relax, Tommy. I'm not going to spend any of your monopoly money, I just need it to get in the door. I will play with my own cash once I am in. But I will need a high rollers suite for the night and a chauffeured car as well." Tommy didn't move from his position.

"What are you talking about? Why should I do this for you? And why do you need to play baccarat all of the sudden. You play poker." Steve held up his hand and waited until Tommy had slumped back into his chair.

"Let's take it one question at a time, Tommy. I need to get into the baccarat room, because I am investigating the disappearance of a young man who is a baccarat dealer over there. Showing up with a marker from your hotel will not only get me in, but they will fall all over themselves, no questions asked. How sweet is that deal? A guy takes out a marker from your biggest rival and loses it in your casino?" Steve held up his hand again as Tommy came half-way out of his chair. "I'm not going to lose it Tommy, I am not even going to play with it. And why should you do this, Tommy? Because it would be a nice gesture between friends, that's why." Steve took another puff of the cigar and looked across at the red faced mobster. After a few seconds, Steve saw Tommy's eyes narrow.

"All right, Slick, you'll get your marker and your room. But let me warn you. If there is any funny business going on here, I am going to own you, you got that? The way I figure it, you lose any of my money, you will be working for me. Maybe you can take Jack's place, huh, Cannon?" Steve smiled and looked down at the Maduro wrapped cigar.

"I knew you would see that angle, Tommy. It's good that we know each other so well, don't you think?" Tommy snorted.

"When do you need it?"

"Now." Tommy shook his head as he picked up the phone.

"It expires at midnight, wise guy, and don't ask again." Tommy pulled down one digit of the rotary dial with his forefinger. He shook his head continually at Steve as he waited for the other party to pick up.

"Myron. Make up a marker that Steve Cannon can take across the street. Two hundred fifty thousand, and make sure there is someone in the cage that can vouch for it tonight if the Stardust checks up on it. Got it?"

"No. He will be down to pick it up in the next ten minutes." Tommy hung up and looked across at Steve.

"I need a drink." Tommy moved from behind the desk and stepped down a level, crossing behind a large billiard table to a bar that sat in front of a long mirrored wall. He returned twenty seconds later with two crystal glasses half full of scotch. He put one down in front of Steve before he sat back into his chair. When he had crossed both legs on the desk, he looked over at the detective.

"So, Jack Cathay. I guess you heard." Steve took a sip of the whisky and held the glass up to admire the color.

"Single malt?" Tommy ignored the question.

"I think it is in both our best interests, Slick, that I continue to believe that you had nothing to do with him leaving. Am I right?" Steve rolled another sip around in his mouth before he answered.

"I just heard yesterday myself, Tommy. Jack stopped by my house, it was news to me." Tommy turned in his chair and looked intently at Steve.

"He say what comes next? He was pretty close-mouthed when he was in here, you know how he is." Steve took a puff from the cigar and placed it in the ashtray.

"I recommended him to Bernie as a good prospect for the head security job at the Casablanca. If you got a problem with that, take it up with Mr. Gold." Steve waited while Tommy finished his scotch and stared out the window at the first tee of the golf course forty feet below. He didn't turn around when he spoke.

"Jack can do what he wants, new blood in here won't hurt." Tommy twirled his chair around. Steve put the glass on the desk blotter and stood up.

"Thanks, for the marker and the room, Tommy, I will see you tomorrow at Bernie's." Tommy grunted and picked up the phone. Steve opened the door with a flourish and strode into the middle of the room, beaming at Miss Horvath whose mouth dropped open when she saw Steve.

"Nice to see that you have returned to your post, Miss Horvath. I think Mr. Carmino would like to see you in his office." Steve stifled a chuckle as he swept past the astonished secretary and opened the big door to the hallway.

Three floors up, he knocked on the white double door. A few seconds later he heard Jack's gruff voice inquiring the name of his visitor. Jack opened the door, and while he wasn't smiling, Steve was having trouble adjusting to the mild expression he encountered whenever he met him. The spacious living room was decorated almost entirely in various shades of white.

"Jack, this is beautiful." Steve walked over to the large ceiling to floor windows that looked across at the Frontier Hotel and the hazy blue Spring Mountains in the distance.

"Yeah, I can't complain."

"Where are you going to stay after this month, Jack?" Jack shrugged. "Don't know. You want me to order us up some coffee?" Steve demurred.

"No, I won't be here that long, Jack. Just got a couple of things to tell you and to get some information if I can. First, I told Bernie that you were interested in the Head of Security job. He's interested and wants to talk, so I will leave it up to you. Secondly, I was just down in Tommy's office. I told him you were considering working with Bernie, kinda heading things off at the pass." Jack chuckled to himself.

"Yeah, I know. That pretty much guarantees that nothing is ever likely to come out of Tommy's mouth about that." Jack grunted and fidgeted in his chair. "They got a new guy in from Cleveland two days ago. Maybe I'll wander down to Tommy's office later and offer to break him in, maybe that will smooth things a bit." Steve smiled.

"Couldn't hurt, Jack. Let me ask you a question. Who's running the casino at the Stardust now?" Jack's pale blue eyes looked intently at Steve for several seconds before he answered.

"Kleinman's out, Hyman Goldbaum's out, I don't know about Johnny Drew, but I heard he can't even go into his own casino. I heard it is the result of some dust-up back east. All I do know is the crew that is running things now are a bad bunch. Don't know the rules and the way things work in this town. Even told Tommy to shove it." Steve nodded thoughtfully.

"I may need you in the next couple of days. Are you available?"

Jack nodded. "Good." Steve stood to go. Jack spun his chair around and looked up at Steve.

"Step carefully if you have to deal with those guys. They are nuts." Steve walked to the foyer with Jack several steps behind. Steve paused after he had opened the door.

"One floor up from the office spaces in the Casablanca, they are halfway through building the luxury suites. Bernie is pressing them because he wants to move into his by the first of May. I think there are two smaller suites on that floor. Something to think about before you talk to Bernie." Steve winked as Jack waved and closed the door behind him.

*

It was nearly five o'clock when Steve arrived home. He went into the bedroom and knelt in front of the safe that sat in the back of the long narrow closet. He removed five thousand dollars in hundred dollar bills from two envelopes, closed the door and spun the dial. He laid the cash on the nightstand next to the marker, a letter from the Desert Inn cage signed by Myron and Tommy, guaranteeing the bearer's losses up to two hundred and fifty thousand dollars. Steve knew the protocol. They would accept it without question, but they would check with Myron and make sure that Steve was a guest at the hotel. The only risk was that someone would recognize him, but he had rarely frequented the hotel, preferring the Desert Inn, the Sahara, and the Sands. Though the Sands and the Dunes usually reported the most baccarat activity, Steve had heard rumors that the new operators at the Stardust had strong connections to the Far East and were very successful in enticing the wealthy Japanese, Chinese and Malaysians to their casino.

An hour later, Steve straightened the tie of his tuxedo in the bathroom mirror. He put the packet of hundred dollar bills in one of the inside pockets of the dinner jacket, two of Tommy's Cuban cigars in the other. It was still light out when he pulled into the Desert Inn

Hotel and parked just inside the entrance for the second time that day. Steve lit a Pall Mall and strolled through the side entrance that was usually used by the casino bosses and security. He stepped into the large lobby and headed for the VIP concierge desk. A young woman smiled up at Steve when he stopped in front of the counter.

"Good evening, Sir, my name is Marion, how may I help you?" Steve smiled back.

"My name is Steve Cannon, Marion and I need to pick up my room key. The Desert Rose suite."

"Certainly, Mr. Cannon." The young woman opened a drawer beside her chair and placed an envelope in front of Steve. Steve turned the open envelope over and let the two keys inside fall into his hand. One was larger and obviously a room key, the other was smaller and round in shape.

"The small one operates the private elevator, Mr. Cannon, in the unlikely event that the floor concierge is not at his post." Steve put both keys in the flap pocket on the side of his jacket and smiled. "Thank you, Marion." He turned and walked several steps to the concierge who was standing in front of the single door elevator.

Steve stood in front of the windows that covered most of the walls of the four room suite. From his third floor perch, he could see past the unfinished Landmark casino and the large hotels and neon signs of Fremont Street, five miles distant. He poured a glass of scotch and sat down on the gold brocade couch with a pack of cards in his hand. He absent-mindedly dealt hands of baccarat to himself. The Punto Banco style of baccarat that most of the Nevada casinos played had never appealed to Steve. It was purely a game of chance and there was little skill that the player could bring to bear on the outcome. However, over the years, Steve had developed a rhythm to his betting that rested upon his innate sense as a gambler and on the few occasions that he had applied it to the game of baccarat, he had done surprisingly well. He also held the personal opinion that all the mystique and exclusiveness of the game was designed to intimidate the gambler and thus gain an edge for the casino. He dealt the players hand, the two cards face down. He then dealt the house or Banco hand and turned both cards face up. A ten of hearts and the king of spades. All tens and face cards had a zero value. A natural nine was the best hand possible. Steve turned over the Punto hand. A six of diamonds and a three of clubs. A natural nine. Several hands later, both hands tied with a seven. If a player had placed his bet on the tie spot, he would have won with eight to one odds. For Steve, if there was a point to baccarat this was it. It took strong gamblers intuition to know when to lay down a tie bet, and the result could often be disastrous, two strong chances out of three that you were wrong is the way a lot of casinos made money. A suckers' game. But it appealed to the well-heeled for one reason: In most casinos and certainly those who attracted the wealthiest clientele there was no limit to the amount the player could bet on each hand. Steve picked up the phone in the foyer of the suite and dialed the number of the concierge.

Ten minutes later, Steve stepped out onto the red carpet that covered the area just outside the front door. He nodded to a bell captain who, after nodding back, blew a short, shrill blast on his whistle and held up his hand. A long black Cadillac limousine pulled slowly up to the front of the hotel from a parking space just down from the main entrance. The captain opened the door with a flourish and Steve slid into the backseat. As soon as the door closed, the driver swung the big caddy in a tight arc toward the entrance to the strip. While he waited for an opening in the traffic he looked in the rearview mirror at his passenger. Steve chuckled as their eyes met.

"Hi Shelly, how ya doing tonight?" The eyes of the black man reflected his large smile.

"I don't believe it! I got the big gun himself in my car. Steve Cannon, what are you doing back there?"

"I had Tommy order you up special, my friend. I hope I am not making you work overtime." Shelly turned and smiled back at Steve just before he turned the Caddy smoothly into the strip traffic.

"Naw, man, I been off for two days, this is a milk and honey run. Double time, my friend." Shelly Cointreu's brow furrowed. "Why the monkey suit? Where we going?" Steve smiled.

"Ultimately, the Stardust, but first take us to the Dunes, you had dinner yet?" Shelly shook his head and held up a brown bag.

"My wife put together a lunch for me. At some point on these jobs, you cool your heels for several hours, pays to have something to nibble and something to read." He laughed and swung off the strip and up the inclined driveway of the Dunes that led to the front door.

"Pull all the way forward, Shelly, and let the valet park it." Shelly stopped several yards past the doors and handed the keys to the car runner in exchange for a numbered slip.

Steve looked up at the bright lights of the huge marquee towering above his head. 'Casino de Paris' blazed in five foot high letters. Below were the words; 'starring Line Renaud'. Steve smiled as he remembered when Remy DeMarche had first come to town and eclipsed Renaud, the first of the celebrity French showgirls. The black Cadillac was whisked away as Steve and Shelly grinned at each other from ten feet away.

"Shelly, you ever eaten at the Sultan's Table?" Shelly crossed over to Steve with a worried look on his round face.

"Are you kidding with me boss? You know they ain't gonna let me in there, I probably would have trouble getting into the coffee shop here." Steve threw an arm around the large shoulders and steered him toward the doors that were opened by two uniformed doormen.

"Relax, Shelly, I had the D.I. make the reservations in Tommy's name. They aren't going to make a fuss." Shelly looked at his friend as they crossed the lobby toward the elevators, and shook his head.

"I hope you know what you are doing here, big gun."

The short maître 'd looked down at Steve and Shelly from his three foot high podium. The lights in the ceiling forty feet above them reflected off his bald head. He took a long look at Shelly before he shifted his gaze to Steve.

"I don 't see Mr. Carmino. Will he be joining you?" Steve smiled benignly.

"He will be a little late. If there is a problem, perhaps we can call him." An ashen look of horror appeared on the face above Steve as the small man's hands fluttered over his reservation book.

"No need, no need, Mr. Cannon. Cherie will be happy to escort you to Mr. Carmino's table." Steve smiled broadly and turned to Shelly, holding out his hand and indicating that he should fall in behind the young woman. The trio walked around the round stage in the middle of the room. When they were seated behind glasses of champagne, Steve held up his glass and waited until Shelly hesitantly followed suit.

"To good friends and to old times at the Golden Nugget." Steve reached forward and gently tapped Shelly's glass before they each took a sip of the French champagne. Shelly looked down at his blue tie and black suit.

"At least I am dressed for it." Steve smiled as two waiters approached the table which was set into a private alcove and was elevated above the rest of the diners.

"Relax, Shelly, I have never been here either. We are going to have a great meal and I am going to have some of their rare scotch and then we are off to the Stardust. Since you are driving, my friend, I would nurse that glass of bubbly as it is all you get tonight."

After the two men had ordered and the waiters disappeared with the menus, Shelly leaned forward.

"So, what's going on, Steve. Why the get-up, the car and all this?" Shelly indicated the rest of the room with his large hand.

"I am working a case and I have to see if I can dig up some information in the baccarat room at the Stardust. Have to look the part, right? I figured why not do it right, just like if I was a real high roller from out of town. I thought maybe you could use a break and some extra cash, plus I need you to do some digging of your own." Shelly's face clouded over for a brief moment.

"Me? What help could I be?"

"You know more people in this town than I do, Shelly. Shoot the bull with the door guys and the car runners. Find out what they know and what they think of the new bosses over there. Guys like you hear and see a lot of stuff." Shelly snorted and half smiled.

"Yeah, it's like we are not there. Invisible." The two men looked up from their conversation as a bevy of waiters descended on the table with salads and appetizers. The head waiter stood at silent attention until he was the only staff person left before he described each dish and the ingredients used to make it. When he left, Steve was just about to eat his salad when he saw Shelly staring at one of the dishes.

"Big gun, did he just say snails?" Steve smiled and nodded.

"You're from the Big Easy, Shel, I can't believe you have never tasted escargot." Shelly made a sour face and shook his head. Steve laughed and grabbed one of the pink shells with the silver tongs and with a small pick, deposited the small succulent insides onto Shelly's plate.

"You like garlic, right, Shel?" Shelly nodded as he slowly picked up his smallest fork. "Well, there you go, I think you will like it."

Several minutes later, Steve called the head waiter over and ordered another dish of escargot. The waiter removed the old dish, stopping for a split second to stare at the pile of shells on Shelly's plate.

As the two men relaxed over the remains of Baked Alaska, Steve sat behind a small flight of scotch glasses, sipping each in turn. Shelly took a taste of his coffee and looked up as Steve spoke.

"Wish me luck at the tables tonight, Shel, because we split the winnings." The big man was startled for a second before he regained his composure.

"What? Now why would you do such a thing?" Steve swallowed a small sip of a peaty Islay whisky before he answered.

"Because you are working with me, Shel. Nobody works for free, at least not in this town." Shelly laughed.

"If it is all the same to you, gun, can't you just play a few hands of poker? No disrespect to your skills as a gambler, but I never heard of anybody walking out of those rooms without leaving it all behind, know what I mean?"

"Yeah, Shel, I know what you mean, but I feel lucky tonight. Let me ask you another question. You happy at the D.I.?" Shelly shrugged and scraped the final piece of cake from his dessert plate.

"Happy as anywhere, I guess. Moving to the strip from downtown has nearly doubled my take, so yeah, it has worked out for me. Why do you ask?"

"Bernie's building a new hotel, kitty-corner to Caesars Palace. You ought to apply for the supervisor of the door and parking lot job. You've met Bernie several times, he is going to need someone good in that position. What do you think?" Shelly smiled and shrugged.

"Yeah, Steve, I'm interested."

"Good. Here is Bernie's number. Call him, tell him you are interested, but don't mention my name. Bernie will remember you and check with me." Shelly looked at the number written on the back of one of Steve's business cards.

"Why not mention you?"

"I have been making a lot of personnel suggestions lately. I don't want it to look like I am a full employment shill for all my friends." Shelly laughed as Steve finished the last of the scotch.

As they left the restaurant, the two men stopped at the podium and waited for a large party to be seated. Steve picked up a box of special 'Sultan's Table' matches. He caught the eye of the maître d'.

"Thanks for everything, I'll make sure that Mr. Carmino hears what a swell time we had." The look on the man's face was wasted on Steve as he and Shelly were already walking to the special elevator that brought guests up to the restaurant.

Steve took his time exiting the limousine in front of the Stardust, the name of the hotel emblazoned along both sides of the building in ten foot high bright yellow letters just above the spinning planets and satellites. By the time that Shelly was inserting the long car into the parking space pointed out to him by the doorman, a hotel executive was extending his hand to Steve just inside the front door.

"Welcome to the Stardust. I am Bill Hanawalt, where may I escort you?" Steve shook the proffered hand and looked around the bustling lobby that opened directly onto the casino floor. He returned his gaze to the beaming smile.

"I like to play baccarat, Mr. Hanawalt, can you accommodate me?" The greeter extended his right arm.

"Right this way … Mr?"

"Cannon, Steve Cannon." Mr. Hanawalt bowed his head slightly as he led the way toward a nondescript door that was built seamlessly into a curved wall of the lobby just past the front desk area. He opened the door with a key he had attached to his belt and stepped aside, grinning, as Steve moved through the door and stepped onto a deep blue carpet.

"Enjoy your game, Mr. Cannon." The door closed behind him, as Steve took three steps into the middle of the room. Curved walls covered with wood paneling from floor to ceiling contained a bar along one side, with glass double doors behind a red velvet rope directly in front of him. Beyond the doors, Steve could see several baccarat tables. A similarly tuxedoed man approached from behind the rope. He stopped five feet from Steve and bowed.

"I am Francois, and I am at your service." The dark olive complexioned man bowed again, something in his French accent striking Steve as forced and unnatural. Steve followed him to the bar. An Asian bartender stood at attention and Steve could see himself and his companion reflected in the antique mirror which sat behind the large array of liquor bottles as he scanned his choices.

"Chivas Regal, neat." As the bartender moved to fill his order, Francois moved closer to Steve.

"Monsieur, have you spoken to our casino manager yet?" Steve turned to his interlocutor pulling the marker from his pocket in the same motion.

"No, I haven't and I don't like wasting time tracking people down. I am sure you can take care of this." Steve unfolded the thick piece of paper and handed it to Francois as he turned back to his drink.

"Of course, Monsieur, I will be but a minute." Francois moved to the side of the bar and disappeared through a thickly paneled wooden door. Steve took a sip of the blended scotch as he moved to the end of the bar where he could see most of the baccarat tables. There were six tables, two being used, but dealers were standing at attention at the four that held no players. All the dealer faces that Steve could see from his vantage point were Asian.

The table closest to him had two players that sat opposite from each other, the dealer between them. One of the men was tall, with swept back salt and pepper hair and wore his tux as if it were a well ingrained habit. The other man was shorter, rounder and his tux jacket was unbuttoned, his plump arms straining the satiny fabric. The only other player in the room sat at the farthest table from the doorway. He was facing Steve, and was dressed in a medium blue business suit with a shortened collar, a fashion Steve was unfamiliar with. His dark skinned face was impassive as his black eyes watched the quick motions of the dealer as the cards were swept from the shoe. The player turned his cards over quickly and sometimes placed a new bet in the same motion. Behind him, two men with even darker skin and identical black suits stood against the wall, their hands folded in front of them and their eyes intent on the player at the table. The player lost four hands in a row. As the dealer pulled two stacks of chips to his side, the man looked up directly at Steve. Steve gazed back unblinking and took a sip of the warm scotch. At almost the same moment, Steve heard the door at the end of the bar open and Francois appeared at his side. One of the black suited men against the wall, left his post, moved between the tables, came through the door and followed Steve and Francois into a spacious office. Steve moved to the far end of the room and turned facing Francois, the black suit, and another man who was smiling at Steve from the center of the room.

"Good evening, Mr. Cannon, I am Harold Warner, director of play here in the baccarat lounge. We are very pleased to have you here. Everything is in order, we just have a small formality to get through and then you may join us at the tables." Steve took a sip from his glass, surveying the three men through the crystal, before he spoke.

"What formality would that be?" His tone and his gaze were even. The man smiled.

"You have come on a propitious evening, Mr. Cannon. One of your fellow players is the Sultan of Brunei. But as a security precaution, we are going to have to ask you to submit to a quick search, just to reassure his highness." Steve grunted and smiled coldly. He stepped into the middle of the room and raised his arms partway toward his head.

"Sure thing. Might even be a good luck omen." The dark skinned man stepped forward and without making eye contact with Steve, ran his hands quickly up and down inside Steve's jacket, feeling in the small of his back for a concealed weapon as he finished. Steve could see the bulge of a handgun beneath the man's coat when he had bent over to pat down Steve's legs. Steve stepped back as the man turned and left the room.

"I have never seen this much falderal just to play a simple game like baccarat." Harold Warner smiled.

"We do things differently here, Mr. Cannon, and I am confident that you will come to appreciate those differences in time if you continue to patronize our casino. Privacy, for instance. Most of the other casinos have big glass windows and put their players on display for anyone that wishes to watch. Some may enjoy that." He shrugged as Francois left the office. "We cater to a different clientele." Steve nodded and followed the director of play as he went to the door and opened it for Steve.

"Enjoy your game, Mr. Cannon."

Steve took the four steps to the velvet rope where Francois was holding open one of the doors for him. Francois followed him into the room. Steve heard the door lock fall with a loud click, indicating that it could be opened from the inside, but not the outside. Francois crossed to a small alcove that Steve had not seen when he had surveyed the room earlier. The small man stepped behind a desk and swiveled a large drawer out from where it was built into the wall. The drawer was lined with green felt and held dozens of tall stacks of casino chips of all denominations, hundred dollar and thousand dollar chips being the most numerous. Francois stepped back. Steve reached into the drawer and picked out four thousand dollars in hundred dollar tokens and placed them in a wooden tray that Francois held out to him. Francois made a notation on a small pad inside the drawer before closing it.

"Mr. Cannon, would you be so kind as to join the other two players at table number three. The sultan usually prefers to play alone." Steve looked at table three and then at the other four unused tables.

"And if I wish to play alone?" Francois bowed slightly.

"That could be arranged, Mr. Cannon, after the quality of your play is known." Steve snorted and moved to the table. He nodded at both players as he approached, the taller gentleman nodding back as he moved to a new position to make room for Steve, the other player gave no acknowledgement. The bartender appeared at Steve's side, replacing his glass of scotch with a fresh one, delivering a martini and a mixed whiskey drink to the other two players.

Steve started his betting slowly, placing bigger bets more often on the player line. Winnings on the bank or house line came back minus a five percent cut to the house. When the play was to him, the sullen player across from him would slowly and carefully bend the edges of his cards up so that only he could see the value, in an attempt to prolong the suspense. Baccarat was the only casino game in which this ploy was allowed, and was considered unsophisticated play in most circles. Steve began to refrain from placing bets when the play came to that side of the table, preferring to start up again when his turn came and then moved on to the gentleman on his left.

After an hour, Steve had turned his four thousand into thirty-three thousand. By his estimation, the player across from him had lost fifty-five thousand and the gentleman to his left, fourteen thousand. When Steve was not betting, he looked around casually at the dealers in the room. One in particular caught his eye. He had been standing beside one of the empty tables when Steve had first entered the room, but since then he had rotated two times with the Chinese dealer at Steve's table. He was Japanese and could not have been much older than Martin Ogawa. Steve also turned his attention away from the table at one point when there was an apparent shift change among the dealers. One of the dealers at the empty tables and the dealer that had been dealing at Steve's table were replaced by two others who had come in through a door just to the right of the alcove in which the chips were stored. The dealers going off shift exited through the small door as well. Steve tried to fix the location of the door into the mental schematic he had of the Stardust casino and where he was in relation to the front of the casino and the parking lot. When a loud Texan with a younger woman on his arm entered the lounge and was escorted to Steve's table, the private detective quietly loaded his chips into the wooden tray and handed them to Francois who made a note of the amount and deposited them back into the drawer.

"You wish to play more, monsieur?" Steve nodded.

"Yes, Francois, but I am going to take a little break." Steve walked out to the bar and was about to order a drink when he saw the Sultan in the mirror standing behind his chair.

"Forgive me, Mr. Cannon, if I am disturbing you, I would like to buy you a drink." The dark face was smiling with white teeth and kind eyes, the English was soft, but clipped. Steve smiled and pulled out the chair next to him. As he did so, he noticed that one of the bodyguards had stationed himself by the door and the other stood directly behind the sultan.

"It would be my pleasure, your majesty. " The sultan frowned and waved his hand toward the ceiling.

"Please call me Ali." The bartender put a fresh scotch in front of Steve, and a tall glass of orange juice in front of the sultan. The sultan held his glass out toward Steve. Steve held his up before they both drank.

"I was watching your play, Mr. Cannon. I play a lot of baccarat and I have never heard of a system, after all it is a simple game of chance at its' heart, no? But there seems to be some reason for your… what is the word?…ah.. consistency. You don't have to reveal it to me, I am just curious that is all." Steve smiled.

"No system, Ali, just betting inside a rhythm and along with that just acting on a gamblers' intuition."

"That is remarkable, Mr. Cannon. In just over an hour you rode the tie line twice. You lost a thousand the first time, but won eighteen thousand the second time." Steve shook his head.

"Sometimes the cards just go your way, Ali." The older man squinted his right eye and nodded knowingly at Steve as he leaned in a bit closer.

"I think that you are a man that makes sure the cards do as you wish." Steve chuckled and took a small sip of the edgy scotch. The sultan looked into his half empty glass and then at Steve in the mirror. When Steve met his gaze, he spoke.

"You are an American, Mr. Cannon, and of a certain age. I think that you saw much of the war, am I right?" Steve turned his head and looked at the Sultan before he took another drink.

"That's right, but there are plenty others that saw more than I did."

"Forgive, me Mr. Cannon, I do not mean to step where I should not. I am very much interested in the second world war, it changed the region where I live and my people in profound ways. Where did you fight?" Steve looked straight ahead into the mirror.

"Guadalcanal." Steve heard the soft intake of breath from the man beside him.

"Were you a member of Edson's Raiders, Mr. Cannon?" Steve nodded again into the mirror.

"That's right, and in answer to your next question, Ali, I was on Bloody Ridge." Ali nodded. For several long seconds, no one spoke.

"You must come to my country, Mr. Cannon, it is beautiful, I will show you around personally." Steve turned and faced the sultan and smiled.

"I imagine I would enjoy that, Ali. I have heard about your gun collection."

"It would give me great pleasure to show it to you, and get the opinion of a man with your knowledge." Steve nodded and glanced over the sultan's shoulder as two more dealers left the tables. One of them was the young Japanese man.

"No special knowledge here, Ali." Ali shook his head.

"No, Mr. Cannon, you are wrong. I have shot at animals and targets, never a man. I want to ask you a question I ask other men like yourself when I meet them. What is it like to shoot a man?" Steve stiffened slightly and turned toward his companion with an appraising gaze. After a few seconds he relaxed and took another sip of whisky before he replied.

"The first time, I have no words to describe it, can't be done. Eventually, it is just the same as when you shoot an animal." Steve put his glass down and pushed his chair back from the bar.

"If you would excuse me, Ali, I would like to take a walk around the casino, stretch my legs a bit. Thanks for the drink." Ali dipped his head in a small bowing gesture and smiled.

"My pleasure, Mr. Cannon. Perhaps when you come back, we can play together."

"I would like that, Ali." Steve waited until the bodyguard moved out of his way before he walked to the door by which he had first entered the private casino.

Steve walked to the far side of the casino to where the rows of slot machines stretched out and curved around toward a bingo parlor on the other side of the building. He looked back toward the door to the baccarat lounge and noticed a narrow hallway adjacent to the area, half hidden by a potted plant and a folding screen. Steve strolled casually across the casino before taking two side steps around the plant and ducking behind the screen. The hallway was not long and lead to swinging metal doors behind which Steve guessed was the kitchen or room service. A smaller hallway branched off to the right. Steve turned the corner and heard voices coming from an open door on his left. Through the glass reflection in the top half of the open door, Steve saw several dealers standing in front of metal lockers. The familiar patter of co-workers at ease filtered into the hallway. Steve moved cautiously until he could see the Japanese man. He was changing from his tuxedo into street clothes. Steve looked past the door and saw the hallway descend a flight of stairs. When the talk and laughter reached a high point, Steve quickly moved past the door and down the stairs. He opened the door at the bottom and found himself in one of the side parking lots. There was a railing ten feet from the door that enclosed a wide concrete ramp leading to the linen department below the hotel. Steve leaned back on the rail and lit one of the Cuban cigars.

After five minutes had passed, the door opened and one of the Chinese dealers that had been posted at an empty table walked toward Steve. There was no look of recognition as the young man passed by and walked to his car twenty yards away. Steve shook his head. How could someone stand in that room for two hours and twenty minutes and later fail to recognize one of only eight other people that had been there as well? He was still mulling over that oddity when the door opened again and the Japanese man appeared. He stopped three steps beyond the door when he saw Steve. Steve stood up straight and smiled. The man hesitated for a few seconds and looked around warily. Steve held up his hand.

"Can I talk to you for a moment?" He kept his voice light and leaned back against the rail. The young man shifted a paper bag from one hand to the other and looked around again.

"Not supposed to be talking to the players." His voice was low and soft. Steve turned and looked out toward the parking lot and took a long pull on the cigar before turning back towards the young man.

"I know that, son. My name is Steve Cannon and I am a friend of Martin Ogawa's father and I need to ask you a few questions." The man' nervousness increased and he started moving slowly toward the parking lot in a wide circle away from Steve. Steve said nothing, but stared into the dark almond shaped eyes. The man came to a stop.

"Not here. I can't talk here." Steve nodded and spoke slowly and softly.

"If you have some time tomorrow, let's meet at Foxy's." The young man looked around the parking lot before looking back at Steve and nodding.

"That's good, son. What time?" The man took a few more steps toward the lot and looked at his watch.

"Noon." Steve nodded and spoke to the man 's back as he hurried down a row of cars.

"See you then." Steve looked out into the dark and the long lines of cars until he heard an engine start up. When a blue Falcon pulled out of one of the spaces and headed toward the strip, Steve recognized the profile of the young man.

Shelly was nowhere to be seen as Steve walked briskly through the front doors for the second time that night. He waited outside the door that lead to the baccarat lounge for several minutes before a young employee with keys to the door appeared and let him in. He stepped up to the bar and smiled thinly at the bartender.

"Do you have any single malt scotch?" The bartender had just shaken his head but not replied when Steve saw movement behind him in the mirror just as he heard his name.

"Mr. Cannon." Steve turned slowly around. In front of him were two men, one dressed in a tuxedo, the other in a gray suit made of a heavy flannel that immediately pegged its' wearer as from the east. The man directly in front of him had a jutting chin and a peculiar way of holding his head back when he spoke.

"I am sorry we can't offer you the beverage of your choice. Most of our players prefer the blends. But if you would like to leave the name of one of those fancy whiskies with Rob there, I am sure that we can accommodate you the next time you play." The man's tone was as icy as his eyes above the fake smile. As he spoke, the other man moved to Steve's right and behind him, just out of his vision. Steve smiled.

"No problem. But if we are going to have a three-way conversation, I feel more comfortable if everybody stands where I can see them." The tuxedo smirked.

"Don't pay any attention to him, Mr. Cannon, he is just here to observe. On the job training, so to speak." Steve moved a half step to his left, his hand braced on the back of the bar stool. He smiled again.

"You seem to know my name, what's yours?" The man sneered and reached inside his pocket. He pulled out a card but did not offer it to Steve.

"My name is: 'I run this place'." Steve squinted at Mr. Place as he took a long pull on the stogie and blew the smoke across the three feet that separated the two men. After several seconds, the man held the card out to Steve. Steve took it from the extended hand and gazed into the dark eyes for a full three seconds before he glanced down at the card.

'Jimmy Rossini, Casino Manager.' Steve flicked the end of the card with his forefinger.

"What can I do for you, Mr. Rossini?" Steve slipped the card inside his cumberbund.

"Why don't you tell us who you really are for starters?" At that moment, Harold Warner came out of the side door, saw the two men in front of Steve and immediately backed into the office and closed the door. Steve noted that as he looked at the elevated jaw and the cold eyes.

"Steve Cannon, just like the marker says."

"Trouble is, Steve Cannon, there doesn't seem to be any background information on you over at the D.I. No player file, no credit check, no bank account numbers, nothing. Just you in a big suite and a two hundred and fifty thousand dollar marker. How is that?" Steve shrugged and smiled.

"Not my business how they do their job. You got a problem with my marker, call Tommy Carmino." Steve turned halfway back toward the bar and took a swig of the whiskey as he gazed at the mobster. Rossini shifted his weight.

"Tommy Carmino don't run this place." As he spoke he pulled the marker from inside his tuxedo pocket.

"Go play someplace else." He dropped the marker on the floor without moving his eyes from Steve's. Steve saw movement in his peripheral vision coming from his right side and braced himself. Again, he heard his name.

"Mr. Cannon, would you do me the honor of playing at my table?" Steve smiled at the soft music of the Arab's voice. He did not break the gaze of Rossini as he replied.

"Sure, Ali, I would be honored." He bent down and picked up the marker at his feet. Rossini snorted with a derisive smile and waited until the sultan had returned to the card room with his bodyguards before he spoke through his teeth.

"Before you come back into my casino, you call and ask my permission." Steve returned the marker to his breast pocket before he walked through the door and over to Francois at the chip drawer.

An hour later, Steve stood in front of the hotel and breathed in the cool midnight breeze. He patted his breast pocket. The last hour had not been nearly as lucky as the first, but he still had sixteen thousand over and above his original four. He nodded to the doorman and approached one of the car runners.

"Know where the big guy parked the black Caddy?" The runner smiled.

"Sure do. Want to me run over there and roust him?" Steve smiled and held out a twenty dollar bill.

"No, I want to surprise him. Just show me where he's parked." The young man laughed, took the twenty, and stepped nearer as Steve sighted down his outstretched arm at the car fifty yards away. Steve smiled and walked behind the long row of cars that the valets had parked. He looked through the back window and watched Shelly as he read a book by a flashlight he had propped up on the steering wheel. Steve opened the passenger door and threw a packet of hundred dollar bills held together with a bank band into the surprised man's lap.

"Big gun! You scared me, man." Shelly laughed and then picked up the stack of bills and held them out to Steve. Steve climbed into the front seat and shook his head.

"Eight grand there, Shelly, all yours. If I had quit an hour and half ago, it would have been more, a lot more." Shelly looked down at the bills in his hand.

"Man, are you sure? That's almost four months' worth of scratch for me." Steve smiled.

"I told you that was the deal. Let's get out of here and back to the D.I. This place gives me the creeps."

Shelly nodded and backed the limo carefully out of the tight space and made a U-turn at the end of the row before heading back toward the Strip. As he pulled out onto Las Vegas Boulevard and headed toward the Desert Inn Hotel, he looked over at Steve.

"Actually know a couple of the guys that work there. Remember Shorty Simmons, the security guard at the Nugget?" Steve nodded.

"Well, he is one of the doormen there. Got some info from him and a couple of the other guys. Ain't nobody happy, big gun. Bad bunch of guys took over. Lot of rules and guys getting their pay docked for nothing, union won't even take their calls." Shelly turned into the wide driveway of the D.I. and drove down the side of the building toward the country club. He turned off the engine and looked over at Steve.

"What else they say?" Shelly shook his head.

"That's about it, man, but I did see something strange about an hour and a half after you went in." Steve looked quizzically at the large round face.

"A guy I know from the Westside walked into the hotel. This guy has been a heroin addict and hustler since I came to town. He ain't never been on this side of the freeway as far as I know, and he was walking in there like he belonged there. You know what I mean?" Steve nodded.

"He have a name?"

"Lucius Freebone." Steve pulled out his notebook and wrote the name down.

"Sorry, big gun, that ain't much, but they weren't amused at me asking questions." Steve smiled and slapped Shelly's knee.

"In this business, you never know, Shel, you never know." Steve opened the car door and climbed out before he turned and bent down smiling at Shelly across the wide bench seat.

"Thanks, Shel, for helping me out tonight, now go get some sleep." Shelly laughed and shook his head as he turned the key in the ignition, and with his other hand he held up the bundle of cash.

"I will give you this kind of help all day long, my friend." Steve patted the window frame twice as Shelly gunned the big engine and disappeared around the corner of the hotel.

APRIL 8

AFTER A QUICK visit to the cashiers' cage, Steve used the elevator key and made his way to the third floor. He stopped at the concierge desk at the end of his hall and ordered a bottle of his favorite scotch. Ten minutes later when the concierge delivered the beverage himself, Steve tipped him a hundred dollar bill. Steve pulled open the curtains and gazed out over the lights of the Las Vegas Valley. He crossed the foyer and retrieved the other Cuban cigar from his jacket. As he poured himself a second glass of the scotch, he picked up the phone and dialed a four digit internal hotel extension. The phone rang four times before Steve heard the sound of a receiver being lifted on the other end.

"Who is this?" The voice was irritated, but did not sound sleepy.

"Hi Tommy, Steve. Steve Cannon." A disgusted sigh was the first sound he heard in reply. "What now? And don't tell me anything bad about my marker, Slick or your…"

"Relax, Tommy, your marker is safely back with Myron without any bumps or bruises. But that isn't why I called."

"I'm sitting here on the edge of my seat, Cannon, what could be so important that you gotta call in the wee a.m.?"

"You have a snitch in your organization, Tommy. The Stardust called over to check on the marker, like we figured, and somebody here went to the file to give them the inside info. There wasn't a file and they got all hostile about it. Thought you should know." Steve heard the same disgusted sound as earlier in the conversation.

"That all you got?"

"Yeah, Tommy see you tonight." This time there was a snort.

"Tonight?"

"Yeah, Tommy, the board meeting." Steve smiled as he heard the receiver drop and the line go dead.

*

The breakfast crowd at Foxy's had cleared out for the most part and the lunch crowd had yet to appear when Steve walked through the doors at ten thirty. The door to the backroom was open and Steve knocked loudly before he poked his head inside and looked around. Bernie was standing with Milton Swanson, his builder and architect. Large sheets of blueprints covered several of the gaming tables in front of Bernie's desk. Both of the men turned around at the sound of the knock. Bernie waved for Steve to join them at the table, Steve smiled and snorted softly as he walked across the room.

"I would think by now that you would be getting sick of looking at those things." Milton smiled and Bernie chuckled.

"Well, unfortunately for my bank account, they keep changing. Just this month we added two floors, a small showroom and another restaurant. Now we are trying to figure out where to put a fountain." Steve looked over their shoulders as Milton and Bernie began rolling up the prints. Bernie tossed them into a pile on one of the tables and sat down at one of the tables near his desk.

"We were just about to have breakfast, Steve, sit and have some too."

"Sure, Bern, after last night I am feeling rather hollow." Milton brought over a carafe and several cups on a tray and put it in the center of the green felt. Steve poured each of the men a cup of the black brew. He handed one to Milton and another to Bernie as he spoke.

"July 17, still the date for the opening gala?" Bernie nodded as he blew softly on the surface of the coffee and took a tentative sip.

"Yeah, that still holds, right, Milton?"

"I don 't see why not." He smiled over at Steve. "I think Bernie has run out of things to change, in that case, we just might make it." Steve chuckled and tossed a business card on the table between himself and Bernie.

"What is this?" Bernie reached for the card.

"The first high roller to add to your guest list." Bernie let out a long whistle as he held the card up for Milton to see.

"How did you get this?"

"I played baccarat at the Stardust with him last night and we hit it off. I told him the vision you had for Casablanca and he wants to be a regular player." Bernie nodded.

"That's great, Steve, I haven't even started thinking about publicity, but the Sultan is a great start, though I don't know what it will do for Middle Eastern relations." Steve and Milton laughed as Walter and another waiter brought in several trays of eggs, toast and a plate of bacon for Milton and Steve. As they were eating, Milton looked over at Steve.

"I haven't even told Bernie this yet, Steve, but your office is ready for you as of yesterday."

"That's pretty quick work, Milton, I figured the week after next at the earliest." Milton waved his fork at the blueprints behind Bernie.

"I flew in fifty new carpenters and a few extra plumbers from Chicago. The Caesar Palace project has scooped up almost everybody that can swing a hammer in this town, and since no one is left to beef, the union couldn't say much, so we got a big push this week. If we can round up some more materials, we will be unstoppable." Steve nodded at Milton, swallowed and looked at Bernie.

"After I saw what the Stardust is doing in their baccarat room, I have some ideas you might consider."

"Of course. That is a just a big empty space on a blueprint right now. I heard they have it closed off to the public, how is that working out?" Steve swallowed another bite of food.

"The serious guys seem to like it. Most of the guys with money also place a big premium on privacy. I was thinking that you could do the same for poker and roulette. Make exclusive rooms for the high rollers with higher limits on the bets, working in the Casablanca theme, with separate rooms." Bernie grinned.

"I hadn't thought of the poker angle. But I heard about a poker game that happened two weeks ago down at the Horseshoe Club. Benny Binion and Jay Sarno ended up playing in Benny's tiny little office, because Sarno hates people he doesn't know watching him play."

"There you go, Bern, our first customer for the poker room. We'll sit him down with the sultan who wants me to show him the finer points of the game. Let's see if Sarno can get to the bottom of that well of cash." They all chuckled at the image and transferred the breakfast dishes to another table and unrolled several blueprints, Milton writing notes for the architect as they decided on new features for the casino.

Steve walked with Bernie back into the main room of the restaurant at eleven forty-five. He took the same seat by the window as the day before and drank coffee while he waited for the young dealer. After ten minutes had gone by he spotted the blue Falcon moving slowly down the row of cars directly across from the deli. A few minutes later the young Japanese man stood blinking just inside the main doors. Walter approached him and led him to Steve's table, stepping back and waiting to see if the newcomer wished something to eat or drink. Steve stood up as the man approached.

"I am glad you came." He held out his hand. The young man started to sit down, but straightened, bowed quickly and took Steve's outstretched hand. Steve sat down slowly and spoke evenly.

"What is your name, son?" The man nodded.

"I am Masumi Yamaguchi." He shrugged. "Mike." Steve nodded. "Can I buy you lunch, Mike?" Mike shook his head.

"Beer or coffee?" Mike looked up at Walter. "Green tea?" Walter smiled.

"Yes sir, I am pretty sure we can accommodate you there, I'll be right back." He winked at Steve and left the table. Steve folded his hands ·and looked at the young man in front of him that he guessed was twenty-four or twenty-five.

"I need to know where Martin Ogawa is, Mike, can you help me?" Mike looked away quickly and shook his head.

"I don't know where he is, ... I don't." Steve lowered his voice.

"I believe you Mike. How well do you know him?" Walter appeared at the table and slid a cup of light colored tea toward Mike. He also filled Steve's coffee cup, before he left. Mike took a sip from the cup.

"We are good friends, Mr. Cannon. We went to different high schools but our families know each other."

"Which school did you go to?"

"Rancho." Steve pulled out his notebook.

"When was the last time you saw him, Mike?"

"The nineteenth, the day his father said he disappeared." Steve frowned. "His Father? Didn't the police talk to you?" Mike shook his head.

"They talked to some of the bosses, but not to any of the dealers. His father was angry, he accused me of talking him into being a dealer."

"Did you?" Mike shook his head again.

"No, it was the other way around. He kept telling me that they needed guys who speak Japanese and I was just going to NSU, not doing much, so I thought, why not?"

"Were you working together the last night you saw him?"

"No, he wasn't on shift, he had just come in to be with some of the players. A junket had just arrived from Tokyo and he wanted to see some people." Steve wrote in his book as he asked the next question.

"That normal? I thought the casinos frowned on that kind of fraternization." Mike took another sip of the tea.

"They don't like it and he is always getting into trouble for it. I speak OK Japanese, but he has the same accent and he has been to Japan several times with his father and he can joke with them and they like him around. Most of the Japanese players he knows also play twenty one or craps or the slots. He just likes to hang around with them."

"When did you know he was missing?"

"He was supposed to work a late shift with me on Saturday, the 20th. He didn't show, there was a new guy they were breaking in instead."

"Nobody on the floor, Francois, Warner, nobody said anything?" Mike shook his head.

"What about the other dealers? What is the scuttlebutt there?" Mike looked down at his tea with his hands in his lap.

"They think he got fired and just took off."

"What do you think?" Mike looked across at Steve and for the first time in the conversation, Steve could see the young man trying to stifle his emotions.

"He didn't run away, Mr. Cannon, he wouldn't do that. I am scared." Steve nodded, brought the cup up slowly to his lips, took a sip and the replaced it carefully.

"What are you afraid of, Mike?"

"I am afraid that something bad has happened to him."

"Did he say anything to you that would make you believe that is true?" Mike shook his head and seemed more agitated than he had been a few minutes before.

"He didn't say much or have much to do with me, the last couple of weeks before he disappeared. I told him that if he kept getting the bosses mad at him, he would make it hard on the rest of us, and he didn't like me saying that, so I could see he was avoiding me a lot." Steve flipped to a new page in his notebook.

"One more question, Mike, when is the next junket from Tokyo coming in?"

"Next Thursday, I think." Steve nodded and pushed his notebook across the table toward Mike.

"Can you write down your phone number and your address? As I learn more, I may need to check some things with you." Mike pulled the small pad across the table and printed out the information. When he handed it back, Steve stood up. He put one of his cards in front of the young man.

"If you need me, call me." Mike put the card in his shirt pocket. Steve waited while Mike stood and walked out of the restaurant. He walked over to Bernie who was chatting with a group of customers at one of the tables.

"Bernie, can I use the phone in back?" Bernie smiled and nodded without missing a beat in his conversation.

Tam Polhaus picked up on the second ring. "Tam, you going to be there awhile?" "Yeah, twenty minutes. I'll see you then."

As Steve drove up Las Vegas Boulevard toward downtown and Fremont Street, he played the conversation with Mike back in his mind. He felt more uneasy than at any time since he had first seen Keno in the Mexican restaurant.

Tam was reading the sports section of the Las Vegas Sun when Steve appeared at his door. Steve sat down in one of the two chairs in front of Tam's desk and began to light a Pall Mall as Tam slowly folded the paper. He looked quizzically at Steve.

"What can I do for you today, detective? New case you want me to solve for you?" Steve smiled as he exhaled the smoke from his first puff.

"No, but I may be able to help some of your guys." Tam sat up straight in his chair and began to absentmindedly rearrange some of the official papers on his desk.

"Really, how so?" He screwed up his mouth and frowned in Steve's direction.

"Who works narcotics that might be willing to trade information?" Tam shrugged.

"Those guys are pretty close-mouthed. They are protective of their sources, especially their snitches, but maybe Al Fonzo would be the best bet. Want me to give him a ring and see if he is in the building?" Steve nodded as Tam reached for the phone.

"Al. Tam. I got a guy here in my office says he might have information for you. You got a few minutes?"

"Yeah, we'll be down to see you, thanks." Tam hung up the phone and looked across at Steve.

"He says OK, but give him twenty minutes. You got time to wait?"

"Sure, Tam, no problem. I'll just sit here and watch you do a crossword puzzle." Tam snorted and leaned back in his chair, his hands behind his head.

"Speaking of puzzles, I heard Jack Cathay quit on Tommy." Steve drew thoughtfully on the cigarette.

"Yeah, he dropped by my place the other day and told me himself."

"What's he going to do now?" Steve looked across at the red faced detective.

"For now, I have some things he can help me with. Long term, there is a good chance he will be working security for Bernie in his new hotel." Tam swiveled back and forth in his chair.

"Sure he is not just clearing the decks so that he can go after Sorelli again?" Steve sighed and crushed out the smoke in an ash tray on the edge of Tam's desk.

"Anything's possible, but when I put it to him directly, he said he had no plans in that direction. But since you bring it up, I assume there is no fresh news on him." Tam swiveled his chair around and dropped his hands to his desk. He sorted quickly through a pile of papers and held one out to Steve. Steve read the lone paragraph and handed it back.

"Who is Grassley?"

"Bureau of Narcotics agent in Phoenix. As a matter of fact, he worked with your buddy down there, what's his name?"

"Leroy. Leroy Blevens."

"Yeah, that's the guy. Anyways, this Grassley has promised to keep us informed if he hears anything about Angelo Sorelli. They had reports of him crossing back and forth last month, but as you can see from the report, there is no confirmation of that. The whole raid in January when Little Moe and the oil guy got killed is still an open investigation, so I guess we can be thankful for that." Steve nodded and looked at the floor. There was silence between the two men for several seconds. Tam slapped his thighs as he rose from his chair.

"Let me show you where the narcotics squad hangs out. I don't think you have ever been down there."

"Nope, never seen it." Steve followed Tam down the corridor to a bank of elevators. When the door opened Steve and Tam stepped in as Tam pressed the button for the level two floors down.

"They like it in the basement. They have their own little back door they scurry in and out of." Steve chuckled as the doors slid open to reveal a large open room with several desks scattered haphazardly around the space. Several mild expressions of derision were directed at Tam from the few detectives that weren't on the phone. Tam waved good naturedly as he weaved through the chaos with Steve close behind him. Tam headed for a glassed in office space tucked in the corner of the room. Tam knocked quickly and then entered. The room was small, so Steve waited at the threshold. Just past Tam, Steve could see a very fat man with black hair and a full beard squeezed behind a desk that took up three quarters of the room. The only chair was opposite the desk against the wall and prevented the door from fully opening. Tam jerked his thumb toward Steve.

"This is the guy I told you about, Al." Al peered around Tam and waved at Steve to come in the room. Tam shuffled over and moved several file folders from a narrow ledge and sat down. Steve stepped in, and with a little difficulty closed the door behind him before he sat down in the chair. Al Fonzo stared at Steve for several seconds, then pointed a finger in his direction.

"I know you. You're that private detective that's always giving Samuels fits." He laughed gruffly from deep in his belly and turned to Tam.

"Samuels know he's here?" Tam shook his head.

"Nope. Since they moved Samuels' office to the other side of the rotunda, things are a lot quieter when Steve here, comes around." The two detectives chuckled at each other as Steve shook his head.

"If you two are done giggling like a couple of little girls, maybe we can get down to business." Al Fonzo stifled a last chuckle and smiled at Steve.

"What you got?" Steve thought about smoking, but decided that there was precious little air in the small room as it was. He pulled out his notebook and flipped back several pages from the last one he had written on.

"Lucius Freebone." Steve was looking at the detective behind the desk for any reaction as he spoke the name. Al shrugged.

"What about him?"

"A friend of mine saw him walk through the front doors of the Stardust last night around eleven." Al looked at Steve impassively.

"I doubt it, Mr. Cannon. It is Steve Cannon, right?" Steve tapped the notebook with his pen.

"That's right and why would you say that, Detective Fonzo?"

"Because I have rousted him and arrested him over a hundred times in the last ten years and I have never seen him more than a hundred yards in any direction away from the Cove Hotel on the Westside. Who is this guy that says he saw him?"

"A guy that has known him probably longer than you have." Al was staring again. "What else he say?" Steve frowned.

"Nothing much. Just like you, he was surprised to see him on that side of the highway, and that he looked like he had a definite purpose." Al sighed.

"Well now I know he is still alive. I haven't seen him for three months or so, and neither have his running buddies or else they're covering for him. Either way, he has changed his pattern for sure." Steve wrote a line in his notebook before he looked at the detective.

"So, we're all pretty smart guys here, what possible reason could a low-life junkie have for walking into the Stardust Hotel? You would expect that if he could somehow get through the front door that he would get a lot of help coming back out faster than he went in." Al looked at Tam and then at Steve. He leaned forward and rubbed his beard and looked about ready to say something.

Tam spoke first.

"They got six guys and one woman down in the morgue, all overdoses, and all long time junkies. What does that suggest to you Al?"

"Could mean a lot of things detective, most of them don't live much past thirty or forty." Tam smirked across the desk.

"And when they die in bunches, it usually means they are getting stuff that is three or four times stronger than their normal fix." Al sat back in his chair and sighed.

"Yeah, it could." A disgusted look that Steve knew well crossed Tam's face.

"Well why don't you try and figure out which it is, Detective?" Tam got up and motioned to Steve that they were leaving. Steve smiled genially across the desk.

"If I get any more sightings of Mr. Freebone, I will let you know." Al Fonzo sneered as he rose to close the door behind them.

"Thanks, you do that." Two more people crowded into the elevator as Steve and Tam rode in silence back up to the third floor. When Tam had closed the door to his office, he crossed over to his desk before he spoke. Steve was just finishing lighting his cigarette.

"Al is part of a new approach to narcotic enforcement, sort of a proactive one. They try to contain the problem rather than eradicate it. They hope by locking up the junkies for thirty and sixty days at a time, they will somehow kick the habit and go straight on their own." Tam snorted and waved a hand in the direction of the door.

"Enough of that." He turned in his chair and looked directly at Steve.

"If this Lucius lowlife was going into the Stardust, it is all about

B. R. Laue

heroin. So how does that work?" Steve stared at the large map on the opposite wall for several seconds before he answered.

"The boys at the Stardust bring in junkets from Tokyo twice a month. The planes stop over in Malaysia, every time. My guess is some unsuspecting tourist gambler arrives at McCarran with an extra suitcase." Tam tapped a pencil on the edge of the blotter as he swiveled slowly back and forth in his chair.

"The mob guys that are involved in trafficking drugs are all back east. That's a big no-no out here." Steve interrupted.

"Except the guys that took over the Stardust last year seem to be making their own rules as they go along. They don't seem interested in falling in line with the way things have been done in the past." Tam persisted.

"But if they are bringing in those amounts from Asia, they have to be sending them back east. Maybe L.A., but how does it end up on our streets?" Steve mashed the last of his smoke in the ashtray at Tams' elbow.

"Somebody is skimming. My guess is that they repackage the shipment and some amount sticks to their fingers. Our Mr. Freebone is part of the local delivery system. Instead of the usual stepped-on crap that floats in from L.A., the local junkies are getting strong stuff straight from Asia." Tam's eyes narrowed.

"How do you know all this? You make this stuff up?" Steve chuckled and moved the chair backward scraping it along the floor as he stood up.

"Just working the missing kid case, Tam. It always amazes me how if you are looking for one thing, you end up seeing another." Tam held up his hand to stop Steve from leaving.

"You think your missing kid and this Freebone character are connected somehow?" Steve stopped at the door and replied before he walked out into the hall.

"Maybe. I'll keep you posted."

"You do that." Tam spoke to the back of his door.

*

Steve sat back in his cushioned seat and watched as Bernie Gold walked from chair to chair in front of the gambling tables he had pushed together to form a sort of conference area. In front of each chair he placed folders, note tablets and pens. The note tablets had the famous smiling fox logo from the deli on the cover. Steve picked up the folder in front of him and began to idly flip through the photostated pages. Carmino Lighting had only been operating for a little over two months and already the number of accounts had nearly doubled. Tommy and Bernie had bought out the only local lighting company and increased market share from twenty-five percent to nearly forty-five. Bernie's formula of better lights at a better price along with local servicing had proved successful. The enterprise had also helped Tommy take the first steps toward legitimacy. Steve looked up when he heard his name being called. It was Clifford Jones, ex-Lieutenant Governor of the state, well connected business lawyer and friend to many of the mobsters in the city. He had also worked with Steve's dad on the Boulder Dam.

"Mr. Jones, how are you this evening?" The middle aged lawyer sat down, dropping his heavy briefcase beside his chair.

"I was somewhat surprised, Mr. Cannon, to hear you were on the board. I didn't think business and its' inner workings was something that would interest a man such as yourself." Steve smiled benignly.

"And what sort of man might that be, Mr. Jones?" The lawyer chuckled.

"Why, a man of action, Mr. Cannon. I am always hearing and reading about your exploits in the world of crime." Steve sat up in his chair and grinned across the table.

"Well, it is a well known fact, Mr. Jones, that business and crime are often found together." Clifford Jones did not reply, but turned and greeted another board member that had just sat down beside him. Steve watched as the rest of the board straggled in and took their seats. Besides Clifford, Tommy, Bernie and himself, there was Andre Malick, who had run the original company, Marvin Littlejohn, who built office buildings and shopping malls, and Chuck Heers, who built housing tracts. Bernie called the meeting to order and held up several envelopes.

"Thanks to all of you for coming here on short notice. This is the first board meeting of Carmino Lighting. I had originally planned to have one each month, but I think every other month will work better, and if there is anything pressing we can call one anytime. Before we start, I would like to hand out the stipends for the year, Tommy wanted to give out casino chips from the D.I., but I convinced him that most of you would prefer real money." There was polite laughter as Bernie started working his way around the table, handing out the ten thousand dollar checks to all present. When he was again seated, the board began working through the agenda that was the first page in the folders.

An hour later, as the meeting was breaking up, Steve was drinking a cup of coffee by the bar and chatting with Chuck Heers about his recent win in the city tennis championships when he noticed Tommy Carmino coming toward the two men. The mobster stopped in front of the bar and smiled at the duo.

"Hey. How are you guys doing tonight?" Without waiting for an answer, he continued. "Hey Chuck, I hear you won that big tennis deal down at Dula Center. Why don't you have your little tournament on my courts?" Chuck looked at Steve and then at Tommy before he stammered a reply.

"Uh… Tommy, that it isn't my decision to make." A look of frustration crossed the builders face. "Maybe if you built more than the two courts you have, the city might consider it." Tommy smirked. "Well how many do you figure I need? Huh, Chuck?" Chuck Heers shook his head and headed toward the door where Bernie was saying goodnight to several of the other board members. Tommy turned to Steve.

"Who cares where they play that silly game." Steve chuckled, as Tommy turned to him with a glare.

"What's so funny Slick? I crack a joke I don't know about?"

"He's right Tommy. Tennis is a growing game, you have a first class golf course, wouldn't hurt to spruce up the tennis part. Jay Sarno has plans to build a tennis pavilion at Caesars Palace and has already lined up Pancho Gonzales as his head of tennis operations." Tommy scoffed, but didn't get the joke at his expense.

"Sarno has plans to recreate the universe, so what? If my tennis pro wants more courts he can say so, and I ain't heard any complaints from that quarter." Steve chuckled again.

"Did you ever think, Tommy, that maybe that is because you don't take complaints too well?"

"You sound like my personnel guy, Slick, and I don't like him much either. I didn't come all the way across the room to exchange pleasantries with you. I need to find out who the informer is in our organization. What time did you hand that marker in over at the Stardust?" Steve took a sip of the coffee and folded his arms.

"Ten fifteen, ten thirty." Tommy drummed his fingers nervously on the top of the bar.

"Myron swears he didn't get any call at all and he was there from six until two in the morning."

"What does the switchboard say?" Tommy made a derisive face.

"They never remember squat. We got it narrowed down to two or three guys, maybe your time frame will help." Steve unfolded his arms and threw his paper coffee cup in a wastebasket on the other side of the bar.

"Always happy to help, Tommy. See, if I hadn't asked you for that marker, you would have been none the wiser."

"Yeah, Slick you are a big part of why I get up in the morning." Tommy turned as he saw Bernie coming toward them.

"Hey Bernie, haven't you got something stronger than this?" He pointed to the carafe of coffee on the bar.

"Sure, Tommy, let me fix you up." Bernie circled around behind the bar and brought up a bottle of Johnny Walker Black Label and a single malt scotch that he and Steve would occasionally share. He retrieved three glasses and poured each glass half full, dropping three ice cubes in Tommy's glass.

"That's more like it, partner." Tommy tipped the glass back and drank half of the contents before he put it down on the bar. He squinted at Bernie.

"You going to the Nessbaum funeral Saturday?" Bernie swallowed the sip he had just taken before answering.

"Yeah, I am. I didn't know that you knew him." Tommy smirked.

"He was in the casino business wasn't he?" Tommy winked. "My boss and his boss go way back." Tommy finished his drink and rapped on the table before backing away. He pointed at Bernie.

"Call me tomorrow." Bernie nodded as Tommy started for the door. Steve smiled as he called after Tommy.

"See you later, Tommy." He could hear the mobster's snort from halfway across the room.

"Thanks for the warning, Slick." Steve turned back and smiled at Bernie as they both shook their heads.

"Tommy was in quite a mood tonight, Bern. He needs to slow down a little." Bernie laughed.

"But then he wouldn't be Tommy would he?"

"I guess you are right about that. I should shove off too. I promised Remy I would take her out to dinner tonight. Thanks for the drink." Bernie followed Steve to the door.

"If you got some time tomorrow, Steve, early afternoon, stop by the hotel site. I want to show you something OK?" Steve turned around and spoke as he continued walking backward.

"Of course I have time. See you between one and two."

APRIL 9

STEVE SAT IN his car for almost thirty minutes before he saw someone moving about inside the little sushi bar. He walked across the deserted street and rapped on the door of the restaurant, a dark blue cloth with Japanese writing on it obscuring his view of the inside. When no one responded, he walked down the sidewalk and turned up a short alley. He knocked on a small wooden door next to several garbage cans. When the door eventually opened, Steve looked into the wrinkled face of a very old Japanese man. The man said something in a high pitched voice that was unintelligible to Steve.

"Suko." Steve repeated the name several times. After the third time the door closed and remained so for several minutes. When it opened again, Steve saw the same thin Japanese girl he had seen the night he and Keno had drunk beer together. Steve stepped back and smiled.

"Suko, I need to talk to you, today." The girl nodded, turning her head and saying something to the old man behind her. She stepped carefully down the two wooden steps closing the door behind her. She turned and faced Steve. She wore a long tweed coat over her waitress uniform, and was more than a foot shorter than Steve. Her cropped black hair was tucked underneath a blue beret. She smiled faintly.

"I can talk, Mr. Cannon, but I have to be back in an hour to finish my work before we open for lunch." Steve nodded and looked toward the street.

"There is a place on the corner next to the casino where we can get some coffee, or tea if you prefer." Suko fell in behind Steve until they reached the street. As they settled into a booth in the small diner, Suko draped her coat over the black vinyl, and sat down. Steve ordered for both of them when the waitress appeared. He waited until she had gone back through the swinging doors to the kitchen before he turned to Suko.

"I need everything you know about Martins' disappearance and what he said to you in the days leading up to the last time you saw him." Steve moved his notebook over as the waitress slid a cup of coffee in front of him. She put down a cup and a small metal pitcher of hot water in front of Suko. Steve watched while the young girl prepared her tea. When she was done, she looked up at Steve, her eyes moist and dark against her white skin.

"Martin is in trouble, Mr. Cannon."

"What kind of trouble, Suko?" She shook her head, as a tear fell on the brown formica.

"I told him it wasn't his business and he shouldn 't get involved, but he wouldn't listen to me, and now I don't know what's happened to him." Steve pulled a kerchief from his jacket pocket and handed it across the table. He waited until Suko had partially composed herself.

"What was he involved in, Suko?" She looked down at her lap as she twisted the white cloth between her fingers.

"At his work. He got to know several Japanese men from Tokyo. He said they were being forced to bring in drugs. He said the men in the hotel threatened their families in Japan if they didn't do what they were told. Martin told them he was going to help them."

"Help them how, Suko?"

"He said he was going to tell them to let the men stay in Japan or he was going to the police." Steve grimaced as he started to write in his notebook.

"Did he say when he was going to do this?" Suko shook her head.

"When was the last time you saw Martin?" She dabbed gently at her eyes. "The day before he disappeared." Steve frowned.

"Did you tell any of this to the police?" Suko shook her head.

"He made me promise not to tell anyone. I kept hoping he would come back. I was afraid to tell my mother or my uncle. I should have said something." Suko buried her face into the kerchief and sobbed heavily. Steve reached across and held her shoulder. Out of the corner of his eye he could see the stern look of the waitress from across the room.

"Suko, you did what you thought was right, what Martin wanted you to do. Whatever happens, Suko, none of it is because of anything you did. Do you understand?" The young girl nodded but did not take the kerchief away from her face. Steve sipped his coffee as Suko blew her nose and composed herself. When she was done, she looked up at Steve again.

"Does my uncle have to know?" Steve folded his notebook and dropped it into his breast pocket. He shook his head.

"No, Suko, this can stay just between the two of us. I will find Martin." He was about to slide out of the booth when he thought of something.

"Suko, do you know Mike Yamaguchi?" The young girl looked up in surprise, her narrow eyelids red from crying.

"He is my boyfriend, Mr. Cannon." Steve stood and laid a dollar bill next to his cup. He held out his hand to Suko as she slid from the booth and stepped down to the floor. He waited until she looked at him.

"You need to convince him to quit his job, Suko." She nodded as they headed for the door.

"I have tried, Mr. Cannon, he doesn't think it is necessary." Steve held the door for the young girl. He spoke as she passed by him and out onto the sidewalk.

"I will help you convince him, Suko." They walked together

B. R. Laue

across the street and he waited until the small door shut behind her. He walked to his car and smoked a cigarette as he read over his notes on the case. After a few minutes he walked into the small casino directly across from the sushi restaurant, weaving his way between the slot machines toward the phone booths in the back that sat next to the newsstand. He pulled out a small black address book and after dropping a quarter in the slot dialed a number.

"Give me room number 423, please."

"Jack? This is Cannon. Can I buy you lunch?"

"No, I thought the coffee shop. Yeah, good, I'll see you in an hour."

*

Steve sat in the back of the Desert Inn coffee shop. He had only been waiting for five minutes when he saw Jack Cathay pass the floor to ceiling glass windows that looked out onto the lobby and into the casino. Jack spoke to the manager who came out from behind his work station. Jack gave Steve a small wave and started walking toward him when the manager pointed in his direction. From several tables, dealers and pit bosses rose and called to Jack as he made his way, nodding and greeting everyone by name that came up to him. When he finally reached the table, Steve was glad he had chosen one that was as far away as possible from any other patrons.

"You are a popular man, Mr. Cathay." Jack grunted as he sat down.

"Yeah, especially since I don't call the shots anymore. Most of them are pretty good guys, though. A lot of them been here for their whole careers. One thing about Tommy, he makes sure the D.I. is a place where everyone in town wants to work."

"You miss it, Jack?" Jack shrugged as he flipped absentmindedly through the menu.

"I miss some of the calls you have to make in the cage and out on the floor, but I am ready for something else." He looked around casually to see if anyone else was listening.

"Speaking of that, I met with Bernie Gold bright and early this morning." Steve sipped a glass of ice water and looked at the craggy face in front of him.

"So how did it go?"

"Good enough, I guess, we came to an understanding. He didn't balk at the suite, and he offered more money that I was making here, which was a surprise. Quite a layout he has, with the gaming spread all over the joint, three different cashier cages, going to make it difficult to keep it all running smooth, but I think it is doable."

"When are you going on payroll?"

"Anytime I want. He says I can move into the suite when I am ready. Things won't really get rolling until the middle of June when most of the construction will be done. Plenty of time to hire the right people. I figure that you and I can work our deal until then."

"That works for me, and speaking of that, I have something I need you to do. Might be a little dangerous, though." Steve waited to judge the reaction of his table mate, as a waiter came to the table to take their lunch order. When he had left, Jack's blue eyes swept the room once more before they turned on Steve.

"Gotta beat sitting around wondering what to do with myself, what you got?"

"I need to know who all the wise guys are over at the Stardust. Where they came from, what their backgrounds are, where they have been arrested and for what, that type of information. Also, who works for whom, the whole pecking order. What do you think?"

"Not a problem. I don't even have to go over there. Five or six phone calls should do it. Those schmucks come to town and think they're invisible. They don 't know how it works around here."

"Good. Let me know as soon as you have all you can get. On another subject, Tam tells me he is in touch with a high ranking federal narcotics guy in Phoenix, who among his other duties, makes it his business to keep tabs on one Angelo Sorelli. He says it is doubtful that Sorelli has come across the border since the raid on the ranch. Tam said he will keep us informed, so I am updating you." Steve stopped talking as the waiter delivered their meals. When they had been eating for a few minutes, Steve spoke again.

"If you got some time, Jack, after lunch, come with me over to the Casablanca. Bernie wants to show me something, it will give us a chance to see the office space." Jack nodded his answer as he chewed.

The Casablanca Hotel sat at former site of the Three Coins Motel on the southeastern corner of Flamingo Road and Las Vegas Boulevard South. The front part of the facade had been completed and the old existing structure had been remodeled and tied in with the new construction. The pale beige stucco, bell tower and sweeping arches were Bernie's paean to the movie by the same name, and as Steve parked in the small fenced in dirt parking lot, it was easy to imagine the palm trees alongside the long curving driveway. Jack and Steve entered the terraced lobby with circular stairways on either side leading to the upper levels. Steve stopped for a few seconds to admire the view as the lobby spilled out onto an expansive inner courtyard where workmen were positioning several pink stone fountains. He had just pointed Jack toward one of the stairways, when he heard Bernie calling his name. He stepped back into the center of the lobby and looked up. Bernie was leaning out from a wrought iron banister and waving at the two men from the second level.

"Up here. Use the other stairway, they are still setting tile on that side." Bernie pointed in the opposite direction from the one in which Steve had been heading. Steve led the way as he and Jack moved up the uncarpeted stairs. When they reached the landing, Bernie was waiting for them.

"Hey, Jack, I am glad you came too. I want to show you your new accommodations." Steve and Jack craned their necks and looked at the curved ceiling forty feet above their heads and one hundred feet from the lobby floor below. Steve stepped over near Bernie.

"This is magnificent, Bernie. You have done a helluva job." Bernie looked at the soaring ceiling and then down to the red tiles of the lobby.

"Milton is the guy who should get all the credit. It is easy to have big ideas, but being able to create all this." Bernie swept his arm across the vista. "It's good to stop and look at what he has done so far. I get so wrapped up in what comes next, I never take enough time to appreciate all that has been accomplished." Bernie turned and motioned the two men to follow him. They turned a corner and found themselves in a wide hallway open on the lobby side. There were several double glass doors on their right and Bernie walked over to the first one and pointed at something. Steve joined him and looked at where he was pointing. Across the stippled glass doors in gold lettering and black shadowing, Steve saw the words: 'Steve Cannon Private Investigations'. For a few seconds he stared at the words, before he turned smiling to Bernie.

"I don't know what to say, Bern, that is great, thank you." He stepped forward and shook Bernie's hand, clapping him on the shoulder at the same time. Bernie laughed and moved his head quickly toward the door.

"Go on in, there's more." Steve opened the door and stepped into the large reception space. There was a built-in receptionists' desk to his left and three large wing chairs in gold silk and a matching couch across from them on his right. A phone sat on the desk and there were several magazines on a table between the chairs. Steve looked at Bernie and shook his head. Bernie pointed to a door in the wall they were facing. Steve took six steps across the room and opened it. He was standing in a narrow hallway facing two glassed in offices, one slightly larger than the other. Bernie stepped in next to him and pointed to the end of the hall.

"Bathrooms down there, and look here." Bernie opened one of the office doors and let Steve walk in first. Inside were two chairs similar to the ones in the reception area, facing a large wooden desk.

Behind the desk was a matching credenza and built -in bookshelves lining both walls. A deep burgundy carpet covered the entire space. Steve walked into the middle of the room and turned toward Bernie.

"I can't believe what you have done here." Bernie sat down on one of the wing chairs and motioned for Steve to sit behind the desk. Jack stood in the doorway until Bernie pointed to the other chair.

"I been ragging on you for years to get an office, I figured it was the least I could do. We just included all this in the furniture order, if you don't like it and want to do it some other way, no problem, we will move it out of here." Steve shook his head.

"This is beautiful, Bernie, I never imagined an office this nice." Bernie waved dismissively as he stood up.

"Don't worry, you will earn it, hanging around here." He looked at Jack and motioned toward the door. "Come on Jack, right this way." The two men left the offices and turned right, leaving Steve alone behind the desk. Steve pushed the chair back slightly and propped both feet up on the edge of his desk. He was still in that position and looking at the box of business cards that Bernie had already made up, when he heard someone enter the outer office and knock tentatively on the glass of the door. Steve walked back across the narrow hallway and into the reception area. A woman in a hat and appearing to be in her early thirties, stood framed by the open double doors. Her face broke into a wide smile when she saw Steve.

"Thank goodness, there is somebody, here. I have knocked on all the doors up here and you are the first person I have seen." She stepped forward and held out a gloved hand to Steve.

"I am Steffi Perone and I am here about the job, are you Mr...." She quickly looked down at a piece of classified ad she clutched in her other hand. "Mr. Gold?" Steve looked down at the plump brown haired woman and shook her hand.

"No, Miss Perone, my name is Steve Cannon. Mr. Gold went up to the next level, you just missed him. May I see that piece of paper, please?"

"Of course, Mr. Cannon." She handed Steve the piece of newsprint and sat down in one of the chairs and began searching for something in her purse. Steve read the ad and then clearing his throat to get her attention, handed it back to her.

"It says there that applicants for administrative jobs were to report yesterday, Miss Perone, were you detained elsewhere?" Steffi looked up and the bright smile was now replaced by a pair of sad brown eyes.

"My mother had one of her spells, Mr. Cannon and it was the nurse's day off, I couldn't leave her." Steve nodded.

"Well, Miss Perone, I think Mr. Gold will take that into consideration. What type of position were you hoping to apply for?" Steffi quickly thrust the piece of paper she had been looking for in her purse toward Steve. Steve unfolded the single sheet and read the contents.

"I was first in my class at typing, Mr. Cannon. Miss Gladys, the teacher, said she would recommend me for a secretarial position. Her phone number is at the bottom." Steve smiled to himself and handed back the certificate.

"What other jobs have you worked at, Miss Perone?" Steve noted that the sad expression had returned. Steffi pursed her lips to stop a quiver that had just started as she looked up at the tall detective.

"I have never had a job before, Mr. Cannon." Her voice was quiet as she shifted her purse nervously on her knees. Steve sat down on the couch facing the younger woman.

"What other skills do you have, Miss Perone? Can you set up a file system, for instance?"

"Yes I can, Mr. Cannon. I can also do books." Steve's brow furrowed.

"Do you mean accounting, Miss Perone?" Steffi nodded.

"But I thought you said you had never had a job?" Steffi nodded again.

"I do books for my uncle. He owns a slot machine company. He lives with us. He brings the bills and receipt books home every night and I balance them." Steve smiled.

"But if you work at the Casablanca, who will do the books?" Steffi Perone shook her head.

"That's just it, Mr. Cannon. My uncle is selling the company. When he told me six months ago, that is when I went to the secretarial school downtown." Steve sat back into the couch and crossed his legs.

"I need someone to run this office, Miss Perone. Would you consider working for me?" Steve smiled when he saw a flush of redness move quickly from the white lace collar at the young woman's throat up to her cheeks.

"I don't know what to say, Mr. Cannon." She looked around at her surroundings, her eyes stopping on the large receptionist desk. She looked back quickly at Steve.

"I always imagined myself in a big room with a lot of other girls, all of us typing and going to lunch together." She readjusted her purse on her lap and sat up straight.

"What does a private detective do, Mr. Cannon?" Steve chuckled.

"Well, Miss Perone, people will be coming through that door with all the problems of the world. Problems that have beaten them down and that are holding their lives hostage."

Steve stood up and crossed over to the chair that Steffi Perone was seated upon.

"Problems that you and I are going to help them solve." Steve held out his hand as Steffi smiled and stood up.

"Yes, Mr. Cannon, I would very much like to work here."

"Welcome aboard, Miss Perone. Have a seat for a few minutes, we need to discuss your salary." Steve crossed over to the reception desk and picked up the phone.

"Hi, who's this?"

"Hi Anne, my name is Steve Cannon. I am up on the second

floor. Are you able to connect me to the Marquis Showroom? Great, thanks."

"Hi, this is Steve Cannon. Could you ask Miss DeMarche to call me when she has a minute? Thanks, the extension here is 9124." Steve hung up the phone and smiled across the room at Steffi Perone.

"How does two-hundred fifty a week and a year-end bonus sound, Miss Perone?" Steffi smiled and nodded.

"That sounds fine, Mr. Cannon, but I have to ask you what time I start work each day. I have to tell Mr. Baxter." Steve crossed to her side of the room and sat down again on the couch.

"Nine o'clock would be fine, Miss Perone. Who is Mr. Baxter?"

"He is my mother's driver, Mr. Cannon. He will be driving me to work each day. My mother was worried because he doesn't start work until seven each morning, so nine o'clock should work just fine." Steve leaned forward and looked quizzically into the round earnest face.

"Where do you live, Miss Perone, if you don't mind me asking?"

"We live in Rancho Circle, Mr. Cannon." Steve smiled and shook his head. Rancho Circle was a small enclave on the northwest side of town that held million dollar houses. Some of the big name entertainers who made Las Vegas their home and most of the casino executives lived there.

"Well, Miss Perone, let's us meet here Monday at nine in the morning and get started." Steffi had just indicated her agreement when the phone rang, startling them both. Steve crossed to the other side of the room and picked up the receiver.

"Hello?"

"Hi, Gem, I'm not interrupting anything am I?"

"Good. I am up here on the second level in my new office. If you can take a break, there is someone here I would like you to meet."

*

It was just past three o'clock when Steve drove down the short narrow street that lead to the municipal golf course parking lot. He drove slowly across the gravel and pulled in next to a car with the trunk open. Two golfers were loading their bags into the vehicle. Steve nodded in acknowledgement at the two men as he locked his car door, and headed for the clubhouse. His friend, Lew Mannion, looked up from the counter when Steve entered the small pro shop. The golf pro's eyes narrowed and his brow furrowed.

"What brings you all the way out to this part of town, Steve? Not bad news, I hope." Steve gazed evenly at his boyhood friend.

"Just need to talk with Keno, Lew, where can I find him?" Lew leaned out over the counter and pointed in a southward direction.

"He's working on the second hole. We had an underground sprinkler pipe break this morning. Take that cart there and follow the path." Steve nodded as he walked by.

"Thanks Lew, I won't be long." The cart was slow but it only took ten minutes before Steve crested a low rise and saw Keno and two other men standing in a mud hole off the second fairway. Steve stopped the cart on the path opposite the men and waited until Keno looked in his direction. Steve waved and watched as Keno gave the men some instructions before he climbed the sloped fairway toward Steve. He wore black rubber boots that came to just below his knees and his arms and overalls were streaked with mud. Steve waited until the man was ten feet away.

"I need to talk to you, Mr. Ogawa." Keno came up to the cart and rested his hand on the roof stanchion as he caught his breath. He looked back down at the workmen and then pointed toward the green two hundred yards away.

"There is a place up there we can talk, Mr. Cannon." He swung himself easily onto the bench seat of the cart, as Steve mashed down on the accelerator to get as much momentum as possible up the long hill. Neither man spoke as Keno directed Steve to take a faint path that branched off from the main cart path. They wound around several trees near the desert border of the course until they came over a rise and dropped into a small bowl. Keno indicated that Steve should stop. He turned the cart off the path and got out. The small depression was about forty yards in diameter with seven cherry trees ringing the area. Ten feet in front of the cart was a concrete bench that Keno slowly walked toward. Steve could see all the way back to the clubhouse from where he stood, but when he moved to the side of the bench, the view was of the Spring Mountains shining in the afternoon haze.

"This is a beautiful spot, Mr. Ogawa. Did you do this yourself?" Keno nodded.

"What do you have to tell me, Mr. Cannon?" Steve shifted his weight off of his stiff right leg and pulled out a pack of Pall Malls. He held out the pack to the sitting man. Keno demurred with a small gesture of his left hand. Steve lit his cigarette quickly and took a deep drag. He looked at the mountains as he spoke.

"Martin is friendly with a group of gamblers who are flown in regularly from Tokyo. Some of those gamblers are being forced by someone at the Stardust Hotel to smuggle drugs into this country. There are indications that Martin is trying to help those men out of their predicament." Keno sat forward and rubbed his hands over his face and through his graying hair.

"He is just like his mother, Mr. Cannon. Always finding people that need help." Steve moved a small rock around with the toe of his shoe.

"The men that run that hotel are dangerous, Mr. Ogawa. They will not let anyone meddle in their affairs." Keno nodded, but did not speak for several moments.

"And you think it is not right for Martin to try and help, Mr. Cannon?" Steve took a short drag on his smoke.

"Everyone knows that Japan does not tolerate drugs. If they aren't smart enough to seek help from their own police, why should he get involved?" Keno shook his head and scowled.

"Why did you take this case, Mr. Cannon? It is obvious to me that you hate my race. It is the same wherever I go. I walk into a room and I can see in an instant those faces who are still fighting the war." Steve turned and looked down at the middle aged man.

"And you think we have no call, right?" His voice was even but his affect was flat and his tone had a hard edge. Steve felt the heat rising from his chest into his throat. When he spoke again, he didn't recognize the hissing sound that was his own voice.

"I spent two days and two nights in a foxhole listening to men I had gone to school and joined the marines with, screaming my name for help while their skin was being peeled from their bodies. Is that enough call for you, Mr. Ogawa?" Steve took two steps backward, painfully unclenching his fists as he turned away. Keno was quiet for several seconds.

"And what about the man holding the knife, Mr. Cannon? Did he have more choices than you?" When Steve did not reply, Keno continued.

"Do you know what Iaido is, Mr. Cannon? It is the art of the sword. The katana. What you refer to as a samurai sword. Swords I have seen your soldiers hack out of the hands of dead officers with their bayonets. And what if the man behind the knife had refused his grisly task? What then, Mr. Cannon? I will tell you. He would have been stripped in front of his whole company and then an officer would have practiced his iaido on him, until his body lay in bloody pieces in the dust. And the worst part, Mr. Cannon? He would go to his death knowing that his name would be stricken from the company rolls, his body buried in a remote spot away from all the other graves and no mention would ever be made of him or his fate. There would be no place for his relatives to find him. He would be lost alone in eternity forever. And you want more choices, Mr. Cannon? What choice did the pilot have that dropped the bomb that killed my father and my wife? Choices are an illusion, Mr. Cannon." Steve turned back from the view of the mountains.

"No, Keno, you are wrong. Choices are real. The choice to

pervert your history to subjugate ancient Asian enemies. The choice to force civilians to be the last line of defense. The choice to place an emperors' vanity above the life of his people. Those are choices and they are no illusion."

"And my brother, Mr. Cannon. What would you make of his choice? He was interred in Wyoming along with my mother and the rest of the family. When the call came, he joined the 442nd and died in Italy for the country that imprisoned his family. The same country your friends fought and died for. Is that the choice that is not an illusion, Mr. Cannon?"

"Maybe, Keno, maybe. All I know is that we were torn out of our lives for something we didn't start and wanted no part of. I understand you were forced to participate against your will, and maybe that sets you apart, I don't know. Those are not my judgements to make one way or the other. I have seen evil up close, more than most people, and when I look at you, I see it all over again."

"Perhaps, Mr. Cannon, but I don't think when we look at each other, we see clearly. We see the creatures and the shapes the war has twisted us into. For me it comes once or twice a year with the sickness. I lie delirious for several days with only my nightmares for company. Then for days afterward, all your faces appear as twisted demons. I am sure you know what I speak of."

Steve pulled out another cigarette, hesitated and then pulled out another one. He turned and held it out to Keno. Keno took it without looking up. They both looked at the Marine 'Globe and Anchor' insignia on Steve's battered zippo as he cupped his hands around it to shield the flame from the breeze. Neither spoke for several minutes until Keno shifted his weight on the bench.

"Will I ever see Martin again, Steve?"

Steve Cannon looked out over the golf course as the breeze stiffened, flattening the grass as it moved toward him. He watched it rake through the trees, sending hundreds of sakura blossoms swirling to the ground.

April 10

STEVE BENT OVER the open hood of the '61 Corvette. He had pushed the bright red car halfway out of the garage and he was working under the partial shade of the open garage door. He had just finished changing the oil and was checking the spark plug connections, when he heard a car rapidly approaching. Steve looked up when he heard the tires crunching the gravel of his driveway. The car was a big black Mercury and Bernie Gold was driving. Steve straightened up and watched as Bernie brought the car to a sliding stop ten yards away. Bernie rarely, if ever, came out to Steve's house and on the one or two occasions that he had, he never drove fast. Bernie slid quickly across the bench seat and climbed out the passenger door. He was wearing a black suit with a black tie.

"Well, look at you, Mr. Gold, I don't think I have ever...." Steve stopped when he saw Bernie's face.

"Bernie. What is the matter?" Bernie shook his head and pointed to the front door.

"Inside." Steve nodded, his brow furrowing as he led the way and opened the door as Bernie pushed past him, turning around as he reached the back of the couch.

"You got scotch, Steve?" Bernie was taking deep breaths. Steve walked into the office and returned quickly with a bottle and two glasses. Bernie took the bottle and one of the glasses and headed down the short hallway to the kitchen, Steve close behind him.

"What's up, Bernie? Are you going to talk to me?" Bernie looked at Steve as he downed three fingers of scotch in one gulp. He let out a big sigh as he slumped into one of the chairs around Steve's kitchen table. He poured the other glass half full and slid it across to Steve.

"Sit down and drink that." He refilled his glass as Steve drank half of the amount that Bernie had.

"Are you going to tell me, Bernie?" Bernie nodded and put his glass down. He pulled a card out of his pocket.

"Drink the rest of that and then I will show you this." Steve shrugged and drank the rest of his scotch. As he put the glass back down, Bernie slid the card across the table. Steve picked it up and studied it. The card was a picture of a middle aged man holding a mortar board hat in one hand and a diploma in the other. The card was edged in black and the words, 'In Memorium', were engraved across the top. Steve held it out to Bernie. Bernie shook his head.

"Look again. Look at the two women in the background." Steve held the card up at an angle to the light and looked at the two women in the background. He looked again before he dropped the card on the table and reached for the scotch bottle. He poured them both the same amounts as before. He took a large sip and looked across the table at his friend.

Bernie took a big drink before he spoke.

"It's her, isn't it Steve?" Steve picked up the card, looking at it once more before sliding it across the table to Bernie.

"Yeah, it's Theresa, all right. How did you know?" Bernie rubbed his hands across his face.

"Man, just one of those things, just one of those quirky things that happen. I am driving Sheldon and Judy Nessbaum, Nathan's brother and sister-in-law to Nathan's funeral, right? Well, Judy has had a few snorts before I get there and she starts in about how the widow is from Boulder City originally and that is how she and Nathan met, right? Then she tells me that this woman, Theresa, was pregnant and married when she met Nathan and Sheldon is not too happy because it is obvious she is spilling family secrets, so he tells her to be quiet. I don't think nothing of it, Steve, until we get to the temple. I'm getting out of the car and see them getting ready to carry the casket in and one of the pallbearers, I swear, Steve, it was like I was looking at you, only it was you twenty years ago. Am I making sense?" Steve sat forward in his chair.

"Bernie, are you telling me…?" Bernie nodded and took another slug of the whisky.

"At the wake, I cornered Nathan and he confirmed it. She was married to a guy named Steve that she met at Boulder High School who enlisted in the Marines right after Pearl Harbor. She didn't know she was pregnant until two months after he shipped out. She was working at the Railroad Pass Casino which Nathan was running at the time. She took up with Nathan and when he went to Reno to run another casino she went too. Divorced her husband while he was fighting in the Pacific and had a son which Nathan adopted. Sheldon says he knows that Nathan isn't his real father, but Theresa told him you died in the war." Bernie stopped.

"Steve, you OK?" Steve nodded. He looked out the window at the sunlit top of Sunrise Mountain.

"Where is she now?" Bernie held out his hands. "Steve.. I…"

"Where, Bernie?" Steve had a strange focused calmness about him that Bernie had never seen and was not sure he liked. Bernie's voice was quiet when he answered.

"The Trop. Nathan says they are at the Tropicana until tomorrow." Steve stood up from the table and looked at his greasy hands.

"Let yourself out, Bernie, I need to take a shower."

*

Steve Cannon sat in a lounge just outside the casino and stared at the white telephone in front of him. The desk clerk had refused to give Steve the room number, suggesting he use the phone. Steve took another sip of his Scotch without taking his eyes off the phone. After a few moments, he lifted the receiver.

"May I be connected to Theresa Nessbaums' room please?"

The sound of his voice and the foreign name sounded strange to Steve in the echoing of the phone line. He had met her as Theresa Reuschel, her family freshly arrived in Boulder City from Illinois, her father transferred to work in the Basic Magnesium plant in Henderson. For a short while she had been Theresa Cannon.

"Hello?" The voice was older, more mature, but it was hers', alright.

"Theresa, this is Steve." There was a pause that grew longer by the second, but somehow Steve knew that first one to speak now would be at a disadvantage. Steve heard a deep sigh on the other end.

"Sheldon warned me to expect this. This isn't a good day for this, Steve." Steve felt the hotness rise in his throat, but took several deep breaths through his nose before he spoke evenly into the receiver.

"I am sorry for your loss, Theresa. But what year, what decade, would suit you better?"

"I am sorry, Steve, I don't want to do this over the phone."

"What room are you in?"

"451, why?"

"Where are you?" There was panic in her voice.

"Downstairs in the casino bar. I will be up in ten minutes." He heard her start to protest as he replaced the receiver. He ordered another drink and finished half of it before he walked to the elevator.

The room was one of the better suites in the hotel. Steve knocked on the door and waited several minutes before it opened. Theresa did not look at Steve but left the door open as she walked back across the room to a small couch and two chairs that were next to a large window that overlooked the strip. The slim girlish body he remembered had been replaced by a matronly one, and her steps were heavy and not light as before. Her hair was still blond, but was sprayed into a smooth bouffant. When she had seated herself on the couch and turned toward Steve, he could still see a little of the girl that had become the middle-aged woman behind the puffy, bloated face. From the redness in her eyes, Steve guessed it was from too much crying or too much alcohol or both. Steve stopped in the middle of the room and stared into her eyes. She shook her head.

"Don't look at me like that. You don't know who I am now or how it was for me." Steve put his hands in his pocket and walked toward the window. Below he saw a gas station on the corner and farther down the strip the Hacienda Hotel.

"You're right, Theresa, I don't know how it was for you. I only know how it was for me." He laughed sardonically, half to himself.

"Most of the company got 'Dear John' letters at one time or another. Yours came after the worst three days of my life. It barely even registered at the time. Later, when I was able to concern myself with normal things again, it didn't matter, I didn't care. I still don't.

When your parents objected to the wedding and cut you off, we both knew it was just a matter of time before you left. So let's dispense with history, I didn't come up here to talk about us." Steve turned and looked down at the woman who had been his wife.

"Where is he?" Theresa put the back of her hand to her mouth and started to cry. Steve pulled out his kerchief and handed it to her. She dabbed her eyes and handed it back without looking up. She sniffled before she spoke.

"I don't want you to tell him like this." Steve shrugged and looked back out the window. "I'm not going to tell him. You are." She looked up quickly, a stricken look on her face. "No… Steve."

"Yes, Theresa. You don't owe it to me, you owe it to him." Steve turned and looked directly into the bloodshot brown eyes.

"I will give you one hour. I will wait down in the bar. After an hour, I leave and you will never see me again." Theresa started sobbing loudly as she threw herself prostrate on the couch. Before Steve could react, a door opposite him that was connected to the suite next door, opened and a young man stepped through. Their eyes met and both stopped moving for an instant. The young man had a concerned look on his face. Steve had no idea what his own expression was. Steve watched as the young man quickly crossed the room and knelt beside his mother.

"Mom, are you alright?" Theresa sat up, nodding her head.

"I'm fine, Michael, I just received a little bit of a shock that is all." Michael looked up at Steve. Steve held out his hand.

"Hi, Michael, I am Steve Cannon. I was sorry to hear of Nathan's death." Michael stood up and shook Steve's hand.

"Thank you, sir. Are you a friend of my mothers'?" Steve looked down at Theresa for a second before he looked back into the brown eyes that were at the same level as his.

"Yes, Michael, I am." He looked back down at Theresa and waited until she met his gaze.

"I am going now." He smiled at Michael.

"Michael, it was nice meeting you, I hope to see you again, soon." Michael smiled back.

"I hope so, too, Mr. Cannon."

Steve sat alone in the bar nursing a scotch for thirty-five minutes, before he picked up the white phone and asked for an outside line. Almost the instant it rang, the line was picked up.

"Bernie, it's me. I know you have been on tender hooks, so I wanted to call you and tell you everything is alright."

"Yeah, I saw them both.

"Yeah, but just for a minute. She doesn 't want to tell him, so I am giving her an hour to do the right thing."

"Up to her, Bern, she can decide. Listen, I don't want you taking this on, I know how you are. You did the right thing, I never want you to think otherwise, OK?"

"At this point I don't...." Steve's voice trailed off for a few seconds. "Bern, I have to go, Michael is here."

Steve stood up as his son approached the table. Steve could see that he had been crying.

"Sit down Michael." Steve pulled out a chair and then moved around to the chair opposite. Michael nodded and sat down. The two men stared at each other for a few seconds.

Michael slowly extended his hand across the table. As Steve grasped it, Michael spoke.

"It is good to meet you, Dad." Steve felt the hot flush and the sting of salt from his brimming eyelids as he shook the strong hand.

"It is good to finally meet you, son." Both men laughed nervously. Steve held up his drink. "What can I get you?" Michael smiled through his tears.

"Scotch would be fine." Steve laughed to himself and signaled the waiter. Steve wiped his eyes with the drink napkin and looked across the table, shaking his head.

"This must be a shock for you. I had to come today, I didn't know how long you and your mother would be in town. You understand don't you?" Michael nodded.

"Is your Mom OK?" Michael nodded again.

"She was on the phone talking to my aunt when I left. She is strong, she will be alright."

"Your aunt Susan?" Michael nodded. Steve waited until the waiter put two drinks on the table before he spoke again.

"It will be rocky for her, Michael, without her husband. You are going to have to take care of her." Michael nodded.

"I will. I have two months before I report, I will stay with her until then." Steve's glass stopped halfway to his mouth and a cold chill moved from the top of his scalp down to his wrists.

"Report? Report to what?" For the second time in a day, Steve felt the heat rise in his throat.

"The Marines. I joined the Marines last month." Steve barely heard the last words as he took a gulp of his drink. As soon as the whisky slid down his throat he took a deep breath through his nose.

"Are you sure that is what you want to do, Michael? They just sent the 9th Brigade to Vietnam a month ago. Things are going to get hot over there." Michael nodded.

"I have just finished four years of ROTC at the University of Nevada. I have had my mind made up for over a year." Michael cocked his head to one side.

"Mom didn't say what you do. I guess she doesn't know anything about your life."

"I am a private detective, son." Michaels' eyes widened slightly.

"You mean murders and things like that?" Steve nodded.

"Yes, sometimes, sometimes missing persons, sometimes missing money, it varies a lot."

"Were you talking to one of your clients when I came in just now?" Steve looked at the phone and smiled.

"No, Michael I was talking to a man, a man you will meet soon, and who very much wants to meet you."

"I was wondering, sir if it is all right with you ..." His voice trailed off.

"What is it, son?"

"Mom is leaving tonight to go back to Reno. I was wondering if I might stay and go back tomorrow night? I have a lot of questions." Steve smiled and reached across the cocktail table and squeezed both of Michaels' shoulders.

"I would like nothing better, son. There are some family members you need to meet, two small ones in particular. Do you and your Mom have plans for dinner tonight?" Michael shook his head.

"Uncle Sheldon and Aunt Judy are picking her up in an hour to take her to dinner and then to the airport."

"If you want, son, I will stay here while you say goodbye to her and then we can go get a bite to eat." Michael stood up.

"That would be great. I won't be long." Steve stood as the young man turned and walked through the lounge toward the lobby. He watched the broad shoulders disappear into the crowds streaming toward the casino.

April 11

STEVE TOOK HIS eyes off the road momentarily as he glanced across at Remy, the breeze from the partially open window moving her hair softly around her face. She smiled back at him from behind her large dark sunglasses. He glanced into the rearview mirror and caught Michaels' eye, 'Mike', as he had requested everyone call him when they had all sat down to breakfast with Bernie at Foxy's. Though he was overjoyed by the news he had received the day before, as he drove toward the city of his birth, he couldn't help thinking of Keno and their conversation the last time they met.

The car swung easily into the dirt and grass two track driveway in front of the modest bungalow three blocks from the Boulder City park. Steve shut off the engine and circled in front of the Jeep and helped Remy from the far side of the car. Mike stepped out of the rear seat and standing on the freshly mowed grass, watched as a slim brunette woman and a tall man with glasses stepped from the small porch and walked toward him. Beside them was a young girl that Mike guessed was about ten. He could also see something or someone behind the woman, hiding behind her full skirt.

Val dropped her husbands' hand and took several quick steps toward Mike, stopping for an instant before reaching up and hugging his neck. She stepped back quickly and smiled.

"Hi, Mike, I am Val." She turned toward her husband and as she did, Mike saw the golden curls and pink bow that had been hidden by the skirt. He knelt down.

"Who is this?" He held out his hand. Betsy took three steps forward and hugged Mikes' neck. He lifted her up in the air and cradled her against his body with his left arm as he gazed down at the dark brown eyes of the older girl.

"I bet you are Susan." The long braids swung off her shoulders as she nodded and pointed up at her sister.

"That's Betsy." Mike smiled at the small child in his arms as she felt his face with her small chubby fingers. Mike held out his right hand to Horace Voorhees as Steve and Remy stepped up beside him. Horace shook the strong hand and looked from Mike to Steve and back again, shaking his head as he spoke.

"It is good to meet you, Mike. You are definitely one of the Cannons, that is for sure." Val took Remy's arm with one of hers and wrapped the other around her brothers' waist.

"Let's go in and get acquainted." Steve turned around as he walked toward the wooden steps and watched as his son trailed behind him, now holding a girl in each arm.

Two hours later, the three men sat behind their coffee cups as Remy and Val cleaned up the kitchen. Susan and Betsy sat on the living room rug, bent quietly over their crayons and coloring books. Steve saw a worried look on Horace's face as he looked at Mike.

"Are you sure that the Marines is what you want to do, Mike?" Before Mike could reply, Horace cleared his throat and continued.

"The commitment has already been made in the Pentagon to widen the scope of the war in Vietnam. The 9th Brigade is just the beginning, and as your father can tell you first hand, there are no Marine battalions left languishing in the states in time of war, especially not a guerrilla war like this one." Mike smiled at Horace.

"Yes sir, you are right. But even before I was elected the leader of my ROTC unit when I was a junior, I had already decided that leading men in combat is what I want to do." Horace looked beseechingly at Steve.

"Do you agree with this?" Steve shrugged, but looking at his son in the same instant, he felt some of the same reservations as Horace. His face held a grim smile.

"If that is what he wants, the Marines will oblige him. I don't know how I feel about the officer part, but had my father been alive, he would have accepted the decision that my brother and I both made." Horace shook his head into his coffee cup.

"Different war, Steve. This is a limited action, much like Korea, and I don't want to see anybody's son get caught up in that kind of meat grinder. I only flew Air Force reconnaissance, but I can tell you the boys on the ground suffered terribly." Steve took a thoughtful sip of his coffee and met the dark eyes of his brother-in-law.

"I know you are concerned, Horace, but if what I read is true and the number of draftees is going to go way up, I would rather see him join the Marines, where everybody volunteers and they take care of each other, not like some thrown together bunch of Army conscripts."

Horace was about to speak again, when he was interrupted by Remy and Val returning from the kitchen. Val carried a large chocolate devils' food cake and a long knife. She placed the platter in the middle of the table and looked at her husband.

"Why are you talking about Korea, Horace?" She handed the knife to Steve without looking in his direction. Horace looked at Steve and Mike out of the corner of his eye, before he returned to the frank gaze of his wife. Steve busied himself cutting the cake into generous wedge sized pieces. Horace forced a smile.

"You know, honey, just war stories." Val frowned and looked at her brother and her nephew, but decided not to press them further.

*

Remy stood in the middle of the airport concourse, five feet away from the two men. Steve handed the leather bag he was carrying to his son. When Mike had deposited it on top of the one at his feet, he held out his hand.

"This isn't goodbye, dad, I will be back in a week and we can spend some more time together before I report to San Diego for basic." Steve clasped the hand in both of his, and looked deeply into the dark brown eyes.

"I don't want to let you get on that plane son. I know you have to go and take care of things, and your mother needs you badly right now... but...there is still so much more to tell you, I haven't even told you anything about your uncle and scarcely anything about your grandparents." He felt the strong grip loosen and then reluctantly let the hand go to the jacket pocket where the plane ticket was partially visible. Mike hoisted a large leather duffel bag over his shoulder and smiled at his father.

"I will call you tomorrow night." He looked past Steve and smiled at Remy. Remy moved to Steve's side and hugged Mike's neck and kissed him on both cheeks.

"Goodbye, Remy, I am glad we met each other." His face reddened slightly at the female attention.

"Goodbye, Mike, take care of your mother." Mike nodded and turned toward the gate where a short line was moving slowly past the ticket agent. Mike turned one more time and waved, just before he disappeared into the tunnel. Steve waved weakly and watched him until he disappeared around the corner.

APRIL 12

EAST SAHARA AVENUE was the same as it had always been in the April sunshine, but this morning it looked very different. Steve was driving to an office for the first time. He had to make a mental note to turn left at the intersection with the Strip instead of swinging into the parking lot of Foxy's. But there was more than that, and as he drove past the Riviera Hotel he felt the new ache somewhere in his chest, an ache that wondered and worried about something that wasn't there, as if his very being had a new dimension that existed inside but was also very much apart. He had felt it the first night he had met Mike as he watched him walk away in the Tropicana Hotel, and he had felt it ever since, and this morning he knew he would never feel any other way or the old way again.

The small parking area in front of the Casablanca only held two cars when Steve turned off the strip. One he recognized as Milton's Buick, the other was a '63 Bentley in two-tone silver and dark blue paint. Steve parked several spaces away from the Bentley and nodded to the driver who was enjoying his morning newspaper. Steve navigated through the construction equipment that was parked haphazardly in the main driveway, waiting for a few moments while a large motorized crane moved noisily around the corner toward where most of the construction was taking place. He walked up the graceful curving staircase instead of using the newly installed elevators and smiled at the signage on the stippled door as he opened it and walked in.

Steffi Perone was standing in the middle of the reception area in a bright yellow dress, her white gloves were folded neatly on her desk, next to a picture of an older woman and what looked to Steve like a dog or horse, he was unsure which from his position just inside the door. Steffi smiled and held out a large lined tablet to Steve. He took it and read each of the handwritten lines on the first page. When he realized there were six pages in all, he looked up from the tablet and down at his new secretary.

"This looks like the list of supplies we are going to need, right, Miss Perone?"

"I hope you don't mind Mr. Cannon, that I took the liberty." She wrung her hands behind her back as Steve continued reading. He smiled when he looked up again.

"Not at all, Miss Perone, might take me a couple of days to find the time to buy them, but the list looks pretty complete to me." Steve saw a hint of apprehension in the pleasant face.

"If you agree, Mr. Cannon, I thought perhaps I would go out now and purchase them."

"But you don't drive, Miss Perone." Steffi giggled as she turned to her desk and picked up her gloves.

"Mr. Baxter is waiting downstairs, Mr. Cannon, just in case you said yes. He can take me, I shouldn't be more than an hour or so." Steve turned slightly and pointed over his shoulder at the door.

"You mean that Bentley down there is Mr. Baxter?" Steffi nodded cheerfully and took the tablet from Steve's other hand.

"Yes, Mr. Cannon. I can use him whenever I want, unless mother needs to go out for something, which is very rare these days, I am afraid." Steve moved away from the door as she removed her matching yellow hat from the coat stand and adjusted her brown curls after she had placed it on her head. She smiled and gave a small feminine wave as she backed out of the door. Steve stood for a few seconds shaking his head before he turned and walked through the door and into the hallway that held the offices. He stopped with his hand on the office doorknob, turned and retraced his steps back into the reception area and over to Miss Perone's desk. He picked up the second photo. It was a picture of Steffi with her arm around a large black thoroughbred horse. Shaking his head again, he entered his office for the first time.

Steve was reading over his notes on the Martin Ogawa case when he heard a sharp rap on his door frame. He looked up to see Jack Cathay filling the door in a tan suit. Steve waved him in and flipped the notebook to a new page.

"Sit down, Jack, sorry, no coffee. Miss Perone has a percolator on her shopping list so maybe tomorrow, huh?" Jack looked around the room and then pulled over one of the wing chairs and positioned it in front of Steve and just to the side of the desk. He waved dismissively as he sat down.

"Already had some in the workers' cantina out back. Bernie has a whole restaurant set up out there, they eat better than any construction guys I ever saw." Jack eyed Steve calmly for a few moments.

"Saw Bernie earlier this morning. Told me something interesting, but if it is none of my business, tell me." Steve sat back in the comfortable burgundy leather chair and looked into the clear blue eyes.

"Not at all, Jack. He tell you about Mike?"

"Yeah, he did. Must be a strange feeling to know you got a kid, hell, an adult kid, you didn't know about."

"Yeah, it is. Took most of yesterday to get over the initial shock. I expect it will take some time to get used to it completely. You ever married, Jack?"

"Yeah, once. Not long though. She decided I wasn't moving up quick enough in the ranks, and she ran off with a wise guy from a rival gang. Some of the guys I know still see her around the old neighborhood once in a while. Turned into quite a handsome married woman I am told." Their eyes met and both laughed softly. Steve held his notebook up.

"You get anything on the Stardust guys?" Jack grunted and pulled a wrinkled piece of paper from inside his suit jacket. He held it up and turned it toward the window.

"Jimmy Rossini, who you already met, was sent out here to run the casino on behalf of Arlen Goldstein, a guy that supposedly has connections to Lansky and a few others. Never heard of him myself, they say he is some big shot lawyer from Miami that wanted his own casino as payment for services rendered. Deal was, he could take over the Stardust, but the other mob guys wanted to staff the place, so ergo; Jimmy and his gang. Rossini is an interesting guy. He has worked for several organizations and was eventually bounced from all of them. Word I get is that he wouldn't stop trafficking in narcotics and brought down too much heat. So safe to say he has set up the same old stand here. Here's a list of the soldiers and underlings and the shifts they work and where in the casino." Jack passed the paper across the desk. Steve read it and then placed it next to his notebook.

"That's quite a set-up. Goldstein must not be too smart if he can't figure out they are going to skim him to death."

"Yeah, and all the guys that were there before, most of them are gone, and the ones that are still there, like that Harold Warner guy you met, he used to be the casino manager, they are all relegated to lower level out of the way jobs. I got feelers out for any more info, but that should get you started."

"That's good work, Jack. Hopefully you didn't have to go too far out on a limb to get it."

"Naw. Like I told you, a few calls to the right people." Steve picked up the paper and with his pen underlined one of the names on the reverse side.

"This guy, Hirsch, Melvin Hirsch. You have him down as 'Casino Personnel', that mean he hires and fires dealers?" Jack nodded.

"He's got points in the operation and he decides who works in the hotel, period. Doesn't even run it by the guys back east. He spends most of his time interviewing showgirls."

Steve wrote for a few minutes in the notebook. Jack shifted uncomfortably in his chair.

"What is the move, Steve?" Steve put the notebook in his jacket pocket.

"I'm going to pay a visit to Mr. Hirsch. I don't think the cops pressed him enough." Jacks' eyes widened slightly.

"You sure that is a good idea? If these guys are up to what we think they are up to, they are not going to like outsiders asking them questions." Steve held up his hands.

"The kid's disappeared off the face of the earth, Jack. Nobody knows anything or saw anything. In my book, that isn't natural, and since he was last seen in their casino, they're elected." Jack sighed and stood up.

"If you say so. Just be careful. Why not let me go as back-up?"

"No thanks, Jack, I want this to be a quiet inquiry, as least as quiet as it can be." Jack moved toward the door.

"You need me to do anything else right now? I have a meeting with Bernie in ten minutes with some guy he needs to interview for the cashiers' cage."

"No Jack, I will brief you when I get back from the Stardust." Jack moved to the door, opened it and then turned back to Steve.

"Thanks for not pressing me about what happened in Sedona, Steve. I am not ready to talk about it just yet. When I am, you and I will sit down over a stiff drink." Steve stood up and put his hands in his pockets.

"I know, Jack. When you are ready, I will be here." Jack nodded slowly and stepped through the door. Steve turned and gazed out the window as he lit his first cigarette of the day. He looked down at the battered zippo lighter, turning it over in his hands. The thin gold plating on the globe and anchor had worn off long ago, leaving a soft pewter insignia on the nicked chrome. He watched as the crane lifted several pallets of gypsum board up to a group of workers on the third floor of the structure that was to become the tower of hotel rooms for the Casablanca.

Two hours later, Steve looked up as Steffi Perone tapped lightly on the glass of his office door.

"Come in, Miss Perone, I was getting worried about you." The woman's bright smile entered the room. She stopped in front of the desk and held out a paper bag.

"I stopped by Mr. Gold's deli and a nice man named Walter said this is what you like for lunch, Mr. Cannon." Steve stood up and took the bag from Steffi's hand.

"That is very kind of you, Miss Perone, thank you. I hope you got something for yourself as well."

"No, Mr. Cannon, I bring mine from home." Steve looked past her out into the reception area.

"Did you get all your shopping done, Miss Perone? Do you need help carrying all that up here?"

"No, Mr. Cannon, I had Mr. Baxter help me and he also convinced two of the workmen to pitch in. Would you like to check everything over and make sure that it is suitable?"

"No, Miss Perone, if you are happy with your purchases, so am I. Do you need help putting anything away?" Steffi shook her head.

"No, but I have a question. Is Mr. Cathay going to be using the other office?" Steve looked blankly at the wall that separated the two spaces.

"I don't think so, Miss Perone. He will probably have an office nearer the casino. What did you have in mind?" Steffi sat down in the chair that Jack had moved closer to the desk.

"I thought it might be a good idea to make that a conference room and somewhere we could put the coffee percolator." Steve sat back and regarded the younger woman.

"I don't see why not, Miss Perone. You might want to check with

Mr. Gold and see if there is a suitable table and chairs somewhere. If I remember correctly, there is already a credenza built in that might work as a coffee center." Steffi stood up and placed her hand on the back of the leather chair.

"Leave it to me, Mr. Cannon, I will take care of it."

"I am sure you will Miss Perone."

"I will let you eat your lunch in peace, Mr. Cannon." She moved to the still open door before turning back to Steve.

"One more thing, Mr. Cannon, I hope you don't mind. I opened an account for us at the stationers on Fremont Street. And before I forget, the workmen are going to install the intercom this afternoon." She smiled expectantly. Steve spoke as he pulled the pastrami sandwich and a cream soda from the brown paper bag.

"That is fine, Miss Perone, you have done well. After lunch, I am going out for a couple of hours. When I get back, perhaps we can go over the telephone procedures."

"I will look forward to that, Mr. Cannon." The door closed and Steve ate the sandwich quickly. Miss Perone was in the other office when he left ten minutes later.

*

The Stardust casino was slow when Steve walked in a little after one. Most of the high rollers weren't even out of bed yet, let alone at the tables. Steve stood by the slot machines watching the pit bosses going about their business. When he was satisfied no one was paying any particular attention to him, he walked casually to the large staircase that led to an upper mezzanine level. As soon as he reached the top of the stairs he was approached by a uniformed security guard.

"Excuse me sir, but these are private offices." The burly guard stood three paces away, but blocked the way down the wide hallway. Steve stopped and smiled.

"I am looking for Mr. Hirsch." He stared directly into the eyes of the man. After several seconds, the guard motioned to a row of plush chairs.

"Sit down, I will see if he is in his office." The man waited until Steve sat down before walking down the hallway and around a corner. Steve crossed his legs and waited. After several minutes, the guard came around the corner and motioned Steve to follow him. When Steve turned the corner, the guard was standing in front of an open door. Steve walked cautiously by the taller man and entered the room, a reception area. A heavyset bald man was leaning over a desk, conferring with a young woman. He looked up when the guard closed the door behind Steve. The guard stayed just inside the door. The man at the desk regarded Steve with a frown.

"Well, who wants to see me?" Steve stepped forward and handed the man his card.

"My name is Steve Cannon, Mr. Hirsch, and I need to talk to you about Martin Ogawa." The man straightened and the frown became a more irritated expression.

"Who?" Steve took a step to his right, turning his body at the same time so that he was equidistant between the two men.

"Martin Ogawa, Mr. Hirsch, one of your baccarat dealers that no one has seen for nearly a month." Hirsch held out his arms and curled his lip.

"He took a vacation, what do I know? Am I supposed to know where every one of the hotel's employees is at all times? Mr..." He glanced down at the card. "Cannon." Steve's eyes narrowed.

"Maybe not, but someone in this joint does, and I want to talk with them." Hirsch motioned to the guard, who gave Steve a sideways look as he opened the door and left the room. Hirsch pointed to the inner office.

"Come in here, Mr. Cannon." He turned to the young woman at the desk. "Run next door and bring whatever there is in the file on this Martin Ogawa." The young woman nodded and Steve heard the door close as he sat down across from a large desk. Hirsch sat behind the desk and gazed passively at Steve.

"So why do you care where this 'Martin' has gotten to? You don't look Japanese to me, so I'm guessing you aren't family." Steve looked around the office. The only way out of the room was the way he came in. Steve decided that even though the cards were bad, it was time to play his hand. He looked intently at the man across the desk as he spoke with a low careful voice.

"I think something has happened to Martin and I think you or somebody in this casino is hiding that fact." Before Hirsch had a chance to react to Steve's words, they both heard the outer office door open. Steve used his body to twist his chair around so that he was facing the door. He guessed who might be coming through the door and when the door opened, he saw he was right, but wrong about the number. Jimmy Rossini had two companions and both of them were standing in the doorway sizing up Steve. Steve leaned back in the chair and positioned his feet so that with one swift move he could be behind the side of the desk. Jimmy Rossini strode into the middle of the room and stared down at Steve. His face was redder than the last time Steve had seen it.

"I thought I told you to check with me before you came in here again?" Steve stood up and moved a step to his right so that the chair was not directly behind him. He stroked his jaw as he looked at the hood.

"I'm not here to gamble, just like I wasn't here the other night to gamble, Rossini. There is a young man missing, and the last time anybody saw him was in your hotel. So I think anybody that knows anything had better start talking." The hood tossed his head back and snickered.

"Is that right, gumshoe?" He turned to his two cohorts. "You guys know anything about this Martin Ogawa?" They shook their heads in unison. He turned back to Steve.

"Well, there you go. You wasted a trip, Mr. Cannon."

"I don't think so, Rossini, and whatever illegal operation you are running here, I promise I will bring it and you down. And by the way, I didn't mention Martin's name, you did." He stared into the black eyes of the hood. Jimmy took a step backward and the two goons stepped forward.

"You're hearing things, Cannon. Make sure you escort him all the way out to the parking lot, Slim." Steve straightened his jacket and pushed by Jimmy, the two hoods following in step behind. By the time they were descending the stairs the smaller of the two men was in front of Steve. They wound their way through the casino and entered the same hallway that Steve had discovered several nights earlier.

Steve was ready as the trio made their way past the dealer dressing room. He took several deep breaths through his nose and took a small sidestep as he came through the doors to the parking lot. When he felt the hand on his shoulder, he instantly pivoted, but instead of stepping forward, he stepped quickly to his left and threw a short punch at the man who was in front of him. The man had turned expecting Steve to be right behind him and was unprepared when the short right cross caught him flush on the chin. Steve followed through with the punch and ducked at the same time, feeling the breeze of the larger man's punch as it sailed over the top of his head. From his crouch, Steve drove his left fist into the off balance man's stomach. Slim sunk to his knees as Steve followed up with a vicious right uppercut that sent the hood sprawling against several garbage cans. Steve heard something behind him, turned and just managed to swing his head back a few inches as the barrel of a police revolver cracked a glancing blow against his right temple. Steve grabbed the man's wrist as the gun flew by his face, and with his right hand smashed the man's nose and with his knee pinned him to the ground. Steve had just wrestled the pistol from the grip of the prone man when he heard a hammer cock just behind his ear.

"Drop the gun." The low voice was just above a growl. Steve

dropped the pistol, but in the same motion swung his arm around his victims' throat and jerked him up off the concrete. The man tried to wriggle from Steve's grip, but Steve clamped down harder on his windpipe. He faced Slim who had the pistol pointing at him from five feet away. Steve laughed.

"Two guys. This the best you can do?" He felt the small trickle of warm blood roll down his cheek from his temple. Slim indicated with several quick jerks of the gun that Steve should let the smaller hood go. His oiled black hair hung over his eyebrows and his nose was bleeding from the scuffle.

"Go on, get out of here."

Steve smiled and pushed the choking man toward his companion, who had to jump quickly out of the way. The hapless hood that Steve had been restraining could not stop his momentum and crashed heavily into the overturned trash cans. Slim reached down and pulled his friend up from the ground still pointing the gun at Steve. Together the mobsters retreated back through the door. Steve shook his hand and made a fist as he reached into his pocket with the other hand and pulled out his kerchief. He held it tight against his sore head as he made his way to the Jeep. He could feel the wound swelling up as he walked.

Steve drove with one hand out of the parking lot onto the Strip, swinging a right hand turn almost immediately into a small lot in front of a liquor store. He pulled open the door of a red and white metal box that sat on the sidewalk and extracted a small bag of ice. He walked into the store and slapped the ice on the counter. The man behind the cash register looked at the bloody kerchief and took a step backward. Steve switched hands on the kerchief and pulled his wallet out.

"You got anything I can put this ice in?" The man hesitated and then put his hand under the counter. When he straightened up he held a rubber hot water bottle.

"This?" Steve nodded, took the bottle from the man's hand and began to shove the ice cubes through the small opening. When he had finished, he pulled a five dollar bill from his wallet.

"Thanks." He carried the bottle and the ice back to the Jeep. He dumped the ice in the gutter in front of his car and with the bag pressing the rag against his temple, he maneuvered the Jeep down the Strip toward the Casablanca. When he had safely parked in the small lot, he went to the back of the Jeep and pulled open the cargo door and lifted out the lid of a small compartment. The quick bending made him dizzy for a few seconds and his vision blurred in his right eye. He grabbed hold of the handle on the metal first-aid box and after closing the door he walked as quickly as he could toward the front of the hotel.

Steffi Perone had her back to the door when it swung open as her boss swept through on the way to his office. She turned in time to see enough and she followed him as quickly as she could, narrowly missing having the door closed on her foot as she pushed her way into the office.

"Mr. Cannon, you are hurt!" Her voice had elevated, but Steve noted that her demeanor was calm.

"Yes, Miss Perone, that is the situation. I need you to help me bandage this wound, if you would, please." He sat on the edge of the desk as Steffi stepped forward and pulled the soaked kerchief carefully away from his forehead.

"No bandage, Mr. Cannon, you need stitches." Steve started to protest, But Steffi held up her left hand as she applied pressure with the other.

"My father worked around horses all his life and my grandfather was a veterinarian, so I know my way around a needle and thread, Mr. Cannon."

"Horses?" Steve tried to move, but Miss Perone pressed harder and Steve groaned and ceased to resist.

"You need to press this on the wound as tight as you can, Mr.

Cannon." She replaced her hand with Steve's and began to prepare what she needed from the kit.

Twenty minutes later, Steve reclined in his chair, holding the water bottle full of ice against the stitches that ran in a jagged row just below his hairline. The pain was better and the throbbing had lessened. Steve did not feel like smoking, but he wished mightily for a glass of scotch. Miss Perone busied herself with tidying up after her procedure.

"You must go to a doctor Mr. Cannon and have that looked after properly." Steve snorted.

"And have them pull out all this beautiful work, Miss Perone?" She stopped what she was doing and stood with her hand on her hip.

"I closed the wound, Mr. Cannon, and a good job it was, if I say so myself, but there is still the risk of infection. I think that antiseptic I used had been in the kit too long." Steve started to shake his head, but stopped when the throbbing increased.

"I survived worse wounds than this in the jungle. If I was going to die from an infection it would have been then."

"That may be, Mr. Cannon, but you aren't twenty anymore and germs are germs." Steve laughed softly as he brought his chair slowly back to an upright position.

"When you are through, Miss Perone, would you please call a Miss Rita Malone at the Las Vegas Sun Newspaper?" Miss Perone opened the door of the office.

"If you stay there and promise not to walk around, I will get her on the line for you." Steve smiled as the door closed behind her. Ten minutes later the phone on his desk buzzed and blinked. He picked up the receiver.

"Hello, this is Steve Cannon."

"Hi Steve, this is Rita Malone."

"How are you, Rita?"

"Fine, Steve, I have just had a most charming chat with your secretary, Miss Perone. Her mother is a good friend of Hank Greenspuns'." Steve shook his head and chuckled.

"Nothing would surprise me when it comes to Steffi, Rita." Rita returned the chuckle.

"Her father was big in oil and gas, mostly in the Middle East, and her grandfather was part owner of Santa Anita racetrack, so you have instant connections there, Steve." Steve chuckled again.

"Well, Rita, I don't want to take up a lot of your time. I was wondering if you are free for lunch tomorrow? Short notice, I know, but there is something important I need to discuss with you and it might be a human interest story you can use."

"Sure, Steve, tomorrow works fine. What time and where?"

"How about noon at the Copper Cart?"

"That sounds good, Steve, see you then."

Steve picked up two pieces of paper he had been working on before he left for the Stardust. He stood carefully and picking up the phone, dialed a four digit internal number.

"Yes, Wayne? Hi, this is Steve Cannon. If you are ready you can bring it up now."

Steve hung up the phone and walked across the narrow hall and into the reception area. Steffi Perone was busy with several stacks of empty file folders that lay in front of her on the desk. She quickly stood up when she saw Steve.

"Mr. Cannon, if you are not going to go home, you should at least sit at your desk and not exert yourself." Steve smiled and motioned for her to sit back down. He handed her the two pieces of paper.

"The first sheet, Miss Perone is a list of the people that should be put through to me right away, whatever I am doing. The second sheet is a list of names that you should call and provide our address and our telephone number. Then follow up with a letter and enclose a business card." The door opened just as he finished and a young clerk came into the room and hoisted a large box from his shoulder, laying it down on Steffi's desk. Steve smiled and handed the young man a twenty dollar bill.

"Thanks, Wayne, that was quick work." After Wayne thanked Steve and left, Steve turned to Steffi.

"Let me open this for you, Miss Perone. You mentioned on Friday that you were going to bring in your old Corona. I thought a new IBM Selectric would be more the ticket." He pulled the flaps of the box open, lifting the typewriter out and placing it on the desk.

"It's beautiful, Mr. Cannon." Steffi expertly cranked a new sheet of paper in the gleaming machine, plugged it in and began to type furiously. Steve smiled and walked back into his office. He sat behind the desk and dialed a number.

"Tam. I need a favor. I just tangled with a couple of guys over at the Stardust. The main guys' name is Slim Atkins. Do you think you can get a line on him?"

"No, don't know the other name, I think he was just back-up for this Slim character."

"Not much, I caught the wrong end of a pistol barrel, the blade sight took a chunk out of my forehead, but I'll live."

"Whatever you can get on him would be helpful."

"What are the chances of lighting a fire under the narcotics boys and getting them to haul in Lucius Freebone?"

"I know. But time is running out, and I need to start putting pressure on these guys from every direction I can."

"Thanks, I will owe you one."

Steve stared into the mirror of the small men's room. He fingered his shirt collar that was stained with several large drops of dried blood. He made a mental note to bring a change of clothes and several extra shirts along with a bottle of scotch to keep in the office. His mind began to idly catalog the guns he kept in the safe in the back closet of his bedroom. After some consideration, he decided that the Browning Hi-Power, a shoulder rig, and the snub-nosed .38 would cover the most bases and could all be locked in the lower drawer of his desk. He splashed water on his face and carefully blotted it dry with a paper towel. He made another mental note to tell Miss Perone to stock the women's room however she saw fit. As he left the restroom he heard voices in the outer office, he walked to the open door and looked inside.

Remy DeMarche didn't need a second glance as she crossed the room quickly and taking Steve's chin in her hand went up on her tip toes to inspect the wound.

"Miss Perone was just telling me what happened, Steve, you should have called me." Steve bent his head forward in an attempt to shorten the inspection.

"It's not as bad as it looks, Gem." He looked past her at Miss Perone with an imploring look. Miss Perone smiled at Remy.

"I told him that he should see a doctor, Miss DeMarche, just in case." Steve rolled his eyes slightly as he removed Remy's hand from his chin, kissing it in the same motion as put his arms around her. Remy smiled, but was still looking at his temple when Steve spoke.

"Fine with me, but I have things I need to do." Remy disengaged the embrace. "It is starting to bruise, Steve, and I can see the swelling. I think Miss Perone's right, you should get that looked at." Steve looked down at the smiling eyes. Remy looked over at Steffi.

"Miss Perone, please call Dr. Aracin, and tell him that we will be at his office in twenty minutes." Steffi quickly picked up the phone book and began to thumb through the listings. Steve started to furrow his brow, but thought better of it.

"Who is this doctor, Gem?" Remy was extracting her keys and sunglasses from her purse.

"He is from France, Steve, and all the French dancers use him. He is wonderful."

"I am sure he is, Gem, but he does speak English, right?" Remy stopped and looked at Steve for a few seconds and then laughed.

"Honestly, I don't know, we always converse in French." Miss Perone held up the phone and caught Remy's eye.

"He wants to talk to you, Miss Demarche." Steffi handed the phone to Remy. Steve listened to a long string of French. When she was done, Remy put the receiver down and turned to Steve.

"He says I should drive, you might have a concussion. We have time to stop by your house and get you a fresh shirt." Steve shook his head as he crossed to the glass door, opening it as Remy walked through.

"Goodbye, Miss Perone, hold down the fort, would you." He smiled wryly at his new secretary and then closed the door.

*

Dr. Aracin did indeed speak English but chose to limit his responses to one syllable when Steve asked him a question. Instead, he and Remy kept up a running dialogue, only occasionally pausing while Remy gave Steve a quick translation. After a twenty minute examination, Dr. Aracin decided that there was no concussion, Miss Perone's stitching job was satisfactory, and all that would be required was a tetanus shot as well as one of penicillin.

As they left the office, Steve took Remy's arm and kissed the top of her head.

"Say, Gem, if you have the time, how about an early dinner at the Golden Nugget. We're only three blocks away and I know Nick would love to see you." Remy snuggled closer to Steve as they walked up to Remy's white Jaguar.

"That sounds good, Steve. I don't have to be back until seven. I gave all the girls the afternoon off, since we are having a full dress rehearsal tonight."

"Visitors, welcome?" Steve smiled at Remy over the canvas top of the sports car. She laughed as she climbed into the low slung seat.

"Sure, but you just saw most of it last week." Steve nodded.

"Yeah, but not with the costumes and the full orchestra." Remy smiled as she revved the engine and turned toward Fremont Street.

Steve and Remy were halfway through with their meal, when

Nick Montero appeared at the side of their table. Two bus boys quickly placed another table next to the one for two that Remy and Steve were sitting at. Nick pulled a chair from an adjacent table and sat down after kissing Remy on both cheeks and shaking Steve's hand. The dark haired Basque was about to speak when he saw the white bandage on the side of Steve's head that was farthest away from him.

"What the hell happened there?" Steve smiled at his friend and waved his fork dismissively.

"It's no big deal, Nick. Two guys took exception to some of my questions and tried to show their lack of appreciation with the barrel of a gun. It is not much more than a scratch." Nick harrumphed.

"It looks like more than that, Stevie boy, I can see the swelling from here." Remy smiled at Steve. Nick persisted.

"What guys, Steve?"

"Two guys from the Stardust. One named Slim Atkins, ever heard of him?" Nick shook his head.

"No, but I'll check on him if you want. I heard a whole new crew took over. Tommy's boss used to keep an eye on things over there for some of the bosses back east, but I guess that deal went away." Steve waited until Nick finished.

"Yeah, it did. A guy named Jimmy Rossini runs things now. Pretty roughly from what I hear."

"Why are you mixing yourself up with those guys, Steve?" Steve smiled and patted Nick on the arm.

"Just working a case, Nick, like always. A young kid who dealt baccarat there is missing, and his father has hired me to find him." Nick shook his head.

"I don't know why you keep this up." Nick turned to Remy. "He can come work for me, name his price, name his hours. Would be a whole lot safer." Nick winked at Steve. Steve laughed and then looked across the table at Remy.

"I almost forgot, I need to call Miss Perone, and tell her I won't be coming back to the office." Steve placed his napkin on the table and started to rise when Nick held his arm and stopped him.

"Perone? Steffi Perone?" Steve stopped and slumped back down into his chair. He shook his head and smiled at Remy before turning to Nick.

"Yes, Nick. Miss Steffi Perone. Don't tell me you know her as well." Nick laughed.

"Of course, I do. She and her mother and uncle live right next door to Margaret and me. She is working for you? Since when?"

"Since today, Nick. It seems like she knows more people in this town than I do." Nick stood up, laughing as he did so.

"I'll guarantee you she does. If I had known she wanted a job, lord knows why, I would have hired her myself. How did you snag her?" Steve leaned back in his chair and looked up at the tall Basque.

"More like she snagged me. She came in a day late looking for one of the administrative jobs that Bernie had in the paper. We got to talking, she seemed perfect for the job." Remy laughed softly and looked up at Nick.

"She is a wonderful lady, Nick, have they lived next to you long?" Nick laughed.

"They were all there when we bought the house. Ida, her mother is in poor health, so they moved here from southern California after Steffi's father died. Better for Ida's allergies. Don't worry, you will meet the whole clan soon enough. Once a month, they put on a big Sunday afternoon soiree, complete with a sit down lunch. Usually the who's who of the valley. I have met some interesting characters there. She always includes Margaret and I and several of the other neighbors, besides that, it is anyone's guess who you'll run into." Steve walked to the front of the restaurant and was still shaking his head when he picked up one of the white courtesy phones.

APRIL 13

STEVE STOPPED THE Jeep on the gravel pullout in front of the rusted cattle guard, twenty-seven miles above Las Vegas. The day had been sunny when Steve started out, but now a low bank of clouds hung over the valley and a cool wind moved through the desert grass and the dwarf pinion trees. He looked down at the two small brown bags on the passenger seat, their tops twisted shut. The casino manager at the Summit Inn had not seen Marcus Boomer for several weeks. That could mean that the old Paiute was in Searchlight at his sister's place, or he was just in one of his unsociable moods. Steve decided to wait for twenty minutes before he left. Steve had just looked at his watch for the fourth time when he saw the small figure walking slowly toward the cattle guard. Steve smiled to himself and pushed the two parcels deep into the pockets of his leather jacket as he climbed out of the Jeep. The ritual was the same as always. Steve deposited the small bags on the other side of the guard, making sure that they stood upright. He backed up two paces and waited while the old man approached, peeking into the top of one of them before picking both up and putting them in pockets on either side of his coat. Steve noted that Marcus now walked with the help of a long staff, which looked to be fashioned from the branch of a bristle-cone pine.

Steve waited until the old man had moved almost fifty yards back up the dirt road before he straddled the low barbed wire fence and followed at a distance. When the pair crested the last rise before Marcus' place, Steve saw that the small wooden table already held three tin cups. Marcus Boomer stood behind the table and watched as Steve walked the last forty yards toward the small clearing that lay in front of the white trailer. The gray fringes of hair left on Boomers' head were swept back by the wind which blew harder on the exposed knoll. Steve pulled out one of the rusted metal chairs at the table and placed it so that he had a view of the mountains to the west. Marcus stood and gazed down at Steve from ten feet away. Neither man moved or made a sound for several minutes. Steve pushed his hand under his jacket and removed the small picture of Martin Ogawa from his shirt pocket. He placed it under the edge of the tin cup that sat closest to him. Marcus turned and gazed at something in the middle distance. Steve hunkered down in his leather jacket, the cold wind made the wound on his head throb.

Presently, Marcus moved to the table and jabbed the pointed end of his staff into the soft dirt. He pulled one of the packages from his coat and placed it on the table before he sat down on Steve's left. He lifted a small flat bottle of whiskey out of the bag and held it out to Steve. Steve held it in his left hand and cracked the seal before he handed it back to him. The old Indian poured both cups halfway full ignoring the third one that kept Martin Ogawa's picture from blowing away and placed the bottle in the middle of the table. Steve waited until Marcus had taken a large drink and nodded his approval. Steve took a much smaller sip and rolled the rough whiskey around in his mouth before he let the fiery liquid slide down his throat. He looked over at his drinking companion when he heard a short laugh and saw the large grin on the wrinkled face.

"What is so funny, Marcus?" The grin slowly disappeared and was replaced by a deep gaze.

Steve waited nearly three minutes for a reply.

"I remember your brother and your father. They are in another place. I told your mother when your father had been dead many years and they had just delivered the yellow paper that told her about your brother." Marcus stopped and took another drink from the tin cup. He moved his tongue around his mouth after swallowing the liquor for several seconds before he continued. He picked up the small picture of Martin, gazed at it for a few seconds and then replaced it under the tin cup. "Your mother and your sister were crying and afraid that you would not return as well." Marcus shifted around in his chair so that he was facing the same direction as Steve. "I told her that I did not know. The future in those days was cloudy. I told her that maybe you won't be back. But there was still a boy who lived, even though he would grow and not know who he was." Marcus turned his head and looked at Steve.

"Now, Steve Cannon, you know too."

Steve looked out over the brown hills and watched a cloud of dust as the wind moved it up a deep arroyo just below the knoll. Steve picked up the small picture and looked at it for several long seconds before he placed it back in his pocket. Marcus stood up and walked slowly to the trailer, returning five minutes later with a magazine in his hand. Steve could hear that he was humming or singing softly under his breath. The Indian resumed his position staring out toward the mountains. For the next twenty minutes, nothing was said as Marcus finished the bottle of whiskey. Just as the sun peeked out from behind the thinning clouds and an edge of light moved across the clearing and the two men, Marcus opened the magazine and tore out one of the pages. He placed it carefully in the middle of the table so that Steve could see it. He held down the corners with the tin cups and the empty whiskey bottle. Steve bent forward and looked at the page. It was a picture of a man and a woman skiing down the side of a mountain and it was an advertisement for the ski resort, Brianhead, which was located in southern Utah. Steve sat back in the chair and gazed at Marcus' profile for a minute before he spoke.

"Is that where Martin is, Marcus?" Marcus nodded. Steve looked again at the picture.

"Is Martin alive?" The old Indian turned and looked at Steve.

"You knew that before you came." Marcus Boomer stood and pulled his staff from the ground in one motion. He gazed at the dirt as he walked toward the trailer, shutting the door behind him. The wind blew harder and a darker bank of clouds moved in front of the sun.

*

The traffic on the Strip was heavier than usual when Steve made his way toward Foxy's just after ten-thirty. The small amount of whiskey that he drank with Boomer had left a bad taste in his mouth, and Steve was hoping that Bernie was at the deli and had time for a cup of coffee. He was relieved when Walter confirmed that Bernie was in his back room office.

"I was hoping you were here, Bern, I never know when you are here or over at the Casablanca." Bernie chuckled as he rose from his desk and came around to greet his friend.

"Sometimes I am not sure either, Steve." He stepped over to the long bar and poured two cups of coffee from the silver carafe. "I try to meet Milton every morning on the site to go over last minute things before he gives orders to the foreman, and then get back here, so that the burden isn't always on Walter, because…" Bernie turned with the cups and looked at Steve. "What happened to you?" Steve reached up instinctively and touched the thick gauze bandage that Dr. Aracin had applied to the wound.

"Just a difference of opinion with a wise guy over at the Stardust. Between Miss Perone, Remy and Dr. Aracin, it is well on its' way to being healed." Bernie made a face and shook his head as he sat down across from Steve.

"I don't why you put yourself at risk like this, for what?" Bernie held up his hand before he continued. "I know, Steve, I know why and I admire that, but it never hurts to think about what comes next, like with you and Remy for instance." Bernie sipped his coffee and glanced over the rim of the cup at Steve. Steve took several sips of the coffee, swishing it around in his mouth a little to take away the faintly metallic taste. He waited until Bernie's attention was off of his coffee and he was looking directly at Steve.

"I am going to ask Remy to marry me, Bern, but when, I don't know. She threw herself into the dance project with you barely two months after Nash died, and it hasn't even been a year yet. I want to let her catch her breath and get the show and your new hotel up and running, before I spring all that on her. But I can tell you, that I plan on spending the rest of my life with that woman." Bernie smiled broadly.

"Glad to hear it, Steve, you two are meant for each other, more than any other two people I have ever known." Steve smiled as Bernie refilled his cup. He sat back and took another sip of the coffee. The second mouthful tasted like Bernie's coffee usually did.

"We have a lot to talk about, Bernie, doesn't seem like we have as much time as we used to. I have to leave in a few minutes, check in with Miss Perone, and then have lunch with Rita Malone." At the mention of the reporter's name, Bernie left the table and after going to his desk, he pulled something from a lower drawer and returned to his seat. He placed a record album cover in the middle of the table. Steve looked down and saw a picture of Rita Malone in sepia, a low cut dress, her hair in a bun with a large flower on the left side. He looked up at Bernie, who was grinning.

"I forgot to tell you that my friend finally sent this from Chicago. I listened to it, she is great, Steve. I mean, a little Billie Holiday, a little Pearl Bailley in the low register, a smooth blues voice. Great stuff. You have to do me a favor, since you know her well. Just mention that I would like her to consider coming over to the showroom and look it over, let me and Remy fill her in on what we have in mind. You do that for me?" Steve picked up the album and turned it over, reading some of the songs it contained. He put it down and looked up at Bernie.

"Of course, I will. What it is the worst that could happen? She gets so mad, she never talks to either one of us again." He stopped as a look of horror crossed Bernie's face. "Steve... I..." Steve laughed and then chuckled at the relieved look he saw across the table. Steve picked up the record and upended his cup, before placing it back on the green felt.

"See ya. Bern, thanks for the coffee, I'll let you know how it goes. Don't get up, I'll show myself out." Bernie smiled and patted Steve's arm as he walked by on his way to the door.

"Thanks, Steve, good luck."

Steve stepped into his office and smiled at Steffi Perone. She was on the phone and Steve waited until she had finished the conversation and replaced the receiver.

"A late good morning, to you, Miss Perone, is everything going all right?" Steffi smiled and held out three small pink slips of paper.

"I was beginning to think that you forgot the way to your office, Mr. Cannon. There are three phone messages for you." Steve quickly sifted through the messages. One was from Tam Polhaus. He looked back down at his new secretary.

"Thank you, Miss Perone, I will make a phone call and then I need to get over to the Copper Cart, which is where I will be until 1:30 or so, if you need to get in touch with me. After that I will come back here and take care of these." Steve held up the slips and smiled as he walked toward his office. Once inside, he took off his leather jacket, switching it for a camel blazer. He sat down at his desk, picked up the phone and dialed the number for the municipal golf course.

"Hi, Lew, this is Steve."

"Fine. How are things with you?"

"I need you to get a message to Keno, if you can."

"Yeah, tell him I will meet him at four o'clock. He will know where."

"That would be great. Thank you, I owe you at least another beer."

"Yeah, let's get together this week, I have some news I need to share with you."

"You, too, bye."

Steve looked down at the record album that Bernie had given him. He bent over and pulled his canvas satchel from a lower drawer. He put the album in the main pocket and walked across the hallway to the reception area.

"Is there anything we need that I can get while I am out, Miss Perone?" Steffi Perone stopped typing and looked up at her boss.

"No, Mr. Cannon, but I would like to ask you something, or more accurately, my mother would like me to ask you something." Steve stood with his hand on the doorknob, a sly smile on his face.

"Of course, I will come to Sunday dinner, Miss Perone, I would be delighted." Steve chuckled as a scarlet hue rushed up from Steffi's collar causing her to quickly place both hands on her cheeks.

"Mr. Cannon.... I don't know....what to...how did you....?" Steve smiled.

"Well, Miss Perone, it is my business as a private detective to know things. Now, what time does your mother want me to be there?" Miss Perone straightened up in her chair and took a deep breath in an effort to regain her composure.

"One o'clock, Mr. Cannon, dinner is at three, and you are to bring Miss DeMarche." Her words were short and clipped and she wouldn't look at Steve.

"That sounds great, Miss Perone, please tell your mother that we will be looking forward to it." Steve smiled and waited until Steffi looked up at him and was smiling as well.

"Make sure you take the time to have lunch, Miss Perone." He gave her a small wave as he went out the door.

Steve drove the four blocks to the El Morroco hotel. He parked his car in the narrow lot in front of the hotel and casino and walked toward the south portico.

The Copper Cart restaurant was half full when Steve stepped into the low light just before noon. He was waiting his turn for the hostess when he saw the owner, Jack Dennison walking toward him from the bar. The tall white haired man's cream colored suit was in sharp contrast to his deep tan.

"Steve, how are you? I haven't seen you in here in quite a while. Been busy?" Steve smiled at the dapper man before him.

"Yeah, Jack, always busy. Missed you at the last shebang at Bernie's. You should call him and get four or five of us together for a private poker game." The older man patted Steve's arm.

"I will do that, always a pleasure to play with you and Bernie. Do you need a table?" Steve nodded.

"Yes, if you have one available. I am meeting someone here for lunch." Jack turned to the hostess station and picked up two menus.

"Right over here, Steve." Steve followed Jack as he led him to the center of the room and over to a large banquette. Steve stopped when he saw the table.

"No, Jack, this is one of your premier spots, anywhere will do." Jack smiled and placed the menus on the table behind the place settings.

"Nonsense, this is perfect. I will bring your guest over when they arrive, let me know if there is anything I can get for you. Tony, your waiter will be with you shortly." Steve smiled and shook Jack's hand before sitting down.

"Thanks, Jack."

Steve had just picked up the menu when he saw Jack approaching the table, with Rita Malone in tow. Steve stood up and waited until they were both standing in front of him.

"Rita, this is Jack Dennison. Jack, this is Rita Malone." Jack took Rita's hand when she offered it.

"A pleasure to meet you Miss Malone, have you dined with us before?" Rita smiled and shook her head.

"No, Mr. Dennison, I have only been in town since last July. But Steve is making sure that I visit all the worthwhile spots. This is a very nice restaurant, I can see why Steve chose it."

Jack smiled broadly and motioned toward the table, pulling it out slightly as Steve stepped back to allow Rita to slip into the curved booth.

"Thank you, Miss Malone, enjoy your lunch and let me know whenever you need a reservation." Rita turned to Steve as Jack left the table and headed toward the front of the house.

"I am sorry I am a few minutes late. Hank gave me directions but he neglected to mention that this place was on the same property as the El Morocco." She looked up from her purse and started to say something and then stopped, her gaze set on the bandage over Steve's right eye.

"Steve, what happened?" Steve waved his hand dismissively.

"Actually part of the story I will get to in a minute." Steve picked up the menu from his plate.

"This is one of those places that mostly the locals know and frequent. Jack is a good guy and a great host. Now that he knows you, he will bend over backward to get you anything you want." Steve sat on the end of the curved bench seat so that he could face Rita. He placed his canvas satchel on the floor near his feet. Steve handed Rita her menu.

"What would you like, Rita? This is a steak and prime rib place, but Jack makes a great Caesar salad if you want something lighter." Steve looked up as the waiter approached. Rita ordered the half order of prime rib and a glass of red wine. Steve ordered a steak and a scotch. When the waiter had retreated, Steve turned to Rita.

"Thanks for coming down here, Rita, I need your help." Rita nodded, her light brown eyes fastened on Steve's face.

"Sure, Steve, you know if I can help, I will." Steve reached inside his jacket and brought out the small picture of Martin Ogawa and placed it in front of the reporter. Rita picked it up, looked at it for a few seconds and handed it back to Steve.

"Sweet looking kid, who is he?"

"Martin Ogawa. He went missing twenty-five days ago. He worked as a baccarat dealer at the Stardust. I have reason to believe he stumbled onto illegal activities at the hotel and I think they have done something with him." Steve stopped and took a drink of ice water as he waited for Rita's reply. Rita reached into her oversized purse and pulled out a steno notebook and a pen.

"What kind of illegal activity, Steve?"

"Heroin smuggling from Asia."

"Can you prove that?" Steve shook his head.

"No. Not at this point, but I would like you to consider writing a 'young boy disappearance piece'. I think that you just putting the questions to some of the execs at the Stardust might be enough to move this forward to where I can figure out what happened to Martin." Steve waited while Rita gazed out into the restaurant and tapped her pen on the top of her notebook. After a few moments, she picked up Martin's picture and looked at it for a few seconds.

"Can I keep this to run with the story?" Steve grinned broadly.

"Yes, of course you can. So you will write it?"

"Yes, I will, pending Hank's approval, but when I tell him what you suspect, I am pretty sure he will insist we run it. But first, I need as much background as you can give me." Steve sat back in the booth as the waiter placed their lunches on the table in front of them. For the next twenty minutes as they ate, Steve told Rita everything he knew about the case.

As they enjoyed their coffee, Steve waited until Rita had put her notebook away before he pulled the canvas satchel up on the bench next to him.

"If you have a few more minutes, Rita, there is something I would like to show you."

"Sure, Steve, what is it?" Steve pulled the album from the satchel and laid it between them. Rita picked it up, a half smile playing across her face.

"Where, pray tell, did you get this?"

"You remember Bernie, right? Well he is from Chicago, and he saw a marquee with your face on it, several years ago, called one of his buddies and here it is." Steve tapped the cover of the album that Rita had put back on the table. Rita shook her head.

"I was quite a bit younger when I recorded that. I worked my way through journalism school at the University of Chicago in the jazz and blues clubs." She looked at Steve with a wry expression.

"But something tells me there is more to it than just wanting my autograph on that, right?" Steve laughed.

"Well, Rita, I am just the messenger, but here it is. Bernie is opening the Casablanca Hotel and Casino in July. In keeping with his theme, he is going to have a small to mid-sized cabaret room devoted to jazz and blues. Opening night is going to feature Oscar Aleman, and Stephane Grappelli. He wants you to perform with them as well, and he wants you to consider regular appearances." Steve sat back and took the last sip of his scotch. Rita rolled the stem of the crystal wine glass back and forth between her fingers as Steve waited.

"I don't know what to say to that, Steve. That is stellar company, I am not sure I am up to the level of those people you mentioned. After college, I couldn't find a newspaper job, and for three years I worked the clubs. I finally left and went to LA because I couldn't handle the late nights and the drugs and the booze that makes everything tick in those clubs. I haven't sung in front of an audience in over four years." Steve sat back and shrugged.

"Like I said, Rita, I am just the messenger. Here's Bernie's card, you decide." Rita picked up the album and read the liner notes on the back for a few seconds before she handed it back to Steve.

"Tell Bernie, I will think it over and if I decide to pursue it, I will let him know."

"That's fine with me, Rita, I will pass that along. Thank you for hearing me out on the Martin story and giving it a shot." Rita waved dismissively.

"If I had known the story, before you told me, I would have done it myself." Steve stepped from the booth and took Rita's hand and purse as she moved from behind the table. They both waved to Jack as they pushed open the heavy wooden doors and stepped, squinting into the bright afternoon sun. Steve walked Rita to her car before he retraced his steps back in front of the restaurant toward the spot where he had parked the Jeep.

Twenty minutes later he sat in front of his desk dialing Tam's number from one of the small pink slips that Miss Perone had laid out in a straight line on top of the green blotter.

Tam answered on the third ring.

"Hi Tam, what is new on your end?" He could hear Tam rustling some paper and figured he was eating his lunch. The detective replied laconically.

"Not much, Cannon. I'm still trying to get information on Slim Atkins, should get some word this afternoon or tomorrow. I just heard from Detective Fonzo and the narcotics guys got a BOLO out for Lucius Freebone. If he hasn't skidadled to greener pastures, it shouldn't be long before we have him in here and maybe see what he knows."

"That is a good break, Tam, things are starting to move in the right direction. Rita Malone is going to write a piece in the Sun about Martin's disappearance, but she isn't going to include anything about the drugs. She will use that information as a hook to get Hank to go along. I promised her that we would tell her if the drug case moves forward."

"That means he will probably be calling my superiors, so I will head over there when we are done and head that off at the pass."

"Thanks, Tam, let me know when you know something."

"Yeah, I will, Cannon. Goodbye."

Steve hung up the phone and leaned back in his chair. He felt the bandage on his temple just below his hairline. It didn't feel as painful as it had the day before. He opened the top drawer of his desk and pulled out the page from the magazine that Marcus had given him. He was still looking at it when the intercom buzzed. Steve pushed down the lever as he had been instructed by Miss Perone, and smiled when he heard the cheery voice.

"This is the first time I get to use this, Mr. Cannon, it is so exciting." Steve waited a few seconds listening to silence on the other end before he spoke.

"That is nice, Miss Perone. Is there something more, or is this just a test." He heard her sharp intake of breath.

"Oh yes, sorry, Mr. Cannon. I got carried away for a minute. Mr. Gold is here to see you."

Steve chuckled softly to himself.

"Send him in, Miss Perone." Steve stood up and opened the door and met Bernie as he crossed the hall. They smiled at each other as Steve closed the door behind them. Bernie walked over to the window and turned when Steve walked into the middle of the room.

"You are lucky, Steve. Miss Perone is just what you need." Steve motioned toward the large wing chair which still sat in front of his desk where Jack had moved it the day before. Bernie sat down, as Steve pulled Rita Malone's record album from the satchel on his desk.

"So, what did she say Steve, is she going to do it?" Steve sat back and looked across the desk.

"Don't know, Bernie. She took your card and said she would think about it. She doesn't seem too thrilled with that kind of life." Bernie's face held a wistful expression.

"But she didn't say no, right?" Steve nodded.

"No, she didn't say no, Bernie. I also got the impression that she was more than a little impressed when I told her who was opening the cabaret. I guess we will just have to wait and see." Bernie nodded thoughtfully as he stood up and walked to the window. There were already four completed stories on the eight story tower. He gazed at the steel for the fifth floor as it glinted in the sun as he spoke.

"You know, Steve, I have been thinking." Steve grinned inwardly.

"Your son, Mike got his degree in Hotel Management, right? Was going to go in with Nathan, learn the business and then maybe one day take over. That isn't going to happen now, so I was thinking, why doesn't he come and help run this joint?" He turned from the window and looked at Steve who had swiveled his chair around and was facing Bernie.

"He's dead set on going into the Marines, Bern. At this rate you will have all of us working here, but I would like to see that happen. I just don't think there is much chance until he gets the Marines out of his system. He grew up in Tahoe. Big difference in the way people act and look at things compared to here, if you know what I mean." Bernie nodded thoughtfully.

"I don't think that will be a problem. I should have told you sooner, but I didn't know how to bring it up, but Theresa is moving back here according to Sheldon. Won't be much to keep Mike in Tahoe, then."

"It's a free country, Bern, I've got nothing against Theresa one way or the other. We should have never gotten married. That's the long and the short of it. She's always going to be his mother, nothing will ever change that, and to tell you the truth, I wouldn't want to change that even if I could. He is a good kid and she raised him right, you have to give her that. I made peace with all of that many years ago. So if you want to propose it to him, go right ahead. He will be back on Sunday night, he might hear it better if it comes from you." Bernie turned and walked to the door.

"Just a thought I had. I am glad you agree. Thanks for talking to Rita." Bernie held up the record as he waved goodbye. Steve sat quietly for several minutes after the door closed. He folded the page from the magazine Boomer had given him and placed it carefully inside the desk.

*

Steve drove slowly out to the golf course. He parked at the far end of the lot and smoked two cigarettes before he opened the door and stepped out from the Jeep. He walked with measured steps the one hundred yards to the pro shop. Lew Mannion was not in, but an assistant was kind enough to let Steve take one of the carts that were parked beside the first tee. Steve drove the half mile to the little bowled out area and parked beside the concrete bench. Almost all the blossoms had fallen from the cherry trees and lay in small pink clumps along the edge of the path where the wind had left them. Steve looked at his watch, he was five minutes early. He was sitting in the same position ten minutes later when he saw Keno walking up the cart path toward him. Steve stood up and busied himself lighting a cigarette while he waited. Keno stopped ten feet away.

"Good afternoon, Steve how are you?" Steve held out the half full pack of Pall Malls, Keno shook his head and came closer.

"I am OK, Keno."

"You have met with some kind of accident, No?" Keno pointed to Steve's bandage and Steve's hand instinctively went to it.

"Yes, you could say that." Keno nodded and walked in front of Steve, bowing slightly and holding his right arm out a short way from his side in a show of deference and sat down on the bench.

"Did this happen because you are looking for Martin?" Steve took a deep drag on the cigarette and looked out at the mountains as he let the smoke out slowly. When it was all gone, he turned toward Keno.

"They don't like people asking questions. That is normal in this business." Keno was quiet for a few seconds.

"Do you know more than the last time we spoke?" Steve took another puff and looked down at Keno.

"I don't know any more facts than I did, but I think I see the case more clearly now."

"Is that good for me, or bad for me, Mr. Cannon?" Steve sighed, dropped the cigarette butt and crushed it out with the toe of his shoe. He pulled a small snuff can from his coat pocket and deposited the butt inside. When he had straightened, he waited until Keno looked up at him.

"You should prepare yourself, Keno." Keno looked at the ground and reached out his hand.

"Perhaps I will take one of those cigarettes now, Steve." Steve pulled his pack out again and lit one with the zippo lighter. He handed it to Keno who took a puff and then held it up and looked at it for a few seconds before he took another puff.

"When I was on Guadalcanal, an officer had confiscated a carton of Lucky Strikes that one of my men had found in the jungle. I remember picking up one of the half smoked butts he had left on the ground. It was the best smoke I have ever had." Steve looked out at the mountains for a minute before he turned back to Keno.

"There is going to be a newspaper article about Martin in the Sun in the next day or two. It will probably contain the picture you gave me. I just want you and your family to be prepared." Keno nodded and flicked some ash to the ground.

"Do you think that will help find Martin, Steve."

"Yes I do, Keno. There are people in that hotel that know where Martin is and this is the first way we are going to put pressure on them." For several minutes neither man spoke until Keno stood up, crushing out the cigarette in his fingers and putting the butt in his jacket pocket. He took several steps away from the bench in the direction from which he had come, before stopping and turning toward Steve.

"When the time comes, Mr. Cannon, will you take me to Martin?" Steve sucked his lips hard up against his teeth for a few seconds before he could answer.

"Yes, Keno, I will promise you that." The older man turned and trudged back over the small knoll and out of sight.

When Steve arrived back in the office there was a message from Rita Malone. He settled behind his desk and placed the return call. It took him two transfers before he finally heard her low voice on the line.

"Thanks for calling me back, Steve. When I got back to the office I ran the Martin Ogawa story by Hank and he was enthusiastic. And as you predicted, he is very interested in the people who run the Stardust and the drug angle. He would like you to keep him updated personally on anything that develops there."

"Sure, Rita, I can do that. When you see him, tell him I may have something for him by tomorrow or the next day. How long before the story comes out?"

"I am working on it as we speak and I am almost done. Unless there are some things that the editor or Hank think need to be changed, I don't see why I can't make tonight's deadline for tomorrows' edition."

"That is good news, Rita, I have prepared the family for the article, I just hope it has the intended effect."

"I do too, Steve."

Steve had just hung up the phone when the intercom buzzed.

"Yes, Miss Perone."

"Mr. Polhaus is on hold, would you like me to put him through?"

"Yes, Miss Perone, thank you." Steve waited for a few seconds.

"Tam, what have you got?"

"Well, first I have to say that having an office makes you a whole lot easier to get hold of. I don't know if that is good thing for you or not, but it is nice to hear a female voice when I call." Steve chuckled.

"I am glad you approve. Impressing you is always at the top of my list. Do you have anything new on Atkins?"

"No, not directly, but maybe something that will turn out to be even better. We have his girlfriend down in one of the cells. She was brought in three hours ago on an assault charge and the booking officer says she called Atkins and he hung up on her. She also has several bruises in the usual places that she didn't get in the altercation, and since he is not her favorite playmate just now, we may be able to get some info out of her."

"Assault? On whom?" Tam chuckled.

"She's a chippy, and a very unlucky one at that. She was with some high roller at the Sands, when the concealed pocket in her fake mink stole burst, spilling several thousand dollars worth of chips on the floor. He took exception, she picked up one of those metal ashtrays and beaned him with it, cracking open his skull. He's not married, so he's pressing charges."

"So how are you going to handle it?" Tam took a deep breath.

"We're trying to locate her lawyer right now. Assuming we can get him in here by tomorrow morning, we can start pressing for some cooperation. She has several priors and the guy is in the hospital, at least for tonight, so she is looking at a couple years minimum. I'll keep steering the conversation around to Slim. If she's smart, she will see where we are going with this and cooperate. I'll let you know how it goes."

"Thanks, Tam, there will be a story in tomorrow's Sun about Martin, so I think with a little luck, it will be a bad week for Mr. Atkins." There was a pause on the other end.

"I also have some information that you and Jack should hear." Steve sighed.

"Should we all meet?"

"Yeah, I think we should. How about seven o'clock tomorrow night at my place?"

"That's fine with me, I will check with Jack and confirm it with you tomorrow."

"Until then." Tam rang off. Steve stretched and walked across the hall into the reception area. He was surprised to find Steffi Perone still there.

"Miss Perone, it is almost six o'clock. You should have left over an hour ago." Steffi smiled.

"I wanted to get a few more things done, Mr. Cannon. Every time I turn around, there is one more thing to do. They told us down at secretarial school that setting up an office efficiently, takes a lot of time and effort." Steve stood with his hands on his hips and looked around.

"I want you to keep track of your hours, Miss Perone, so that you are paid overtime." Steffi giggled softly.

"No need for that, I am just making sure everything is in its' place."

"Nonsense, Miss Perone, I don't want your mother thinking I am taking advantage of you." Steffi's face clouded over for a moment before she turned toward Steve.

"Mr. Cannon. When you come to Sunday dinner, I should tell you that my mother will address me as 'Stephanie'. I want to make sure you know who she is talking about." Steve smiled to himself as he began to make his way back into his office.

"I don't think there would be any chance of missing that, Miss Perone. I am going to leave now and go down to the showroom. Please don't stay too long. Is Mr. Baxter here yet?"

"Yes he called from downstairs. I won't be long, I will see you tomorrow, Mr. Cannon."

A few minutes later Steve descended into the spacious lobby, his footsteps echoing in the emptiness. He crossed through one of the wide courtyards that led past the pool area that was still under construction and into the building that held the smaller showroom. There were several groups of workmen still putting the final touches on the walls and the stage. Large piles of furniture were in the middle of the space covered with plastic. He saw Remy and Bernie along with Donn Arden sitting at a table on the stage. Steve waited until a lull in the conversation before he approached the trio. He put his arm around Remy and squeezed her shoulders before extending his hand to Donn.

"Hi, Donn, how are you?" The famed choreographer stood and smiled.

"Doing good, Steve, your timing is perfect, we have just finished." He patted Remy on the shoulder as he walked around the table.

"I will see you two, tomorrow." Steve looked down at Bernie as Donn walked away.

"Bernie, let's go to dinner, my treat. The three of us haven't been out in a long time. What is that Italian restaurant you are always talking about? Let's go there." Remy smiled across at Bernie.

"That is a great idea, Bernie, you are always promising." Bernie smiled.

'Villa D' Este. Sure, why not. I can take a break. Let me call Joe Pignatello and see if we can get a good table." Bernie walked off the stage toward the phone. Steve looked down at Remy.

"I don't know how you can look so beautiful after a twelve hour day." Remy smiled.

"Well, thank you Steve, a girl likes to hear that even if it isn't true. Lucky for me, we had pictures taken this afternoon or I wouldn't be going anywhere in public tonight. I am going to powder my nose, tell Bernie I will be right back." Steve waited alone on the stage until Bernie came back.

"All set. Where's our girl?" Steve jerked his head toward the dressing room.

"Let's have a seat, Bernie, it could be a minute or two."

The Villa D' Este sat on Convention Center Drive, the short street that connected the Strip to Paradise road and was the main artery leading into the Convention Center complex. Bernie's baby blue Thunderbird made the wide turn into the parking lot which was almost full even though it was six-thirty on a Tuesday evening. When Bernie announced his name to the maître d', the man told him to wait for a minute as he disappeared behind the large mirrored bar. A few seconds later, Joe Pignatello smiled as he came around the small check-in table to shake Bernie's hand. Joe put his arm around Bernie and beamed at Steve and Remy. Bernie handled the introductions before Joe looked down at the shorter man.

"I'm glad you called, Bernie. Frank is here and unless he knows them personally, he won't let me seat anyone next to him at that middle table. Solved my problem, heh?" Bernie laughed and fell in line behind Remy and Steve as Joe led them into the softly lit dining room. The three of them waited while Joe stepped up to Frank Sinatra's table and whispered in his ear. Frank was sitting with two women and his body guard Jilly Rizzo. Frank looked at Bernie, winked and snapped his fingers. He said something to Jilly and then waved the trio over.

"Hey Bernie, don't think Joe has matzos, but sit down over there anyway." He looked at Remy for a long second and then at Steve.

"Hey Cannon, you and your friend are looking well tonight. Can I buy you a round of drinks?" Steve laughed.

"Sure, Frank. Frank, this is Remy DeMarche. Remy, this Mr. Sinatra." Frank waved his hand and shook his head as he stood up. "Frank." He shook Remy's hand across the table. He indicated his dinner companions.

"Jilly, you know. This is Marilyn and Judy." Remy and Steve nodded at the two women and Steve shook Jilly's hand. Steve and Remy followed Bernie to the table right next to Franks' and sat down. Bernie smiled and looked around the smoky room.

"I told you this was a great place. Joe makes the best raviolis I have ever tasted, and on the south side of Chicago, there were some good raviolis." Several tuxedoed waiters descended on the table bringing water and the round of drinks plus a bucket of champagne that Frank had ordered. Steve sipped the Jack Daniels and looked at Remy.

"What do you think, Gem, drinks bought by the great man himself." Remy smiled.

"He is more of a gentleman than I would have thought. I think I danced with Marilyn in the revue at the Dunes six years ago. This is a nice place, Bernie, thanks for bringing us." Bernie said something that was drowned out by laughter from Frank's table. Steve turned to see the comedian Joe E. Brown and Frank laughing at one of Joe's jokes. Just as their dinners came, Frank appeared at the table as the rest of his party was preparing to leave.

"I gotta leave for the dinner show, but I wanted to propose something to you, Cannon." Steve smiled over his plate of osso bucco.

"Sure, Frank, what's on your mind." Frank smiled thinly.

"I still haven't got a chance to get my ten G's back. When's that going to happen?" Steve looked over at Bernie.

"Bern. Do you think that we could use your back room Saturday night for a few hands of poker?" Bernie looked at Steve and then at Frank.

"Sure, no problem. Do you trust me to deal, Frank?" Sinatra smirked.

"Sure, Bernie, that would be swell, but I'll bring the cards." Steve smirked back.

"Fine, Frank, just make sure there's only fifty-two of them." Frank's icy expression was lost on Steve as he filled a fork with a bite of his dinner. Frank looked at Remy.

"Very nice to meet you, Miss DeMarche." He stepped back from the table to where Jilly was standing. He pointed.

"I'll see you two after the midnight show on Saturday." Steve waved at his back as the two men walked toward the door where Joe stood with their coats. Remy looked at Steve.

"What was that all about, Steve?" Bernie leaned in toward Remy.

"Frank can't stand the fact that Steve is the better poker player. Steve took ten grand from Frank three years ago and he has never forgotten it. There were all the wrong guys there that night and they are always ragging on Sinatra about it. Even Joey Bishop works it into the shows when he really wants to get under Franks' skin." Remy looked at Steve.

"Ten thousand is a lot of money, Steve. What if you lose?" Steve put his arm around Remy.

"There are a lot of variables in poker, Gem, but style of play goes a long way toward deciding the winner. Some guys just never figure out they play a bad game. He may beat me, but it will take him all night and a lot of good cards and better luck." Bernie chimed in.

"Frank might bring some funny decks and try to get by that way, but he always brings the ones' from the Sands. If I suspect any funny business, I always have several of those decks on hand to make sure things are fair and square." Steve nodded and looked at Bernie.

"Let's try to keep this as quiet as possible. Too many people in there always make it worse in the end." Bernie smiled.

"Don't worry, I will keep it down to the bare minimum." Bernie looked at his watch.

"I gotta go, too. Milton left me with a big stack of bills to get through, or nobody will get paid." He started to get up, then a blank expression crossed his face.

"I just forgot, I drove you guys over here." Steve held up his hand.

"No problem, Bernie, we will catch a quick cab back to the Casablanca."

"You sure? I can wait." Remy patted Bernie's arm.

"Don't worry about us, Bernie, we still have quite a bit of champagne to kill." Bernie smiled as he got up to greet Joe Pignatello as he approached the table.

"How was everything? Frank's picking up the tab, so enjoy." He laughed and clapped Bernie on the shoulder.

"I've got to go, Joe, but the kids are going to stick around." Joe beamed as Bernie said his goodbyes and left. When they were alone again, Steve and Remy chatted, glad that the noisy room had quieted. They had just finished the champagne when Steve saw the round form of Jay Sarno approaching the table. Steve stood up and greeted the hotelier.

"Mr. Sarno, this is Remy DeMarche. Remy, this is Jay Sarno,

Bernie's competition across the street." Jay gave Steve a cold look as he shook Remy's hand.

"Nice to meet you, Miss DeMarche." Steve waited until Jay looked his way.

"You want to sit down and have a drink, Jay?" Jay smiled at Remy as he shook his head.

"No, Cannon, I just stopped by to see if you and I could have a little chat sometime. I didn't know you were so thick with Sinatra." Steve held a steady gaze on the portly, balding man in front of him.

"I'm not. In fact, away from the poker table, I would say we barely get along at all." Jay snorted.

"Don't think so, you wouldn't be sitting where you're sitting unless he ok'd it. So how about it? We get to powwow soon?" Steve shrugged and pulled one of his cards from his jacket pocket.

"Sure, Jay, but you'll have to come over to the Casablanca." He smiled when Jay took the card and with a sour look, walked away. Remy waited until he was out of earshot.

"Why the face when you mentioned Bernie and the Casablanca, Steve?" Steve looked across the table into the soft brown eyes.

"Bernie bested him in the land deal that gave Bernie enough land to build Casablanca. Jay wanted to keep that property for himself and build it out after he opened Caesars, and then he would own two of the four corners on Flamingo and the Strip. Bernie put an end to that dream, plus Milton and Bernie are a good team and Casablanca will open a year before Caesars, and steal even more of his thunder. There are rumors that Jay and his partner are always at odds." Steve picked up the empty champagne bottle and caught the eye of a passing waiter. He smiled at Remy.

"Since Frank is paying, let's have another." Remy laughed and took Steve's hand. They moved closer together in the large booth and kissed.

APRIL 14

STEVE SAT IN the warm early morning sunshine that streamed through the windows of Foxy's. He ate his plate of eggs, potatoes and toast slowly as he read Rita Malone's article in the Sun. Hank Greenspun had given her a section of the front page just below the fold to start the story, and three long columns on the back page. Steve was confident that it would garner quite a bit of attention. He was hoping the right people were also reading along this morning. While the article stopped short of accusing the executives of the Stardust of wrongdoing, they had initially refused to comment to Rita when she called them repeatedly and only after they were tipped that publication would be today, did they try to get their viewpoint included. But what came across loud and clear was that the hotel not only didn't seem to care much about what had happened to Martin Ogawa, there was a very strong impression left that they were hiding something. Steve made a mental note to include Rita the next time he and Remy went out to dinner. He had just finished the article when Bernie sat down at the table, a damp dishcloth slung over his shoulder. Steve looked up and smiled into the pale blue eyes. Bernie picked up the paper and looked at the picture of Martin.

"I read it this morning with my first cup of coffee. Too bad about the kid, though Rita does write almost as well as she sings." He looked across at Steve.

"You kids get home OK?" Steve nodded as he brought his coffee cup to his lips.

"Yeah, we did. We sat and had another bottle of bubbly on Frank." Steve smiled at the chuckle the comment elicited from Bernie. "Jay Sarno stopped by the table after you left. Wants to come over and talk to me about something or other. He was pretty put out we were sitting next to Frank's table, and it killed him when I gave him my card and told him he would have to come over to the Casablanca." Bernie wiped part of the table with the damp cloth.

"Yeah, I heard from Stan Irwin that Sarno keeps trying to push the date of his opening up, especially since it looks like Hoffa might be indicted. Sarno promised him he would be the center of attention at the opening. Word that Milton gets is that Jay keeps changing things and it is impossible for him to make a decision. Wants to design everything from scratch. Want to hear something funny? I had an engraved invitation sent to Jay, inviting him to our opening." Steve laughed and gathered up the paper.

"Next time I see him, I will ask him if he is coming." Steve stood up and moved toward the door with Bernie right behind him.

"Going to the office, Steve?" Steve stopped with his hand on the door.

"I told Miss Perone that I would be in by eleven o'clock. I have to go downtown and pow wow with Tam. I hear your canteen has pretty good food, maybe we can meet for lunch."

"Sure, I'm heading over there in a few minutes. I'm taking Walter with me, I have a surprise for him." Steve laughed as he pushed open the door.

"Too bad for him, I don't have time to warn him." Steve could hear Bernie's laugh as the door closed behind him. The inside of the Jeep was warmer than usual, a sure sign that the hot weather was not far off.

Tam finished reading the story in the Sun and handed the paper back to Steve. Steve folded the front section and slipped it into his inside jacket pocket. Tam leaned back in his chair with his hands behind his head.

"Well, that is a good start. If I was Jimmy, Slim and the boys, I would be pretty ticked off if I read that. If you want to cause a stir, I am pretty sure you are going to get your wish. By the way, how is your head feeling?" Steve rubbed the wound which was now covered by a band aid. He smiled wryly at the implication.

"Sooner or later, they have to react, I just hope you are there to bail me out of trouble." Tam snorted and sat upright in his chair. He picked up a mug shot that was clipped to a file folder and tossed it in front of Steve. Steve looked at the hard eyes that stared back at him from beneath the bottle blond locks.

"Lois?" Tam nodded.

"Here's what I suggest. Visiting hours start in ten minutes. I put in a call now that you want to visit with her, and I meet you down there. All unofficial, no one can squawk. She spent time with her attorney yesterday and got her bail hearing. Judge is not buying her story, so I think she wants up and out from underneath pretty badly. Bad news is that her attorney has also represented Slim in several scrapes according to the file, so we have to include him out as much as possible." Steve looked thoughtfully at the floor.

"Might be a long shot, but the way I look at it, we don't have anything to lose by taking a run at it." Tam held up his hand.

"I almost forgot. Narcotics made some inquiries and the Stardust doesn't have the usual Far East junket scheduled for tomorrow, but they have one coming in on Monday. They're working right now, trying to get someone undercover in the baggage area to keep an eye on things. Looks like there is a chance the feds will get involved." Steve sat back in the chair and looked up at the ceiling.

"Let's hope they don't get too ham-handed and get them wise." Tam shrugged as he picked up the phone.

Ten minutes later, Steve stood in front of a large steel door as it slid open with a loud clanging. He had been frisked and signed in and now he walked toward Tam who was waiting for him outside a large fenced-in area inside the jail. Tam led him to a table in the corner where a petite blond sat in a yellow jumpsuit. Tam turned toward Steve.

"Steve Cannon, Lois Pittman. Lois, this is Steve Cannon, he is a private detective, he would like to talk to you." Lois ignored Steve and looked up at Tam with an angry expression.

"Where are my cigarettes?" The voice was low and husky. Tam rolled his eyes at Steve and pulled a new pack of Camels from his pocket and tossed them on the table in front of the woman.

"I said three packs. Where are the rest?" Tam pulled out a chair and motioned to Steve to take the other one beside him.

"One now, Lois, more later, if you cooperate." Tam gazed directly into the hard dark eyes.

"My lawyer know he is here?" She jerked her head toward Steve. Tam smiled.

"I don't know, why don't you ask him? There is a phone right over there. Here I have some change, why don't you give him a call, we'll wait." Lois looked grumpily at Steve.

"Forget, it, he wouldn't answer anyway, Slim tells him what to do." Steve threw one arm over the back of the chair and tapped a new pack of Pall Malls on the table.

"Why don't you get yourself a new lawyer, Lois?" The woman smirked as she made a gesture toward the cigarettes. Steve unwrapped the cellophane and handed her one of the cigarettes as she answered.

"With what money, pretty boy?"

"Seems like you'd be better off than you are now." Steve pulled out his lighter and lit Lois's smoke as she leaned over the table, squinting up at him as he sat back and put the lighter away. She scoffed.

"That is a one-way ticket to the big house. No, I'll take my chances." Steve regarded her evenly as he lit one for himself.

"If you help me with something I am looking into, maybe I can help your chances." She shot a disgusted look at Steve.

"You? You ain't even a cop. What could you possibly do to help me?" Steve let out a long stream of smoke toward the wall, as he waited until the hard eyes were looking at him again.

"There is young man that is missing from the Stardust. I think there is foul play involved. A case like that gets solved, many people are grateful, Miss Pittman." She shook her head, the cigarette unattended in her mouth.

"I get it, you want me to roll over on Slim, right?" She scoffed again and turned her head as she took another puff on the Pall Mall. "You know, you're right. If that kid is dead, it was probably Slim that did the killing, but you will never get me to swear to that. I'm in trouble, sure, they can't kill me for palming chips, but Slim sure as hell will if I squeal."

Steve looked at her arms and the bruise on her neck.

"Looks like he is doing a pretty slow job of it anyway." Lois flicked the ash from the cigarette into a shallow metal tray in the middle of the table, her eyes narrowed.

"That's the breaks in this town."

"You live with Slim, Lois?" She shook her head.

"Nah, he kicked me out last month. He lives in a house on the Stardust golf course. I live in a crappy studio downtown, unless the landlady has already heard I'm in jail and tossed my stuff out in the street." Steve took a deep breath.

"So, Lois, let me see if I got this right. This Slim character beats you whenever he feels like it, throws you out of the house, won't take your phone calls, let alone go your bail, and controls your lawyer. That about right?" Lois looked down at the cigarette in her hand but didn't say anything. Tam leaned forward.

"We can offer you protection. Lois. You and I both know that sooner or later, Slim is likely to maim you or worse. Why not give it a chance?" Lois looked down at the floor and shook her head.

When she looked back at Tam, Steve could see tears brimming from her eyelids.

"I had to hear it from some other broad in here that he already has another girl." Steve slid his kerchief across the table. He and Tam sat quietly while Lois cried into the cloth. After several minutes she stopped and looked at Steve.

"The young man you were talking about. He Japanese?" Steve nodded. Lois again buried her face into the kerchief for a few seconds before she straightened up.

"Jimmy Rossini came over to the house a month ago. They didn't see me sitting out by the pool. They were talking about what they were going to do about some Japanese kid who was threatening to go to the police about something."

"Do you hear what they decided?" Lois shook her head.

"Slim got a phone call, and I didn't hear anything else after that." Steve sighed.

"Does the word 'Brianhead', mean anything to you, Miss Pittman?" Lois looked at Steve blankly for a few seconds before she nodded.

"Slim has a cabin there. Way out in the woods, I've never seen it. He goes up on weekends sometimes to play poker with his buddies." Steve gave Tam a look with his eyebrows raised. Tam stood up and pulled two more packs of Camels from his pocket and placed them if front of Lois.

"You think of anything else you want to tell us, Lois, let me know." Steve stood up.

"Goodbye, Lois, I hope you remember something that will help Martin Ogawa." He placed the Sun article next to the cigarettes.

"Keep the kerchief, Lois." Tam and Steve walked back to the large metal door. Tam nodded to the guard and the door clanged open. Steve and Tam walked back across the rotundra to Tam's office. Tam shut the door behind them and sat down behind his desk. He picked up several yellow slips of paper and shuffled through them quickly, picking out two and placing them by his telephone. Steve busied himself writing in his notebook before he looked up at the detective. Tam spoke first.

"What is this about Brianhead? Where did you come up with that one?" Steve smirked and lit a Pall Mall with a lighter that sat next to Tam's ashtray.

"You don't want to know." Tam stopped what he was doing, and swiveled around in his chair.

"Are you trying to tell me, that old Indian came up with that?"

"I'm not trying to tell you, Tam, so much as I am telling you. I asked. That was what came back. Martin is there or was there."

"What do you mean 'was there'? Is he alive?" Steve let out a long trail of smoke and looked at Tam.

"No." Tam looked at the desk and shook his head slowly.

"You seem pretty sure of that."

"I am. The only thing I am not sure about is whether I am going to kill that scumbag Slim myself or let justice take its' course. What do you think?" Steve smirked and tipped off the ash end of the cigarette with his index finger as he looked up at Tam.

"I think you know what I think, and I think I am going to forget what I just heard." Steve stood up and looked down at the Irish-German cop.

"Well, Tam, you just keep living in the valley of the unconcerned. If I decide to go the legal route, I will make sure you get the collar and the credit. See you tonight." Steve walked to the door and sent back the same glare he was receiving before he stepped into the hallway.

*

Miss Perone was busy talking on the phone when Steve stood in front of her desk for the first time that day. She smiled and handed him three phone messages. One was from Larsen, the assistant DA, the second was from Clifford Jones and the third was Jay Sarno.

Steve draped his jacket over his office chair and pulled the telephone to the middle of his desk. He dialed the DA's number first.

"Steve, how are you?"

"Fine Jim, how are you doing?"

"Can't complain. I was glad to get the message from your secretary yesterday that you now have an office. I am sorry that my first call to you there might not be so pleasant."

"Oh? How so?" Steve could hear Jim take a deep breath.

"It concerns a matter in which you and I were involved in the first part of the year. A grand jury has been impaneled, and as I predicted then, your name is on the list of witnesses that will be called. I just thought I would give you a heads' up before you were served." Steve swiveled his chair toward the window and looked out toward the room tower.

"I assume the subject is Tommy Carmino."

"Yes, I'm afraid it is, among others." Steve shook his head.

"Did you read Rita Malone's story in the Sun this morning?" There was a slight pause on the other end.

"Yes, yes I did." Steve interrupted.

"Don't you think that your brother-in-law and the other FBI agents would be better employed investigating the hoods that have taken over the Stardust and are flooding the Westside with Asian heroin?" There was a longer pause this time.

"I know your feelings on the subject, Steve, I was just calling out of professional courtesy. I hope you don't take the same attitude before the Grand Jury as you did last time." Steve snorted.

"I'll be a part of their fishing expedition because I have no choice, but as I told you last year, if they truly had something they wouldn't need this circus."

"I am sorry you feel that way, Steve. Again, congratulations on the new office and I hope to see you soon." The phone clicked in Steve's ear.

Now the purpose of Clifford Jones' phone call was clear. He left a return message with the firm's secretary and dialed the number that Jay Sarno had left.

"Jay, this is Steve Cannon."

"You left a message with my secretary, I am just calling back."

"No. Saturday night is a private game, just the two of us."

"I have no objection, but that will have to be another time. And if you want to pursue it, you are going to have to call Bernie Gold to set it up. Getting Benny Binion, Frank and you in the same room is going to take more coordination than I got the stomach for." Steve listened for several minutes.

"I don't understand that attitude, Jay, Bernie deserves the same respect as any other casino owner. His project may not be half as grandiose as yours, but it will be a well run place, the people that work here will all be cared for properly and the casino won't be run by wise guys. Can you say the same?"

"What about Sinatra?" Again Steve listened. He swiveled his chair and watched the work on the tower to pass the time.

"I told you last night, I have no pull with Frank. He and the Sands are almost the same thing for chrissakes, he still owns points in the joint. Last I heard, you are at least a year from being able to open, thinking about getting Frank over to perform at your place is a little premature, don't you think?"

"Look, like I told you the first time I met you, I appreciate what you are trying to accomplish and I wish you luck, but there are ways that things are done in this town and not everybody is going to be happy when an outsider comes in here and tries to tell the local rubes what they are doing wrong." Steve swiveled his chair around as Miss Perone knocked softly on the door frame and came into the room. He put his hand over the receiver and Jay's excited voice became muffled.

"Mr. Cannon, a Miss Horvath is on the phone and wants to speak with you." Steve nodded and smiled. He removed his hand from the receiver and spoke loudly into it.

"Jay, I have to go take another call. Call Bernie." He pushed down the buttons on the cradle and took a deep breath. The phone buzzed, he picked up.

"Mr. Cannon, this is Mr. Carmino's secretary, Miss Horvath." Steve chuckled to himself.

"Yes, Miss Horvath, what can I do for you?"

"Mr. Carmino would like an appointment to come to your office as soon as possible."

"Uh,… Miss Horvath, that is why Miss Perone, whom you have just spoken with, is employed here. I am somewhat surprised that fact is lost on you of all people."

"Mr. Carmino insisted I speak only to you about this." Steve sat back in his chair looked at his watch and sighed.

"It's eleven o'clock now, Miss Horvath, I will wait for him and when he gets here he can join Mr. Gold and myself for lunch. Does that meet with your approval?"

"Yes, Mr. Cannon." The short clipped response was followed by the click of her receiver. Steve snorted as he looked at the black phone in his hand.

*

The loud voice that Steve heard coming from the reception area twenty minutes later announced the arrival of Tommy Carmino. Steve stood in the doorway of his office and watched as Tommy hung up his gray fedora. His dark gray suit had a sheen that matched the shine on his Italian shoes. A dark burgundy shirt was highlighted by a light gray tie. Tommy smiled as he turned from the coat rack and saw Steve. He smiled down at Steffi as he looked around the office and started walking toward Steve. He stopped and glanced up and down the hallway, grinning as he stepped past Steve into Steve's office.

"Well, Slick, I am very impressed if I do say so." Tommy frowned at the gold brocade wingchair that sat off to one side of the desk. He quickly scooted it to the middle of the desk and stepped back to see if it was centered. When he was satisfied, he turned and motioned for Steve to sit down.

"Let's see how you look behind the big desk, killer." Steve snorted and walked past Tommy as the hood sat down in the wing chair. Steve lowered himself slowly into the large burgundy desk chair and stared at his visitor. Tommy was looking around the room. His gaze stopped on Steve. He held up his hands.

"No bar?"

"This is a working office, Tommy, next time bring your own." Tommy chuckled and unbuttoned his suit coat as he sat back in the chair.

"There's work and then there's work, Slick. Making people feel comfortable makes them more willing to hear what you have to say, don't you think?" Steve swiveled his chair slowly back and forth.

"Maybe. What is it that I am going to have to hear?" Steve looked at his watch. Tommy leaned forward.

"What is that you're wearing? Let me see that. Christ, Cannon, that looks like something you give a kid for Christmas because he was a good boy and learned how to tell time." Steve scowled at the timepiece.

"It's government issue, Tommy, saw me through a lot of long dark nights." Tommy sat back and raised his eyebrows.

"If you say so, Slick." He held up his wrist and pulled back his shirt cuff. "Maybe when you retire, I will get Mr. Rolex to make you one of these for you to look at in your old age." Tommy laughed to himself as he pulled his arm back and admired the gold watch.

"So, Tommy. You didn't come all the way down the Strip to compare fashion accessories, right?" Tommy reached into his suit coat pocket and pulled out one of his Cuban cigars. His searching look around the desk prompted Steve to pick up an ashtray, walk to the middle of the room and come back with a small oval side table that he placed beside Tommy.

"Need a lighter?" Tommy shook his head.

"No, Slick, I got one. I would offer you one, but after you left my office the other day, I noticed my cigar box was a little light, so I figure you smoked your quota of my Cubans for the week." Steve sat down and pulled a pack of Pall Malls from the top drawer. Tommy leaned back and looked up at the ceiling as he inhaled the rich smoke. He looked back at Steve for several seconds as he slowly released the smoke from his lungs.

"This isn't my idea, Cannon, I have been sent." Steve held out his hand in a gesture he hoped would hasten the conversation.

"Sent? By whom, and for what reason?"

"For several. My boss wants to make sure you are OK for one. I told him that you only cried a little when you got that scratch, but he wanted me to make sure." Steve nodded knowingly.

"Ah, yes, I wondered when we were going to get around to the guys over at the Stardust. I think everyone in town is wondering how that deal went down, Tommy. You guys oversaw that operation since it opened. If I were your boss, I would be a little concerned about how that looks." Tommy took another small puff and held the cigar up in front of his face.

"Not a problem, Slick. Just business as usual. Those that matter, know the score. My boss told them that they were asking for trouble sending those guys out here, so he ends up looking like a genius."

"Maybe, Tommy, but they seem to be cheesing everyone off and so far, you and your boss seem pretty disinclined to do anything about it." Tommy smiled.

"Well, why should we get involved when we got you willing to take one for the team? And speaking of that, I am supposed to ask you if you need our help in your little endeavors. I told him about the marker and your one-man crusade and after he read the story in the Sun, he is just inquiring." Steve swiveled back and forth several times before he replied.

"Yeah, he could do something. He could send word back up the pipeline that Jimmy Rossini is not only importing heroin from Asia on his junkets, but a lot of it is sticking to his fingers and ending up on the Westside."

"That so? Says who?" Steve smiled wryly and tapped his chest. Tommy scoffed.

"Gotta do better than that, Slick. That's not enough weight to swing the deal."

"Oh, I think it is, Tommy and I will tell you why. Importing heroin is Jimmy's little trick wherever he lands and I think some of the guys back east protest too much. The skim, however, that is what you and your boss will run to teacher with. My guess is before nightfall. Am I wrong?" Tommy shrugged.

"Not my call, I just work here. But out of curiosity, how did you figure all this out by just by playing a few hands of baccarat in your little penguin suit?" Steve looked at Tommy and shook his head as he inhaled deeply on the cigarette and let it out slowly.

"You just don't get it, do you, Tommy." Tommy threw up his hands and rolled his eyes.

"Oh, please enlighten me, Slick."

"Your problem, Tommy, is you never ask questions, or more precisely, you never go out and ask questions yourself. You have all these people around you that keep their jobs by figuring out what you want to hear. As far as I can see, the farther you move up the food chain, Tommy, the less you know." Tommy nodded and contemplated his cigar for a few seconds before smiling up at Steve.

"Got it all figured, right, Slick? Let me ask you something. You ever stop and wonder why I waste my time with you? Because my ego gets a boost hanging around with somebody that dresses like you do? No. I'll tell you why. Precisely because you don't work for me, that's why. You think I would have stood you to that marker to play high roller at the Sahara? You provided me a useful service just like I do for you by pretending I know you." Steve chuckled.

"Yeah, Tommy, it's a real fair trade, right? Is that why I am waiting for a subpoena so I can go get grilled by a grand jury?" Tommy's face darkened for a brief moment.

"You talk to Clifford?" Steve held up the pink telephone slip.

"No, but he called. I got the word from the Assistant DA. You seem a tad more concerned than the last time we covered this ground."

"Naw, you're wrong. They got no more than they had last year. What are you going to tell them? That Miss Horvath is mean to you? You think that you and I ran into each other by accident four years ago at Bernie's? No, Slick, I had your number way before that. Though you are a big pain in the rear at times, you got what Bugsy had, God rest his soul. You can look past the surface and put things together that make other things make sense. You know what I mean?" Steve smiled.

"So I should be happy that you came along and now my life is worthwhile?" Tommy snorted, stood and walked to the window, taking two quick puffs on the Cuban as he looked out over the Casablanca.

"No, Slick. You should be happy that you have a good woman and a good friend like Bernie who's got your back. And you should be happy that when you wake up in the morning your first thought isn't about what friend or employee is being squeezed or paid off to hasten your demise."

The door opened widely and Bernie walked into the room. He grimaced and stepped back into the hallway, waving his hands in the air.

"Wow, that is a lot of smoke. It's like a Turkish hookah party in there." Steve stood up and laughed.

"Don't worry, Bernie, Tommy won't burn the place down. Stay right there, we'll come to you." Steve and Tommy followed Bernie into the reception area. Miss Perone stood up when the trio arrived in front of her desk.

"Should I turn the fan on in your office, Mr. Cannon?"

"Yes, Miss Perone, but let the smoke clear for a few minutes." Bernie smiled at Steffi.

"Miss Perone, when you have had enough of this guy, you can always come over and work for me." Steffi sat down to her typewriter and waved the three men off with her hand.

"I have work to do, Mr. Gold, and Mr. Cannon suits me just fine, thank you." Tommy stepped forward and removed his hat from the coat rack. He held out his hand.

"It was good to see you again, Miss Perone and give my regards to Ida." Steffi stopped typing and smiled.

"Thank you, Mr. Carmino, I will certainly pass that along." Steve waited until Bernie and Tommy exited the office.

"Miss Perone, we will be in the cantina if any of us are needed."

"Thank you, Mr. Cannon, are you coming back?" Steve looked at his watch.

"Yes, I have some calls to make this afternoon." He smiled and waved as he closed the door behind him.

He caught up with Tommy and Bernie on the wide curving stairway. Through the windows he could see workmen planting the twenty foot tall palm trees.

"How do you know Miss Perone and her mother, Tommy? Why do I get the feeling I am the only guy in town who has never met this woman?" Tommy waited two steps below Steve and then continued as Steve arrived.

"We get most of our slot machines from Anthony, her uncle. Top drawer machines. The Gaming Control Board boys like them, easy to check the calibrations, never break down." Bernie was waiting at the bottom.

"I've been trying to get some of those. Seems they are all spoken for." Tommy slowed as he approached the last few steps.

"Well, Bernie, I am all ears, how badly do you want them?" Bernie smiled as Steve and Tommy joined him.

"I don't know, maybe we can work out some kind of trade, you think?"

"Maybe, Bernie, there is always a way to make any deal."

*

Steve returned to his office just before two o'clock. He sat down in front of the phone and called a number that he did not have a pink slip for. He waited while someone went to find the man he was calling. After a few minutes he heard the warm southern Louisiana accent and he smiled into the phone.

"Shelly. I'm not interrupting anything am I?" Steve heard the big man laugh from his belly.

"No way, big gun. I have been looking for an excuse to take a break. Breaking in some new guys, good time to see what they can do. And speaking of that, what can I do for you? My wife asks every day when am I going to drive you around again." Both men laughed before Steve spoke.

"I need you to find Lucius Freebone for me. The cops are useless, and I need to put the squeeze on him. Do you think you can find him?" Shelly chuckled.

"If I can't, I'll give you back your money. Stay right there I will call you back." Steve pushed down the lever on the intercom. When Miss Perone's pleasant voice came on he made a request.

"Miss Perone, I am expecting a Mr. Shelly Cointreau to call me. Interrupt me as soon as he does, please."

Steve went quickly to the men's room and when he had settled down at his desk, he picked up the small pile of slips. He was just about to call Jack Cathay when the intercom buzzed.

"Mr. Cointreau, Mr. Cannon." Steve picked up the receiver and punched the lit button.

"Shelly, seven minutes, you have to be kidding me." Shelly chuckled.

"You know the neighborhood you play in, big gun, I know

mine. Write this down." Steve moved a writing pad near the phone. He wrote down the address and asked Shelly a few particulars about directions and the neighborhood.

"Shelly, you are worth every penny."

"Always glad to help, gun. I still have twenty minutes left on my break. Let me know if you need anything else."

"I will, Shelly, goodbye." He quickly called Tam. The detective answered on the third ring.

"Tammy boy, how lucky do you feel today?" Steve heard the exhalation through the nose that met his use of the diminutive.

"I never feel lucky, what have you got?"

"I got Lucius Freebone."

"What? Where?" Steve chuckled and pulled out his pack of Pall Malls with his free hand.

"Pays to pick up the phone once in a while, right? He's not sitting right here, Tam, you are going to have to work for him. The question I put to you is, do you do it, or do I call Fonzo?" Steve flicked the zippo open and lit the cigarette.

"I'll do it, teach those lazy SOBs a lesson." Steve read him the address and gave him the details that Shelly had relayed.

"I'll let you know what I find, if anything. You didn't get this from the old Indian, right?" Steve snickered.

"The old Indian has a name, Tam. His name is Marcus Boomer, and the answer is: No." Tam ignored the retort.

"I'll call you later." Steve hung up the phone and sat back in his chair. He had barely finished his cigarette, when Miss Perone announced another call. Steve reluctantly picked up and greeted the caller.

"Mr. Jones. You called earlier."

"Yes, Mr. Cannon, I did. Do you have a few minutes for me now?"

"Yes, I do."

"I am calling as a legal representative for Mr. Carmino. A grand jury has been empaneled and several lines of inquiry are to be opened. I have in front of me the witness list and three names down, your name appears. Now the question I have, Mr. Cannon is whether you are a hostile witness to my client or not." Steve sighed.

"I have heard your voice on recordings too many times for my liking, Mr. Jones, so I have a suggestion. Let's not do this over the phone and I want Tommy present when I answer whatever questions you might have. That OK by you?" There was a three second pause.

"If that is what you want, Mr. Cannon. Where and when?"

"Tommy's private steam room. You set it up and leave the date and time with my secretary, Miss Perone."

"Fine, Mr. Cannon, I will get back to you in a day or two, goodbye." Steve noted the time and recorded it on his calendar.

Two hours later, Steve locked the office door and walked up the stairway to the suite level. He knocked on the second door, just past Bernie's suite. He heard a muffled request to enter. He opened one side of the white double doors and stepped into a semi-circular foyer, closing the door gently behind him. Through the open arch, he could see Jack Cathay at a small writers' desk near the window talking on the phone. Steve waved and stepped onto the white carpet, gazing around the room. Except for the view and a curved wall here and there, it looked very similar to Jack's rooms at the D.I., all the furniture were the same pieces he had then. Steve busied himself with his notebook, while Jack finished up the call. He looked over at Steve for several seconds, sighed then stood wearily on his feet.

"I don't know about you, Cannon, but I need a drink. I never put a cashiers' cage together from scratch, let alone three, I just ran 'em." Jack walked over to a large cabinet that was anchored on the wall next to a small curving zinc topped bar. When he pulled both doors open, Steve saw two shelves filled with liquor bottles. Jack selected one and brought it over to the couch for Steve's inspection.

"This suit you, Steve?" Steve looked at the bottle of scotch and whistled.

"That is some expensive stuff, Jack, also very peaty, smoky and strong. You sure you want that? I thought you were strictly a bourbon man." Jack scoffed as he returned to the bar and pulled out two short crystal glasses from beneath the cabinet.

"I've had enough at your house that it finally grew on me. Walter gave me a short list, said this is the best, so this is what we drink." Jack returned to the couch and put a coaster on the glass table before setting Steve's drink on it. Steve waited until Jack had settled into one of the large wing chairs before he hoisted the glass of whisky.

"Here's to new beginnings, Jack." Jack grunted and took a large drink, immediately standing up and heading to the bar for a refill. When he seated himself again, he looked across at Steve with a bemused expression.

"Think we should get something to eat before we head over to Tams'?" Steve looked at his watch, chuckling to himself as he turned the scratched dial toward the window to read the time.

"Yeah. Tam said seven, so we got some time to kill. Where you want to go?" Jack shrugged.

"You pick. I'm tired of making decisions, anywhere is fine as long as I can get a steak."

"Fine, let's go to the Flame Pit. It's close to Tam and the steaks are good." Jack nodded into his drink.

"What do you think he has to say?"

"Probably some new intelligence on what Sorelli is up to." Jack stood up.

"I'm hungry, finish your drink, let's go." Steve took the last half inch of the strong whiskey into his mouth and smiled after he swallowed.

"I think I need a key to this place, Jack. I can just stop by here every day after work and drink your wonderful booze." Jack snorted as he swung his sport coat over his shoulders.

"Any objections we take my car?"

"No, no problem, Jack." Steve led the way out of the suite and waited while Jack locked the front door. Jack had a half smile on his face as he moved past Steve.

"Bought a new car yesterday. New Lincoln, with the continental package and the suicide doors. Figured you might like a change from jouncing around in that Jeep of yours." Steve chuckled as the two men descended the stairs quickly, their footsteps echoing on the tiles when they reached the bottom and walked toward the doors.

"Bernie must be paying better than I thought. You need some help in the cage?" Jack shook his head at the detective as he waved to the security guard who was standing in the lobby.

Jack pulled the long black Continental onto the Strip and started heading north. In the side view mirror, Steve saw another car pull away from the curb and move into the traffic keeping in the same lane as the Lincoln but two cars back. Steve could not see who the occupants were, but he could see that there were three of them. He turned to Jack.

"Jack, take Desert Inn Road." Jack scowled.

"Why? Sahara to Maryland Parkway is faster. We'll get caught in the traffic on Paradise."

"Yeah, we will, that is the idea. I think we're being followed." Jack sat abruptly forward craning his neck to look in the rear view mirror.

"Which car?"

"Tan Chrysler Imperial, two cars back, same lane, three men."

"I see 'em. Yeah, they look hinky all right, trying to pretend they aren't there." Jack slowed for the turn onto Desert Inn. Steve watched as the Chrysler turned as well, but it changed lanes and fell back behind two slower cars.

"I got an idea, Jack. When you get on Paradise, stay in the middle lane until just before we get even with the Convention Center and then pull quickly into there. We will drive around the back and come out front again and then back to Paradise. That will either get rid of them, or force them to make a play." Jack looked over skeptically.

"If you say so, but let me ask you a question. Are you packing?"

Steve shook his head as he watched the Chrysler change lanes and pull closer.

"No, I'm not. But something tells me that isn't their intent right now." Jack snorted and turned left at the green light onto Paradise.

"I don't know how you figure that, Cannon, but get ready, we are almost to the center."

"When this car passes us, Jack, I'll tell you when." Steve took one last look at the Chrysler.

"Now!" Jack turned sharply into the lane closest to the curb and with only ten yards in front of him, squealed the tires as he twisted the wheel, pushing the heavy car around the corner. Steve braced himself, keeping his eyes on the Chrysler that had braked, but was unable to turn in time and continued on toward the intersection with Sahara Boulevard. Steve turned around in the seat and watched them disappear through the rear window. He turned back around and looked at Jack.

"Pull all the way around the back of the Convention Center and come out on the far side." Jack shook his head and slowed down.

"I can just cut through the back lots and hook back onto D.I., ditch 'em for good."

"No, I want a chance to see who these guys are. If they know we have made them, they will tread more carefully, either way, we will have to deal with them sooner or later." Jack sighed audibly and pulled behind the huge dome shaped building and drove through the back parking lot. They followed a pair of cars down the extension of Convention Center Drive and slowed to make the right turn back onto Paradise Road. Just as Jack turned, Steve saw the tan Chrysler across the street in the parking lot of the unfinished Landmark Hotel.

"When you get to the corner, Jack drive a little faster. I see them, but they are tucked behind the construction fence. It will take them awhile to catch up with us." Steve was peering through the back quarter window. He recognized Slim Atkins sitting in the front passenger seat. Jack drove quickly, rounded the corner and sped up

Sahara Boulevard, the big V8 roaring beneath the hood. Ten minutes later, they cruised slowly down Tam's street in the Huntington district and pulled to the curb in front of the tidy two story home. Though they had not seen the tan Chrysler since they left the Convention Center parking lot, Steve convinced Jack to sit quietly in the car for ten minutes. When the time was up and no cars had even turned onto the quiet tree lined street, Steve jerked his head toward the house and got out of the car.

"Let's get Tam and all go to dinner. It should be safer, if nothing, else." Steve and Jack knocked on the door and waited as Tam looked quickly from behind the curtain covering the back of the glass door, grimaced and opened it partway.

"You guys are an hour early, what gives?" Steve jerked his thumb toward the street.

"Jack's got a new car he wants to show off and we're hungry, so grab your coat, we're going for a ride." Tam was still wearing the grimace when he shut the door behind him and followed the two men to the long black Lincoln parked at the curb.

"Jeez, Jack, you got a wife and eight kids nobody knows about? How much car does one guy need?" Jack sneered.

"Just get in, copper, I don't need your wise guy remarks." Tam smiled at Steve and climbed through the wide back door and settled down in the black leather. Steve turned around and looked at Tam.

"Keep an eye out for Slim and a tan Chrysler Imperial. They followed us halfway here from the Casablanca. We lost them by the Landmark, but I got a feeling we haven't seen the last of them tonight." Tam craned his neck to look out the back window.

"So you figured bringing them to my house was the best idea you've had today?"

"Relax, Tam, we shook them." Jack drove slowly through the quiet neighborhood and then sped up when he reached Charleston Boulevard. Steve instructed him to pull through the restaurant parking lot and circle around the block before parking under a street light in the small lot. Tam got out and looked around.

"Why don't we put a big sign on the corner with an arrow pointing at the car, Cannon?" Steve turned toward the restaurant.

"We're going to sit right by that window and keep an eye on Jack's car and anything else that moves in this parking lot." Tam looked at Jack, who extended his arm and fell in behind the detective. They settled into a booth in the corner where they could see the car and most of the lot, but were partially hidden from view. They ordered steaks and beer and engaged in a small bit of small talk until they were almost finished with their dinners. Tam pushed his plate away and looked across the booth at his two companions.

"Here's the deal. I got word that Sorelli was seen in Phoenix by an informer. He described the car he was in along with two Mexican body guards. They found the car yesterday at the Phoenix airport. They are checking the flights out of there to see if they can come up with something. Not much, but as we all predicted, he didn't stay in Mexico for long." Steve looked sideways at Jack.

"Well I guess we pack from here on in." Jack snorted and caught the waitress' attention. After he had ordered scotches for the three of them he looked at Tam as he lit a cigarette.

"Cops. Always a day late and a dollar short. I'm going to hit the head." Jack stood from the booth, looked carefully around the restaurant and then disappeared around the corner toward the men's room. Tam jerked his head in the same direction.

"What's his problem?" Steve moved his plate as the waitress arrived and began to serve the scotches.

"He's not the same Jack, Tam. He hasn't got over what happened to Little Moe in Sedona." Tam took a sip of the golden-brown liquor.

"What did happen out there? Why all the hush hush?" Steve pursed his lips and looked into his glass.

"He hasn't said. I guess he will when he thinks the time is right." Tam shook his head.

"On another subject. I arrested Lucius, he was right where you said he would be. I ended up taking Al Fonzo along just for instructional purposes." Steve snorted into his glass and smiled. Tam continued. "Caught him with twenty grams of the stuff. Fonzo says it is high quality and definitely Asian, not Mexican. Al is grilling him as we speak and pulling out all the stops, even got the DA involved already. Mr. Freebone thinks he can bargain by telling us where the rest of his product is, but it's Al's job to get him to turn on the Stardust guys. His lawyer showed just as I left. Definitely hired by someone else, so my guess is that your Mr. Atkins knows the score by now, since we have his girlfriend and their main dealer both downtown. Hope you didn't heat up this pot too quickly." Steve held out his hands and glanced out at the parking lot.

"There's even more heat than you know. Tommy Carmino stopped by today and I think I got him and his boss to put a bug in the ears of the bosses back east about Jimmy and his activities. So, if I am right, they should be feeling the heat from everywhere. When I get home tonight, I am going to call Hank Greenspun and let him know he can follow up with you guys and print the drug allegations as a follow-up to the Martin Ogawa story."

"I guess it doesn't pay to hit you upside the head with a pistol, right?" Tam looked up as he saw Jack coming back to the booth. Tam started to say something to the older man, when Jack waved him off and slid into the booth and leaned his head toward Steve.

"You got that piece of paper I gave you?" Steve nodded and pulled his notebook out from his inside jacket pocket and flipped to the back where he had the paper clipped to the back cover. Jack took it from his hand and underlined a name halfway down the page.

"Don't anyone move a muscle. There is a guy sitting on the third stool in at the bar." Jack tapped the name on the page turning it so Steve and Tam could both see it. Steve reached his hands over his head, stretched, yawned and looked casually around the restaurant.

"See him. He was with Jimmy Rossini the first night in the

baccarat room. Fresh from the coast. They wised up and switched cars on us. Three to one, they are nearby."

"Want me to call in for back-up?" Steve shook his head.

"No, Tam. I got a better idea. Jack, you take Tam back to his house and then go back to the Casablanca. I'll call a cab. If I can keep this guy away from a phone, they will be half way across town before they realize I am not with you." Tam looked at Jack and shrugged.

"Your call. I hope you know what you are doing." Steve motioned for Jack to slide out of the booth.

"I am going to use the pay phone by the men's room. Hang tight, enjoy your scotches, act like you're going to be here awhile." Steve strolled toward the swinging doors and once inside peered back through the small windows to make sure that the man at the bar hadn't moved before he crossed the short hallway and picked up the phone. When he returned to the table, he picked up the check and spoke to the two seated men as he pretended to add up the figures.

"There is a back door that comes in past the restrooms. Let's all leave together and I will slip back in that way." Jack and Tam got up and Steve put a twenty dollar bill under the check as they made their way to the front door. Steve peeled off from the small group as they neared the corner of the building and ducked back in the side door. He stood inside the swinging doors and watched as the hood at the counter quickly paid his tab and walked outside. Steve saw the Lincoln glide by in front of the window. The man averted his face then walked to the far end of the lot and opened the door of a dark blue Chevrolet. He drove toward the entrance to the lot, slowing for the yellow cab that had the right of way as it pulled in front of the restaurant. Steve hung back until the Chevy had left before he pushed open the glass door and entered the cab.

"Take me to Ringe Lane." He settled down in the backseat, keeping his profile low as the cab moved down Charleston Boulevard heading east.

*

Steve closed the front door of his house behind him as he heard the cabs' tires crunching in the gravel as it swung back onto Ringe Lane. He had just entered his small office when he heard the same gravel noise coming from the opposite direction. The bright headlights in the mirror told him everything he needed to know. His hand closed on the butt of the 1911 .45 just as the first three shots hit the front of the house, one smashing through the window four feet away and burying itself in the ceiling. Steve rolled onto the floor, scrambling on all fours toward the kitchen as rounds continued to slam against the walls. He tumbled out the back door and rolled into a crouch. Holding the pistol pointed at the ground with two hands he swung his body around the corner and sent three fast rounds toward the tan Chrysler that was only twenty yards away.

Almost before the rounds impacted the vehicle, the driver stomped on the gas, sending the car fishtailing toward the road, sending sprays of gravel out from under the tires. Steve waited until the car was broadside to him for a fleeting moment before he sent three more rounds toward the back seat where gun flashes were still erupting toward the house. The car hit the leading edge of the asphalt at a sharp angle launching it two feet off the ground, it's suspension sending off sparks on landing as it bottomed out on the pavement. Steve sprinted toward the street trying to cut off the gunmen. The driver straightened the car out and was fifty yards down the road and almost over the small crest in the road when Steve knelt in the middle of the road and squeezed off one more shot, the rear window shattering as the car disappeared over the rise.

Steve stood up, his breath coming in ragged wheezes. He wiped the sweat from his brow and tried to fight down the surge of adrenaline coursing through his body. He forced himself to walk calmly back toward his house. On the way, he extracted the near empty magazine from the handgun and pushed the slide back, locking it into the battery position. As he came slowly up to his house he could see that every window facing him was shot out, and the front door was splintered by pistol rounds as well as buckshot. He walked back in through the kitchen and picked up the phone. As he was dialing, he reached into a cupboard for a bottle of scotch, pulling out the cork with his teeth and taking a large mouthful. The police operator came on the line just as he swallowed the liquid fire in three short spasms.

"There has been shooting on Ringe Lane." Steve gave the address and added that there were no casualties at the location. He hung up and dialed Tam's home number.

"This is Cannon. They just shot up my house, I think you better get over here." Steve hung up the phone, placed the gun on the kitchen table on top of a hand towel. He was standing outside his front door when two black and white police cars nosed down the incline, their headlights blinding Steve for a few seconds. Another black and white unit came from the opposite direction with full blue and red lights as well as the siren. When it turned toward the house, the loudness of the shrill siren doubled in intensity. Two city cops opened the doors of the first patrol car and walked in front of their car surveying the damage in the bright lights. One of them walked toward Steve, his hand resting on the butt of his pistol. He stopped four feet away and cocked his head toward Steve. He swung his arm toward the house.

"You call this in?" Steve nodded his head in a slightly exaggerated fashion. The other cop and one from the second car were walking in widening circles on the gravel driveway with their flashlights, bending down and picking objects up off the ground.

"Yes, officer, I did. Happened maybe ten minutes ago. Three men in a tan late model Chrysler Imperial pulled up and…." Steve gestured with his arm toward the bullet holes in the splintered door. Before the cop could answer, one of the other cops called to him from the corner of the house and started walking toward him, shining his flashlight on something in his hand. The officer was intercepted by the occupant of the third car, who had exited and left the lights and siren going. Steve saw the silhouette of the small physique and the fedora before the man stepped into the circle of light. The fedora looked down at the officer's hand and then smiled at Steve. He said something to the officer and held out his hands as the objects were transferred to him. He walked over to Steve, taking in the damage as he moved closer. He stopped when he was five feet away and grinned up at the private detective holding up one of the spent casings from the .45.

"Looks like we might have some discrepancy here about who shot at who first. How many times am I going to have to take that Colt away from you?" Steve's eyes narrowed and he spit on the ground.

"I guess until your bosses figure out that you are one lazy cop, Samuels. Kind of hard to explain this as some kind of hunting accident, don't you think?" Steve turned around and looked at several bullet holes just above his head in the sideboards near the front door. He turned back toward the detective.

"Even you couldn't mistake this house for a deer." Samuels tossed one of the spent shells up in the air, catching it and then repeating the process as he gazed with a small smile at Steve.

"You always have some cock-n-bull story, Cannon. After this, I don't even think your buddy the sheriff is going to let you keep your guns. Where is it?"

"On the kitchen table." Steve jerked his head toward the house, his eyes narrowed on the small man in front of him.

"Go get it." Steve again spat on the ground.

"Go get it yourself, Samuels, if you want it so badly." Samuels gave Steve a long look as he moved in a shallow semicircle toward the front door, keeping the same distance between himself and Steve.

As Samuels walked through the front door, Steve's attention was drawn back to the driveway as two more cars pulled up and parked. Tam parked his car beside Samuels' and began walking toward Steve with a small smile on his face. The second car was a Sheriff's car and as soon as the white cowboy hat appeared, Steve grinned. Sheriff Ralph Lamb said something to one of the city cops who was kneeling and sweeping his flashlight back and forth over the dusty gravel. The sheriff joined Tam as they walked onto the small concrete pad where Steve was standing. Tam jerked his head toward the cars.

"Samuels here?" Steve nodded as he turned and pointed toward the open door. Lamb walked over and was examining the bullet holes when Samuels appeared in the doorway holding the pistol with the towel. For a long moment both men stared at each other. Sheriff Ralph held out his hand.

"I'll take that, Detective Samuels." The sheriff leaned toward the smaller man. Samuels looked past the door at Tam and Steve. He held out the gun. Ralph took it and turned back toward Steve, holding the pistol out to him.

"Who did all this?" Steve stepped forward and took the gun and smiled at the sheriff.

"A guy named Slim Atkins. He works for Jimmy Rossini at the Stardust, along with two of his cohorts." Ralph pushed his hat back on his head and looked at the broken windows.

"Let me go call a description in." He looked at Steve.

"Join me at the car?" Steve nodded and fell in behind the sheriff. Tam gave a sidelong glance at Samuels and trailed along behind Steve.

The sheriff sat in the car with the door open while Steve leaned against the hood. Steve gave Ralph the basic description of the car, several of the numbers on the license plate, and the two men he had seen. Tam went over and spoke to one of the police officers before he came back to the sheriffs 'car.

"I didn't see them following us after we left the restaurant."

"That's because the guy at the bar left right after you in a dark blue Chevy." They were interrupted by the sheriff climbing back out of the car.

"Just got a call from dispatch. A guy was dropped off at Sunrise

Emergency, two bullet holes in him, serious condition. I am going to head down there." The sheriff looked at Tam.

"Can you handle Samuels?" Tam chuckled.

"I'll just tell him you're coming right back, that should scare him off." Ralph smiled and climbed into the car. He spoke to Steve before he closed the door.

"Make sure you give a full statement, as much as you can remember to George over there." He pointed to one of the cops that was standing by a patrol car talking with Samuels. "He will make sure that my office gets a copy." Steve gave him a small wave as the Sheriff put his car in reverse and powered up the incline, swinging onto the asphalt. He waved as the lights and the siren came on, both still assaulting the senses even after he was out of sight over the small hill. Steve and Tam walked over to the trio. Tam lead and stood directly in front of Samuels.

"How did you get the call?" Samuels was trying to hear the conversation between Steve and the other two policemen, he looked up at Tam when the detective moved to cut the others from view.

"Heard it on the radio. Recognized the address, figured your buddy was up to no good as usual. Bad luck, the sheriff got involved." Tam frowned at the smaller man, and reached for a pack of cigarettes.

"What would your response have been, detective, if these three guys began shooting up your house?" Samuels looked at the red face illuminated by the flame of the match as it touched the end of the cigarette.

"I would let the proper authorities handle it, of course." Tam grunted and blew a long stream of smoke toward the brim of Samuels' hat.

"That would very likely get you killed. No, detective, Cannon has a right to defend himself, and if that hood dies tonight, the world will be a better place for it, and I think Assistant DA Larson will agree, especially after I brief him personally." Samuels smiled and pursed his lips as he pushed the gray fedora back on his head.

"Suit yourself, Polhaus, I am a patient man, your sidekick will step over the line someday and I will be there to bust him." Tam took a half step forward and turned his body slightly to one side as he stared into the small black eyes.

"Yeah, Samuels, you may get your chance, but if you take it, you will have me to deal with." Tam flicked the half-smoked cigarette just past Samuels ear, the butt leaving a trail of tiny sparks as it arced toward the ground. Tam watched as Samuels spun on his heels and walked the short distance to his car. Tam continued to stare at the detective until he had turned the patrol car around and was headed for the street. He followed Steve and the two cops into the house. He helped himself to the scotch as he listened to Steve relate the nights' events to the two cops who had taken seats at the kitchen table. When they had gone and Steve had bolted the front door, he returned to the kitchen and poured some of the scotch into two fresh glasses. Tam gave a sideways glance toward his friend as Steve sat down across from him.

"My advice is to back off and let Sheriff Lamb do his job. This is the county out here, nothing official Samuels can do now, and Ralph will get any information there is to get from that guy if he is still alive. Meanwhile, you should keep a low profile and see what happens." His voice ended on a less than positive note. He wasn't surprised at the look he got back from across the table.

"You know as well as I do, Tam, that Slim is already gone from this town. When Ralph shows up at the Stardust, Rossini probably won't be there either and they will just wait it out until the whole thing blows over. If the guy dies, it will just be that much easier to put it on him and forget about it." Tam took a sip of the whisky.

"Yeah, maybe, it could go down like that, but I wouldn't under-estimate Sheriff Ralph when he thinks he is being played for a patsy." When Steve didn't reply, Tam looked at the clock on the wall, upended his drink and stood from the table.

"It's almost midnight, I'm gonna go. We should be able to get

Lucius to see the light tomorrow. Give me a call." Steve stood and followed Tam out through the front door.

"Thanks for coming, Tam and thanks for running interference with Samuels." Tam turned and smiled as he kept walking toward his car.

"Think nothing of it. That guy gives me the creeps as much as he does you." Steve stood at the front door until Tam's taillights disappeared. He stood in the darkness for a few minutes and smoked a cigarette. When nothing happened, he went back inside. An hour later, he had finished shoring up the broken windows with some pieces of plywood from the garage. He poured the last of the Bowmore scotch and plugged in the desk lamp from the office, placing it on top of the kitchen table. He spread out a towel and field stripped the 1911 semi-automatic. When he had cleaned and reassembled the pistol, he slid it into his shoulder holster and loaded two more magazines. Just before he turned out the light, he spread his topographic map of Utah on the table top and studied the contour lines for several minutes.

APRIL 15

STEVE SAT AT his desk and finished his first cup of coffee. He heard Miss Perone's sunny voice come over the intercom.

"Yes, Miss Perone, what is it?"

"Mr. Jones' office just called. You are to meet with Mr. Jones and Mr. Carmino, today at eleven. She said you know where the meeting is to take place." Steve smiled to himself.

"Thank you, Miss Perone." Steve dialed the office for the cantina. He recognized the voice that answered.

"Good morning, Walter, how are you? I guess congratulations are in order. Bernie told me that he made you food and beverage manager for the Casablanca."

"Thank you, Mr. Cannon, yes he did, though the job means I have to run the deli as well."

"I am sure that you can handle it just fine, Walter. By the way, is he around?"

"Sure, he is here talking to Milton Swanson, you want me to get him for you?"

"No, Walter, that is OK, just tell him I am on my way down." Steve hung up the phone and eased his sport coat on. He walked down the short hallway and into the men's room, checking the back and sides of his profile in the mirrors to make sure it was not obvious that he was carrying a gun. Satisfied, he presented himself to Miss Perone as the ultimate test.

"I will be downstairs with Mr. Gold in the canteen, if you need me, Miss Perone." Steffi looked up from her purse.

"Are you alright today, Mr. Cannon? You don't seem yourself to me." Steve laughed.

"I'm fine, Miss Perone, I just didn't sleep too well last night. I will be back in an hour."

Steve found Bernie and Milton having rolls and coffee over a set of blueprints when he arrived. He went over to the long buffet tables that Bernie had set up and filled a mug with coffee from the large silver dispenser. He sat down at the head of the table as the two men finished their conversation.

"Hi 'ya, Steve, how you doing?" Bernie's face was wrapped in a large smile, his blue eyes fastened on his friend. Steve held up his cup.

"Fine, how are you? Hello Milton." Milton pointed to the blueprint.

"The casino is all laid out, should be done in another month. Then all that's left is finishing the room tower which should take another six weeks' tops."

"Sounds right on schedule. It will be nice when the money starts flowing in, instead of out all the time, right, Bern?" Bernie laughed and rolled up one of the blueprints. He held up his hand.

"Say, Steve. I got a call yesterday from Shelly Cointreau. He wants to apply for the job of overseeing all the parking operations. You know him pretty well, right?" Steve nodded.

"Yeah, Shelly and I go way back to the Golden Nugget years."

"So, what do you think? He up to the job?" Steve smiled.

"You couldn't get another guy that would know that job better. Plus, he knows every car park and doorman in town. You won't have to lift a finger and you will have the best run operation on the Strip."

"Yeah, that's my thinking too. Alright, I'll call him back and get him in here and get him started." Steve smiled his assent and slid over several seats picking up the morning paper that Milton had just laid down. The second column on the front page was a brief story on the previous night's shooting. Steve picked up the paper and tucked it under his arm as he stood up from the table.

"I'll see you two later, perhaps. If Shelly drops by and you have time, Bern, bring him up to my office."

"Will do, Steve, take care." Steve paused for a long moment before he walked away from the table.

On the way out of the cavernous room that would soon be the main casino, Steve dropped the paper in a large bin by the door that held scraps of lumber and drywall. He picked up a house phone just outside the entrance.

"Hello, Miss Perone. I am going downtown to see Mr. Polhaus. I will probably be back before my meeting with Mr. Carmino." Steve hung up the phone, looking back into the casino where Bernie and Milton were staring up at the ceiling and pointing something out to one of the foremen. He figured it was a long shot that Bernie would not eventually find out about the shots fired the night before, but something had held him back and as he watched him laughing with Milton and the foreman, he felt it was the better decision.

The radio had said the high temperature for the day would be 91 degrees and as he passed the Sahara hotel, the temperature board already was displaying 80 degrees. After a colder than normal winter and early spring, Steve knew it would take several days or even a week or more to adjust to the warmth. He turned the air conditioning on and shifted in the seat, nudging the heavy pistol forward to a more comfortable position.

Tam was meeting with Al Fonzo in his office when Steve stopped and leaned against the doorframe. Tam stopped talking and waved Steve into the room, pointing to the empty chair across from the narcotics detective. Steve pulled out a pack of Pall Malls before he sat down. He offered one to Al Fonzo, when he saw him looking at the one he held in his hand. Al lit both of them with the lighter from Tam's desk. Tam was in an expansive mood and was grinning impishly at Steve.

"How is the East Las Vegas Pistol Range this morning? Pretty quiet, I'm guessing. I was just telling Al, here how Sheriff Ralph spanked Samuels and sent him to bed." Al Fonzo chuckled, his large belly shaking in the too small chair. Steve took a short drag on the cigarette as he looked over at Al.

"So, what does Lucius Freebone have to say for himself this morning?" Al pointed at Tam.

"I was just telling Tam, here, that Lucius is still trying everything he can to keep from giving up anybody over at the Stardust. He keeps pushing his list of small-time dealers and addicts on the Westside. Haven't been able to convince him that we can get all those guys anytime we want, so the DA's office is laying it out to his lawyer in no uncertain terms as we speak. Either take the deal or go up north for five to ten." Tam waited for the detective to take a breath, before he looked over at Steve.

"Sheriff Ralph drug Jimmy Rossini through his casino by the collar and out the front door last night. Booked him and stuck him in a cell for a half an hour, his lawyer was right on their heels, so he wasn't a guest of the county for long. Seems Jimmy broke Ralph's rule about checking with him before he brings in wise guys from out of state." Steve opened his notebook, noting in his peripheral vision that Al was giving him a quizzical look.

"What about the guy in the hospital?"

"Oh yeah, him. Still alive, though barely. The final count was four slugs you put in him. His name is Romo Kiner. He is out of Miami, small time loan shark and torpedo. Did four years in Attica for driving the car on a contract murder. Lovely guys you attract." Steve ignored the remark as he wrote several of the particulars in the small notebook. He looked up at Tam and then at Al.

"No word on Slim?" Tam shook his head.

"The same time that the Sheriff hauled Jimmy Rossini out of the casino, the deputies searched the premises for Slim. Not there, not at his house, either. I guess they learned enough from Romo Kiner to put out a warrant on him, so everyone is looking, at least theoretically." Steve snorted.

"Yeah, that's the problem. Unless he stops in here for lunch, he is free as a bird."

"Maybe, but everything that can be done is being done, but here is some better news. After several days of thinking it over, Lois is ready to roll over on Slim. Assistant DA Larsen is working a deal out with her lawyer sometime later today. If it all works out, she will testify to what she heard that day, and she will press charges for domestic assault." Steve stood up and crushed his cigarette out in the ashtray. Tam looked up quizzically.

"Leaving already?" Steve was almost to the door.

"Yeah. I try not to stay in one place too long these days." He made a pointing gesture at Al.

"See you two later."

*

A half hour later, Steve sat in his office. He had waited until Miss Perone left after delivering the phone messages before he slipped the pistol from the holster and secured it in the top drawer of his desk. He picked up the phone and dialed quickly.

"Hello. Is this Mike Yamaguchi?"

"Mike, this is Steve Cannon."

"Yes. I do."

"You need to stay away from work for the near future. In fact, you would be well advised to resign right now. I don't ever think it is going to be healthy for you to work there again."

"I don't know yet, but I will tell you the same thing I told his father. Prepare yourself for the worst."

"I will tell Suko if you don't want to."

"Let me know. The main thing is that you stay as far away from the Stardust as possible. In fact, if you have some way to leave town for a couple of weeks, that would be even better. Barring that, at least keep a very low profile."

"Here's my office number, call me if you need anything."

"Yes. Goodbye."

Steve paused for several seconds with his hand on the receiver before he lifted it and dialed again.

"Hi Lew, how are you doing?"

"You read that, huh?"

"No, no real big damage. Got a guy and his crew out there now replacing the windows and patching up whatever holes they can."

"Comes with the territory."

"Yeah, it's connected to Martin's case."

"Don't know, there are a lot of curly cues in this case. Just have to keep after it until we get to the truth."

"Yeah, I know it is hard on everybody."

"That's why I called. You have some time after work?"

"Yeah, let's do Bernie's again. But Lew, do me a favor. If Bernie is there, don't mention what happened last night, OK?"

"He's got a lot on his mind these days, the less he has to worry about the better."

"I know, you're probably right, it probably isn't fair, but there it is."

"Yeah, see you then." Just as he hung up the phone, the door opened and Miss Perone entered and walked slowly to the middle of the room. She was holding the front page of the Review-Journal in her hand. She held it out toward Steve.

"My mother just called and asked if I had seen this." She tapped the article with her index finger. Steve sat back in his chair and put his hands behind his head.

"If you would like to sit down, Miss Perone, I will answer any questions you have." The brown curls bounced as Miss Perone shook her head.

"I will not sit down, Mr. Cannon, but I have as many concerns as I have questions. How often does this sort of thing happen and does Miss DeMarche know about it?" Steve smiled warmly at the earnestness in the round face.

"Yes, Miss Perone, I called Remy and told her about it first thing this morning. And as to your first question, I am afraid I don't have a good answer. You and your family have lived here long enough to know there are many types of people in this town. Everybody knows the rules of the game and we all get along for the most part, but nobody with any intelligence ever forgets the background of some of these people and the way that they resolve conflict among themselves. Unfortunately, my work puts me in the middle of things sometimes that many people in this town consider none of my business. So, to answer your question, Miss Perone, I am afraid that incidents like the one that happened last night are more than occasional." Steffi walked toward the desk and slumped down in the chair that was directly in front of Steve, still where Tommy had positioned it. She looked sadly down at the paper in her hands. Steve spoke softly.

"I am sorry, Miss Perone, I think I may have done you a disservice by not telling you all the aspects of what I do, before we decided to work together." Steffi looked up at the rugged, handsome face across the desk. She managed a weak smile.

"No, Mr. Cannon, I think it is more my fault. Mother always says that I am too naïve to go out in the world. Believe it or not, this type of thing has happened to me all my life. I guess I just see every day as a sunny day, and...." Her voice trailed off. Steve rose from his chair and came around to the front of the desk. He knelt in front of the chair and clasped both of Steffi's hands in his. He waited until the moist dark brown eyes looked into his.

"I am going to tell you something, Miss Perone and I want you to remember it as long as we work together. Do I have your promise?" Steffi looked down at her hands completely enveloped in his before she nodded.

"The way that you see the world is exactly why I want you to work for me. One thing I brought back from the war is that this is all too short to do anything but appreciate the good things there are, in people and in life. I made myself a promise when I was sure that I would survive to come home, that I would never let anything or anyone keep me from living the rest of my life that way, and you should make yourself that promise as well." Steffi sniffled quietly and nodded her head. Steve handed her his kerchief and she blew her nose softly.

"Thank you Mr. Cannon. I promise I will do better." She looked up at Steve as he stood up before her. "And I do like working here, I really do." Steve patted her shoulder.

"I know you do, Miss Perone, I can't imagine this place without you." Steffi took a big sniffle and stood up.

"I have some work to do, Mr. Cannon, I can't be away from my desk all day." Steve smiled as the phone rang in the outer office almost on cue. Steve replied as she walked through the door on the way back to the reception area.

"Yes, Miss Perone, we must all soldier on."

*

Steve was the last one to enter the private steam room in the Desert Inn country club. He had been there once before, and though he had survived his first experience in the steam, he was not looking forward to it, nor to the subject of the meeting. He waited for a few seconds as his eyes adjusted to the half-light of the room. He could dimly see the two men sitting across from each other. He moved to the left side of the long rectangle filled with rocks and sat down on the bench next to Clifford Jones and directly across from the semi-reclining figure of Tommy Carmino. He nodded to Clifford and looked across at the mobster who had his eyes closed and a small towel draped over his head. The steam seemed thicker than he remembered. Tommy spoke without opening his eyes.

"Nice, you could make it, Cannon. I told Clifford, here, that you would try to spend as little time as possible in here, but you are a Marine, so time to tough it out, mister." Steve snorted.

"If you want to have a contest to see who can stay in here the longest, Tommy, fine by me, just let me know, but it was my suggestion to meet here. You told me before that this is the one place there would unlikely to be any bugs, and my guess is that anything they got on you is probably the result of you being too loose with your lip around a microphone." Tommy sighed and spoke as if he was trying to conserve energy.

"Well, now that we have the gospel according to Slick, maybe we can get on with this. Clifford has some things he wants to share with you and I am here mainly to judge your reaction to those things." Steve shrugged and turned slightly toward the lawyer. The strong face was sweating more than the other two men's and Steve thought that maybe he had underestimated Clifford Jones' real age. The lawyer smiled benignly at Steve.

"We are entitled to a list of potential charges and a list of witnesses, in addition to certain other types of information. We have contacts, shall we say in certain areas of the state and federal government that also provide additional information, informally, if you know what I mean. You already have a pretty good idea of the areas they are likely to cover when you are called to testify. That is not why you are here." Tommy held up his hand and Clifford stopped and looked across at the mobster. Tommy groaned slightly as he turned his torso toward the wall and flipped up a plastic cover revealing a small white phone. He lifted the receiver and pressed down rapidly three or four times on the cradle arm.

"Who is this?"

"Where's Earl?"

"Never mind who this is, get Earl on the phone or start looking for a new job." Tommy muttered to himself as he waited.

"Earl. Listen to me. Don't ever let that guy, whoever he is, answer the phone again. And if I run into him, he's history, so if you want to see him keep his job, keep him the hell away from me. Three scotches. Now." Tommy slammed the plastic lid down on the phone sending a small shower of water drops across the small space that separated the three men. Tommy glowered at the two men across from him.

"What you gawking at, Cannon?" Steve smiled and leaned forward slightly adjusting his towel so that the flesh from his backside was not sitting directly on the hot wood.

"Tommy, you seem all agitated this morning. I thought you told me this was no big deal." Tommy ignored the remark and leaned forward his hands on his knees. Steve breathed through his nose as the heat began to permeate his body. The door opened and a small draft of cooler air washed over Steve when Earl swung the door closed and set the tray down next to Tommy. Steve nodded at Earl who was ignored by the other two men in the room. When the door closed again, Tommy handed the cool glasses across the small space to Clifford and Steve. Steve always took his whisky neat, but this was one time he wouldn't have minded a few ice cubes. The three men sipped their drinks in silence for a few minutes before Tommy motioned to Clifford. Tommy sat back against the hot boards of the wall. Clifford Jones began again.

"As you may or may not know, Mr. Cannon, the bar is rather high when it comes to the type of evidence the Feds need to make any kind of racketeering charges stick. There are no paper trails, so they are prevented from pursuing that avenue. They are unlikely to get anyone to accidently incriminate themselves or Tommy, by questioning them directly on the stand." Tommy took a big swig of the liquor and abruptly sat forward.

"For chrissakes, Cliff, spit it out already." He looked at Steve and his eyes narrowed as he pointed with the near empty drink glass.

"This is the deal, Slick. They got somebody to turn states' evidence against me." Tommy paused for three beats.

"The question for you, my detective friend, is this: Who is this person?" Tommy kept his eyes locked on Steve's. Steve kept his expression as blank as he could. After nearly thirty seconds, Tommy looked down at his glass and sat wearily back against the wall. He shook his head and sighed.

"Well?" Steve leaned back as well. He could hear Clifford breathing heavily beside him. He kept his eyes steadily on Tommy's.

"Haven't the foggiest, Tommy. If you don't know, why would you think I would?" Tommy waved his hand dismissively when Clifford Jones made a small noise as if he was preparing to say something. Steve saw Tommy set his jaw. In Steve's experience, that usually meant the mobster was going to get to the nub of the issue.

"I think Jack Cathay is going to testify against me." Steve breathed through his nose as the words came across the small space and impacted upon him. He willed his face to remain as placid as it had been seconds before. When he spoke, he could not feel his mouth moving.

"You are entitled to your opinion, Tommy, but I think you are way off base here." Steve made an effort to sound as casual as possible. He raised his glass and took a sip of the Johnnie Walker. Tommy said nothing but studied Steve's face. Again, Clifford made a small movement, and Tommy raised his hand. He looked across at the lawyer.

"I think you can leave, Clifford. If you need to talk more with Cannon here, you can do it on your own time." Clifford looked down at Steve as he stood and slipped past him, Steve holding up his legs slightly so that the lawyer could pass by. Clifford hesitated at the door, looked back quickly at Tommy, and then left the steam room. Steve leaned back against the wall and studied Tommy. Tommy looked casually around the room before he fastened his eyes back onto Steve's face.

"It all fits, Cannon. Jack lays in the hospital for all those weeks, starts to think. Comes to me and tells me that he wants to do something different, wants to leave. Seems queer to me, 'cause what is a guy his age gonna do, right? But fine, I say, because Jack and I go way back and at one time he was partners with my boss. Who else could it be?" Steve started to speak, but Tommy held up his hand and pointed across the small space at Steve with his glass.

"If you're gonna tell me that it ain't Jack, save your breath. If you want so badly that it is someone else, you better come up with that somebody else pretty damn quick." Steve leaned back against the wall and sipped the scotch slowly. He didn't say anything, his gaze fastened on the clear plastic bubble just above Tommy's left shoulder. He could see Tommy fidgeting.

"Well, Slick?" Tommy's normal tone of voice was back. Steve leaned forward and looked directly into the dark brown eyes eighteen inches away.

"You're right, Tommy. I owe it to both of you to find out who this person is, or even if he exists." Tommy held the gaze for a full three seconds.

"He exists alright, Cannon, and I don't give a dollar poker chip why you are going to do it, just do it." Steve drained the last few drops of the liquor and stood up.

"I've reached my limit of heat for today, Tommy, I'll be in touch." Tommy draped the towel back over his head and leaned against the wall, his eyes closed. Steve moved to the door.

"Thanks for the scotch, Tommy."

*

Steve drove the two blocks back to the Casablanca as slowly as he could. When he swung the Jeep into the fenced-in parking lot just off the Strip, he parked beside Jack's Lincoln. He walked into the lobby and picked up a house phone that was just inside the door at the security guard's station.

"Hi, Sarah, do you know where Jack Cathay is?"

"Thanks, Sarah." Steve replaced the phone, nodded to the guard and walked toward the courtyard and the main casino space.

Jack was standing in the middle of the large empty casino, watching as workmen were putting up the walls of the cashiers' cage. Rather than having the main cage against a back wall as in most casinos in the town, Jack and Bernie had decided that a central location made more sense for the players as well as for added security. Steve walked up and stood next to his friend. Jack glanced over and waited until the front portion of the cage was carefully lowered into place.

"Heard about the shenanigans last night after we left." Steve looked at Jack through his peripheral vision.

"Who told you?" Jack shook his head as several workmen rushed to keep the newly placed front of the cage from falling.

"Nobody. I can read." Steve turned and faced the craggy faced man.

"Jack, I need a couple hours of your time, right now." Jack gave a small dismissive wave.

"Not now, maybe later, or tomorrow." Steve moved to within six inches of the impassive face, his eyes narrowed on the gray ones below the silver shaggy eyebrows.

"No, Jack. Now." His voice held an edge that made Jack take a half step backward." He shrugged.

"Fine, where?" Steve pointed toward the entrance. "Follow me. You need to check with Bernie?" Jack shook his head and fell in behind Steve. Steve waited until they were out of earshot of the workmen.

"You packing, Jack?'

"Yeah, and my guess is that you are too." Steve turned and faced the ex-hood.

"Your .45?" Jack patted the gun under his left arm.

"Yeah, why?" Steve jerked his head toward the front of the hotel.

"I'll tell you later. We're going for a ride." Jack opened the front door of the hotel and looked back at Steve.

"I would have figured that you had enough driving around last night." His face held a quizzical look as Steve brushed by him without comment.

When they arrived at the Jeep, Steve opened the door and motioned for Jack to get in. He went to the back and opened the cargo door. He pulled a black cargo net away from its' place just behind the wheel well and pulled out a canvas bag with leather straps. He quickly spread out the contents of the bag on the deck of the Jeep. There were six boxes of .45 ACP ammunition and four extra magazines plus a speed loading tool. He looked up when he saw Jack looking at him from the front seat.

"When was the last time you practiced with that lump of iron you're carrying?" Jack snorted.

"I don't remember. Do we have to do this now?" Steve stuffed the bag back behind the net before he looked up.

"Yeah, Jack. We have to do this now."

Steve pulled onto the Strip and headed south. When he was ten miles south of town he pulled left across the other direction of travel and onto a small dirt road that headed in the general direction of the small town of Jean. Jack looked up at the dirty brown hills in front of them.

"Never been on this road. It come out at Jean?" Steve looked over briefly.

"Yeah, eventually, but that is not where we are going." Jack shrugged and held onto the door handle as the Jeep bounced over a washed out section of the road. Five miles later, they rounded a small hill and nosed down an incline toward a cliff face and the remains of a borax mine. Steve turned the Jeep in a wide circle and parked with the front pointed back up the road they had just come down. Steve gazed silently at Jack for a few seconds.

"I've often wondered just how good a shot you are, Jack." Jack's eyes narrowed and he rubbed his chin.

"Better than most, I'd say." Steve smiled thinly and climbed out of the car. Steve opened the tailgate and then busied himself dragging several old timbers that were lying about toward the face of the chalky white cliff face. He pointed to a pile of rusted garbage that was twenty yards away in a clump of grease wood.

"Jack, see if you can find some tin cans in that pile." Steve pointed and Jack walked slowly toward the rusted metal.

A few minutes later, Jack returned with four old cans and two bottles. One of the bottles was dark brown and had once held Fischer beer, the other was a delicate lilac color and was likely from the back bar of an old barber shop. Steve took the small lead crystal bottle from Jack's hand.

"Not this one. It's valuable." Steve held it up to the sun, shaking some of the dirt from the vessel. Jack squinted at it.

"Why's that?" Steve put it in his pocket.

"Part of the state's heritage, Jack. I know a guy over at NSU that runs their small museum. He's always looking for stuff like this." Jack scoffed.

"If you say so. How far away do I have to be?" Jack pointed toward the timbers that Steve had set up as a sort of crooked table. Steve looked around and pointed toward a flat spot just in front of a small knob thirty yards away.

"That should do." Jack looked at the spot and then back to the timbers where Steve was busy setting up the cans and the bottle.

"That's a long way, Steve." Steve patted him on the arm on his way back to the Jeep.

"Well, Jack let's start there, you can always move closer."

"I don't know why this is so important, Cannon." Jack was muttering under his breath as he joined Steve at the back of the car and accepted the canvas bag. Steve walked over to the flat spot and waited for Jack to join him. Steve pointed toward the cans.

"You first, Jack, slow and easy, let's try for accuracy." Jack shook his head as he pulled the .45 from his shoulder holster. He pointed the muzzle to the ground, pulled back the slide and raised the pistol with both hands toward the target. Steve took two steps behind him and pushed two .45 rounds into his ears.

"Jack, you don't want hearing protection?" The gray head moved slowly from side to side just before the sound of two quick shots bounced sharply off the cliff wall. Other than two small white puffs of alkaline dirt behind them, the cans were undisturbed. Jack looked down at his weapon. Steve stepped forward as Jack swung his muzzle in a safe direction.

"It's a poor workman that blames his tools, Jack." Steve moved into a slight crouch and sent four bullets toward the cliff in as many seconds. All four of the cans flipped into the air and were rolling on the ground when Steve looked over at Jack. Steve took a step backwards and slowly replaced the pistol in the holster under his right arm. He squinted at Jack. For several seconds the two men stood five feet apart, Jacks' hands still holding the pistol, his eyes searching Steve's. Steve took a deep breath.

"Tommy Carmino thinks you have gone to the Feds and are going to testify against him." Jack looked down at the pistol in his hand and then back into Steve's eyes. He replaced it in the holster without looking at it. His voice was quieter than usual, but Steve could hear the small edge of tension.

"Why does he think that?"

"Because someone in your old outfit who has their hooks into the Justice department says that is what is behind the grand jury. By some kind of process of elimination that only makes sense to Tommy, you're elected." Jack turned and looked over the hills as he fished a pack of cigarettes out of his coat pocket. He lit a cigarette with a small gold lighter, letting the breeze pull the smoke from his mouth as he bent over and picked up one of the cans that had landed at his feet. He examined the hole that was centered in the middle of the brown flaky metal before he turned back to Steve.

"What do you think?" Jack's eyes held a small sadness as he looked at Steve. Steve stepped forward and took the can from Jack's hand, running the tip of his finger over the jagged edges of the hole. He flipped it toward the cliff as he looked back at Jack.

"I think the Feds probably have someone in their pocket, but even though I have not known you long, I know it isn't you. I brought you out here less to tell you, then to figure out what we need to do. The target practice was just a way of getting us to focus on the problem." Jack laughed softly.

"You don't know Tommy as well as you think you do. If that is what Tommy thinks, I am a dead man. If you don't believe me, look closely at Bernie's face when you tell him. No, I'm getting out of here, today." Steve stepped forward and grabbed Jack's shoulder.

"No. You're staying put. Why do you think I was given this information? Tommy knows that I would come straight to you, no two ways about it. Any move like that will only confirm what he thinks he already knows." Jack squinted at Steve and wiped a bead of sweat from the side of his cheek.

"Let's get back in the car, I'm roasting out here." Steve followed him over to the Jeep. When Steve was seated he waited until Jack spoke.

"What's your plan?" Steve shrugged.

"Haven't got one handy at the moment. Tommy isn't a patient man, but I figure we have some time to figure this out. Let's secure the guns and get back to town." Steve started the car and watched out of the corner of his eye as Jack slipped a new magazine into the .45. When they were only a block from the Casablanca, Steve slowed the car down and looked over at Jack.

"You need to do us both a favor, here, Jack and think hard about who in the organization could be the snitch. Somebody who has a gripe or got kicked out, and would know how the skim works." Jack didn't say anything until Steve parked beside the black Lincoln.

"What makes you so sure it is about the skim?" Steve opened the door as he looked over at Jack.

"Because the Feds are obsessed with it, that's why. If they can prove the skim, they got Tommy, his boss, and everybody else all the way down the line. So think of someone who used to get cut in, but now is denied the gravy train, and do it quick." Jack grunted as he took the long step down from the Jeep.

"I will see you later. I am going upstairs and have a few drinks." Steve leaned against the front of the car, lit a cigarette and watched Jack walk slowly through the tall glass doors.

*

"What?" Bernie's eyes were wide and staring at Steve. Steve had called him up to his office and closed the door. He had not beat around the bush, but laid it out straight to his friend, who now sat stunned in the gold brocade chair. As the message sunk in, Bernie looked up at Steve.

"Jack has got to get out of town now." Steve held up his hand and shook his head.

"No, Bern, I have thought this through and that would be the worst move possible. Jack has to stay put and act like he is not guilty. You and I both know that Jack is not a snitch, and I think deep down, Tommy wants to believe that as well." Bernie looked down at the floor before he stood up and went to the window.

"What are we going to do, Steve?"

"Tommy has given me a little time to come up with the name of the real guy, but you and I both know that there are several guys in that organization from here to Cleveland and down to Miami who could be the snitch, or worse, guys who aren't as slow as Tommy to shoot first and ask questions later, so whatever I come up with, it had better be fast." Bernie turned toward Steve.

"Any thoughts?" Steve sat back in his chair and put his feet up on the desk.

"Well, if the guys that Tommy and his organization have inside the justice department know who this is, then the FBI agents here know who it is, which could mean that Agent Hurley's brother-in-law, Larsen, the assistant DA, likely knows as well."

"I don't follow, Steve. The assistant DA isn't going to tell us who the guy is." Steve nodded assent as he spoke.

"You're right, Bernie, but he might tell me who it isn't." Bernie's face bent downward as he shrugged.

"Maybe an angle there, just maybe. But you're still only halfway home, Steve, Tommy wants the whole hog, I know him, he has an old timer's attitude when it comes to this kinda thing." Steve looked at his watch.

"Bernie, I have to get over to Foxy's, I am having a beer with Lew Mannion. You want a lift over there?" Bernie turned and waited until Steve looked up for a reply.

"I heard about what happened last night." Steve had just started to get up from the chair. He sat back down slowly, his brown eyes on Bernie's face.

"Bernie..I.." Bernie held up his hand.

"I don't care about that, I know you are always trying to spare my feelings and because I'm a little over protective sometimes, that is a normal reaction. But I just want you to think about something you told me the other day."

"What was that Bernie?"

"You said that you were going to ask Remy to marry you, remember?" Steve nodded as he swung his chair toward the window.

"All I ask is that you think about what happened and then you think of her. At some point, she will be with you when the bad stuff happens." Bernie walked to the door and stopped before he opened it.

"Yeah, I should check in on the restaurant. I'll take that ride if the offer is still good." Steve sighed to himself and swept his keys off the desk.

*

Lew Mannion was already sitting at a window table when Steve and

Bernie walked in the front door of Foxy's. Steve waved and then asked one of the waiters to bring over a pitcher of Coors from the tap. He shook Lew's hand and then sat down heavily in the chair opposite the golf pro.

"You look bushed. Did you get any sleep at all after the fireworks last night?" Steve grimaced and watched the beads of condensation run down the sides of the pitcher that the waiter had just placed on the table. He motioned to the waiter that he would pour and then he filled both of the large steins to the top, turning the glass at an angle to reduce the head. He handed the first across to his boyhood friend.

"No, I slept OK, just been a tough day. How's Keno holding up?" Lew took a long slow drink as Steve spoke. He put the glass down and removed some foam from his lip with a paper napkin.

"Quieter than usual. He hasn't ever been a big talker, less so nowadays." Lew leaned in toward Steve.

"Is he ever going to see Martin again?" Steve had almost taken his first sip of the beer, but lowered his glass to the table instead. Steve stared at the top of the table for a few seconds before he looked up. Lew's face darkened when he saw Steve's expression. He sat back and held up his hand turning his face to the side and looking out the window. He spoke without turning back.

"Forget it, I don't want to know." Steve slowly raised the beer to his lips and took a small sip. The usually light and fresh tasting beer was all sour notes today. Lew sighed and turned back toward the table. They finished their glasses and Steve had filled them again before he spoke.

"Something else I need to tell you, Lew, kind of important." Lew took a deep breath and smiled slightly.

"Shoot." Steve sat back in the chair and crossed his legs.

"I saw Theresa last week." Lew's head moved perceptively backward and his expression went blank for a few seconds.

"Theresa Reuschel? Where?"

"She was here for her husband's funeral." Lew shook his head and whistled softly.

"Jeez, how many years has it been, Steve? Since the first year or two of the war at least, right?"

"Yeah, Lew, that's right. But that's not all." Steve took a long drink of the beer.

"She has a son. Mike. He's twenty-three." Lew had an uncomprehending look for five seconds, before Steve saw his fingers moving in a silent count. His face reddened.

"Steve, are you trying to tell me...?" Steve nodded slowly.

"Yeah, Lew, that's what I am trying to tell you."

"You gotta be kidding me, right?" Steve smiled and shook his head.

"Nope. Not kidding you Lew, I swear." Lew sat back and threw up his hands looking from side to side taking deep breaths.

"Does that not beat all, or what?" He pointed at Steve. "You, a son!" Lew grinned widely, reaching across the table to slap Steve on the shoulder, before sitting back and shaking his head.

"So, what's he like? He look like you?" Lew held up his beer glass, waiting until Steve clinked the two together.

"Well, Bernie and my sister think so. I think he looks a lot like my brother Pete, but you'll meet him soon enough, and then you can decide for yourself." Lew was still shaking his head.

"He play golf?"

"Good question, I didn't think to ask."

"Well, if he does, you, me and Bernie will show him around the course, whadda' say?"

"Sounds good to me, Lew." Steve sat back in the chair and listened as his friend extolled all the joys of being a parent. He looked out at the dusty parking lot and thought of Keno and Jack Cathay.

APRIL 16

THE GOLDEN MORNING light filtered through the gauzy curtains as Steve sat up in bed. He looked over at Remy's bare back and saw that she was still asleep. He slipped carefully out from under the covers and put on a blue silk robe that Remy had bought for him for just such occasions. He let himself quietly out of the bedroom and descended the stairway to the kitchen. He had almost finished making the coffee when he heard the light rustle of Remy's night-gown behind him. He turned toward her as she entered the kitchen and wrapped his arms gently around her waist, pulling her to his chest. He looked down into her brown eyes and bent to kiss her lips as Remy stood on her tiptoes and put her hand behind his neck.

"Good morning, Gem, how did you sleep?" She placed her cheek on his chest and let out a small happy groan.

"Just fine, Steve, I am glad you stayed. Too bad I am due at the showroom by nine, otherwise we could just grab a bottle of champagne, go back upstairs and take the day off." She turned her head and smiled impishly up at Steve. Steve kissed her lips, more passionately this time, gently rubbing her nose with his as she lowered herself.

"I would like nothing better, Gem, but duty calls us both. Maybe tomorrow, we can spend the day together." Remy stood on tiptoes again and kissed Steve's forehead.

"It's a date." She turned and placed the carafe of coffee and two cups on a tray.

"But first, I feel like coffee in bed."

*

Sheriff Ralph Lamb was sitting in Steve's normal seat in front of Tam's desk when Steve walked through the doorway of the office just after ten. Ralph's legs were crossed and his white Stetson was perched on his knee. He smiled when he saw Steve. Steve pulled the other chair back away from the desk and nodded at Tam as he sat down.

"Sheriff, how are you doing this morning?" Ralph laughed and pointed at Tam.

"I was just telling Detective Polhaus, here, that I am feeling a whole lot better than our friend, Romo Kiner. He had another surgery yesterday and was still a little groggy when I saw him this morning. Doc says he should pull through." Tam was cleaning his fingernails with a pen knife and looked up when Ralph finished.

"Assistant DA Larsen is counting on him to be the final nail in Slims' coffin. He's counting on Slim to give us Jimmy Rossini." Tam looked closely at Steve as he talked, while trying to appear as casual as possible. Steve's eyes narrowed.

"Once the rest of the organization back east find out about Jimmy's little scam, Slim is going to be the least of his problems. I am more interested in where Slim is hiding out." Ralph stood up and put his hat on.

"Well, that is my cue to get going." He pointed at Tam. "I will keep you posted on Kiner's condition. You can tell Larsen that he will likely get a crack at him on Monday." He held out his hand to Steve.

"We've got everybody on the lookout for Atkins. If he is still around here, we will get him." Steve stood and shook the sheriff's hand.

"Thanks, Ralph, and thanks for the other night. Not often you

B. R. Laue

get the sheriff himself sticking up for you." Ralph snorted a laugh as he headed for the door.

"Well, it's my county and I take it seriously." He smiled and saluted as he walked out of the door and turned down the hallway. Steve sat back down and pulled out a Pall Mall as he grimaced in Tam's direction.

"I saw what you were doing there, Tam. You're afraid I will get to Slim before you do and queer the Rossini deal, am I right?" Tam opened the top drawer of the desk and dropped the knife into it, before he looked at Steve.

"Don't know what you're talking about, Steve. You want Atkins, go get him. Rossini is DA Larsen's problem, one less hood on the street is not going to make me lose any sleep." He watched as a large cloud of smoke wafted toward the ceiling before he continued. "My guess is that you have a pretty good idea where Slim-boy is hiding out anyway, and if my guess is right, it ain't anywhere near my juris-diction." Steve turned his head and studied the large map on the wall as he took several short puffs on the cigarette.

"As my father used to say: 'wanting ain't the same as getting' and no matter how many ideas I have, Slim is still out there as free and unfettered as Sorelli is." At the mention of the killer's name, Tam's mood darkened and he pulled cigarettes of his own out of his desk drawer. Steve waited until Tam had taken a long pull and settled back in his chair.

"Lucius come around yet?" Tam nodded and flicked a small length of ash into the large tray that was on the far edge of his desk and was shared with Steve.

"Yep. Gave his statement yesterday. Fonzo thinks Larsen will file charges against Rossini on Monday, so you see, Slim or no Slim, I doubt Jimmy Rossini is going to be able to avoid prison." Steve shrugged.

"Maybe, maybe not. They all seem to have nine lives when it comes to getting jail time. You hear anything about the grand jury that is looking into Tommy and his organization?" Tam swiveled slowly in his chair and looked at Steve with a passive expression.

"No, not much, those aren't circles I move around in. But you hear things from time to time and I would say that this time it looks serious for Tommy." Steve kept his voice as casual as possible when he replied.

"Oh? How so?" Tam smiled thinly.

"Oh, just scuttlebutt, mostly, but the word I get is that the Feds are confident they got enough on Tommy to get him to turn on his boss, and they also think that might get them in a position to take down Meyer Lansky." Steve snorted.

"Never happen. The last thing Tommy Carmino would do is to give evidence against his boss." Tam shrugged.

"Don't be too sure. I have seen tougher guys than Tommy fold their cards when they are looking at big jail time." Steve stood up and crushed the butt out in the ashtray while he peered down at Tam.

"We'll see." He had crossed the room and was partway out the door when Tam spoke again.

"You'll let me know if you get a line on Slim, right?" Steve turned into the hall without a reply.

Steffi Perone was glad to see Steve when he came through the door for the first time since the previous afternoon. She followed him into his office and waited while he took a sip of the coffee that was waiting for him on his desk. He smiled at his secretary as he took his seat behind the desk. Miss Perone sat down in the gold wing chair.

"Here are your messages, Mr. Cannon." She handed the stack to Steve and gave a running commentary on each one as Steve flipped through. When he was done, he looked quizzically at her.

"Something else, Miss Perone?" Steffi nodded her head.

"A man has called here twice, once yesterday after you had left and once today. He is very rude and won't leave his name or number. I told him that he would not be able to talk to you unless he gave me his particulars." Miss Perone sat up straighter in her chair and gazed at Steve. Steve sat back and smiled.

"That is good, Miss Perone, I support you fully." For the second time that morning, Steve tried to keep his voice casual.

"But the next time he calls, and I am here, put him through to me, would you do that?"

Steffi nodded her head.

"Of course, Mr. Cannon."

"I am going over to Sunrise hospital, Miss Perone, if anybody needs to know." Steve followed Steffi across the hall and into the reception area. He adjusted the shoulder rig under his jacket while her back was still to him and the entryway.

"If Mr. Gold calls, ask him where he might be around lunchtime. If his schedule permits, I would like to have lunch with him." Miss Perone nodded.

"Of course, Mr. Cannon, if you are near a phone, call me before you leave the hospital and I will relay any messages I have." Steve had just started to reply when the phone rang.

"Good morning, Mr. Cannon's office, Miss Perone speaking." Steve smiled at the friendly efficiency that Steffi exuded.

"Yes, Mr. Greenspun, he is standing right here, would you like to speak with him yourself?" Steffi smiled and handed the phone to Steve.

"Hank, how are you?" Steve nodded a few times, wrote something down on a pad that Miss Perone handed him and then rang off. He tore off the top sheet of the pad and handed it across the desk.

"Hank Greenspun will meet me here at two o'clock." Miss Perone pulled a long appointment sheet out of her top desk drawer and wrote the information down.

"Thank you Mr. Cannon." Steve waved from the doorway and quickly descended the stairway.

*

Steve searched along the cool corridor looking for the room number that he had been given at the front desk. He turned a corner and stopped when he saw a city policeman sitting on a chair halfway down on the right side of the hallway. He quickened his pace when he saw that it was one of the faces he was familiar with. He slowed to a stop across from the cop and smiled.

"Hi, Jerry, what did you do to get on this duty?" Jerry laughed as he stood up.

"Nothing, thank God, I just had to pull a two hour stint to stop gap between shifts. What are you doing here?" Steve pointed to the door over the cop's right shoulder.

"Just need a few words with Kiner." The smile faded from Jerry's face.

"Sorry, Steve, you need permission from higher up." Steve stepped back and nodded.

"Tam Polhaus high enough?" Jerry resumed his position in the chair.

"Yeah, if he authorizes it, yeah, OK." Steve grinned and started to move down the hall to the nurse's station as he pointed back toward Jerry.

"Stay right there, I'll be back." By the time Steve had hung up with Tam and arrived back in front of Kiners door, Jerry was talking on a white phone that hung just over his shoulder on the wall. He looked up at Steve and nodded as he replaced the receiver. Steve patted him on the shoulder as he pushed the heavy door open and stood in the same room he had spent the better part of three weeks in the year before. This time there were two beds in the room, though only one was occupied. Steve walked over to the bed by the window and looked down at the man lying with oxygen lines in his nose. The man slowly opened his eyes and looked toward Steve.

"Who are you?" Steve turned and dragged a chair from the end of the bed, turning it around and sitting down, resting his arms on the back, his hands clasped.

"I'm the guy whose house you shot up the other night." Steve took in the pallor and the labored breathing. The man's reddish hair was matted around his ears and his pale skin was heavily freckled. The gray eyes looked up at the blue sky and the top of a tree that could be seen through the window.

"What do you want?" Steve waited until the eyes shifted back toward him before he replied.

"A trade."

"What kind of trade?" The pale face grimaced as the man shifted his body slightly in an effort to sit higher in bed.

"Simple one, Kiner. You tell me one little piece of information I need to know, and I use that phone there to tell Assistant DA Larsen, that you were cooperative in finding a missing person." Kiner breathed heavily for several seconds before he mustered the strength to speak.

"Why should I help you?" Steve shrugged.

"No reason, unless saving your skin is a hobby of yours. Let me lay it out to you so you can make the right choice." Steve stood slightly and scooted the chair a few inches closer.

"I don't know if you had any involvement in the disappearance of Martin Ogawa or not, but it hardly matters. Rossini will say you did and that will be that. Now I think Slim Atkins is the guilty party, but unless you cooperate, there is no way anybody else is going to care one way or the other. Did anything I just said suggest a reason why you might give me what I want?" The hood's eyes closed for several long seconds and Steve was just about to get up and see if he had fallen asleep when his eyelids fluttered open and he spoke.

"What kind of information?" Steve leaned forward.

"Where is Slims' cabin in Utah?" The man nodded slightly.

"Near Brianhead." Steve looked around the room and felt his pockets.

"That I already know. Draw me a map." He placed his pen and his notebook open to a new page on Kiners' chest, who slowly picked them both up and in a shaky hand began to draw. Five minutes later, he handed the notebook back to Steve. Steve studied it for several minutes, at one point turning it slightly sideways as he tried to orient it to the contour maps he had pored over each night. He held the page in front of Kiners' face.

"What is this feature, here?" Kiner coughed and groaned before he spoke.

"A bar and store." Steve nodded and stood up. Kiner's eyes followed him and he raised his hand weakly.

"The DA." He pointed in the direction of the phone near his head on the nightstand. Steve looked down at Romo Kiner as he put his notebook back in his pocket.

"I find Slim Atkins there, then I make that call." He turned and crossed the room stepping aside as a nurse came through the wide door with a tray of medications in her hands. He glanced back at the bed before the door closed behind him. Jerry had been replaced by another cop, one that Steve had never seen before and the man's brow furrowed as Steve swept by his chair and quickly disappeared around the corner.

At his car, he folded the map carefully and placed it in his glovebox. He walked back into the lobby of the hospital and slid the door closed on one of the three payphones just inside the front door.

"Hello, Miss Perone, I am just checking in. Any calls I should know about?" Steve listened for a few minutes, thanked her and hung up the phone, moving away as the extra coins fell noisily into the chute. Back at the Jeep he sat for a few minutes smoking a Pall Mall. The man had called again. This time Miss Perone used the adjectives; deep and gruff, to describe the voice she heard. Steve was now certain that the caller was Angelo Sorelli and the game that the killer had initiated last year which nearly cost Steve his life was being played again. Steve started the car and drove slowly out of the lot, turning left onto Maryland Parkway, and after passing the Boulevard shopping center, he turned right onto Flamingo road. The cloud of apprehension darkened even more the closer he got to the Casablanca.

*

Bernie was in an expansive mood as the two men sat across from one another in the hotel canteen. Steve had walked through the casino and was amazed how much had been done since the day before when he had pulled Jack from the floor. All around them was the buzz of conversation and as Steve turned his head from side to side, he could see the reason, as there were almost one hundred and fifty workers on one of the two lunch breaks that occurred each day. Milton had filled up almost all of the cheap motels up and down the Strip with construction workers from the east coast, and though it was costing Bernie a pretty penny, the hotel was moving toward completion faster than any local could remember seeing on any other project that had come before. Steve's thoughts were brought back to the table as he had to ask Bernie to repeat something he had just said.

"One of Frank's people called this morning. Just making sure that everything is still on for tomorrow night." Steve nodded as he cut into the small ribeye steak in front of him.

"Everything is still go from my side, Bernie, what about you?"

"Yeah, me too, but I was thinking there should be a time limit on this one. Maybe three hours, then stop. What do you think?" Steve looked up blankly for a few seconds.

"Yeah, it might tone things down a bit. If Frank is up at that point, he might go home happy. If he is losing, at least it won't be a whole lot more than what he is down now. Think he will go for it?" Bernie shrugged.

"With Frank, you never know, but since it is my place, it will be my rules." Bernie took a small bite of his steak and looked across at Steve as he swallowed.

"You have quite a busy weekend, Steve. The game with Frank, the party that Miss Perone's mother is throwing and on top of all that, Mike's coming back into town." Steve sat back and sipped the last of his beer. Bernie's face clouded over as he saw the expression on Steve's face.

"What's the matter, Steve?" Steve looked into the bright blue eyes as a half smile played across his downcast features.

"I am pretty sure that Sorelli is back in town." He tossed his napkin onto the plate in front of him as he heard the sharp intake of air from across the table. Bernie looked around quickly as he leaned forward.

"Man, that is the last thing you need, are you sure?" Steve shook his head.

"No, but someone keeps calling the office and won't leave his name. From the description of the voice that Miss Perone gave me, it is very likely." Bernie sat back in his chair, letting out a disgusted sigh.

"What are you going to do?" Steve stood up and looked down at his friend.

"Nothing. The last thing I am going to let him do is restrict where I go or what I do. If he is planning on more than just phone games, he will have to make the first move. I thought about what you said yesterday and I thought you should know." Bernie stood up and slapped Steve's arm lightly as he walked by. Steve craned his neck toward his friend.

"Thanks for lunch, Bernie, I should open a tab, and by the way, what is the rent on the office and when is it due?" Bernie waved as he moved away from the table.

"When the hotel opens, we will sit down and talk about all those things." Steve shook his head as he watched Bernie walk through the still open side of the hotel on his way to the room tower that was just two floors away from completion.

As Steve climbed the stairway he saw Hank Greenspun entering the office just ahead of him. As he came through the door he heard

Hank and Miss Perone in animated conversation. He stopped and waited until they noticed he was there. Hank turned around and smiled.

"I was just telling Steffi Perone what a delight it was to see her here when I opened the door. Her mother and I go way back." Steve held up his arms in mock exasperation as he smiled at Hank.

"Of course you do. Sometimes I feel like I am the only one in town that wasn't on a first name basis with Miss Perone and her mother." Steffi blushed.

"Well, Mr. Cannon, that will all be rectified on Sunday. That is if you are still coming." Her eyes held an impish gleam.

"Of course, Miss Perone, I wouldn't miss it for the world." Hank frowned.

"I should hope so, Steve, Grant Sawyer is in town and I'm sure he will be there, right, Steffi?' Miss Perone smiled and nodded at Steve who then looked at Hank.

"The Governor?" Hank nodded and smiled down at Miss Perone.

"Always been there before. If he is in Las Vegas on the second Sunday of the month, you can count on him being there." Steve shook his head and held out his arm toward the hallway and his office beyond. Hank smiled once more at Steffi Perone and followed Steve into his office. Steve closed the door and caught himself about to remove his jacket. He crossed the floor instead and motioned to the chair, before he sat down carefully behind his desk. Hank settled into the soft chair and looked past Steve at the window and the room tower beyond.

"Bernie isn't wasting any time, is he?" Steve swiveled his chair and gazed at the new structure, craning his neck to see the workmen on the top section.

"No, Hank, he isn't. Once Bernie makes up his mind, it is pretty much his only focus until he accomplishes what he set out to do." Steve gazed evenly at the intense face on the other side of the desk. Hank crossed his legs and cleared his throat.

"Thanks for your time, today, Steve, I know you are busy. I just need to know if there is any update on the Stardust deal." Hank stopped talking and looked at Steve expectantly. Steve leaned forward slightly in his chair.

"Quite a lot to update, though it is still playing itself out. The narcotics squad is trying to catch them red-handed with the heroin shipments that come in from the Far East. So far they have been pretty cagey about it, and might have even gotten wise or been tipped. The DA is working the other end with a dealer they are squeezing and pressure is being brought to bear from other quarters, so I guess it is just a matter of time." Steve stopped and waited for a reaction. Hank squirmed a little in his seat and frowned.

"Not much to base a follow-up story on, Steve, what about the missing boy?" Steve leaned back in the chair, taking care not to expose the shoulder rig under his arm.

"I am pretty sure I know what has happened to him, but I need some more time before I am able to comment fully. I would say that by the middle of next week, I can give you and Rita the scoop." Hank nodded and Steve made a small move to stand up, but stopped when he saw that Hank was getting ready to say something. He sat back down and waited.

"I am sure you have heard about the Grand Jury that has started operating this week." Steve concentrated on keeping as neutral an expression as he could. He nodded casually as Hank continued.

"I think that finally they are going to put some of the mobsters that operate in this town away." Steve frowned.

"Really? Why do you say that Hank? How is this time different from all the other times they tried and failed?" He was hoping that his voice conveyed the right amount of polite indifference. Hank smiled.

"Well, this time they finally have someone on the inside that is willing to talk." Steve scoffed.

"You and I have both heard that one before as well. If there was such a person, I would wager that he or she would not live long enough to make it worth the while." Steve reached in his pocket and pulled out a new pack of Pall Malls. He gestured with the pack toward Hank, who shook his head gently. Steve began to light up as Hank spoke.

"The beauty of this one, Steve, is that the guy is still part of the organization and nobody even suspects he exists." Steve smiled at the newspaperman.

"Are you sure about that Hank?" When he received a startled expression in reply, Steve took a deep drag on the cigarette and let most of it out before he continued.

"You and I both know that the Feds are riddled with guys who plan on retiring early in Costa Rica on the juice they get to pass this type of information along. I doubt this goes all the way, Hank." Hank sighed and stood up.

"I hope you are wrong, Cannon. The governor gave up his weekend at his ranch to come here and get briefed on the case." Steve waited until Hank turned toward the door before he rose from his seat and followed. Hank stopped at the door and faced Steve.

"I look forward to seeing you on Sunday." Steve smiled and held out his hand. Hank shook it and crossed the hallway into the reception room. Steve could hear Miss Perone's voice as he closed the door. He crossed to his desk, pulled out his sheath of maps and spread them out on the green felt. He spread the map that Kiner had drawn on top of the desk and reached into the top drawer for a magnifying glass.

*

An hour later, the intercom crackled on. There was a silence for a few seconds.

"Miss Perone?"

"That man is on the line." Steve took a deep breath through his nose.

"Put him through, Miss Perone." The next voice he heard was unmistakable, and instantly confirmed his suspicions.

"Steve Cannon, the man who refuses to die. Know who this is?" Steve snorted and his voice held a hint of a growl.

"The scum of the earth always has a distinct sound and smell, don't you think, Sorelli?"

"Wouldn't know myself, Cannon, that is more your line. I just called to say hello, tell you I was in town, and catch up. You know what I mean?"

"Really? Where you staying?" Sorelli's manic cackle caused Steve to pull the phone away from his ear.

"That's right, Stevie boy, you keep pitching. Maybe someday, somebody will be dumb enough to let you catch them." The laugh was repeated. Steve wished he had taken the time to set up his reel to reel recorder. He decided to try a different tack.

"Surprised you survived the raid on your ranch, Sorelli, not to mention the escape from the desert." Sorelli scoffed and laughed.

"Italian luck, my friend, and speaking of the desert, you looked pretty dead to me before I left. Imagine my surprise when I heard you were still kicking." Steve smiled into the phone.

"You should have made sure that you finished the job before you left, Sorelli. You will regret that mistake."

"I doubt it, Cannon, I got all my lives left. But the reason I called was that I heard something interesting and I thought I would check it out for myself. I heard that you are in the family way, that right? A son. Imagine that." Steve did not reply, but watched the blood leave the hand that clenched the receiver.

"You still there, Cannon? I would give anything to see the expression on your face, right now."

"This conversation is over, Sorelli." Steve slammed down the phone. He was still staring at it a few seconds later when Miss Perone knocked softly on the door.

"Mr. Cannon, are you alright?" Steve looked up from the phone.

"Yes, Miss Perone, I am fine. Sit down, please, I need to show you something." Steve used a key from his ring and opened a side drawer as Miss Perone seated herself. He pulled out a manilla file folder and placed it on the desk. He quickly thumbed through it, drew out two pictures and laid them across the desk so that Miss Perone could see them clearly.

"Look closely at these two pictures, Miss Perone. The man in the picture is Angelo Sorelli, and he is the one who just called." Steffi picked each of the pictures up in turn, studying them both closely. When she was done, Steve waited until he had her full attention.

"This is important, Miss Perone. If you see this man anywhere on this property, you are to call security immediately. If he tries to come into the office, and I am not here, pretend that you have to go elsewhere in the hotel to find me, and then head for the nearest security guard. If he insists on going with you, let him, and continue with the first plan. I will alert security and make sure they have copies of these pictures. Is that clear, Miss Perone?" Steffi Perone nodded.

"Mr. Cannon? Who is he?" Steve slipped the photos back into the folder.

"He is a murderer, Miss Perone, and will stop at nothing to get his revenge." Steffi waited for a few seconds biting her lip as she contemplated her next question.

"Mr. Cannon, do you think it would be wise if I kept a pistol in my desk drawer?" Steve stopped what he was doing and stared across the desk at the petite woman.

"Do you know your way around firearms, Miss Perone?" His voice was low and deliberate. The curls began to shake immediately.

"Oh, yes, Mr. Cannon. I accompanied my father on several safaris and hunting trips. I have fired every weapon from a .22 to a .416 Rigby, the latter out of a Mauser action handmade for me in England." Steve sat back in his chair and chuckled to himself.

"You never cease to amaze me, Miss Perone. I will leave it up to you, but let me check first with Sheriff Lamb and see if there is some paperwork he would like to see prepared." Miss Perone stood to go.

"Thank you, Mr. Cannon, for trusting me with this information." Steve shook his head thoughtfully as he watched her stride across the dark red carpet and through the hall to the reception room.

*

Steve drove toward the lights of the Strip through the darkness. He slowed a block short of the glow of the casinos and pulled into the curved driveway. He parked at the end of the drive and walked slowly up to the black door. A few seconds after he rang the bell, he saw Remy sweep into the foyer from the living room. Her long white dress swirled softly around her legs. Steve took a step toward the door and smiled.

April 17

STEVE ARRIVED BACK home at two in the afternoon. He had not told Remy about Sorelli. Three times he had started to work his way up to it, each time deciding at the last minute that now was not the time. As he turned onto the gravel driveway, he wondered if he had made the right choice. He took a beer from the refrigerator and made his way to the small office just off the living room. He took out his address book from the top drawer of the desk and sat on the small couch, the telephone in his lap. After a few minutes he dialed the number that had most recently been copied into the small book. After four rings the phone was answered.

"Mike? This is your father."

"I am fine, Mike, listen to me for a minute, I have something important to ask you. Is there any way that you can enter the Marines early?"

"Because a situation has developed concerning an old case I worked on and Las Vegas has become a very dangerous place for you."

"That's all I can tell you. You have to trust me on this. Can you report early?"

"Yes, call me back as soon as you can and tell me what they said." Steve hung up the phone and drained the last half of the beer. He dialed again. This time the phone picked up immediately.

"Tam, this is Steve, sorry to bother you on the weekend, but I got a call late yesterday from Sorelli."

"No, very short. He made veiled threats against Mike."

"Yes, he said he was in town, who knows, he could have called from anywhere, but it didn't sound like long distance."

"Yeah, do that. If he is here, he can't resist showing himself around town, especially out on the Strip. I'll call Jack." Steve pressed the buttons down on the cradle and dialed Jack's number. When the receiver was picked up, he could tell the owner of the voice had been drinking.

"Jack, this is Steve. I know you have a lot on your plate, but you need to know that Sorelli is in town."

"No, Jack, I talked to him myself. He has been calling for two days now, refusing to leave his name, and yesterday afternoon I was in when he called."

"It was a short conversation, Jack, I don't have any answers to your questions. I called Tam and he is going to issue an all-points bulletin, today, nothing much else he can do. The guy could be anywhere and nowhere, just like last time, except he has a lot more money to hide with, this time."

"Yeah, I will keep you posted. I will be making a trip to Utah on Monday."

"Yeah, see ya."

Steve walked wearily into the living room. He retrieved another beer from the kitchen and sprawled across the living room couch. He flipped on the TV and started watching a pro basketball game. The game was over when he awoke two hours later. He rose from the couch and went to the shower.

April 18

STEVE RAPPED ON the door of Foxy's deli just after one in the morning. Through the half light of the dining room, he saw Bernie's figure moving through the tables with the door key in his hand. He stepped back as Bernie swung the heavy glass door toward him.

"You're early, Steve, get any sleep?" Steve moved in front of his friend and turned just inside the entrance.

"A little, Bern, being keyed up is better than too well rested." Steve stepped back and let Bernie lead the way into the back room. Bernie had moved all of the green felt gaming tables to the walls, leaving one in the middle of the room, directly under one of the long rectangle lights which Bernie had lowered until it was only four feet above the table. Bernie walked to the middle of the room and turned around. He pointed to a row of chairs that were lined up against the wall. The poker table held a chair at each end and one along the side.

"This time, no one sits at the table except you, me and Frank." Steve walked over to the table and rubbed the back of his hand across the green felt.

"What about Jilly? Frank isn't going to like him way over there." Steve indicated the chairs which were eight feet away. Bernie thought for a few seconds and then walked to the line of chairs, pulling one across the carpet and positioning it three feet behind one of the end chairs.

"What about that? Jilly can cover Frank's back, and get him whatever he wants from there." Steve nodded.

"Looks Ok to me, Bern, we'll see if it flies. A lot depends on Frank's mood." Steve looked up as Walter opened the door and looked in.

"I'm here, boss, you want the usual bar set-up?" Steve smiled at the tall waiter.

"I'm sorry we had to drag you out here at this time of morning, Walter. Win or lose, I'll make sure it is worth your while." Walter laughed.

"Think nothing of it, Mr. Cannon, just goes with the territory. Besides, how often do you get to watch Frank Sinatra play cards?" Bernie pointed toward the bar.

"I laid most of it out, Walter. Let's wait and see who Frank brings with him, before we add to it. I got Rocco working on sandwiches in the kitchen. Keep an eye on the door, please." Walter disappeared behind the door as Bernie put two new packs of cards in his pocket.

"Jack Entratter called just before you came in. Frank should be here in the next ten minutes or so." Bernie pointed to the large rack of poker chips on the table. "You want to use those or just go with cash?" Steve slid several of the tokens back and forth in their slots.

"Let Frank decide." Steve pulled a thick stack of one hundred dollar bills from his coat pocket and counted them out on the table in stacks of ten. He reassembled the bills in four stacks of five thousand each and deposited them into separate pockets of his sport coat. Bernie watched him from the other side of the table.

"Twenty grand your limit, Steve?" Steve nodded. "If Frank has a hot night, it is all his." Bernie smiled.

"That would have to be a hotter night than I ever heard of him having." Bernie was interrupted by Walter.

"Boss, Mr. Sinatra is here." Bernie quickly crossed to the door and was gone for a few seconds before he reappeared, opening both of the doors wide. Steve leaned against the table smoking a cigarette as he watched the six men enter the room. Besides Bernie, Frank and Jilly Rizzo, Frank had brought Jack Entratter, Dean Martin and Benny Binion. Dean stopped in the middle of the room and dead-panned while he spun around with a cigarette in his hand.

"What? No ladies?" He stopped his spin in front of Steve. He walked close to the private detective and hugged him with the arm holding the cigarette, while he spoke in a low tone.

"Hi ya, Steve, you going send him to bed early?" He jerked his head back toward the door where Frank was taking off his coat and looking at the large empty space around the table with a scornful expression. Steve patted Dean on the back, before he started for the door.

"Hopefully we can all go home early tonight, Dino." He held out his hand to Jilly who was standing in front of Frank.

"Jilly, nice to see you. Frank. Well here we are." Steve held out his hand. Frank held out his, but Steve had to take the extra step forward before he could grasp it. Frank nodded to Steve and looked around the room.

"Looks like a fire sale in here, Bernie, what gives?" Bernie laughed as he pointed Benny Binion toward the line of chairs.

"Just want to make sure that you don't feel crowded, Frank." Sinatra walked over to the table and threw three packs of Sands Hotel cards on the table.

"Where's Jilly sitting?" Bernie clasped the back of the only chair near the table.

"Right here, Frank, right behind you." Frank turned around and looked at Jilly, jerking his head slightly toward the chair. He then looked over at Benny who had already selected his seat and was accepting a bourbon and water from Walter.

"You see from there, Benny?" Benny took a drink, smacked his lips and thanked Walter before replying.

"Yeah, but who cares, you aren't playing Texas hold'em, so what's the point." Frank bristled as he tore the wrapper off one of the decks.

"No one twisted your arm, Benny. Maybe after I wipe the floor with Cannon, here, you can show me how it's done, right?" Benny laughed and pointed at Steve.

"If you wipe the floor with anybody in this room, Frank, I will stake you myself next week in a big game I am putting on downtown." Frank scowled across the table as Bernie stepped in front of his seat, cutting off Frank's view of the Texan. Bernie reached for the pack of cards. Frank scowled for a few more seconds before he reached across the table and let Bernie take them from his hand. Steve sat down and took a small sip from the glass of scotch that Walter had put down in front of him. Bernie waited while Jilly returned to the bar and retrieved the bottle of Jack Daniels from Walter and set it beside the glass that Frank had already half emptied. Frank still stood, and when he caught Walter's eye he beckoned him over to the table. He pulled several bills from the stack in front of him and handed them to the surprised waiter.

"Keep it coming." Walter smiled and bowed slightly as he backed away from the table. Steve could see that he held ten one hundred dollar bills in his hand. Frank sat down and smiled thinly at Steve before he looked over at Bernie.

"So, Bernie, what are the house rules. How much can I bet?" Bernie shrugged.

"Whatever you want, Frank, no limit there, but it's almost one thirty now. I am limiting this game to two and a half hours, so last hand just before four o'clock." Frank looked at Steve.

"That OK by you?" Steve nodded and pulled two of the stacks of bills from his pocket, laying them down beside his glass. Frank's smile grew wider, and Steve noticed his eyes looked a little bluer under the bright light.

"You bring enough, Cannon? You know your markers are good

with me." Steve chuckled and tapped a fresh pack of Pall Malls against his fist before he selected one and put it between his lips.

"Yeah, Frank, I brought all you need." Bernie shuffled the cards and looked at Frank.

"You want the hole card up or down?"

"Down. Are we doing ante or bring-in?" Bernie shrugged and looked at Steve.

"Why not do both, Frank? Thousand dollar ante OK with you?" Frank snorted as he took a drink.

"You in a big hurry, Cannon?" Steve shook his head slowly and smiled.

"No, Frank, I just want every pot to be worth your while." Bernie placed the cards in front of Frank. Frank kept his eyes on Steve as he cut them.

For the next hour, Bernie dealt the cards. It was obvious to Steve that Frank was taking his time more than usual, and fighting his normal tendencies to play quick and hard. Steve had won more hands but had Frank just barely in the hole. Dean and Benny had lost interest and were sitting at the bar while Walter served them drinks. Steve had invited Jack Entratter to sit across from Bernie and pressed him into service for four or five hands to give Bernie a breather. Just after three thirty, Frank got four hot hands in a row and went up $12,000 on Steve. A few minutes later, Bernie called last hand. Frank looked at his stack of bills and smiled across the table.

"How much you carrying, Cannon?" Steve riffled the stack of bills next to his glass.

"Eight thousand, Frank." Steve could see the gamblers gleam in Frank's eye, that euphoric state where you are convinced that lady luck has chosen you and no one else. Frank picked up all the money in front of him and threw it in the middle.

"What say, we play one hand for it all?" Steve pursed his lips and looked at the singer. Benny and Dean moved back to the table and stood just behind Bernie.

"You're up Frank. You got your ten grand back plus two more of mine. Were I you, I would call it a night." He saw the wince that quickly crossed Bernie's face. Franks' eyes narrowed.

"You're not me, Cannon, nobody is. Are you scared that tonight is the night I take you down?" Steve shrugged.

"No, Frank. I came with twenty grand, win or lose. You play a hand like the last two, it's all yours." Steve picked up the stack of one hundred dollar bills and dropped them in the middle of the table. Frank turned his glare on Bernie.

"Deal, Mr. Gold." Bernie cast a sidelong glance at Steve and began to shuffle. After the cut, Bernie spun the cards out in a deliberate fashion. Steve's table card was a jack, Frank drew an ace. Bernie slowed the pace as he flicked the next two cards. Ten to Steve, eight to Frank. After the next deal, Steve had nine, ten, jack showing, Frank had a pair of aces and an eight. Bernie looked around at the six men, now all intent on the next two cards to come from his hands. He turned Frank's over: Ace. He dealt Steve's last card: Queen. All eyes went to Steve as he turned over his hidden card: King. Every eye in the room moved to the last hidden card that lay just in front of Frank's left hand. Frank flipped it over and stood up: Deuce. Steve sat back in his chair and pulled out his pack of cigarettes. His dark eyes watched as the singer took a big gulp of Daniels and looked at Jilly. When Frank turned back to the table, his face was flushed and there were several beads of sweat on his upper lip. Bernie casually swept the forty thousand in hundreds over in front of Steve. Frank looked at the lost pot for several seconds. When he spoke, his voice was low and strained with anger.

"Put it back." Steve snorted and began to push the money into one neat stack. Bernie stood up, looked past Frank and shook his head very slightly at Jilly. Frank picked up the cocktail napkin that had been under his glass. He took out a pen and wrote quickly across the damp surface before throwing it into the middle of the table. Out of the corner of his eye, Steve could see Benny Binion move in front of the chair Jack Entratter had just left. Steve finished stacking the bills and looked up at Frank. The singer's face was redder than a few seconds before.

"Forty thousand marker, Cannon, let's go again." Steve stood from the table as he broke the bills into two equal stacks depositing each of them in separate pockets of his sport coat. Jilly Rizzo made a small exclamation and moved behind Frank when he caught a glimpse of Steve's shoulder rig. Bernie held up his hand and motioned for Jilly to stay back. Steve looked evenly across the green felt at the shorter man, "No, Frank. You may not know when to quit, but I do." He held his gaze fastened on the icy blue eyes until the singer turned toward his bodyguard.

"C'mon, Jilly, let's blow this joint." Frank strode to the coat stand grabbed his coat and opened the door letting it bang shut behind him before Jilly had even reached it. For a few seconds nobody in the room said anything. Dean Martin raised his glass toward the door.

"Well, there goes my ride." Benny Binion picked up the cocktail napkin from the middle of the table.

"I think I just might hold onto this. Might be good for a few laughs down the road." Steve lit the cigarette he had pulled out of the pack five minutes before. He smiled at Bernie through the smoke. Bernie shook his head and sat down, forgetting his guests who slowly filed out of the room. Walter began to stack the glasses on the bar as Steve sat down and patted Bernie's arm.

"Thanks for dealing, Bern, and thanks for hanging in there." Bernie looked at Steve with a blank expression and shook his head.

"Man, that could have gone either way, Steve." Steve patted the shorter man's shoulder and laughed.

"No, Bernie, it was always going to be OK, but my guess is that it isn't over yet. Frank will want another shot, so lets him sweat for a year or so and then do it again. What do you say?" Bernie stood up and shook his head.

"This keeps up, the pot will be a hundred grand in no time."

Steve reached in his pocket and pulled out a folded stack of twenty, one hundred dollar bills. He walked over to the bar and waited until Walter stood up from behind the polished surface.

"Here, Walter, thanks for all your hard work." Walter blushed when he saw the thick roll.

"That's too generous, Steve, just doing my job." Steve stepped back and rapped his knuckles on the wood.

"We were all just doing our jobs tonight, Walter, time to clock out." Steve waited for Bernie at the door and walked with him through the darkened restaurant. The sky was just a little paler in the east when Steve swung the Jeep out of the deserted parking lot and onto the Strip.

*

Steve awoke at ten o'clock after four hours' sleep. He quickly showered and shaved, dressing in a pair of khaki dress pants, a linen sport coat with a light blue shirt and dark tie. He traveled the six mile distance to Remy's house in good time owing to the lighter Sunday traffic. He let himself in and waited in the living room while Remy finished getting ready. Presently, she descended the stairs, her pale yellow dress flaring from the knees. She carried a matching sun hat and stood smiling in the foyer while Steve joined her.

"You look beautiful, Gem." He kissed her cheek, being careful not to smudge her make-up or her lipstick. She stepped back still holding his hand and looked him up and down.

"You don't look half bad yourself." She giggled as he pulled her back into his arms, and playfully kissed her neck.

"Want to take the Jag?" She nodded and took the keys from her purse, placing them in Steve's hand.

"If you don't drive too fast, we can put the top down."

"It's a perfect day for it, Gem, it will only take me a minute." Steve walked into the garage and waited while the automatic garage door swung upward into place. He stood just inside the opening and looked carefully up and down the private street. Seeing nothing untoward, he backed the car into the curving driveway and quickly took the top down and stowed it in the trunk. He removed the .45 from the Jeep and slid it into the Jaguar's glovebox. Remy came out just as he finished. She had on her oversized dark sunglasses, and she was adjusting a silk ribbon under her chin that would hold her hat in place as they drove. Steve opened the passenger door for her and checked the street once again as he rounded the back of the car.

Steve drove the two miles up the Strip to the intersection with Charleston Boulevard. Two turns later he was on Alta, the last street before the entrance to Rancho Circle. Having the top down, had allowed him to drive slower than most of the traffic, making it doubly hard for anyone to follow without being detected. He knew the Perone house, if only because he had recently been to Nick Montero's house which was right beside it. Most of what he remembered was the huge back acreage which contained several levels of grass and tile patios leading down to a large pool, tennis courts and riding stables. He pulled the white Jag beneath the large stone archway which guarded the long circular driveway. As he neared the apex of the curve he saw Mr. Baxter standing in the center of the roadway, directing him to pull up and stop. Steve got out and went around to Remy's side of the car, next to two long black limousines that were parked close to the curb. He gave her his hand and helped her exit the car, handing the keys to Mr. Baxter at the same time. Mr. Baxter held up his hand.

"I will be right back with your keys, Mr. Cannon. Parking is a little tight today." Steve smiled and nodded, holding out his arm to Remy.

"No hurry, Mr. Baxter, we will wait here for you." Steve looked at the small crowd that was standing just outside the double doors. He did not recognize anyone that he knew.

"I wonder how many people are coming to this shebang?" Remy looked at the crowd and then back at Steve.

"Steffi told me this week that her mother typically invited between eighty to one hundred guests to her second Sunday dinners." Steve whistled.

"I didn't realize it was that many." He pointed to the limo parked next to them. The front bumpers sported two small Nevada state flags.

"The governor is here." Just then Mr. Baxter huffed up to them, quickly handed Steve the keys and moved toward two more cars that had just pulled up to where they were standing. Steve smiled down at Remy.

"Shall we?" Remy smiled back and lead Steve toward the entrance to the mansion, the arched double doors opening onto a circular patio with a fountain in the middle surrounded by tropical flowers and plants. Steve and Remy circled around the fountain and into the main doors that led to the foyer of the house. Just inside, a tuxedoed waiter nodded at each guest extending his arm toward the main great room. Just beyond him, two waiters stood on either side with trays of champagne. Steve took one of the light glasses and held it out to Remy. Steve looked around the crowded room, where at least fifty people, mostly in couples, milled around, forming small conversational groups. The side doors of the great room were open.

"Gem, would you like to see the grounds? They are pretty impressive." Remy nodded and he led the two of them out onto a very large tiled patio that was surrounded on all sides by a marble balustrade. Steve and Remy walked over to the low wall and looked out over the huge property. Remy had just pointed out the central fountain that sat on the third level just before the property sloped gracefully down toward the horse stables, when they heard someone coming toward them. Steve turned as he heard his name.

"You must be Mr. Cannon." The speaker was approaching in a rhythmic gait, using a silver topped cane to facilitate her locomotion. The woman's silver hair was swept back from her tanned face in a tight bun that was fastened with a turquoise comb. Her long white dress had a scooped neckline that was set off by a necklace of turquoise beads that lay in several stands below her neck. The woman's gaze quickly went to Remy and she smiled as she moved forward to grasp her hands.

"Miss DeMarche, how lovely to see you. I have admired your dancing for many years." She kissed both of Remy's cheeks and held on to her hands as she looked over at Steve.

"When Stephanie told me that you were involved with Remy DeMarche, I knew you couldn't be all bad." Steve chuckled and smiled politely as he took one of the hands that Ida Perone had offered.

"It is nice to meet you, Mrs. Perone. Thank you for inviting us." Ida waved dismissively and looked back at Remy.

"Nonsense. And you must call me Ida." She looked behind her at the few people that had filtered out onto the patio.

"Stephanie must be around here somewhere. These aren't her favorite afternoons, I'm afraid, she is much like her father. He preferred peace and quiet and as few people as possible in the house." Her face brightened. "There she is." Steve turned and saw Miss Perone coming toward them from one of the center doors. She was dressed in a pale green dress and had a gold shawl around her shoulders. She smiled at Steve and Remy as she stopped beside her mother.

"I see you have met my mother, Mr. Cannon. When I saw her out here with the two of you, I figured I better join you quickly or she will spill all the family secrets."

"I don't think you should be concerned, Miss Perone, I have discovered a great deal about you in just the few short days we have worked together." Steve was interrupted by one of the waiters who required a consultation with Ida Perone. She excused herself and followed him from the patio. Remy took Miss Perone's hand.

"You look beautiful, Steffi, I wish I could wear that color." Miss Perone blushed slightly as she cast her gaze down at her own dress.

"Thank you, Miss DeMarche. I just wish I could just once look as elegant and beautiful as you." Steve took Remy's empty glass from her hand and looked at Steffi.

"Miss Perone, may I get you some refreshment?" He held up the glass. Steffi shook her head.

"No, thank you, Mr. Cannon, I don't drink." He turned to Remy.

"How about you, Gem, another?" Before Remy could reply, Steffi stepped closer and put her hand on Remy's arm.

"Would you like me to give you a tour of the house?" Remy glanced quickly at Steve.

"Of course, I would. How about you Steve?" Steve shook his head.

"No, you two go ahead. I am going to get a drink. I will come and find you later." He watched as the two women moved among the guests and disappeared into the great room. He flagged down a waiter and gave him his drink order. Over the waiter's shoulder he saw a small group gathered at the far corner of the balustrade. He smiled to himself and strolled over, waiting for a break in the conversation before he approached the circle. Nick Montero was the first of the group to notice him.

"Steve, I was looking for you." Nick looked over Steve's shoulder. "Where is Miss DeMarche?"

"Sorry, Nick, you'll have to do with me for awhile. Miss Perone is taking her on a tour of the house." Nick turned to the others in the group. "Steve you know everybody here?" Nick nodded and extended his hand to the only person he did not recognize in the group of four which included The Sultan of Brunei and Clifford Jones.

"Steve this is Joel Ciro, He is one of Governor Sawyers' top aides. Joel, this is Steve Cannon, private detective par excellence." The younger man, shook Steve's hand.

"I believe I am familiar with some of your exploits, Mr. Cannon. I am glad to finally meet you."

"Likewise, Mr. Ciro." Steve turned his gaze to the Sultan, as he took one step forward and grasped his hand, placing his other hand on the Sultan's forearm. "Ali, it is good to see you again. Any luck at the tables?" The Sultan shook his head solemnly.

"No, Steve, the last time we played together was my last night of winning." Steve put on a mock face of concern. "I hope I didn't take all your luck with me, Ali." Steve's face dissolved into a grin as he heard the reply. "No, I don't think so, but just to be sure, we should play together again before I leave, just you, me and the dealer." Steve nodded his assent.

"That would great, Ali, I would like that." Ali turned to the governors' aide. "Mr. Cannon is one of the best baccarat players I have ever seen." Before Joel Ciro could react, Steve heard a dismissive snort from the man beside him, but decided that Clifford Jones was best ignored for now. Joel pointed his drink glass at Steve and waited for a few seconds as the waiter stopped and handed Steve a glass of whisky and served Nick Montero another gin and tonic.

"Have you met the governor, Mr. Cannon?" Steve shook his head as he took a sip of the liquor. "No, Mr. Ciro I have never had the pleasure." Joel indicated Clifford.

"I was just about to take Mr. Jones in to greet him, why don't you come along?" Steve demurred with the hand that was not holding the glass tumbler. "I don't want to take up the governors' valuable time." Joel shook his head emphatically. "Nonsense, Mr. Cannon, the governor likes to meet as many people and get as many opinions on things as he can. Come along." Steve smiled and fell in behind Clifford as the aide led them back across the great room, down a short hallway and into a large library with French doors at the far end that opened to yet another large patio separated from the one the three men had just left. The governor sat in one of five club chairs that were arranged in a circle in the middle of the room. Three of them were empty as the governor was in close conversation with a man Steve had never seen before. The room held two other groups of men conversing with cigars and drinks. Steve recognized a county commissioner and a state legislator among them. Joel went over to the governor, bending over the back of his chair as he whispered something in his ear. The governor looked over at Clifford and Steve and smiled broadly.

"Come on over, gentlemen, sit down for a few minutes." Steve settled into the chair that was the farthest away from the governors'. Clifford sat down right next to the governor on his right side. Steve silently appraised the man as he finished his conversation in low tones with the man on his left. The governor had a commanding voice that he was having trouble keeping low enough so that only his conversational partner could hear him. His black rimmed glasses and his dark wavy hair gave him a professorial look that went with his black suit, white shirt and dark navy tie. The conversation ended, the man gave the governor his card which the governor handed over his shoulder to Joel as he grasped the man's hand and wished him well. Joel came over and sat beside Steve.

"Governor, this is Steve Cannon, you already know Clifford." The governor laughed at the joke, nodded at Clifford and looked at Steve directly. "Yes, Mr. Cannon, I am glad to meet you, I have read about some of the cases you have been involved in. One or two concerned malfeasance on the part of elected officials, and while one of them was a democrat, I was still glad that your investigation led to his removal." Steve crossed his legs and accepted a cigar from a waiter who had just entered the small circle.

"No, the pleasure is mine, Governor Sawyer, thank you for your hospitality." The governor sat back and swept his arm indicating the room. "Ida puts on these functions for a lot of reasons, but she has always been kind enough to include me and provide me with a venue to meet people such as yourself and hear your thinking on current events." Steve was about to reply, when the governor continued. "You are good friends with Mr. Bernard Gold, am I correct?" Steve started to respond, but settled for a nod as the governor didn't pause. "Now, there is the type of casino owner-operator we welcome in this state. I may relate too much sometimes to those who come from humble beginnings like myself and go on to make a success of themselves, but I think not, at least not in this case. If we could encourage more people like Mr. Gold, I think the all too frequently talked about mob influence would fade away. What do you think, Mr. Cannon?" Steve looked at the governor and the earnest face of Mr. Ciro, who had taken the chair vacated by the first man, while also aware of the smirk on the Clifford's face. Steve indicated the room with the unlit cigar.

"Well, Governor Sawyer, I think you might get an argument or two from your constituents in this town if they ever had a chance to express how they truly feel about what you have just said." Steve brought the cigar to his lips and waved the flame from his lighter in front of the thick, dark brown cylinder. The governor sat back in his chair, a questioning expression on his face. He held out his hands and smiled as the positive aura returned.

"Well, Mr. Cannon, you are among friends here, why don't you elaborate on what you just said and give a voice to those who are not present." Steve smiled and blew a cloud of smoke into the middle of the circle.

"Well, Governor Sawyer, I would put it this way: The average citizen of this town likes things just the way they are. By that I mean that there is no street crime to speak of, everyone knows what is expected of them and they are comfortable that the 'mob influence' as you term it, is a benign, and on the whole a beneficial presence in their lives." Steve stopped and took another puff on the cigar, breaking the gaze of the governor, he looked up at the coffered ceiling and the sky blue paint on the curved surface. The governor sat forward in his chair.

"Are you telling me, Mr. Cannon, that the residents of Las Vegas don't see the mafia and the casinos they control as a problem?" Steve nodded and quickly replied before the governor could get started again. "That's exactly what I am saying, but there's more. If you really want the mafia influence out of the state, then your best bet is to allow corporations to own and run the casinos." Governor Sawyer waved his hand impatiently back and forth in front of his face. "No, No, Mr. Cannon, that is impractical. How could you vet all the thousands of shareholders?" Steve cut in evenly, so as not to appear rude. "That's already taken care of by the fact that shareholders are a matter of public record. Vet the members of the corporate board and let the market take care of the rest. If ABC corporation wants to hire hoods to run their casino, their profits or lack of them will reflect that fact, and the market will punish them appropriately. One decade of corporate ownership, and I bet that you will never see another mafia run casino." Steve sat back, sipped his scotch and watched as the governor cocked his head and smiled.

"Well, Mr. Cannon, it might surprise you to know that Mr. Jones here, completely agrees with you and has been pushing me and my predecessors rather forcefully to do just that. But wouldn't that destroy this 'benign', whatever it is, the locals see as a benefit to having the mob around?" Steve shrugged. "Sure, it probably would, and that is why, as I said, the mob is not an issue that anyone here thinks about one way or the other. After all, who is hurt by skimming? The tax revenue folks? Hardly a sympathetic victim, wouldn't you say?" The governor smiled and turned to his aide.

"See, this is precisely why this type of gathering is so valuable." The governor stood up.

"Gentlemen, I see it is about that time, and unless we want Ida in here shooing us all out, I suggest we go to lunch." Steve stood and joined the line of men as they filed out into the great room. Steve saw Remy and Miss Perone talking with Nick Montero and his wife Margaret. He felt a presence at his side and looked back to see the Sultan.

"Hi, Ali, would you do us the honor of sitting with us at lunch?" The monarch smiled at the invitation. "Of course, Mr. Cannon, I would be delighted." Steve tugged at his elbow. "Come with me, there is a lady I want you to meet."

Ten minutes later, Steve, Remy, Ali and Miss Perone, had all gone

B. R. Laue

through the buffet line and were seated at one of the twelve round tables that each held eight people. Nick Montero and Margaret along with Buddy Hackett and his wife, Sherry, were already sitting there when the foursome arrived. Steve introduced Remy to Buddy and his wife. The Sultan had known the comedian for many years as they were friendly competitors when it came to their gun collections. Remy frowned as she looked at Steffi's plate.

"Steffi, you have hardly taken anything at all." Miss Perone looked down at the half-empty plate and smiled at the rest of the table. "My mother wants to make sure that I visit all the tables, before everyone is done eating, so I'm afraid that I won't be able to stay here long." Steve paused before he took a bite of salad. "I am sure that she won't mind if you spend a little time with us. I bet you have already greeted most everyone here." Steffi nodded her head. "Yes, Mr. Cannon, but unless you have put one of these types of gatherings together, it is hard to imagine how many little things there are to do."

*

Steve stood at the balustrade and watched Remy, Margaret and Steffi grow smaller in the distance as they made their way to the stables. Miss Perone wanted to show the other two women her horses, and Steve had demurred. He had never seen the point of horses and the few times he had been around the animals, they had always seemed to sense his ambivalence. He had just lit a Pall Mall when he saw Joel Ciro coming toward him, drink in hand. Steve nodded as the younger man joined him. Steve held out the pack of smokes, but the aide politely refused.

"I just wanted to make sure that you understand the governor is always happy when his constituents feel comfortable enough to be candid with him." Steve turned his head so that his exhalation of smoke was directed away from Joel. "I am sure that is true, Mr. Ciro." The aide shrugged. "He just hates the mob, always has, always will." Steve's eyes narrowed slightly as he looked at the other man.

"Well then, he must be pretty pleased by what is going on with the grand jury." Steve watched the man's face closely, trying to gauge the effect of his pronouncement. His gaze was met by an innocent smile. "Yes, he is, actually. He is very confident that this time they will get results." Steve decided to take a chance. He squared himself and looked directly into Joel Ciro's eyes. He spoke with just a hint of gravity in his voice.

"If he thinks that, Mr. Ciro, he is going to be mighty disappointed." Steve stopped and held the man's gaze. Joel took a step backward and Steve thought he saw an unsteadiness, perhaps from too much alcohol. Joel's face was turned down into a deep frown. "Why would you say that?" Steve took a deep breath through his nose.

"Because the Feds think they have someone that is going to roll over on some of the bigger bosses in town, right? If I know that, don't you think that the mob knows it as well?" Steve raised one eyebrow. He was hoping the bait was wriggling and that Joel could not see the fishing line attached to it. Joel shook his head and took a big sip of his vodka. "This time is different, Steve. This guy will testify." Steve shook his head. "I don't think so, Joel and I'll tell you why. At some point, if it hasn't already happened, this guy whoever he is, is going to decide he needs protection, big protection. The Feds will have to comply or lose their witness. The guys' pattern will change and the wise guys here will see it." Joel shook his head. "Not this time." Steve looked at him firmly.

"Why not?" Joel smiled, and when he replied, Steve heard a definite slur in the deep voice. He tapped Steve's chest as he spoke. "Because he is far, far, away, Steve." Steve turned and looked out at the fountain and the stables beyond. He snorted.

"There is no place far enough away, Joel, there just isn't." He turned when he saw Joel smile drunkenly and raise his glass.

"Oh, no? I think Syracuse is far enough away, don't you?" Steve smiled to himself and turned to the young aide. "You might be right, Mr. Ciro, it just might be." Steve looked over the man's shoulder as

Ida Perone moved toward the two men. She stopped a few feet away and addressed Joel.

"The Governor would like you to join him, Joel, he is ready to leave." Steve turned and held out his hand. "Good to meet you, Mr. Ciro, I enjoyed our conversation." The inebriated man nodded and began to move unsteadily toward the open doors that led from the patio into the house. Ida watched him for a few moments, before she turned back toward Steve. "His father worked for my husband. Couldn't hold his booze either." She looked up at Steve. Her face was pleasant, but Steve could sense the resolve under the surface. He decided to stay quiet as he guessed that Ida had something to say. He was right.

"Let me start by saying that I am very glad that Stephanie is working for you. I was against her going out into the work-a-day world, but she is stubborn like her father. But she is also very sensitive, Mr. Cannon, and I fear for her as her big heart sometimes gets her into trouble. She has always confided in me, and since I don't get out as much as I used to, she uses the events of her day to entertain me in the evenings. That is why I know that even though your work is sometimes dangerous, you have her best interest at heart and will protect her. I hope I am not putting you in a difficult position by saying that, Mr. Cannon." Steve smiled down at the earnest face.

"No, Ida, not at all. In the short time we have worked together, she has been such a big help to me, I sometimes think she has been with me for years." Steve watched as a smile spread over the sun-wrinkled face. His own turned darker as he thought of Sorelli. There were more people in his life to protect now than just a year ago, he suddenly had a thought he needed to share with Bernie. He made a mental note to himself as he tuned back into the one-way conversation Ida was having.

"That is why you and Miss DeMarche must make sure you come back." Steve nodded and smiled, trying to recall the words that had come before. When he failed, he tried to cover.

"And what day is that, Ida?"

"The second Sunday of next month, of course. The weather will be warmer and the pool and tennis courts will be full. Stephanie wants to do a Mexican celebration theme. You promise me that you will come?" Steve pointed out toward the paddocks at the three women approaching.

"I can't speak for Remy, Ida, but I don't see why not." The three women were laughing and talking as they ascended the wide marble steps to where Steve and Ida were standing.

*

Steve had kept one eye on the traffic behind him as he had driven Remy home and then crossed town again to reach his house. He settled on the couch in the office with the phone on his lap. His first call was to Bernie.

"Bernie, I'm sorry, I know this is your one day off, but I wanted to run something by you."

"Thanks, this will just take a minute. Do you think that one of Milton's skilled guys can rig up the door to my office so that Miss Perone can buzz people in?"

"Yes, exactly, like that. Also take out the stippled panes and put in the heaviest, thickest glass and the heaviest door frame they can find, right?"

"Thanks, Bernie, I will leave it with you, and one more thing. I am leaving for Utah early tomorrow morning, might be gone for a day or two. Could you look in on Miss Perone once or twice while I am gone?"

"Thanks, Bern, I'll let you go." Steve hung up and thought for a minute before he dialed the next number.

"Hi Earl, this is Steve Cannon. You know where Tommy is?"

"Thanks, I will see you in a half an hour." Steve had just set the phone down on the desk when it rang.

"Hello?"

"Mike. I am glad you called. What did you find out?"

"A week? That is good news. Does that create any problems for you?"

"Good. I want to fly to Reno and go down to San Diego with you, if that is OK with you?"

"I will see you on Friday." Steve hung up the phone and walked through the house to his bedroom. He switched the sport coat for a dark blue windbreaker, looking in the mirror to make sure the bulge from the .45 was not obvious. He locked the front door and swung the red Jeep southward toward the Desert Inn.

Earl was sitting in a golf cart just outside the starter's shack when Steve walked up. Steve jerked his head toward the golf course behind him.

"Think you can give me a ride out to the hole Tommy is playing." Earl shook his head and pointed down the eighteenth fairway.

"Don't have to. There's Tommy's foursome now." Steve turned around just in time to see Tommy's third shot on the par five land short of the green. Steve nodded at Earl.

"Thanks, I see him." Steve strolled over to a bench that sat beyond the green just behind a large sand trap. He watched as Tommy's next shot ran past the cup over a small hill and trickled down into the sand in front of him. A few minutes later, Tommy's cart screeched to a halt in front of Steve. Tommy Carmino peered at the private detective from behind a pair of dark sunglasses.

"What you want?" Steve stretched his legs out in front of him and buried his hands in the pockets of his light jacket.

"Need to talk. Privately." Tommy snorted.

"Another perfect end to another perfect day." Tommy exited the cart and grabbed his sand wedge and putter. Two shots and two putts later he stood in front of Steve.

"So, Slick. What is so important that you have to track me down out here?" Steve stood up and looked toward the clubhouse.

"You want a drink, Tommy?" Tommy turned and looked at the green tinted glass windows.

"Yeah, but not in there." He smiled, patted his back pocket and pulled his putter back out of his bag.

"I got a hip flask and five hundred bucks that says I beat you two out of three putts." He pointed down the asphalt cart path to a large practice putting green that was surrounded by jasmine bushes and was deserted in the falling twilight. Steve shrugged.

"Sure, Tommy, why not?" Tommy laughed and handed Steve the putter.

"Get in, Slick and hold on." Steve braced himself as the cart rocketed forward down the short pathway. Tommy took two new balls from his golf bag and tossed one to Steve.

"Pick a hole, loser picks after that." Tommy took a big swig from the silver flask and handed it to Steve. Steve held the flask up to Tommy in a small salute and took a short drink before handing it back. He dropped the ball at his feet and pointed with the putter to the far end of the green.

"Number eight, Tommy." Steve lined up the putt and rapped the ball sharply, sending it on a large arc toward the small flag. It came to a stop two feet below the hole. Tommy took the putter from Steve's hand, his ball following the same trajectory but stopping a foot short of Steve's. Steve looked at Tommy.

"You're away." Tommy's eyes squinted as he pulled the sunglasses from his brow and dropped them into his shirt pocket.

"So, talk, Slick." Tommy started walking toward the two balls. Steve followed and then waited until Tommy's ball rattled into the bottom of the hole.

"Met the governor, today Tommy." Tommy straightened up, the ball in his hand.

"That hayseed? Where was this?"

"At Ida Perone's. He was in town getting briefed by the FBI and the DA on the case they got on you." Steve bent over his putt and tapped it nonchalantly into the hole.

"And?" Steve peered across the green into the setting sun.

"Number two." Steve took the putter back an extra two inches and swept it gently forward. The ball rolled slowly, climbing a small rise in the middle of the green, before picking up speed as it curved sharply to the left, traveling ten feet before disappearing into the hole. Steve looked up at Tommy.

"And a lot of things, Tommy. Had a conversation about casino ownership. Clifford was there." Steve stopped talking as Tommy lined up his putt. The ball didn't make the top of the rise, falling away too soon and ended up ten feet from the cup. Tommy swore under his breath as he walked toward his ball.

"So far, I'm not entranced, Slick." Tommy's half-hearted second putt grazed the edge of the lip and stopped two feet away. He stepped up behind the ball and pointed.

"Number five." He putted the ball three feet past the hole and turned toward Steve.

"That's what you came out here to tell me? You and the dummy governor trading casino stories?"

Steve took the putter from Tommy and leaned on it as he looked at the mobster.

"I also met one of his aides who was half in the bag and wanted to chat. Found out who they got waiting to rat you out, Tommy." Steve dropped the ball at his feet and started to line up his putt. Tommy grunted.

"And who might that be?" Steve looked over at Tommy and smiled.

"Syracuse." Tommy stepped back and cocked his head.

"Syracuse. You sure that was what he said?" Steve nodded. Tommy turned and looked out at the course. After a few seconds, he nodded to himself.

"Yeah, that all makes sense now." He turned toward Steve with a pensive look on his face. Steve sensed that something had yielded inside the mobster. Tommy's voice was low and quiet when he spoke.

"Well, I guess you got Jack off the hook." Steve turned back to his putt.

"I didn't do it just for Jack."

The ball jumped from the face of the putter, gathered speed across the short grass and curled into the hole thirty feet away.

APRIL 19

STEVE CLOSED THE front door to his house and shivered in the pre-dawn chill. The moon was full but hung low in the sky and was hazy behind a thin layer of clouds. Steve sat in the Jeep and checked his maps with his flashlight. He had used a razorblade to carefully reduce the topo map of the Brianhead area to small squares that he glued to pieces of pasteboard and finally attached them to a spiral ring that allowed him to flip easily through the map as he hiked. He carefully buttoned the book of maps into the large front pocket of his dark blue wool shirt. He had almost four hours of driving ahead of him before he reached the edge of the forest where he could park the Jeep and start his hike.

He was ten miles south of Cedar City, Utah when he pulled into a gas station to fill the tank of the thirsty Jeep. If the course he set himself was right, he would see the turn-off he needed a few miles north of Cedar City. After he replaced the gas nozzle, he sat for a few minutes and drank a cup of coffee from his thermos. He pulled the small canvas day pack onto his lap and went through the items he had carefully placed there the night before. He shook the canteen to make sure it was full and adjusted the forty-five under his canvas jacket. He unbuttoned the breast pocket of the wool shirt and flipped the pages of the map with the hand that wasn't holding the red plastic cup. When he reached the last page, he looked for several long seconds at the picture of Martin Ogawa. The sun peeked over the ridge a mile ahead of him and turned the meadow around him into a blaze of rainbow diamonds as the rays passed through the dew.

*

Steve drove carefully down the rutted logging road for several hundred yards before he found a space between two trees that was wide enough to slip the Jeep through and make it less conspicuous from the road. He spent several minutes with his maps and a compass making sure that the first part of his hike brought him from the east to within two miles of the cabin. When he was satisfied, he placed the straps of the canteen and the pack over his shoulders and started a slow place along a deer trail that led roughly along the same course he had laid out. He took precautions to walk as silently as possible and slowed when he had to move through the undergrowth. In the far distance he heard the whine of a chainsaw and stopped for a few minutes when he caught a faint whiff of wood smoke. After forty-five minutes he came to a dry stream bed that afforded easier walking and he followed it for a mile and a half before it veered from his line of march. The next hour was spent bushwhacking his way over several tall hills. When he stopped for a water break it was ten o'clock and after consulting his maps, compass and picking out the landmarks he had memorized, he figured he was an hour away from the cabin. He turned and looked back down the hillside he had just come up. He was not looking forward to the return trip if the cabin was empty. From his perch, he could see a small wisp of smoke and the chrome reflection from a car parked in front of a building a mile below him and to the west. If Romo Kiner had not led him wrong, that was the gas station and small store that was the last thing you passed before the turn-off to Slims' cabin.

An hour later, Steve knelt beside a small stream and peered through a tangle of chokecherry bushes. Fifty yards across the river and partially visible through the large pines, Steve could see a cabin. He rechecked his maps carefully before he waded the small waterway in a crouch and slipped into the undergrowth on the far side. He moved in a wide semicircle around the structure keeping at least a hundred yards away and out of the line of sight at all times. After a mile of the circumnavigation, he climbed a small hillock that afforded Steve a concealed vantage-point from where he could take in the whole property at once. He carefully parted the lowest branches of a large Douglas Fir and rested an elbow on the prickly needles as he brought the binoculars into focus.

The cabin was an A-frame, a configuration much favored by week-enders that flocked to the resort areas in the west. A wooden walkway circled the structure leading to a wide deck below the large trapezoid windows that held a southern exposure. Steve had picked his observation spot because there were no large windows on this side of the cabin, and the rough terrain made approach from this direction the least likely of the four. The only other building was a small garage with no windows, forty yards away from the main house and twenty yards from the dirt road that Steve guessed led down the mountain for three miles to the store and the junction with the main logging road. He glassed the cabin and the area immediately surrounding it carefully for a half an hour. There was no smoke coming from the chimney, and Steve could see no sign of movement from inside, though he could clearly see the front third of the house through the large front windows. A half hour passed with no sign of movement from inside the house. He was almost ready to move to another position when something startled a pair of blue jays resting on a tree branch just outside one of the bigger windows. A thorough glassing of the ground and the trees immediately adjacent to the one that birds had just left revealed no other animal or anything that could account for the quick exodus. Steve pulled the binoculars from his face and swung them behind his back as he sat against the large trunk sipping from the canteen. A few minutes later he quietly climbed down from the small hillock and followed a shallow ravine that intersected the road one hundred yards away. When Steve was even with the garage, he began the slow process of covering the thirty yards between himself and the structure without revealing his position to the house. The only way was the slow way. Quick darting movements across the numerous open areas between trees and under-growth would catch an eye even if the watcher wasn't focused on that specific area. Steve used the shadows of the dwarf pine trees and the numerous large rocks to conceal his progress as he crawled along the ground as flat as he could make himself. After another twenty-five minutes, Steve was behind a large pine tree in the shadow of the garage, ten feet below the graded level of the road. He dropped to his belly and crawled up the red dirt slope until he was shielded from view by the weathered wood of the garage. He quickly inspected the side of the garage and found a fissure between two of the boards. The flashlight beam cut through the gloomy darkness and played over the surface of a car. Steve pressed his face close to the crack. The light revealed the side of the tan Chrysler. The back window had been repaired, but Steve could see at least two bullet holes in the door nearest him.

Steve had just dropped the flashlight into his pack and taken a small step backward when he heard the sound of a car in low gear coming from somewhere behind him. He ducked down behind a pile of leftover lumber that had been abandoned against the side of the garage. When he heard the engine noise stop, he raised his head a few inches and peered through a space between two large timbers. Thirty yards away and just off the road but still out of sight of the house, a black and white police car was parked in the shadow of the overhang. Steve watched as the cop opened his door and walked out into the middle of the road. He knelt down and disappeared from Steve's view. Steve crawled carefully to a new vantage point and again raised his head. The cop was inspecting a newly killed mule deer that lay in the red dust of the road just short of the turn-in to the cabin.

The cop stood up and looked around. He was young, maybe twenty-five or so, Steve guessed. Blond hair and moustache, Steve figured he was a Cedar City cop by his uniform. The young man, brushed off the knees of his khaki pants and looked toward the cabin. Steve's next breath was a sharp intake as he realized what the cop was going to do next. He didn't see the man's first steps up the slope toward the cabin, as he slid from under the woodpile and crawled to the farthest corner of the garage. He pressed his back against it as he slid up the wood to his full height. The cop was below him and out of sight for the moment. He bent down and picked up a softball sized rock that lay at his feet. Taking care to stay out of sight of the cabin, he heaved it high into the air with his right hand, the rock arching upward before it fell, bouncing heavily in the middle of the dirt driveway. The third bounce ended at the feet of the cop who had just come into Steve's view. The young man stopped and looked at it for a second before swinging his head in an effort to figure out the direction it had come from. Steve waited for a few seconds until the cop looked toward the garage. Steve held his arm over his head and waved. The cop put his hand over his eyes as he fought to see what was in the dark shadows beneath the bright morning sun. Steve waved again and motioned for the cop to get low and off the driveway. The cop took two steps toward Steve. His hand went to rest on the top of his pistol. Steve heard the thud of the bullet at the same time that he heard the crack of the rifle. Even as he watched the cop's body wrench around and fall to the ground, his mind cataloged the sound as that of a .30 caliber, probably an M1 carbine. The man had made no sound as his body turned toward the road and fell face down in the dirt. Steve had to stand on his tiptoes to see the fallen man. The right hand was moving. Steve slipped the .45 from under his arm. He crouched and ran toward the far corner of the garage. He took a deep breath as he swung the gun around the edge of the building and squeezed off three quick shots toward the cabin. As he ducked back behind the building in almost the same move, he caught a glimpse of a figure

on the walkway diving for cover. Steve crammed the gun back into
the holster as he ran in a crouch down the short slope to the officer.
He bent over quickly and locked his arms under the unconscious
cop and with all the strength he could muster he pulled him back
up the slope toward the safety of the garage. Two shots rang out
and the bullets sent up puffs of dirt next to Steve's right foot. Steve
made one last effort and pulled the officer into the shade behind the
garage. He turned him on his back and tore open the man's coat. His
uniform shirt was soaked from so much blood, that Steve could not
readily see where the bullet had impacted. He felt for a pulse and
feeling none, began to do CPR. Five minutes later he realized that
the young man was probably dead before he had gotten to him. He
stared down at the name badge. Larry Hiram. Steve shook his head.
A local Mormon kid from one of the big families. Steve bit his lip
and through hot tears pulled the .38 special from the dead man's
holster. He slipped it into his belt in the back of his pants, crossed
the cops' arms over his body and stood up. He crossed to the side of
the building, counted three and sent one bullet toward the cabin as
he jumped from the top of the slope down into the green underbrush
of the ravine.

Steve rolled into a ball just before he hit the bottom of the ravine.
Before he could get to his feet, a bullet impacted a tree trunk right
next him, but six feet off the ground. Steve got ready to move as a
small shower of bark fell on his shoulders. The M1 was a light and
portable weapon but was not very accurate past seventy yards. It had
traditionally been issued to officers and tank crews on the theory that
if they had to use their weapons it would likely be very close combat.
He hesitated and decided to wait for ten seconds or so. Another shot
cracked across the ravine, but this one was twenty yards ahead of him.
Steve dropped to the ground and began to crawl carefully through
the underbrush. There were two more shots in the ten minutes it took
Steve to reach the shade underneath the cabin. Both shots were well
behind him and proved to Steve that his instinct had been right, and

the gunman had no real idea where he was in the ravine. Steve waited under the deck next to one of the six-by-six pylons that anchored the cabin and allowed it to hang off the mountain side. After several minutes he heard a slight creaking on the front deck where he had caught a glimpse of the assailant, a small piece of shadow moved on the ground twenty feet in front of him. Steve breathed in through his nose and concentrated on not making any sound. As his eyes became accustomed to the darkness under the cabin, he began to assess his surroundings. All around him were large chunks of concrete left over from the construction of the A-frame. Ten yards away he could just make out the outline of the wooden stairs that led from the deck down to a dirt pathway that circled toward the front of the house. Steve slowly oriented his body toward the stairs and planned out his moves so that he could cross the distance with as few movements as possible. Above him he heard the creak of the boards as the gunman moved to a new position. Steve used the killers' own noise to cover any he might make as he stretched one leg out as far as he could and carefully set it down. He was able to get both of his feet together just as the creaking above his head stopped. A few seconds later, another shot crashed into the ravine and the killer took several steps to a new position. Steve stopped and tried to control his breathing. He willed his muscles not to move as a long shadow grew on the ground to his left. The gunman was leaning out over the railing of the deck trying to see under the cabin. For several seconds nothing moved. Steve took a shallow breath as he heard a board squeak right above his head. Steve slowly tilted his head back and looked up through the thin shafts of light that slipped between the boards and provided the only light he could navigate by. The bright sky above made Steve squint for a second, but just as his vision adjusted, his blood ran cold. Slim Atkins was staring down between the cracks directly at Steve.

Steve concentrated on keeping the muscles of his right arm loose. If Slim made one move, Steve would immediately swing the heavy Colt up and attempt to shoot through the cracks. Even if the bullet failed to penetrate, it would affect the gunman's aim. Several seconds, later, it was clear to Steve that Slim could not see him, but was listening for any sound that might come from below. The gunman was dressed in deer hunting clothes and had a four day growth of beard on his thin sallow face. Steve knew that time was more of an ally to him than to Slim. Though Slim knew that Steve had more than enough time to traverse the ravine, he could not be sure that the approach was not being made from another direction. Just as that thought cleared Steve's mind, the cruel black eyes disappeared. Slim moved rapidly across the deck and ran until he reached the catwalk on the front of the cabin from where he had shot the cop. Steve took three large steps and was beside the stairs. He moved to his left and hugging the rough sideboards of the cabin, he began to quietly ascend the stairs, the .45 pointed with both hands toward the corner where Slim would appear. When he reached the last step he pressed the left side of his body against the cabin and peered around the corner. Slim was thirty feet away, his back turned, and he was using a small pair of field glasses to study the ravine. Steve stepped noiselessly off the top step and with one long stride, stood in the middle of the deck, the small white dot on the back of the front gunsight centered squarely between the shoulders of the gunman.

"Freeze, Slim." The words growled out of Steve's throat. Slim hesitated for a split second and then began to turn around. The Colt bucked in Steve's hand and a large chunk of deck railing flew up, just missing Slims' eye. Slim quickly held the short carbine up over his head with one hand, the other was held out on front of him in an act of supplication.

"Don't shoot." Slims' voice held a distinct quaver. Steve lowered his center of gravity and moved two quick steps closer, the gunsight steady on Slims' nose and his own ears ringing from the report. Steve jerked his head to the left and toward a small table that sat against the side of the cabin wall.

"Grab the rifle by the barrel, take two slow steps and put it on the table, the barrel pointing toward you and then walk backwards, back to where you are now." Steve followed the nose with the white dot while Slim did as he was told. When Slim was again facing him with his arms halfway up, Steve jerked the gun barrel.

"Take off your jacket and throw it over the railing." The garment quickly disappeared from view and Steve heard it land with a thud in the small thicket below. His supposition was right, Slim had at least one other gun in the pocket of the jacket. Steve took three more steps until only ten feet separated the two men. At the closer range, Steve could see the mixture of fear and anger in Slims' black eyes. For a few seconds both men stood in the cool breeze, before Slim spoke.

"What are you going to do now?" Steve snorted.

"This deck is covered with spent shells. There is a dead cop lying behind the garage, I could kill you right here, and no one would be the wiser." Slims' lip curled into a sneer.

"I don't think so, Cannon. That's not how guys like you play the game." Slim spit toward Steve. "No, you're going to have to take me in, and the nearest phone is over three miles away. A lot can happen in three miles." Steve smiled and his response was registered instantly in Slims' eyes as a shadow of doubt flickered across them.

"You aren't going to be in any shape to run, Slim, because you are about to get the worst beating you have ever seen anybody get in your whole miserable life." Steve stepped quickly to his left and deposited his pistol on the table next to the M1 carbine. He slowly returned toward his spot ten feet in front of the grinning hood. Slim spit again and smiled.

"Didn't figure you for such a sporting type, Cannon, but it's your funeral." Slim spread his arms away from his body and sank into a semi crouch, circling slowly to his right in an attempt to get Steve to counter and move in front of the railing. Steve took two small steps in the direction that Slim wanted him to go and then stopped, leaving his weight on his left foot, the one farthest away from the rail. He waited for a full second as Slim made his charge, before he pivoted back into the center of the deck and sent a left fist crashing down hard just behind Slims' ear as the killer fought to stop his progress. Slim fell to his knees but instantly the tall man twisted, shot upward and grabbed Steve's legs, pushing both their bodies heavily to the wooden deck. Steve had just enough time to bring his left knee up and now he kicked violently outward, his foot planted squarely on Slims' chest. Slim slid across the deck, his head crashing against the railing supports. Before he was able to move, Steve was standing over him swinging a right hook to Slims' jaw. At the same time as Slims' head snapped to the side, the hood swept Steve's feet with his left leg. Steve fell on his right side and was barely able to get his right arm out from under his body and turn over before Slim crashed heavily on top of him his hands attempting to encircle Steve's neck. For several seconds the test of strength was even as each man labored, their forearms locked against each other. Slowly, Steve began to push Slims' arms backward toward his chest causing his center of gravity to rise. With one last effort, Steve let out a growling yell and pushed Slim over onto his side. Steve used his momentum off the deck to scramble to his feet while his left hand grabbed Slim by his thick black hair. He sat down heavily on the prone man's back and with quick moves pounded Slims' head and face repeatedly into the deck. With Slim slipping in and out of consciousness, Steve reached behind his back and retrieved the police revolver that belonged to the dead cop. He twisted the hood's head to the side and pressed the barrel of the gun into his ear. He bent over and hissed into the man's other ear.

"You had your chance, Atkins, more than the chance you gave that cop and Martin Ogawa."

Steve felt the first wave of heat sweep up his chest and explode in his ears. He pressed down harder and twisted the barrel against the side of Slims' head. Blood was now flowing freely from Slims' nose and he was taking large jagged gasps in an effort to breathe. Steve pulled back the hammer on the .38 special and leaned closer.

The pool of blood and the barrel of the gun began to rotate slowly in his vision, picking up speed as the deck turned to the green of the jungle and Slims' grunting pleas echoed off the walls of the cabin and bounced back against Steve's ears as Japanese shrieks. Successive waves of heat pulsed through Steve's throat as he fought to slow down the rotating circles. The shrieking was now mixed with explosions and gunfire, Steve heard his own voice from a long way away.

"How do you like it now, Slim? How does it feel now, big man?" Steve felt the cold steel of the trigger as his finger tightened around it. A small part of his mind was idly wondering how many pounds of pressure the young cop had set it at, when the last wave of heat was replaced by the chill breeze that swept the deck. Steve sat up as the circles slowed to a stop and the deck became the dirty gray brown color it was before. Steve looked down at the trickle of blood that ran from Slims' ear and heard the soft groaning coming from the face that was still being pushed into the wooden decking.

Steve released his grip and staggered to his feet. He stuck the pistol in his belt, walked backward toward the table, keeping his eyes on the prostrate man. He pulled the magazine from the carbine and put it in the pocket of his jacket. He picked up the .45 and looked down the barrel at Slim.

"Get up." Slim moaned but did not move. Steve walked behind him and grabbing Slims' collar roughly turned him on his back before he backed away and leaned on the rail. Slims' eyes blinked open and he slowly rolled onto his side and laboriously pulled both of his knees underneath him. He slid one of his boots unsteadily under his chest and then rose to his feet, his long torso weaving in small circles over his legs. His eyes were nearly swollen shut and his nose and lips bled steadily onto the front of his shirt. Steve waited until the eyes focused and turned toward his attacker. Steve motioned with the gun toward the stairs.

"You're going to take me to Martin's body. Any bad moves, I kill you and leave you there for the black bears and mountain lions."

Steve indicated the stairs again, this time less patiently. Slim wiped his mouth and looked down at the bloody smear on his hand. He turned unsteadily to his right and slowly walked to the stairs. He leaned his weight heavily on the railing as he half stumbled down the wooden steps. Steve stood at the top of the steps and monitored his progress. Slim reached the bottom and turned gasping as he leaned against the railing. He spat out a glob of blood before he spoke.

"Long ways. Too far." Steve raised the Colt and pointed it between the black eyes.

"I don't care how far it is. There are at least six hours of daylight left. If you don't show me where he is buried before nightfall, I am going to kill you." Slim staggered backwards a few steps and swung his arm wearily toward the back of the property before sinking to his knees. Steve walked down to the last step and waited until Slim had regained his feet. He pointed in the same direction.

"Get moving. Now." Slim turned and looked back at the cabin before he started taking small, uncoordinated steps towards the tree line thirty yards away.

The first twenty yards of the trail led to a small outhouse, before it broadened out and gently sloped down under a long grove of aspen trees, the leaves from the previous year a spongy carpet under the feet of the two men. As Steve had guessed, Slim was not used to being in the woods and the distance was actually only four miles by Steve's reckoning, though it took them the better part of three hours to reach the spot. Over the second half of the journey, Slim recovered somewhat and rested at the frequent stops that Steve took along the way to check his map book and make notations. The final half mile required a long climb over rock outcroppings to a small stand of cedars that clung precariously to the side of a mountain. Slim staggered into the small clearing beneath the trees, pointed to a rock in the center of the clearing and collapsed. Steve moved cautiously to the side of the prone man and checked his maps again, looking out between the trees to the mountains on the other side of the valley. He noted several landmarks before he closed the book. He walked quickly to the far side of the rock, keeping Slim in his vision at all times. The rock was actually two rocks with a five foot wide oval shaped space between them. The ground had clearly been disturbed as the soil was darker and pine needles had been haphazardly and unnaturally spread on the surface. Steve picked up a small branch and probed the soft dirt. When he struck something hard, he brushed the top layer away and tugged gently on a brown piece of material. After a few more minutes, Steve had satisfied himself that the grave held a body. He stood up and looked over at Slim who lay flat on his back, his arms splayed out and his eyes staring at the sky. Steve walked over and looked at the blood-caked face. He kicked the nearest boot.

"Get up. I need to get you back down and into custody before dark which is…", Steve held up his watch and glanced at the sun overhead, its' light filtering through the trees.

"Three more hours, tops. Let's get going." Slim rolled painfully onto his side. He stared at the nearest tree trunk.

"Water." Steve snorted.

"We get back to the cabin, maybe some water, maybe not. But you aren't going to find out sitting here. Get up." Steve kicked the boot harder this time, bringing a cry of pain from the hood.

*

The journey back went quicker, as the trail sloped in gentle curves almost all the way back to the cabin. Halfway, the sun dropped behind the mountains and the gloomy path beneath the trees grew darker. Steve stayed behind the killer and ten feet away at all times, varying his position in case a move was being planned. It was nearly seven o'clock when Slim sank to his knees in front of the cabin. Steve made him get up and walk another forty yards to the garage area, where he collected the canteen as Slim sat with his legs out in front of him and his hands behind his back. Steve kept him in view as he carefully unpinned the gold badge from the young cop's shirt. He buttoned it into his own shirt pocket. When he stood over the killer, he had to kick one of his boots to get him to look up at him. Steve dropped the canteen between the man's legs and watched as Slim greedily poured it down his throat, most of it falling onto the ground. When Steve figured that the container was still half full he yanked it away and replaced the top. Steve backed up two yards and pointed the .45 at Slims' head.

"Where are the keys to the car?" Slim spat and looked up angrily. He did not speak but jerked his head disdainfully toward the cabin. Steve moved around behind him.

"Get up. You're going to show me. Any false moves I shoot. I got what I came for, so don't push it." Steve's voice was husky with anger. Slim slowly rose to his feet and wearily began plodding toward the cabin.

The keys were hanging on a hook just inside the door. Steve lifted them off without taking his eyes from Slim. He stepped away from the door on the doorknob side and motioned for Slim to walk through. Something in the way Slim averted his eyes alerted Cannon and he was ready when Slim made a quick move just as he came to the doorsill. Steve calmly stuck his boot out and caught Slims' foot just above the ankle. The hood's momentum launched his body forward horizontally his face cracking against the struts of the deck railing five feet away. Steve walked out and looked down at the unconscious man. He pulled the strap of the canteen over his head and poured the rest of the contents on the bloody head and face below him. After several seconds, Slim came to, but lay there moaning for several minutes. Steve leaned against the door and switched magazines in the Colt. Slim raised both hands and grasped the top of the railing. Slowly and painfully, he struggled to his feet and turned toward Steve. Steve could see the torn lip and the gap where two front teeth were missing and now lying somewhere in the dirt below the deck. Steve pointed the gun at Slim and then down the stairs.

"Let's go. You just refuse to wise up, don't you? It's all over for you Slim, and were I you, I would start thinking about how I am going to frame this to the cops so that Jimmy Rossini takes the fall. Just a little friendly advice." Steve raised the pistol to eye level and centered the front sight on Slims' forehead. "Of course, maybe you would rather keep pushing it. Get it over quick. If that's what you want, I will oblige you here and now. Otherwise get moving." Steve jerked the pistol toward the stairs before pointing it back at the killer's face.

Slims' eyes dropped toward the ground and he moved slowly down the stairs. Steve crept behind him, the gun pointed at Slims' back. Steve moved quietly and varied the distance between the two men so that Slim could not be sure exactly where Steve was.

When they reached the garage, Steve instructed Slim to kneel on the ground with his hands behind his back. Steve kept him in sight as he pulled the heavy wooden door up on its' rusty springs. He opened the trunk of the dusty Chrysler and stepped back.

"Get in." Slims' eyes were even blacker than normal, and he let out a low moan when he saw the open trunk. Steve stepped away and pulled back the hammer of the .45.

"Now!" He stepped behind Slim as the killer stood up and roughly shoved the upper half of his body into the spacious trunk.

"Get in now or I will coldcock you and throw you in." Steve held the gun steady as Slim slowly folded his legs into the space and Steve slammed down the trunk lid, locking it securely. Steve found a Hudson Bay blanket in the back seat. He returned to the side of the garage and folded it in half and laid it carefully over the body of the young cop.

Steve backed the long car out of the garage and executed a two-point turn to get the car faced downhill towards the road. Steve glanced over at the body of the dead cop, a lock of blond hair visible beneath the blanket, as he let the heavy car glide slowly down to the end of the dirt driveway. As he turned left onto the dirt road, he wondered if the cop had been able to call in his location before he left his patrol car. A few seconds later his question was answered as the patrol car was still parked in the lee of the cut hillside. Steve guessed that there was a wide search underway as there had been no word from Larry Hiram for the last eight hours. Steve steered the car carefully through the hairpin turns, keeping his touch light on the wheel as the car gathered speed on its' own down the mountainside. There was no sound from the cavity in the back of the car.

As Steve rounded the last curve, he saw the small store and the two patrol cars parked in front of it. He pulled slowly into the parking lot and stopped the car thirty yards away. One of the cops was standing just behind a low rail fence talking to two men. He turned his upper body with his arms still folded across his chest and looked at Steve for a long second when he heard Steve's door close. Steve had left the .45 on the seat of the car and had buttoned his jacket before he stepped out onto the asphalt parking area. He walked as casually as he could toward the cop. The man turned and looked at him again and with his cops' intuition held up his hand to stop the conversation he had been having as he unfolded his arms and walked to meet Steve.

*

Two hours later, Steve sat near the fireplace in the store and looked down at his coffee cup. Across from him a plainclothes detective sat at the plank table and wrote in his notebook. Steve lit a cigarette and watched through the smoke as the detective's partner came in the front door and headed for the large coffee pot on the counter. He walked over, dragging a chair from another table and sat down between Steve and his partner. He glanced at Steve out of the corner of his eye while he waited for his partner's attention.

"Looks like his story checks out, so far. Officer Hiram's wound suggests a thirty caliber weapon, the coroner will know for sure. They are getting a team in from St. George at first light to check out the site where he says a body is buried." The detective's head jerked slightly in Steve's direction at the reference. The other cop looked up with a passive expression, first at his partner and then at Steve. He sat back in the wooden chair and stretched before his eyes fastened on Steve.

"We've gone over your story several times, Mr. Cannon, and I just have a few more questions." Steve nodded and picked up his cup with the hand holding the cigarette. He gazed evenly at the young detective.

"So, I guess one question is: If you were so sure that this Atkins character was in the cabin, why didn't you inform law enforcement?" The detective tapped the pencil on the table, his partner shifted his chair so that he was looking at Steve. Steve smiled and flicked the ash off the end of his Pall Mall into a small metal ash tray.

"I needed some information. Information I had promised my client and that only Slim knew. You guys had the same amount of time as I did to come up with him, and now I have saved you the trouble." The detective's eyes narrowed.

"But a policeman is dead. How do you square that?" Steve glanced up at the beamed ceiling before he answered calmly.

"My guess is it would have been worse if you had found out where he was and sent more of your men up there. He was prepared and waiting. The only reason I was successful was because I came in from an unexpected direction. That young cop was only ten paces up the driveway before he got it." Steve looked closely at each of the detectives in turn. The detective dropped Steve's gaze and flipped a few pages over in his notebook before he spoke again.

"This Slim character is in pretty bad shape, he give you any trouble?" Steve chuckled and stubbed out the butt.

"It's a long hike to where Martin Ogawa is buried. Slim was pretty clumsy, especially in the rocks." The second detective snorted and Steve smiled benignly at him. The lead detective stood up and looked down at Steve.

"I think we have as much as we need right now. The Las Vegas police will be here later tonight or tomorrow. If I need more information, I will contact you through them." He slapped his notebook across his hand before he dropped into his coat pocket. Steve watched as the two detectives moved towards the door of the tiny store. They had a brief conversation before they both looked back at Steve and walked out onto the large board and log deck.

*

Steve drove toward the lights of St. George and considered pulling into a motel, but pushed on instead toward the pinkish orange glow of Las Vegas.

APRIL 20

IT WAS NEARLY ten o'clock when Steve rolled over and looked up at the ceiling. He stretched slowly and tried unsuccessfully to shake out the pains in his body. Even after a long hot shower he was limping noticeably as he entered the kitchen to make coffee. As the brew began to percolate Steve placed three calls in quick succession to Remy, Bernie and Miss Perone. The message to each was the same: He was back in town and safe. As he worked on his first cup and his first smoke, he dialed Tam. Tam was not surprised to hear from him.

"You made quite an impression on those Mormon hicks, Steve. All they can talk about." Tam chortled, but then grew quiet when Steve did not reply. Steve's voice was flat with no affect as he spoke.

"I need to know as soon as you hear something, Tam. The team from St. George should be at the burial site by now." Steve felt as if he could go back to bed for another eight hours. He rubbed his eyes and sat back in his chair.

"Unlikely to hear today, Steve. Those backwoods coroners usually take their sweet time if you know what I mean." Tam waited, but when he didn't receive a reply, he began again.

"Of course, I will call our guy up there and make sure he calls me when he hears something. That work for you?" Steve nodded and replied tersely.

"Yeah, make sure you do that." He hung up the phone and looked around the room for a few seconds before he knew what was missing. He returned to the bedroom and retrieved the .45. He came back to the kitchen table and over the second cup of coffee he carefully cleaned the pistol and the two magazines before he slipped the black semi-automatic back into the leather holster under his arm.

Steve parked in the expanded parking lot in front of the Casablanca. With the steady hiring of the hundreds of people that would be needed to fully staff the hotel by the opening date, there were several long rows of cars parked on the fresh asphalt. Steve walked across the wide sweeping road that lead off the Strip and lined with tall palms, curved gracefully in front of the fake sandstone of the entrance before it sloped away back toward Flamingo Road. Steve reached the second floor of the staircase and continued on to the third floor. His knock on the door of the suite brought a reply several seconds before Jack's face appeared behind the now open door. The craggy face nodded knowingly.

"I was hoping that you would pay me a visit today." Jack opened the door wider as Steve walked into the cool interior of the four room suite. Jack pointed to one of the two chairs that along with a matching couch, sat in the middle of the large great room. Steve sat down, noting the .45 pistol with mother-of-pearl grips that lay on the table just inches from Jack's hand as Jack settled into the opposite chair, laying the morning paper he had been reading on the floor beside him.

"Coffee, or some booze?" Jack pointed toward the bar and the liquor cabinet. Steve demurred.

"No thanks, Jack, already had coffee, too soon for liquor, but don't let me stop you." Jack shook his head.

"Naw, too early for me as well." He glanced at the pistol before he looked over at Steve.

"Where you been?"

"Utah." Jack scoffed.

"Why the hell for?" Steve laughed.

"Just bringing the case to a close that's all. You might like to know that Slim is behind bars, but not before he killed a young Utah cop." A disgusted look crossed under the shaggy brows as Jack shook his head.

"That yellow dog. I hope it was you that got him and I hope he was a little worse for wear when you handed him over."

"Yeah, his mother would be upset if she saw his face, and he is on a soft food diet for the foreseeable future, but he should be in good enough shape in a few days to finger Rossini." Steve paused for a few seconds and looked openly at Jack.

"You talk to Tommy?" Jack nodded his head gravely.

"Yeah."

"And" Steve waited.

"And the Syracuse situation is being taken care of as we speak." Steve crossed his legs and settled deeper into the chair. Jack's demeanor grew grim as Steve waited for him to speak.

"I have probably said thank you and meant it ten times in my life, and in the space of two weeks, I have had to say it to you twice." Steve snorted softly and smiled wryly.

"Well to paraphrase what I told Tommy, I didn't just do it for you, Jack." Jack nodded, but the demeanor still held.

"I know, Steve, but you were stuck in the middle and you came through. I won't ever forget that."

"Just like war, Jack, you go through things with people, you do what you have to." Jack nodded and looked at the floor. His face brightened as he thought of something that would help change the subject.

"Hey, I heard about the poker game the other night. Word on the Strip is that Frank is not real happy about the outcome." Steve laughed and stood to go.

"Big fuss about nothing. Frank is alright. It will blow over. People have to cut him some slack at some point. That whole 'chairman of the board' stuff is a tiger by the tail for the guy, anybody would get a little wacky behind that." Jack stood up and agreed.

"Yeah, you're right. Who would want to be him for more than one night?" The two men looked at each other briefly and laughed softly as they both headed for the door.

Steve saw the new door when he was twenty feet away. Milton's workmen had not only replaced the glass, but the door frame itself was now made of metal and was two inches thick. Steve peered through the glass after he pushed the buzzer next to the door. Miss Perone looked up from her desk and smiled. A loud buzz was followed by a short click as the door unlatched and swung open four inches. Steve stepped through and smiled down at Steffi.

"Good morning, Miss Perone, I hope all this work didn't make for too much racket." He stepped backward and turned one of the wing chairs toward her desk.

"No, Mr. Cannon, I just worked out of the other office. I am glad you thought of it. Mr. Gold was here before I was on Monday morning and they finished at two. It works perfectly and I feel much safer now." Steve smiled to himself. After the last thirty-six hours it felt good to have normal conversations again.

"I am glad, Miss Perone, I should have thought of that from the start. The same procedures I mentioned last week still apply if you see any suspicious characters appear at the door." Steffi smiled and held up her index finger.

"I forgot, Mr. Cannon. Mr. Gold and Mr. Swanson added something." Miss Perone, pushed a small lever on a new box that sat on top of her normal intercom. She leaned forward.

"May I help you?" she intoned. Steve heard her voice clearly from a speaker on the outside of the wall next to him. He smiled.

"Leave it to Bernie." Miss Perone also smiled.

"Isn't that neat, Mr. Cannon? If someone can't give me a good explanation for why they are here, they don't get in." Steffi shook her head and the dark curls moved from side to side. Steve stood up.

"I want to thank you and your mother for the wonderful time Remy and I had at the party on Sunday. I hope she invites us back."

"Of course, Mr. Cannon. Now you are expected every second Sunday and no more discussion." Steve snorted and shook his head.

"Give me a few minutes, Miss Perone, then I would like to fill you in on recent developments." Steve walked across the hall and sat down wearily in the comfortable leather chair. He had just retrieved his address book from the top drawer of his desk when Miss Perone's voice came over the intercom.

"Mr. Polhaus would like to speak with you, Mr. Cannon."

"Thank you, Miss Perone." Steve sighed and picked up the phone and bid hello to Tam.

"You sound tired."

"I am. I'm not in good enough shape to go six rounds with every hood who crosses my path." Tam was silent for a moment.

"Just got a call from our guys on the scene in Utah. A wallet was found on the body and they are confirming it is Martin Ogawa. The coroner will make his official determination by tomorrow, but I figured that will probably be enough to go on for you and you can decide from there." Steve let out a long breath and sat back in the chair. Even though he knew that this was to be the outcome from the start, he realized that even he had held out hope. He thought of Keno, before he turned his attention back to the phone.

"Thanks, Tam, this will give me a chance to break it to his father before he gets an official visit or phone call."

"Yeah, that is what I thought, too. Don't envy you, but I think he would rather it come from you than from someone he doesn't know in the coroners' office." Steve thanked the detective again and put the receiver down. He stood up and swung the sport coat from the back of the chair over his shoulder before he walked across the hall to the reception area.

*

The parking lot of the municipal golf course was filled to the brim when Steve eased the Jeep into one of the few empty spaces just past one o'clock. A sign attached to the chain link fence announced the annual spring tournament. Steve had to ask two people before he located Lew Mannion. Lew was handing out box lunches down the long row of golf carts as the participants queued up to tee off. Lew smiled when he saw Steve.

"The women went out this morning, now the guys. You want a lunch?" Steve forced a smile and watched while the expression on Lew's face darkened as he handed the lunch to an extended hand from the cart next to him.

"Keno around?" Lew pointed back over his shoulder.

"He's been here since three this morning. Over at the maintenance sheds. Not much for the guys to do out on the course on a day like this." Lew eyed Steve closely.

"Bad news?" Steve sighed and looked back blankly at his boyhood friend.

"Yes, Lew, I'm afraid that this time it is." Lew looked at the ground and shook his head. When he looked back up, he couldn't look directly at Steve, but the tears in his eyes were still visible. He suppressed a choking in his throat when he spoke.

"Stop back here when you are done, I need to go see him." Steve nodded and patted Lew's arm lightly as he passed down the long row of happy golfers.

Steve peered into two of the sheds before he found the one that held Keno. He stood in the doorway for several seconds and watched as Keno stood hunched over a long table, his short fingers quickly dismantling a water pump, laying the parts out on the flat surface in the same sequence in which they had been removed. Keno looked up when he heard Steve's shoe scrape on the rough concrete floor. Steve stopped five feet away and gestured toward the parts in front of the Japanese man.

"I often wondered, Keno, if Japanese soldiers could break down their weapons and reassemble them in the dark." Keno glanced down at his handiwork. He wiped the caked mud from his hands on a red rag that he picked up from the table. He turned and faced Steve squarely, his gray eyes unblinking.

"I have always been good with machines, Mr. Cannon, not so with people." Steve nodded slightly and looked up from the table and met the gray eyes. When he spoke his voice was barely above a whisper.

"I found Martin, Keno, I'm sorry." Something flickered darker in the brown eyes before they turned their gaze back to the table. Keno picked up one of the larger parts and slid a chrome cylinder slimy with mud from the middle. He weighed it in his hand for a few seconds and looked blankly at the wall.

"Where?" Steve shifted his weight off of his aching leg and leaned against the edge of the table. He looked at Keno who was still staring at the wall.

"He is in a grove of aspen trees, in southern Utah, near Brianhead." Keno nodded and began cleaning the cylinder with the rag. For several seconds, neither man spoke as Steve watched the water pump come back together under Keno's expert hands.

"When can I see him?" Steve sighed and stepped back, he put his hands in his pockets and stared at the door.

"I'm not sure, Keno. What I have just told you is unofficial. Someone from the coroners' office will contact you, probably tomorrow. He will have all the information you need." Keno looked at Steve and nodded.

"I am glad that it was you that found Martin." Steve nodded back.

"When you are ready, Keno, I will take you there." When Keno didn't answer, Steve laid one of his new business cards on the table and walked to the door. He stood for a minute and watched Keno at work. He slid the thin metal door shut behind him and walked across the muddy path toward the pro shop.

Ten minutes later, he found Lew at the first tee. He watched while Lew answered a question from two golfers who were waiting to tee off. Lew walked slowly down the grassy slope toward Steve.

"You tell him?" Steve nodded and looked at the ground.

"How'd he take it?" Steve looked up and shrugged.

"I don't know him that well, but I would say pretty badly. He is in the small shed beside the cart barn. You going over?" Lew turned and looked in the direction of the sheds.

"Yeah, as soon as I can get someone to spell me here." Lew waited until Steve looked up at him his eyes squinting against the sun.

"Brenda and I would like you and Remy to come out for dinner sometime." Steve took a deep breath and nodded.

"Yeah, Lew, I would like that." Steve stepped back off the slope onto the asphalt pathway.

"If you think of something I can do for Keno, let me know." Lew waved as Steve turned to go.

"Sure, Steve, I will." Lew watched his friend as he made his way through the waiting carts. He was limping badly on his right leg as he disappeared into the parking lot.

*

Steve stood beside his desk and watched as the yellow cranes heaved large square window panes to the third floor of the new tower. The first two floors had already been fitted and their golden mirror finishes glowed as the sun lowered itself behind the Spring mountains. He looked down at the empty scotch glass in his hand as he turned away, slumping into the leather desk chair. He was stretching his leg into a more comfortable position when the phone buzzed straight through as it normally did after hours. Steve frowned and stared at the yellow blinking light for several seconds before he picked up.

"Steve, I was hoping you were still around, this is Tam." Steve grunted a greeting and waited for the next utterance from the cop which would announce the purpose of the call.

"Several developments you should know about. You there?" Steve cleared his throat and sat up in the chair.

"Yeah, I'm here."

"Well, first off, they have cleared Slim Atkins for extradition and as soon as he is able to travel he will be transported back here for prosecution. As if his luck couldn't get any worse, they found Jimmy Rossini's body in a cornfield in Iowa eight hours ago. Shot three times with a bag over his head. That leaves him to take the rap all by his lonesome." Tam waited for a few seconds and when there was no reply, he continued. "Maybe the strangest news, is that I just received photos over the wire of Angelo Sorelli coming out of a meeting with other drug kingpins in someplace called Rancho Bernardo, so maybe he was just passing through. The feds who were monitoring the meeting didn't know who he was until Grassley in Phoenix saw the photos, so they missed out once again on nabbing him. What do you think of that?" Steve sat back wearily in the chair.

"Business as usual, Tam, I guess. Nothing to stop Sorelli from coming back here, so nothing's changed on that front. The coroner make the ID on Martin Ogawa official?"

"Yeah, he did. He used the fingerprints from the Gaming Control Board's file. Saved the old man from having to come down." Steve nodded to himself.

"I was hoping for that. You got anything else?"

"Nope, that's all for now." Steve bid goodbye and hung up. He glanced at the empty glass on the green blotter and was just about to reach for the scotch bottle in the lower drawer when the front door buzzer sounded with one short burst. Steve stood and walked through the hallway, stopping just inside the doorway of the reception area when he saw the figure that was framed by the bullet proof glass. He walked slowly to Miss Perone's desk and leaning over the typewriter he pressed the brown button. The short buzz was followed by the front door swinging open slightly. The visitor walked through the doorway and stood before Steve, letting the door swing closed behind him. The horn rimmed glasses sat above a bemused smile and below a jaunty white golf hat. The visitor removed the hat with a careful motion, revealing the slicked back brown hair that was starting to recede on both sides.

"Good evening, Mr. Cannon. Am I catching you at a bad time?" Steve turned sideways and extended his arm toward the hallway and his office beyond.

"No, not at all, come in." Steve followed the man's lean, compact physique through the reception room and into his office. When he was seated in front of Steve's desk he crossed his legs and plucked at the crease of his light blue golf pants.

"Forgive my informality, Mr. Cannon, I have just come from the golf course, I had a few minutes and I thought we could chat and catch up. You look much more in the pink than the last time I saw you." Steve nodded as he recalled how the world had looked through the gauze that had encircled his head the last time they met. He held up his glass.

"Would you like some scotch?" The man smiled and demurred.

"No, thank you, not today. I am on my way to my niece's sixth birthday party and I don't want to hug her smelling of booze." Steve nodded, but retrieved the bottle and poured himself a short drink. He looked up after his first sip as the visitors' smile widened.

"Well, Mr. Cannon, you have been busy as usual. I was glad to hear that you had successfully concluded the case you have been working on. I have been following your progress in the paper." The smile lessened as he shook his head. "Terrible business. If there is anything I can do for the boy's family, I would appreciate it if you would let me know." Steve swung his glass in a quick motion.

"No, nothing I know of at this point." The visitor nodded and continued.

"I was surprised that you found Slim Atkins where you did. I was led to believe that he wasn't there." Steve shrugged.

"Seemed like the logical choice. Sometimes I don't think people look as hard as they might." The tanned face moved up and down in agreement, the brown eyes magnified by the thick lenses narrowed slightly.

"I am sure you are right, Mr. Cannon, but why put yourself in such danger? As I am sure Mr. Carmino made clear, you could have come to us, but I know…" He held up a hand in a grandfatherly gesture. "The justice system." He smiled widely again. "You see, Mr. Cannon, I understand you perfectly, even if each of us know ourselves imperfectly." Steve took a sip of the whisky and put the glass down before he spoke.

"And Mr. Rossini. How imperfectly did he know himself?" The visitor permitted himself a small chuckle.

"Ah yes, the late Mr. Rossini. I daresay if he were to materialize in front of us right now, he would agree that he knew full well the possible consequences of his actions, and perhaps you are right, he may have known himself more perfectly than all of us." Steve snorted.

"All's well that ends well, right?" The visitor's eyes danced as a bemused expression crossed his face. He switched the position of his legs and ignored the sardonic tone.

"That's where you and I are the same, Mr. Cannon, we see the natural progression of things, the way things should be and we use our energies to help channel events to that end." Steve sat back and put his hands behind his head, his smile matching that of the man in front of him.

"I will have to remember that line, the next time I get called in for a grilling from the DA or the FBI." The visitor flicked a bit of grass from the edge of his pant cuff.

"I daresay, Mr. Cannon, you have been very resourceful in avoiding just those types of unpleasant experiences." He looked up at the private detective and when he spoke again the tone of his voice was flatter and more direct.

"Your association with myself and my colleagues has been beneficial to your interests, am I right, Mr. Cannon?" Steve gazed straight ahead and only his lips moved when he replied.

"I see it as more of a quid pro quo. I think you would agree that I have given as much as I have received, especially in light of recent events." The visitor slapped his thighs lightly as he stood up.

"I do agree, Mr. Cannon, and perhaps we are even in your debt. As always, I find our talks productive. Don't stand, please, I will show myself out." The visitor moved to the door, turned and gestured toward the window.

"Please tell Bernie that I think he is doing a wonderful job with this property." Steve watched as the white golf hat moved through the outer door and disappeared around the corner.

April 26

STEVE SAT IN the back of the small sushi restaurant sipping on his second cup of coffee. It had been a week since he apprehended Slim Atkins and he still felt twinges of pain in his leg. The sun was just beginning to peek through the white curtains that hung on the window next to him when the door swung open. Keno Ogawa swept the blue cloth aside as he stepped into the room. Suko appeared from behind the curtain that led to the kitchen. She lowered her eyes and bowed in greeting to her uncle. He bowed slightly in her direction and uttered several long sentences in Japanese before he looked to his left and saw Steve. He walked to within five feet of Steve's table and stood in the narrow aisle way. He bowed slowly.

"I am ready, Mr. Cannon." Steve looked down at his coffee cup and turned sideways in his chair taking care not to jostle the low table as he stood up. He nodded to Keno as he took a last long sip from the cup and appraised the attire of his companion.

"We won't be back until late tonight. It will likely get cold up there." He shrugged as Keno turned expectantly toward the door. Steve followed the shorter man to the doorway, nodding to Suko who had come out of the kitchen and quickly moved past Steve, tugging on her uncle's sleeve. She bowed quickly and handed him a small bundle wrapped in a stiff maroon cloth. Keno turned and accepted the package with both hands as he bowed slightly. Steve walked to the Jeep and stopped when he saw the large pack leaning against the back wheel. He wrapped his hand around one of the stout pieces of maple that formed the frame and lifted the pack off the ground a few inches. He frowned as he turned to Keno.

"This is too heavy for the distance we have to go, Keno. Let me carry some of this in my own pack." Keno looked up at Steve and shook his head.

"No, Steve, I must carry it myself." Keno bent over and opened the large flap on the top of the pack that was fastened with a thin cord. He placed the bundle that Suko had given him carefully into the interior of the pack, taking great care in replacing the cord. Steve opened the window of the Jeep and dropped the tailgate. He stepped back as Keno hoisted the load into the cargo bay. Steve opened the passenger door for Keno and circled behind the jeep, making sure the tailgate was securely closed. He pulled away slowly from the curb and drove toward the highway two miles away.

For the first hour of the drive, Steve pointed out landmarks and historic sites after Keno had remarked that he had never been on the road or visited Utah. As they neared St. George, Keno became quiet and seem to prefer taking in the landscape in silence as it moved past his window. Steve stopped at the same gas station he had exactly a week before. He stood in the morning sun and watched Keno sitting alone in the front seat as gas flowed into the tank. He took out his notebook of maps and laid it on the hood of the car. He had pulled out the metal spiral the night before and rearranged the order of the maps. Deciding to spare Keno the trauma of starting from the cabin, he had plotted a path that would start from the small store and while it was a little bit longer than the alternative, it avoided two long uphill climbs. Steve looked at the top of the pack frame visible through the side windows and wished that he had put more effort into starting the trek closer to the small grove of aspens.

Steve parked in the outer asphalt area in front of the store. He waited while Keno pulled his pack from the back of the Jeep and resisted helping when Keno struggled under the weight as he pulled the thin leather straps over his shoulders. Steve pointed toward the trailhead which started just beside the store, and lead the way, trying to judge the pace that would be the most comfortable for his companion. Thirty yards up the trail, Steve stooped to pick up a walking stick that someone had fashioned from a tree branch and abandoned at the end of their sojourn. He waited until Keno came to his side and held out the stick. Keno hefted it and nodded. Steve held out the book of maps.

"There are three parts to this hike. This trail will take us for two miles in that direction." Steve pointed due east. "Then we will have to cross these two hills here." He traced across the densely packed contour lines with his finger in a southerly direction. "There is another half mile of improved trail that curves around back of this mountain, before we start the last climb here." Keno stared down at the map.

"Where will we find the place where you found Martin?" Steve moved his finger around the curving lines and stopped on the eastern facing slope of the mountain. "There." Keno nodded and took a step backward as he gazed up at the mountain whose top was just visible to the southeast. Steve buttoned the map into his shirt pocket and pointed up the slightly inclining trail.

"I will stay in front. I will check where you are every one hundred yards or so. If you need to stop, use this." Steve held out a chrome whistle that hung from a leather lanyard. Keno nodded and wrapped the leather thong several times around his wrist, pushing the whistle back between his fingers so that he needed to merely lift his hand to signal Steve. Steve nodded, turned back to the trail and with measured steps began to move toward the mountain.

By the time that they came to the point where they were forced to leave the trail and began to make their own way through the underbrush, Steve had stopped several times to wait for Keno. It was obvious that his companion had not spent much time in nature outside of his work on the golf course. The gardener and cultivator in him had gotten the better of him and at one point Steve had rushed back down the hill when he turned and there was no Keno, only to find him several yards off the trail on his knees, inspecting some white blooms that were growing out of a rotting log. Steve surveyed the hillside in front of him and dropped his pack. From a side compartment he pulled out a long war surplus machete and tested it on the nearest clump of four foot high bushes. Satisfied, he stepped back and indicated the top of the hill with the blade.

"We have two hundred yards to the top of that hill, a small downhill and then another one just like it." He stabbed the machete blade into the soft dirt beside his foot and lifted the canteen strap over his head. He handed the flat, round receptacle to Keno. Keno took three small sips and handed it back. Steve took a long drink and pulled it back over his head and adjusted it so the flat part of the canteen rested comfortably behind his hip and out of the way of any errant branches.

Steve immediately saw the effect of Keno's heavy pack on the older man. A third of the way up, Steve began to clear a way for twenty or thirty yards while Keno waited below. He would then descend back down to escort Keno, holding back some of the larger tangles that had resisted the machete, to let Keno pass. By this method they reached the top of the second hill two hours later. Steve dropped his pack and began to lift the straps off Keno's shoulders before he could protest. When his companion was no longer encumbered, he led him to the edge of a rocky precipice and pointed downhill to the faint outlines of an improved trail fifty yards below the two men.

"We'll rest here for twenty minutes." He pointed to the east where the whole mountainside was visible. "The wind has picked up and it will be cold on the exposed slopes." When ten minutes later after they had finished chewing on some of the jerky that Steve had packed, Steve made a point of pulling a rough-out leather jacket from his pack, Keno still made no move to add to the wool shirt he had worn since they left. Steve looked at his watch. It was just past two. He pushed his hand deep into his pack and touched the two miner helmets and operated the switches on the headlamps to make sure that both shone brightly. Steve insisted that Keno drink several mouthfuls of water before they set out, skirting the cliff outcropping and descending to the trail.

Forty-five minutes later they reached the bottom of the mountain. Steve pointed with the machete toward a faint game trail that weaved back and forth up the slope in a lazy switchback pattern. He replaced the machete in the pack and led the way through the lichen that grew on either side of the trail. An hour later, they crossed over to the east side of the mountain and walked into the shadows. The wind rippled through the sparse vegetation. Steve waited for Keno to catch up with him. Keno stopped and leaned on his stick for support as he caught his breath. The deep shadows and the wind wicked away the warmth that the climbing had generated. Steve didn't want to rest long. He borrowed Keno's staff and pointed ahead a half mile to where the edge of the aspen grove could be seen just before the side of the mountain curved out of sight.

Twenty minutes later, they stood inside the ring of aspens, their small leaves exposing light green undersides in the wind. Steve stood beside Keno as the shorter man peered into the dim light of the small grotto. Steve noted the ground had been disturbed and there was a muddy trail that lead to the two rocks in the middle of the clearing. Next to the gray granite boulders a large pile of dirt had been left on the ground. Steve let his pack slip to the ground as he knelt, feeling for the small folding shovel he had carried all through the war. Keno walked slowly forward and pulled a large white cloth from underneath his shirt. He spread it on the ground a few feet from the rocks and carefully placed his pack on top. Steve joined him as they stared down at the shallow hole that had once held his son.

Keno returned to his pack and began to carefully lift several objects from its' interior and lined them up as he did so on the white cloth. Frequent gusts raked the small clearing and both men were forced to turn their faces away from the blowing leaves and dirt. Steve stood a few feet away from the rocks as Keno sat on his knees in the same position that Steve had seen the night he observed the kendo practice. He pressed his head against the ground several times and Steve could hear the murmuring of the prayers, but could not make out the words in the wind. Keno rose, went back to the cloth and returned with a small bamboo dipper and a round container. Keno knelt beside the rocks and carefully unscrewed the top of the canister pouring half the contents into the dipper. He repeated a portion of the prayers and then poured the water back and forth into the hole. He refilled the dipper and repeated the ritual. From his shirt pocket he pulled a small bundle which he unwrapped, pouring the contents into his hand. Steve stood up as Keno spread the small handful of salt evenly into the depression. He stood up and nodded to Steve. Steve unfolded his small shovel and slowly began to fill the hole from the dirt pile next to him. When all the dirt was gone, Steve smoothed the top and stood back a few paces as Keno returned with a small lacquered cabinet that sat twelve inches tall and had two doors in the front. He placed it snugly against the biggest rock at the end of the grave, scooping out a little of the loose soil to make sure that it was anchored and would not move. He placed a small bowl on top of the shrine, filled it with a fine sand from a box in his pocket and lit two long sticks of incense, placing them upright in the bowl. He returned to the white cloth and came back with three more objects, one Steve recognized as the bundle that Suko had handed her uncle just before they left the restaurant. Keno lifted a small stone urn up before him, bowed and placed it on the shelf inside the two doors. He slowly undid the bundle and lifted the top of the lacquered box he found inside. One by one, Keno examined each object before he placed it next to the urn. Two baseball cards, a thin gold band and a small ivory carving of a bear. Keno sat back on his knees, his gray hair fluttering over his forehead from the wind. He bowed once more before he took a small picture of Martin and placed it on the shelf. He closed the doors of the shrine, bowed and then placed a long thin piece of wood with kanji printed vertically along its flat surface into the soil beside the shrine. For several minutes, the Japanese man stared at the shrine and the grave marker. Steve stood silently on the other side of the grave. After a large gust of wind, rattled through the clearing, Keno looked upward searching for Steve's eyes.

"We must call my son by his new name, Mr. Cannon: Maseo no mikoto. Otherwise his spirit will hear his name and turn around, interrupting his journey." Steve nodded. Keno continued. "I will say more prayers, Steve and then we will leave." Steve nodded again and stepped away from the grave. For the next twenty minutes, Steve busied himself repairing the damage the recovery party had done to the small clearing. He filled in the muddy footprints with fresh dirt from under the trees. His last act was to cut several boughs from a douglas fir farther down the mountain. These he dragged around the area in concentric circles, in an effort to return the gravesite to as close to the natural condition as was possible. He waited for Keno just outside the small circle of white-barked trees. The wind had died in the last half hour, but Steve felt the chill of the late afternoon on his head and shoulders. Keno stepped from the clearing his now empty pack on his back. Steve held out the walking stick to his companion. Keno bowed slightly and accepted it.

Twenty minutes later, they rounded a large boulder and were in the sunshine. For the next mile the sun warmed them until they left the trail and began to climb the two hills. They made it to the last trail in half the time it had taken on the outbound trip, but by the time their boots hit the hard pack of the improved trail, it was nearly dark. Steve took off his jacket and insisted that Keno put it over his shoulders and then placed the pack straps over it to secure it. Steve also retrieved the two miner helmets and placed the brighter lamp of the two on Keno's head and fastened the chin strap for him. The full moon rose as they got underway on the last leg of their journey, but provided little light. The lamps on their helmets kept them in an illuminated ten foot circle as they walked along much closer together than before. It was another two hours before Steve saw the lights of the store just below them. He looked back at Keno who was trying in vain to keep his teeth from chattering. Steve lead the way until their boots clomped across the board porch on the front of the store. Steve opened the heavy log door for Keno and felt the welcome rush of warm air on his face.

Steve dropped his pack and canteen just inside the door and looked around the deserted store. The proprietor leaned out over the counter and quietly surveyed the pair. Steve pulled a small silver flask from his pack and walked to the counter. He held it out to the older man.

"Do you have a couple of glasses, I could use to pour this in, please?" The man looked at the flask and shook his head.

"This is Utah, mister, I can't do that." He glanced over at Keno who still had his pack on and was leaning unsteadily against the counter. When he looked back at Steve, his eyes were softer.

"But, I don't mind if you and your friend sit over there by the fire and pass it back and forth among yourselves. Just make sure that if anyone else comes in here, you hide that thing quick." Steve nodded, stepped behind Keno and helped him slip out of the pack. He walked over to the fire dragging two chairs from the nearest table and waited while Keno settled himself into the one closest to the crackling flames. Steve watched until Keno was comfortable and then held out the flask of rum. Keno looked at Steve and then at the flask before he took it and tipped a small amount into his mouth. For the next few minutes they sat transfixed by the fire, stirring as little as possible when they passed the flask between them. It was Keno who first broke the silence.

"Thank you for taking me to my son, Steve." Steve looked the older man in the eyes and nodded. Keno nodded back and handed the nearly empty flask back in front of the fire before he spoke again.

"I must come back this time next year. Perhaps you will let me use the maps you have." Steve smiled and rested the flask on the stone hearth.

"Perhaps you will let me come along with you." Keno glanced sideways as he nodded his head slightly.

"I would like that. It was a good walk." Steve bent over and picked up the walking staff that Keno had set by his chair. He tapped it gently on the hearth, testing its' flexibility.

"Perhaps you would enjoy a walk in the desert sometime." Keno looked at the stick before he turned his face toward Steve.

"Yes. That would suit me."

The moon cast the stronger beams across the dark highway as Steve steered the Jeep down the mountain by the glow of the head-lights toward the desert and home. He turned to see Keno's head slumped on his chest in deep slumber. Steve reached over and pulled the leather jacket up until only the man's face could be seen.

EPILOGUE

Steve sat back in the white wooden chair in the early morning sunshine and reached for Remy's hand. He smiled into her dark brown eyes as she smoothed the light pink dress over her knees. At the first notes from the organist, they both stood and looked up the aisle as the bride moved slowly toward them. Suko's satin dress shimmered in the June sunlight. Steve caught a glimpse of Keno's profile as he passed, his head high and his eyes forward, his arm guiding his niece down the gentle slope to where Mike Yamaguchi waited, his eyes shining with nervous joy.

www.ingramcontent.com/pod-product-compliance
Lightning Source LLC
Chambersburg PA
CBHW021341250626
47155CB00002B/726